INTERSTELLAR FLIGHT MAGAZINE BEST OF YEAR SIX

INTERSTELLAR FLIGHT PRESS ANTHOLOGIES
BOOK 6

EDITED BY
HOLLY LYN WALRATH

CONTENTS

ORIGINAL ARTICLES

REVIEWS

INTERVIEWS

ORIGINAL ARTICLES

UNDROWNED HISTORIES: A RETROSPECTIVE READING OF THE DEEP (2019) AND FLOWERS FOR THE SEA (2021): THE BLACK AQUATIC IN SPECULATIVE FICTION

LIZA WEMAKOR

> "The ocean, for many African and African diasporic peoples, is not only a source of fear and violence, but a source of awe, reverence, and veneration for Earth, the universe and our ancestors. The ocean is capacious, capricious, and deep like we are. Do you remember?"

The reality that black people have particular connections to water and oceans (the Middle Passage, river lynchings, segregated pools, stereotypes that black people can't or don't swim) could go without saying. But I will say that black people have particular connections to water and oceans throughout this essay.

My reasons for doing so are that:

1.) *The black aquatic* is a subject we could stand to think more deeply about,
2.) In a time when we can observe marine mammals engaging in acts of protests (pursuing and attacking private and commercial boats), it is worthwhile to consider the ocean from every angle, and
3.) It is no secret that many speculative fiction fans (across racial cate-

gories) struggle when reading speculative fiction that is *abstractly* informed by black histories and cultures.

When I say *abstractly*, I am referring to works that respond to an *idea* that recurs across black histories and cultures, as opposed to works that represent a particular moment or era. For example: a work of historical fiction set on an early 1800s Jamaican plantation offers more concrete storytelling, whereas a story set in a never-before-seen mermaid civilization, consciously and subconsciously inspired by centuries of black people's engagements with water, may register as abstract.

Brief engagement with Goodreads reviews of the two novellas I'll prioritize in this essay, Rivers Solomon's and clipping's *The Deep* (*S&S/Saga Press*, 2019) and Zin E. Rocklyn's *Flowers for the Sea* (*Tordotcom*, 2020), evidences this pattern of readers struggling to comprehend aquatic abstractions of black histories and cultures—even when they enjoy the writing itself, or sense that there *is* profound meaning in the text below the surface, just beyond their grasp.

In this short essay, I will consider the cultural and historical foundations of aquatic themes that feature prominently in black speculative fiction, with the agenda of encouraging us all to read these fictions more confidently and carefully. The scholarly and creative work of Dr. Alexis Pauline Gumbs, a queer Caribbean black feminist philosopher, writer, and self-proclaimed love evangelist, will be formative to our exploration of the black aquatic.

Let us note that "BlueBellow" (2017), the sole short story Gumbs has published in *Strange Horizons* (or any pro-rate speculative fiction magazine) to date, features a trans-Atlantic voyage that culminates in a movement called the Reconnection, wherein black people reconnect with the Atlantic Ocean en masse, "reuniting with the part of us that drowned" after the world-changing atrocity that is the Middle Passage. This story not only engages with the trauma African diasporic people incurred through and in the Atlantic Ocean (enslavement, colonization, torture, dehumanization), but suggests we have another historical and cultural relationship to the ocean that supercedes the trans-Atlantic slave trade. The ocean, for many African and African diasporic peoples, is not only a source of fear and violence, but a source of awe, reverence, and veneration for Earth, the universe, and our ancestors. The ocean is capacious, capricious, and deep like we are. Do you remember?

Gumbs asks us, throughout her body of work, to recover memories of the black aquatic that existed long before we were born into these bodies. She asks us to remember what water has meant to us not only in "BlueBellow" but in the "Archive of Ocean: Origin" section of *M Archive* (Duke Press, 2018), which is the second installment in her black feminist triptych, and in the entirety of *Undrowned: Black Feminist Lessons from Marine Mammals* (AK Press, 2020).

Near the beginning of *M Archive*'s "Archive of Ocean," Gumbs writes the origin story of the ocean as she knows it. Attributing the ocean's beginnings to black feminine pain rather than the aloof, Zeusian gods many of us have been trained to worship, Gumbs writes that an unnamed *she* "cried and it became the ocean. and out of the ocean came life as we know it. life as we be it. the salt in our veins. the who we are and the who we are not. we have not yet seen the bottom of it, the depth of mourning that birthed us here" (109).

There is a long history of black feminine spirits birthing and mothering the ocean in African diasporic cultures. We know Mami Wata in West Africa, La Sirene and Erzulie / Ezili in the Francophone diaspora, and Yemaya / Yemoja / Yemanja in the Hispanic and Lusophone diasporas. All of these spirits are especially drawn to *fluid people* who place faith in the spirits' beauty, strength, and gendered excess, which are reflected in the qualities of the ocean itself. These water spirits are syncretizations of African and European cultures and practices, and are likely part of what Gumbs had in mind as she wrote this passage, given her longstanding personal and scholarly interests in black divination.

Gumbs extends her maritime interests in *Undrowned*, moving the frame of the black aquatic to potential parallels between black and queer cultural sensibilities, and the experiences and ontologies of marine mammals. Floating between scientific studies, news reports, high theory, and personal observations, she convincingly demonstrates how black people, queer people, and community organizers (which are often overlapping categories) have ways of operating in the world that resemble marine mammals. We travel together, we look out for each other, and we have a way of seeing in the so-called dark. Dr. Kevin Dawson mirrors this idea in his own study of the black aquatic, *Undercurrents of Power: Aquatic Culture in the African Diaspora* (*Penn Press*, 2018), which considers the connections African people already had to the ocean through water rites and sports well before colonization and the transatlantic slave trade.

These notes should provide us with enough context to return to our novellas, Solomon's *The Deep* (2019) and Rocklyn's *Flowers for the Sea* (2021), which both build their narratives around black merfolk, or hybrid, human-marine beings who are racially coded as black.

Dr. Jalondra Davis provides a historical analysis of black merfolk in her article "Crossing Merfolk Narratives of the Sacred" (Shima Journal, 2021), in which she traces the mythos of enslaved African people becoming merfolk after jumping or falling from slave ships in acts of rebellion and tragedy. In her work, Davis finds that black merfolk stories are rooted in historical trauma, but they also "reclaim history and seek to heal trauma" through "depictions of care" (67–68). This interpretation of black merfolk certainly applies to both *The Deep* and *Flowers for the Sea*.

The Deep

> "Let it wash over you—when you get to its optimistic end, you won't feel like drowning."

— Sean Dowie's "REVIEW: The Deep by Rivers Solomon" (*Fiyah Magazine*, 2019)

In a nutshell, *The Deep* (based on a clipping song of the same name, which was itself inspired by the black electronica duo Drexciya) follows merfolk descendants of pregnant African women who were thrown from slave ships. This backstory is outlined in the intro of the clipping song, which describes a people "who were born breathing water as we did in the womb."

Rivers Solomon adapted this source material and deepened its lore, introducing readers to a merperson named Yetu who has the responsibility of remembering her people's difficult, six-hundred-year history in its entirety. She is an underwater griot of sorts, a historian whose "role was to carry the memories so other wajinru wouldn't have to" (Solomon, 7). Yetu resents the pain she's been made to carry for most of the novella, since "The Remembrance took more than it gave" (Solomon, 8) in her estimation. She felt possessed by the historical pain of the wajinru, a people borne from death and mothered by whales, as if "Her body was full of other bodies" (Solomon, 28). By the end of the novella, however, Yetu's friendships with Amaba, Nnenyo, and "two-leg" humans named Suka and Oori teach her to rely upon other people instead of bearing the weight of remembering by herself. Indeed, intellectual work does not have to entail individualism or loneliness. As I share these reflections with you, I feel a bit like this matured version of Yetu.

One of my favorite chapters in *The Deep* is the fourth one, where we see an earlier incarnation of the wajinru rescue a brown woman from drowning in the ocean. The brown woman gives them the name zoti aleyu ("strange fish"). I like that this woman says, after meeting the zoti, that she "has always known there was a world beyond this world, a world where the unseen happens" (Solomon, 45). It affirms the African, spiritual roots of this novella.

"But we are a people who do not forget, we nims." (Rocklyn, 11)

Flowers for the Sea

Flowers for the Sea is perhaps more gruesome than *The Deep*, though it similarly syncretizes black people with sea creatures—challenging the notion that being more-than-human is so bad after all.

Like Yetu, the protagonist of *Flowers for the Sea*, Iraxi begins her story in loneliness. And she is lonely because of what she remembers. She hails from an unnamed land that resembles precolonial West Africa, and finds herself thrown into a dark, filthy ark after she refuses the advances of a prince. Before she is forced onto the ark, whose claustrophobic conditions resemble the squalor of slave ships, the vengeful prince has her family's home set on fire, and she loses most of her skin and hair in a failed attempt to save her loved ones. Heartbroken and miserable, Iraxi delights in her putrid physical state, taking pleasure in the discomfort it must cause her male and female lovers. She eventually finds herself pregnant with a strange, tentacled child.

The birth of this child is gruesome—accompanied by back-arching seizures and oozing slime. And Iraxi rejects the sinister, purple-eyed baby at first. But when she accepts the child, the fruit of her trauma, and its plans for her, she gains power. Her burnt hair and skin regenerate, and she has a certain sway over plants. The fearsome sea creatures that have crowded the ark, like the sharks that were said to trail slave ships (awaiting fresh bodies), answer to her power and wrath.

Both Yetu and Iraxi experience tumultuous passages en route to self-actualization, in which they struggle to stay connected to people. Iraxi arguably fails in this struggle, allowing her new powers to subject people on the ark to attacks from sea monsters, while Yetu's sojourn away from her people and memories comes full circle when she meets people who are both like and unlike her—people who lead her back to the necessity of community and togetherness.

Outsider-ness is a mirror that can refine one's self-perception and one's sense of possibility. When Yetu looks into the face of Oori, one of her human friends, the tribal "scars and markings cut into [Oori's] face in elaborate patterns" (Solomon, 84) remind her of her own beautiful, aquatic scales. And eventually, she returns to her true self and quells the storm of memory that threatens to flood Earth's lands.

Iraxi didn't have a comparable experience in the hold of the ark, and her antipathy hardened into total alienation; she bore too much pain on her own, and lost contact with the "knowledge, beauty" (Solomon, 145) of her history. She became little more than her anger.

> "We must save one another," said Yetu. (Solomon, 148)

The black aquatic teaches us about ourselves and reminds us of our connectedness to everything in the world—including darkness. We need one another, and we must save one another.

Notes

This essay is not comprehensive, so please continue exploring the black aquatic. For example: I didn't even touch upon Samuel Delany's *The Motion of Light in Water* autobiography (*Arbor House*, 1988), and how its gorgeous prose entangles black queer life and history with water and fluidity. And I'm curious to see how recent releases, such as Akotowaa Ofori's *The Year of Return* (Android Press, 2024), will further enrich our impression of the black aquatic.

For academic studies of the black aquatic, I encourage you to return to the scholars I've cited in this essay (e.g., Jalondra A. Davis, Alexis Pauline Gumbs, and Kevin Dawson).

GENIES AND HUMAN NATURE: EXPLORING ROBERT LEWIS STEVENSON'S 1891 FANTASY STORY ABOUT GENIES

HENRY L. HERZ

It struck me that Beetlejuice from *Beetlejuice Beetlejuice* (starring Michael Keaton, 2024) is a form of genie. In addition, there have been several other recent movies and TV shows featuring more traditional genies, including *Genie* (starring Melissa McCarthy, 2023), *Three Thousand Years of Longing* (starring Tilda Swinton and Idris Elba, 2022), and *The Lamp* episode (2022) of *What We Do in the Shadows*.

All these genie-centric shows brought to mind the 1891 fantasy short story, *The Bottle Imp*, by Robert Lewis Stevenson. Stevenson was a Scottish author known for his acclaimed poetry, short story collections, and literary and genre fiction, including *A Child's Garden of Verses, New Arabian Nights, Treasure Island*, and *The Strange Case of Dr. Jekyll and Mr. Hyde*. He considered himself sharing the literary goals of fellow Scottish novelist Sir Walter Scott—"a storyteller with an ability to transport his readers away from themselves and their circumstances." His essays, *A Gossip on Romance* and *A Gossip on a Novel of Dumas's*, demonstrated a focus on entertainment rather than instruction.

Yet I would argue that genie stories, in general, and *The Bottle Imp* in particular, not only entertain us but also teach us something insightful about human nature. Since not everyone has read the story, here is the salient element.

The magic item in *The Bottle Imp* is (surprise!) a bottle containing an imp. Not just any imp, but an imp who grants all the owner's desires—a genie without a three-wish limit, just like Barbara Eden in *I Dream of Jeannie*. Mansion,

Lamborghini, Learjet 45, your own private island, health, stunning good looks. They can all be yours! But unlike with sweet Barbara, there's a catch.

Well, actually several catches, and, oh, what a devious trap they set. First: the bottle can only be sold for less cash than the owner purchased it. Nice try, but no fractional Bitcoin transactions are permissible. Second: the bottle may not be given away or discarded. Not so bad. Third: the owner must explain all the rules to prospective buyers. That seems fair enough. Fourth: If the owner dies without having first sold the bottle, then his soul will burn for eternity in Hell.

Well, that isn't very appealing at all. Hard pass.

Still, the bottle is quite alluring, being reputed to account for the successes of Napoleon and Captain James Cook. Over the years, its price has diminished to fifty dollars. Not a huge price, but still, it leaves room for up to 4,999 transactions if the price is reduced by one penny per sale. So far, so good.

Assume for the sake of discussion that, even if you're an atheist, the penalty is indeed an eternity of torment. Also, assume you're not a masochist, so an eternity of torment is to be avoided at all costs. Also, assume you cannot outsmart the imp's rules by subsequently wishing to cancel the transaction, wishing someone buys it for more than you paid, wishing the bottle's penalty nullified, or wishing you can abandon ownership without selling the bottle. In other words, the rules are the rules. If you want to own the bottle, there is no way to avoid the concurrent risks. Personally, I wouldn't suggest owning it for more than a couple of minutes. Make your big wishes and get out. Lastly, and I beg your pardon if I'm wrong, let's assume you would not buy to bottle with the intent of consigning yourself to eternal hellfire in order to altruistically wish away all the world's illness and war.

With those ground rules, would someone buy the bottle for $49.99?

The story's protagonist, Keawe, buys it, and I suspect many real people would, too. After all, they could purchase it for $49.99, use it briefly to fulfill all their wishes, and then sell the bottle for $49.98. Let's ignore the fact that, at least in the story, your gain can come at someone else's loss.

Is there a way to analyze whether it would be reasonable to follow Keawe's example? Yes, we can consider the situation with a logic technique called recursion. Recursion involves a base case along with a series of recursive steps that reduce all successive cases toward the base case. This explanation will be clearer with an example.

Starting with the base case, would someone purchase the bottle for one cent, knowing there can be no more buyers? Hell, no! Literally, because buying it without the ability to sell it is consigning oneself to hell.

Next, consider whether someone would buy the bottle for two cents, knowing that, by the unbreakable and unavoidable rules, they would have to sell it to someone for one cent? Logic would insist no, since we just established in the base case that no one would be self-destructive enough to buy the bottle for one cent. This is the first recursive step.

If no one would buy the bottle for two cents (for the reasons just explained), then who would be foolhardy enough to buy it for three cents? Logically, no one! Ditto for a price of four cents, and so on. Recursion thus proves that there is NO price at which a *logical* person (by my definition, someone who wishes to avoid eternal damnation) should buy the bottle.

Yet multiple bottle sales happen in the story. Further, when I presented the theoretical offer to buy the magic bottle for $50, real-life people consistently accepted. Why? Two reasons come to mind, neither of them shining a flattering light on human nature.

First, a lazy thinker might buy the bottle without making the effort to conduct the analysis just covered. They may figure, *there are plenty of sales prices lower than $50, so I can easily find the next buyer*. And who knows, maybe they'd make their wishes and get lucky enough to find a similarly minded person to buy it from them. Very risky.

Second, a selfish person could buy the bottle fully understanding the risk but planning to sell it to either an intellectually lazy person (as described above) or planning to take advantage of someone incapable of comprehending the peril their purchase would entail. Risky and jerky.

In conclusion, despite his stated goal of solely entertaining, it appears Mr. Stevenson has used a genie to demonstrate something very unflattering about human nature—that we have among us a plentiful supply of slackers and jerks. But don't lose hope. The main characters of his story also demonstrate noble behavior. How? I hope you'll read his story to find out.

SLEEPY HOLLOW RETROSPECTIVE: SOCIAL PANIC AND HORROR IN THE 1790S

GRANT BUTLER

> "*Sleepy Hollow* endures as a piece of American cinema not just because it's well made and has superb atmosphere, incredible visuals, and excellent performances but also because of its groundbreaking source material and what it has to say about America as it came to be."

The fall of 2024 marks 25 years since *Sleepy Hollow* (*Paramount*, 1999) was released to the public. Directed by Tim Burton, it's a loose adaptation of the Washington Irving story "The Legend of Sleepy Hollow" that centers around New York City police constable Ichabod Crane (Johnny Depp) being tasked with getting to the bottom of several murders committed in the town of Sleepy Hollow. Received favorably by fans and critics alike, its accolades include an Academy Award for Best Art Direction. Looking back after all this time, there is no doubt that *Sleepy Hollow* has endured in the minds of cinema fans because it's incredibly unique. But what exactly makes it stand out from numerous other films?

Part of that is due to Tim Burton's direction. The subject matter suits his personal style and interests incredibly well, and it results in one of the most uniquely atmospheric movies out there. From the moment it begins, *Sleepy Hollow* completely immerses you in its world.

But that isn't the main reason *Sleepy Hollow* is such a unique experience. It stands out from most other movies because of the time period it takes place in, as it's about a very specific period in time, right after the American Revolution but before the dawn of the Nineteenth century. This is important because while there have been numerous films about American history and the American Revolution, this unique era has not often been seen in cinema.

When we first meet Ichabod Crane, he's imploring people to move away from the superstitions of the past. But he isn't just talking about the past in a historical sense; he's talking about finally doing away with all the old ideas that were taken from Europe but weren't entirely discarded after the Revolution. To people of that time, "the past" meant not just a time before American independence; it meant ancient European ideas and methods. Ichabod's speech to the court right before being assigned to investigate the Sleepy Hollow killings highlights this point because he specifically references the use of "medieval devices of torture."

What Ichabod is really saying to his audience is that he wants them to solve crimes by discarding outdated and unhelpful methods taken from Europe and instead adapt new techniques for a new American society. The Burgomaster (Christopher Lee) understands this because he wants not just to send Ichabod to solve crimes using these methods but to do it in an area where the people are more likely to be open to them. When assigning Ichabod to Sleepy Hollow, the Burgomaster specifically notes that they are not just farmers but mostly Dutch. This is significant because not only does it highlight how strongly what country you originally came from meant in terms of your identity and how you were perceived, but the Dutch Republic was one of the countries that contributed aid to the Revolution. So this means that the Headless Horseman (Christopher Walken) is not only the ghost of a mercenary who fought for the British during the Revolution, he is killing some of the most prominent people in a community who originally came from a country that gave aid to the American colonists fighting for independence.

The fact that Ichabod is a New York City police constable and the exchange over getting rid of outdated methods takes place there is equally important. During the American Revolution, both the State of New York and New York City were well known to have a significant number of citizens who opposed American Independence and wanted to remain British subjects, known as Loyalists.

Sleepy Hollow has much in common with John Carpenter's *Halloween (Sony, 1978)* because they both revolve around what are essentially ghost stories that represent a very specific image of America and what was on the minds of Americans at a given time. *Halloween* is a tale about the social panic of what may have been lurking behind every well-maintained suburb in America in the 1970s, whereas *Sleepy Hollow* is all about the Revolutionary War and the founding of America as we know it today. It's explicitly stated to Ichabod Crane that the Hessian mercenary they know as the Headless Horseman not only specifically came over to fight for the British against the American Revolution, but he came because it was a perfect opportunity to satisfy his appetite for killing.

Halloween's Michael Myers and the Headless Horseman have much in common, not just because of a seemingly endless desire to kill but also because they are both faceless threats lurking in seemingly prosperous and respectable communities. In many ways, the two films are bookends of the first two hundred years of the United States. While *Sleepy Hollow* is all about the uncertainty lurking behind the new nation, *Halloween* was filmed and released soon after the American bicentennial in 1976 and shows how, despite everything seeming tranquil, there could be darkness lurking there.

Aside from the general plot, *Sleepy Hollow's* focus on the American Revolution is even more striking because, with the exception of Johnny Depp, Christina Ricci, Christopher Walken, and several others, the cast is filled with British actors. Even the specific point in the film takes place—in the 1790s—it is important to remember what was happening at that exact moment in American history. Since *Sleepy Hollow* is set in the fall of 1799, the events Ichabod is sent to investigate happened just before the death of George Washington in December of that year.

The final aspect that makes *Sleepy Hollow* so unique is its source material. The original story by Washington Irving was published in 1820, just two years after the publication of *Frankenstein* by Mary Shelley. The idea of a uniquely American cultural identity is at the heart of both the film and the original story because, at the time of its publication, American literature and American fiction, in particular, were in their very early stages. "The Legend of Sleepy Hollow" predates virtually all the most famous American literature of the Nineteenth century, whether it's by Mark Twain, Nathaniel Hawthorne, or even Edgar Allan Poe.

What the original story does that the film captures (despite all the surface-level changes) is how it takes ancient literary storytelling elements and uses them to tell a story that is uniquely American and connects to America's past specifically. It wasn't just literature; it was part of what was then a brand-new concept called American literature.

Sleepy Hollow endures as a piece of American cinema not just because it's well made and has superb atmosphere, incredible visuals, and excellent performances, but also because of its groundbreaking source material and what it has to say about America as it came to be.

THE LE GUIN STORY THAT'S SCARIER THAN OMELAS: WHY "WAKE ISLAND" DISTURBS ME

PRIYA SRIDHAR

A dystopia hidden within a travelogue to other worlds.

I'm surprised when people talk about Ursula K. Le Guin, they don't mention her short story "Wake Island". It comes from her collection of short stories, *Changing Planes* (Harcourt, 2003), which is about how certain people can travel while their flights are delayed. I read it as a kid, and the implications of the story stayed with me as an adult. It also explores why sleep procrastination, when your own mind turns against you, remains scary.

Most people talk about "The Ones Who Walk Away from the Omelas," which is more a thought experiment than a story. "Wake Island," however, shows a world that is not an experiment; the societal horrors are very real. You can believe that Omelas is a true paradise that doesn't have a dark underside; Wake Island does not have that privilege. Far from being an escape, it is a logical nightmare.

The Changing Planes Gist

Most of *Changing Planes* focuses on different worlds that the narrator ventures into, using the power of her mind and boredom. They tend to be harmless for the most part, such as in a world where teddy bears are reared as actual pets for children of royals and the rich who desire to be poor to get the status that goes with it. A few worlds have more sinister sides, like those who engage in arms races over a small piece of land or have locals exploited for tourism. Each plane's dark side is a mirror of our own.

Generally, there are no consequences to this sort of travel. You can spend two weeks on one plane and return just in time to make your flight without having to rush. And the narrator talks about how this experience can expand your worldview, or narrow it if you're that kind of tourist. Slowly, however, the tales start edging away from a comedic angle to one that is truly disturbing.

"Wake Island"

In "Wake Island," one plane comes up with an experiment to free people from sleep. They start with willing test subjects: parents who are expecting children. Then, this new generation will learn never to sleep. Surely, nothing can go wrong. After all, if you don't sleep, then you can get more work done! Perhaps you can create a more functioning society. Or, as this plane theorizes, you can unlock "lateral genius" and shed a part of an evolution that no longer seems necessary. Humans evolved, after all, and we can keep progressing.

In a compound, the scientists start teaching the babies and children to go without sleep for hours. At first, it seems to go well. Then, the growing children start demonstrating erratic behavior. Without sleep, they don't respond to education or demands. They barely seem to be aware of their surroundings while keeping their eyes open and their bodies moving. Instead, they walk like zombies and act independently of the adults who are brought to monitor them. Both the scientists in charge and the parents come to lose control, with tragic consequences.

For those who know science, sleep is the time when the brain recharges. Cells repair torn muscle tissue and address injuries, if any, acquired during the day, while the mind clears our subconscious with dreams. Sure, our brains sometimes lie to us by saying that being awake has many benefits. In most cases, however, a good night's rest can make all the difference. And when you have insomnia, sleep procrastination, or both? You become paranoid that your own mind is trying to sabotage you.

Le Guin makes this an analogy about parenting. Each family wants the best for their kids in an ideal world. They may, however, have some misconstrued ideas about what that means. And when a parent imposes that idea on a kid who rejects it, the clashes of wills can lead to verbal or physical altercations. The child is raised broken, with resentment and hurt. And for the kids without sleep? They don't have the means to process such trauma and have to act it out in other ways, hurting their parents in turn. The children also don't know the meaning of boundaries with each other, becoming practically feral.

The worst part about the story is that the experimental children are left to fend for themselves after they were raised that way. While one can visit from a distance, apparently, the government that ordered this nurturing has written them off as an embarrassment. We don't hear if anyone has taken accountability, apart from some of the parents who didn't need intensive therapy after the experiment. No one paid for the consequences, except the children rejected by a world that made them that way.

Sleep Tight

With all this context, I maintain that people should be talking more about "Wake Island" when going into Le Guin's more dystopian works. It shows actual horrors that can happen with science gone wrong and what the cost of a "perfect" society and progress may be. And it's a reminder to embrace our imperfections because perhaps they exist for a reason. Sleep helps us survive, while dreams allow us to live.

WRITING ROMANCE AS AN AROMANTIC WRITER: SAILOR MOON AND HOW PORTRAYING LOVE AND ROMANCE IS COMPLICATED

RAMI UNGAR

I'm fascinated by romance. I have been since I first watched *Sailor Moon* as a kid. Watching Usagi and Mamoru (or as they were known then, Serena and Darien) fighting to protect each other and, at times, even sacrificing themselves because of the intensity of their love, I was in awe. Unlike the Disney movies I'd seen before, where "love" and "romance" weren't really explored beyond a cog to keep the plot moving, *Sailor Moon* showed me what love was: a desire for another person and a need for them to always be nearby, but also a willingness to fight and even die for their beloved's life and happiness. That love set a high bar for me and would influence the romantic subplots I would include in the stories I would later write.

It would be several years before I realized that while I loved the idea of romance and loved writing it, I had no desire to experience it personally. I was, and still am, aromantic.

If you're unfamiliar, aromantic people, or aro for short, are people who do not desire or experience romantic love or attraction. Some of us are also asexual and have no interest in sex, though not always (I myself am bisexual). And no, this cannot be changed by just trying to fall in love or "meeting the right person." Aromanticism is as genetic as hair color, eye color, or sexuality. Even if I could change it by finding "the right person," there are seven billion people on the planet. That's way too much work! I have a better chance of winning the lottery.

That being said, there are aromantic people who do have long-term relationships that resemble romantic ones. The couples care for one another, enjoy each other's presence, and do a lot of normal couple things. But they may not have sex, feel the need for romantic gestures, or have the emotional intimacy that a romantic couple would display or need. It's not for every aro person, but there are people like that out there.

And guess what? You do sometimes see characters and couples like this in our media. In *The Owl House*, supporting character Lilith is confirmed aromantic and asexual, though she becomes very close to her sister's house demon Hooty. In Japan, a TV miniseries called *Koisenu Futari*, or "A Couple Without Falling in Love," followed a pair of aromantic, asexual teens in a relationship. And last year, Marvel's character Gwenpool (basically Gwen Stacy meets Deadpool), realized she was asexual and aromantic while in a brief relationship with Julie Powers.

Now, returning to the main subject of this article—writing romance as an aromantic writer—let me be clear: I am not a romance writer. I am a horror writer. Ghosts, monsters, serial killers, and malevolent entities that prey on humanity? That's my thing. But I enjoy putting in a romantic subplot or strong romance element to the stories I write. This can be seen the most in my Victorian Gothic horror novel, *The Pure World Comes*, about a maid who goes to work at the home of a mad scientist. In between terrifying manifestations of monster hands in the bathroom and Jack the Ripper in the library, several pages are devoted to the budding attraction between the main character, Shirley Dobbins, and Griffin Avondale, the nephew of Shirley's master.

Now, you may be wondering how someone who cannot feel romantic love and has no desire to be in such a relationship can write those plots and subplots. Well, it helps that, unlike other aro people out there, I can at least understand romance from an intellectual standpoint. For others like me, even a theoretical view of romance is a bewildering one. But even with that advantage, I still don't have any personal experience and am unlikely to seek it out any time soon. And I can't exactly follow my friends or family around and study their interactions. I don't want to be charged with a crime.

So, how do I learn about romance, let alone portray it in my stories? The same way any writer learns about a subject they are unfamiliar with or unlikely to experience themselves: lots and lots of research. And, for better or for worse, there is a plethora of material to use for research. The romance industry is a billion-dollar-a-year industry, with tens of thousands of new titles released every year. And outside of the romance genre, books, movies, comics, TV shows, music, manga, plays, and art often have romantic subplots that help carry the main stories and keep audiences interested.

Through this glut of materials, I have been able to learn not only the tropes of romance but also what counts as a good or bad portrayal and how to recognize them. For example, I've come to reexamine my beloved *Sailor Moon* and realize that as much as I idolize the love affair of Usagi and Mamoru, it's pretty messed up in some areas. Depending on the adaptation, Mamoru is a lot older than Usagi, which makes it kind of creepy, and Usagi is kind of possessive when it comes to her man. Even her own friends or their future daughter aren't immune from her ire if she thinks they're getting too close to him. It's played for comedy, but still, Usagi, chill out!

It's also made me realize that a lot of famous "love stories"—Romeo and Juliet, Cosette and Marius Pontmercy, Cinderella and her Prince Charming, etc.—are based on love at first sight. This has led to a further realization that these characters aren't in love or in a romance: they're feeling a crush or initial sexual attraction. And while that's good enough for fairy tales or for formats where the main romance must be established quickly, like ballets, it's something that I've come to realize doesn't usually work in real life. And it's not something I like writing into my stories, even though I write about much more unbelievable things every day.

And finally, maybe it's because I'm aro, and outside that experience, I've come to realize how much emphasis many people put on finding and staying with a romantic partner, sometimes to their own detriment. I read advice columns every day, and many letters come from people, men and women, who are wondering how to fix a relationship that doesn't seem to benefit them in any way, but they love their partner, or the latter makes them feel good, or they don't want to leave for one reason or another. It makes me realize that, while I can't feel that sort of love and attachment, I can sympathize with how difficult their situation is and how there are many reasons for any one person to be in these relationships. Even if doing so might not be in their or their partner's best interests.

All this has helped me come to an important conclusion about romance and its fictional counterparts: love and romance are complicated. They require hard work, constant communication, and are never perfect. Love at first sight is popular but unrealistic and is more likely a sign you want to sleep with someone rather than spend the rest of your life with them. Also, portrayals of love should more often portray important factors such as partners being on the same page about work, finances, children, and all the other things that are not incidental or can't be compartmentalized in life. Not just how passionate they are for one another or how long that fluttery feeling in your chest lasts.

And perhaps we can do more to portray romances dying. Not because of a lack of passion, but for all the normal reasons. Differing life goals, disagreements that can't be resolved, even the darker things that normally aren't talked about. That should be portrayed, too.

This is how I, as an aro writer, approach romance in my work. Granted, how well I do this will vary from story to story, and my experience is different from other aro writers. And, in the future, I do want to write more characters who are openly aro like myself. Maybe even ones who are in relationships with partners who, if not also aro, are at least understanding and accepting of an aro partner. More likely, I would like to write characters who are happy as they are and don't feel the pressure to change or lie to themselves.

Still, I know one thing for sure: when I'm writing a romantic subplot, I want my readers to look at my characters and have the same reaction I had as a child to Usagi and Mamoru on *Sailor Moon*. I want them to think, "Now, this is how you portray romance."

HEAVENLY CREATURES, 30 YEARS LATER: A HORRIFIC CRIME BORN FROM FRIENDSHIP

PRIYA SRIDHAR

Heavenly Creatures (*Miramax*) is 30 years old. The movie is a 1994 biopic directed by Peter Jackson (before LoTR fame) about Pauline Parker and Juliet Hulme, two girls convicted of murdering Pauline's mother, Honorah Parker, in 1954. A friendship blossoms between the two girls, bonding over childhoods spent with chronic illness and wanting to write about a fantasy world where Orson Welles inspires a murderous prince and fictional royalty revels in tormenting plasticine masses. Yet this friendship ends in tragedy, as life circumstances and concerned adults worry that the relationship will lose its healthy boundaries. The concerned adults, however, are just as flawed, and their actions make the relationship even less healthy.

I first heard about the film when an art teacher mentioned I was like a character in *The Simpsons* parody of *Heavenly Creatures*. Naturally, I was offended when I understood the full context, but I did want to see the movie to form my opinions about the tale. It is also fascinating to see Peter Jackson's work before *The Lord of the Rings* cemented his director's reputation.

For the record, while I am listening to videos and reading about the real-life murders to inform this article, most of my analysis will come from the movie. The real-life case has more history and nuance than I can cover, requiring presumption about the girls' motivations. In addition, murder is still murder, and no one can condone such an action.

A Driving Question

The movie deals with the horrors of matricide and the motives for a cruel murder. According to documentaries, the crime shocked the surviving parties, as well as Christchurch. Eyewitnesses claimed they saw Juliet and Pauline laughing when they washed off the blood after the deed at a tea kiosk in the park. Pauline's diaries provided the motive that she was sure her mother was an obstacle to the happiness she and Juliet would share.

Jackson mainly wants to ask why. Why did these two girls engage in such a crime, and what motivated them? Jackson simplifies reality to emphasize that the murder was not okay or justified in any way, while still humanizing both protagonists. As Azar Nafisi would say, he used the power of story as a democracy to give people involved a chance to speak their piece long after many of them had passed in real life. One could argue that he succeeded, as Kate Winslet transitioned from a child star role to a starlet icon in the movie *Titanic*, which came out a few years later.

The Hazards of Social Isolation And Generational Trauma

Both Pauline and Juliet's parents note that the girls are not good at making friends. At the least, Juliet isn't; Pauline gets along well enough with her classmates at the beginning of the film. She does well enough in school, at least before becoming obsessed with the Fourth World. Yet she lives under the shadow of her mother Honorah's affair and determination to give her daughter a better life. Honorah's good intentions border on both emotional and physical abuse.

Juliet displays arrogance due to her wealthy background and class. She has never known the financial hardships of having parents who work long hours. Instead, she nurtures abandonment issues and resentment about her life. Juliet's main struggles are physically traumatic since tuberculosis necessitates her isolation, and her parents tend to travel when she has to stay.

Juliet's arrogance rubs off on her best friend; Pauline starts failing her classes, which leads to her parents pulling her out of school and making her get a job. Pauline believes she can access another world where she and Juliet rule together. Nothing matters but the Fourth World, the royals that drink wine and explode banners.

Sickness bonds the girls. Juliet has sustained tuberculosis since she was young, with flares that crop up at the worst possible times. Even in the 2020s, TB is contagious, and during the 50s, the disease isolates her by default when she has a flare. She has to go to a sanitarium to recover, with only letters as her form of communication and no visitors. Pauline sustained osteomyelitis since she was a child and bone infections in her leg. This means that she had to sit out of many school activities and still has scars. Juliet claims they both understand what it's like to be sick and singled out.

The other part of the bond is that their parents have a certain image of how girls should act and are aghast when neither of them conforms. Honorah Parker and Herbert Rieper believe that Pauline should stay quiet, finish her studies, and listen to the records they gift her; she only appreciates the last part. While Dr. Hulme and Hilda Hulme try to show reason and patience for

Juliet, who is a teenager and a little spoiled, their mistakes also affect the tragedy and the motivation behind the murder.

Rebellion becomes liberation, but without temperance, they both cross the line. Namely, the girls forget that other people exist. Juliet's own brother disappears at some point in the movie, and she barely mentions him. (He's alive in the film, but he was just sent to another place to finish his schooling.)

The girls lack healthy outlets to process their mutual traumas. Neither of them trusts therapists, for a good reason, and as a result, they can trust no adults. Pauline lashes out at her mother, Honorah, when her status quo is threatened, while Juliet vents at her father for leaving her when her sickness becomes contagious and her mother for nurturing a selfish affair with a lodger. While they use fictional characters shaped from Plasticine to create heroes and villains, Diello and their royal lives dictate the girls' lives in their fantasy novels concerning the Fourth World. One could argue that creating evil characters allows for cathartic control, something their actual life lacks.

Juliet has abandonment issues combined with chronic illness. She notes with bitterness that her parents left her in the Bahamas "for her health" and rarely visited. New Zealand was supposed to be a fresh start. Yet her idyllic family life falls apart in a matter of months with her mother's affair and Dr. Hulme losing his job at the university. No one states it, but the implications hang that Hilda's affair forced Dr. Hulme to resign. Juliet yells at her parents that they plan to send her to South Africa, where the climate is better, and her father can support her while working in London. In her mind, Pauline is the only one who has never left her. Pauline wrote her letters when she was sick and stood by her when teachers deemed her arrogant.

Types of Love

One irking scene is when Pauline's parents take her to a therapist after suspecting that her relationship with Juliet is unhealthy. Dr. Bennett does have some sensible advice, primarily that there is no shame in having more than one friend, and you don't have to limit yourself. Yet he is dated by the homophobic beliefs and tells Honorah that Pauline is in love with Juliet. He believes the crush will fade over time, as Pauline insists that girls are "silly" and lies that she prefers boys. It seems that he and Honorah have forgotten that Pauline was dating a boy earlier and pursued a semi-serious relationship with him.

Some reviewers have talked about viewing the film through a queer lens; they discussed the sense of rage that builds when you're a teen being told your existence is immoral and that you can't be your real self. They also expressed how the Fourth World felt safe in what it represented, where the girls could relish the arts and be celebrated as queens. At the time the film was released, there weren't many films showing the gray areas of LGBTQ relationships, so it makes sense that some viewers took that interpretation.

As a queer person, I don't believe that the movie shows a queer relationship. Why? Because I have been in friendships that have become obsessive or toxic. In some cases, a person will try to take over your life with their trauma and input, and you use up all your energy to accommodate them, or vice versa. That doesn't need to be romantic. And to a lesser extent, the implications of having two girls commit murder because they were in love are a bit too homophobic for my liking, even for 1990s Hollywood.

There is more than one type of love, and many can become obsessive. Some friendships can become this way, as can familial bonds.

Did Pauline and Juliet's relationship go this way? Yes, I believe so. One of their final deeds before the murder is burning Pauline's records, an act of commitment. They both loved the tenors who crooned arias, who were real people and entertainers. Yet that love of a healthy hobby didn't matter in the face of planning for such a deed.

Toxic Enabling And Further Isolation

The relationship between the girls is unhealthy, but not in the way that the parents think. Instead of a romantic love gone wrong, it's an obsessive friendship that becomes all-or-nothing for both girls. They don't have any outlets besides their novel writing and dreams of going to Hollywood to become actresses. They drop any other healthy outlets, such as socializing in school or playing. LARP-ing in their fantasy world isn't necessarily bad, as we see in movies like *Labyrinth*; the issue is when you choose to think that you are the protagonist and that only you matter, that you can do no wrong.

Juliet doesn't have anyone besides Pauline and her parents. She inadvertently isolates Pauline by showing jealousy over the latter, who has a lover in John, whom Pauline calls Nicholas. Sure, Nicholas is a bit of a douche and a creep with the way that he uses a pretense to sneak into bed with Pauline and starts putting moves on her after he gets the boot, but when Juliet talks about it, she doesn't seem to care about the details of consent or age gaps. She gets jealous that Pauline has a "normal" romantic relationship and a tether to the real world.

Her parents also don't set a good example for her. Juliet's mother has an affair with a lodger, Bill Perry. When Juliet confronts her, Hilda matter-of-factly states that her husband already knows and they have an arrangement in place. Dr. Hulme looks like a kicked puppy for the rest of the movie as he tries to make decisions regarding what's best for Juliet, with Honorah's murder taking the choice out of his hands. Even so, all of his good intentions falter in the face of Juliet's rage.

The Riepers aren't much better. Pauline's grandmother lets slip that Honorah Parker was a home-wrecker, breaking up Herbert Rieper's first marriage when she was seventeen. She has siblings that she has never met and a stepmother who paid the price for the affair. When Pauline confronts Honorah about this after the latter slut-shames her for letting John cuddle in bed with her, Honorah's response is to slap her across the face. Honorah breaks up this relationship and kicks out the boarder without considering that John could have easily molested her daughter or asking Pauline for her side of the story. We saw how it went, that Pauline was trying to push John off her. While the film doesn't outright state this, Honorah's physical and emotional abuse motivates Pauline to seek out John despite his creepy ways, only to dump him when Juliet is no longer contagious and can return home.

This experience makes Pauline believe real boys aren't worth the fuss compared to tenor Mario Lanza or Orson Welles. She can see Juliet anytime she likes without seeing her mother's hypocrisy. John, or "Nicholas" as she calls him, is fun but also chaotic and unstable. He represents a danger she doesn't want to risk unless absolutely necessary. The bicycle scene shows this perfectly when he follows a bus, screaming at Pauline that he loves her. John crosses the line from potential molester to full-on stalker, and police chase him for causing a public disturbance. Meanwhile, Pauline smiles at Juliet while the latter is next to her. Juliet is safe and predictable.

Honorah inadvertently isolates Pauline further by pulling her out of school when the latter stops doing her work. She has a point that Pauline can't be failing her classes but orders her to get a job to make something of her life rather than obsess over a fantasy world. The real world has older women typing away in an office, with Pauline quietly imitating them to earn some income. She is still a child but is forced to grow up all too quickly.

Pauline can only find refuge in Juliet's house, where no one judges her for the person she has become. Because of these actions, however, Dr. Hulme believes it would be healthier to separate the girls. It is ridiculous that neither of them has the necessary space to process these teenage horrors of an affair that breaks up a seemingly perfect household. The judgment comes from a position of medical authority rather than about parenting.

The Final Straw

I don't condone either Pauline or Juliet's actions. They didn't think through the moral implications of their actions or how they would harm others. While I don't think the girls in the movie are narcissists, they do lose their empathy and compassion as their obsessive friendship grows. They both think the real world matters less than the Fourth World, where princes like Diello will kill for them. It says something that Diello, a murderous prince who stabs and executes people on any whim, is their hero of choice. Pauline starts to imagine Diello as her savior by killing the psychologist who evaluates her.

And here is the thing: The film emphasizes that while one can understand Juliet and Pauline, they aren't the only people who matter. Diello would not save them, and emulating him only made things worse. Their actions affected more than one person in a deleterious way. Juliet had a younger brother and a father affected by what she later did, while Pauline's sister Rosemary lost her mother thanks to the former's actions.

Let's also talk about the reason for the murder: the Riepers wouldn't allow Pauline to apply for a passport so she could join Juliet in South Africa. The Hulmes and Riepers make the point that Pauline coming to South Africa would be a daunting journey for a child. Pauline would be separated from her family, starting school in a new place, or having to get a job on a visa. She may think she can handle it with Juliet's friendship, but she is still very young. Approving the passport is one thing, but making all those arrangements is quite another. What doesn't help is that she and Juliet think they will both make it as actresses if they send enough nudes to Hollywood agents. They're still minors while taking photos in the bathroom.

What about the illegitimate point that the adults think if the girls are in love, they are suffering from mental illness? The film implies that this bias was the final straw that led to Juliet and Pauline planning to murder Honorah in cold blood. Pauline embraces being "mad," complete with a Fourth World banner that seals the deal. She then proceeds to write a journal about the plot and, in real life, talks about what it was like planning a "surprise party." Pauline didn't seem to comprehend the gravity of the situation, only caring that she'd be separated from her best friend. Juliet wasn't thrilled that half her family would go to London, the other half would be in New Zealand, and she couldn't stay in either place.

What makes it worse is that in the scene, Honorah is quite nice to the girls after spending most of her screen time berating Pauline. She advises Juliet to button up her coat since it's chilly and thanks Pauline for helping her along the rockier parts of the trail. Juliet's expression becomes thoughtful as Pauline starts to hesitate. Yet they are both too committed to this plan to consider it a bad idea. They use the same stone that Diello uses to kill a random courtier. Only Honorah is not someone casually impaled. She screams the whole time as the girls beat her to death with a brick in a stocking.

The girls don't realize the implications of what they are doing in the film until it is too late, and their last fantasy features them separated as Juliet's parents take her away on a ship. All they can do is scream each other's names as Honorah bleeds out onto the ground beneath them. Diello's clean stabs in plasticine are very different from hitting someone with a brick over and over again. Pauline and Juliet are both crying as they do the deed, screaming loudly.

In real life, the court documents and witness testimony maintain that they did know what they were doing was wrong, but as an adult, Juliet, who went by the name Anne Perry until her death, says that she didn't understand the implications of such a murder until serving her prison sentence. The movie allows the audience to interpret how aware the girls are of their heinous actions, and their fantasy dies with seeing Honorah's body and screaming in remorse over what they did.

Living In The Real World

A fantasy can only protect you so much from what happens in reality. When escapism impedes your empathy rather than expanding on it, then you have a problem. Yes, you should call out people who are not kind to you. You should know the truth about what happens. But when you are not kind in turn because you believe that only you matter, those actions have consequences.

Pauline and Juliet's flaw is that they let an obsessive friendship and a desire for another world deprive them of empathy for other beings. By thinking they only mattered, they stopped being kind and considerate to others, leading to their worst possible act. Their attempt to reshape a reality that conforms to what they want, regardless of how other people see it, instead separates them forever.

Heavenly Creatures is an unsettling film as a character study in empathy. Even thirty years later, it reminds viewers that you still have agency and choices.

FRANK-N-FURTER, IT'S ALL OVER: HAS SOCIETY PROGRESSED PAST THE NEED FOR ROCKY HORROR?

ALEX KINGSLEY

> " . . . as the saying goes, satire requires clarity of meaning lest it be confused for that which it seeks to mock."

Taking a Look at the Queer Horror Cult Classic Nearly 50 Years Later

When I first watched *The Rocky Horror Picture Show,* I hated it. Years later, I was an assistant stage manager for a live production of the show, and my perspective shifted. For one thing, hearing the text every night, I caught a lot of things that I didn't initially understand when I first watched it. But more than that, I got to experience the conviviality of a live, interactive show with an audience that was excited to be there. Now my perspective on it is more nuanced. I see the aspects of the show that are quite brilliant, but I still see flaws. Is it a product of its time? Absolutely. But as with all works that have aged poorly in some respects, it is worth examining: Is this something we should still be performing? This is a particularly scary question to be asking, especially given just how much people love the show. I've known many people (mostly fellow queer people) who refuse to hear any criticism of their beloved *Rocky Horror,* and while I respect that people want to enjoy what they enjoy unmolested, I do think it's a topic worth examining.

On a conceptual level, *Rocky Horror* is excellent satire. Our setup is a familiar B-movie plot. The young, innocent—and most importantly *pure*—couple find that their car has broken down in the middle of nowhere (you know, that rope that started man hand hook car door) and the only place around is a spooky mansion which, as the audience knows, is full of horrors. The horrors here, however, are rampant sexuality and gender-bending—which, to a conservative audience, *is* horrific. Instead of creating a monster, Frank-N-Furter is just making a really hot guy that he can marry.

However, as the saying goes, satire requires clarity of meaning lest it be confused for that which it seeks to mock. The second act of *Rocky Horror* is where clarity of meaning declines rapidly. Broadly, unclear meaning is not a bad thing. *Rocky Horror* is not just satire, it is also avant-garde, and the search for meaning in the avant-garde is often not only fruitless but also antithetical to the whole idea of avant-garde. One of the reasons I'm such a big David Lynch fan is that *I* get to decide what *Mulholland Drive* (2001) is about because no one really knows, least of all David Lynch. When satire and avant-garde combine, however, messaging gets murky.

To begin with, the second act starts with Frank-N-Furter sexually assaulting both Brad and Janet. It's played for laughs, and also, the idea is that this assault is what makes both of them decide to give in to their sexual desires. On the one hand, the idea of trans people as rampant assaulters is definitely one that still gets circulated, and it could definitely use some making fun of. But let's go back to the original conceit for a moment: that the things conservative America sees as horrific, like free love and queerness and gender fluidity, are not actually all that bad, so framing them as bad is comedic. Sexual assault, however, I think we'll all agree, is pretty bad. The message that "it's okay to desire physical pleasure" is a good one, but much of the physical pleasure we see in the show is not actually consensual, thus conflating assault with the concept of simply "giving into your desires."

This extends beyond the top of the second act and into the floor show, in which all of our characters have been drugged and made to dance in corsets and fishnets. Frank-N-Furter is framed as a martyr who dies in the name of free love, but it's hard to feel sympathy for a martyr who has been forcing people into his vision of sexuality and gender.* The floorshow ends with the empowering message, "Don't dream it, be it," but the whole thing feels a little hollow when, in context, the characters are singing this against their will. If this is a story about liberation, shouldn't the characters actually desire that liberation?

Now I know many will say: hold on, that's the point. Frank is the embodiment of everything conservatives fear trans people to be, not what they actually *are*. So the fact that he's forcing people into sex-related activities actually makes total sense because he's a manifestation of projected fears (kind of like the Gremlins, which I also wrote an article about that you can view here). I accept this rebuttal. My other issue, though, stems from the way that *Rocky Horror* equates liberation with sexual liberation specifically. As an asexual person, I find the story very difficult to relate to. It's a very sex-positive show, which, hey, sex-positive is great, but at times, the implications of "we *all* have these deep dark desires that we're holding in" can feel isolating because, well, we don't all have that. I understand why it was radical in its time, but now it feels as though we could do with telling stories that are more inclusive of the wide variety of sexual experiences that we now know to exist.

Not every piece of media is for every audience, and that's perfectly reasonable, but given that *Rocky* is often treated as a bastion of the queer and trans community, it seems a little strange for it to involve aspects that come off as alienating to some queer and trans people. The sense of isolation I get from the show is compounded by the fact that there is such genuine joy in the participatory aspect of the live performances. Whether it's a shadow cast or a full production, there is a sense of group togetherness that comes from yelling "slut!" and "asshole!" and other such things. I only wish that some sense of group participation could exist for a different story that was perhaps not so sex-centric or so questionable with its treatment of transgender stereotypes.

So, if it has the potential to perpetuate harmful transgender stereotypes due to its unclear messaging, and it no longer feels like a symbol of the queer community, given that it is unrelatable to many asexual people, why do we still put it on? For one thing: people love to feel sexy. Especially young people. In the production I worked on, I saw college students taking a lot of joy in getting to dance around in corsets and fishnets in front of their friends. And there's nothing wrong with wanting that! Young people are going to want to explore their sexuality no matter what. I simply wish that the hallmark of participatory queer cinema was not something that was, in fact, so alienating to a decent chunk of the queer community.

So, should we stop putting on *Rocky Horror*? I don't think we have to. And I know that even if I did, that certainly wouldn't stop anyone. It's a beloved classic, and far be it from me to tell anyone to stop loving it. I just think that if you are considering putting on your own production, perhaps consider other options. It's not that I think you'd actively be doing harm by putting it on, but that there are other works by queer and trans writers to choose from that you may find speak more authentically to a contemporary cast and audience. What new stories could we be exploring? What new ways can we explore the possibilities of interactive live performance? These are questions that I believe are worth answering. It would be lovely if we could find a community event that is truly for the whole community.

**Also a martyr who inexplicably hacks someone to death with an ax? I was honestly never able to fully understand that part, but I always chalked it up to the avant-garde aspect.*

THE END OF NANOWRIMO: AFTER ALLEGATIONS OF INAPPROPRIATE RESPONSE TO ABUSE, THE ONLINE WRITING COMMUNITY STRUGGLES TO MAKE SENSE OF IT ALL

PRIYA SRIDHAR

If you have heard of NaNoWriMo, you probably know the challenge is to write 50,000 words in one month. NaNoWriMo is an abbreviation of National Novel Writing Month, an event that happens every November, with summer camp versions in April and July. Some published authors have even made their debut with such works.

Being part of NaNoWriMo has formed a portion of my volunteering time. I've been working with my local group since 2019 as a Municipal Liaison (ML) after the previous ML moved to another state. She is awesome, and I miss her dearly. I took her example to try to support fellow writers, and I was supported as well.

Now, I'm following her example again by leaving the organization after being an ML for four years. Why? The organization is punishing volunteers for upper management's lack of accountability and oversight regarding allegations of a moderator grooming minors.

Back in November, I posted thoughts about the challenge and organization after hearing terrible allegations. Now, in May 2024, I still can't comprehend what happened. NaNoWriMo is supposed to be a fun challenge where you and your friends find out if you can write a novel in a month or at least 50k. Somehow, it has changed into an organization that focuses on protecting itself rather than the minors who were targeted.

A Difficult Departure

This year, in 2024, I made the hard decision to step down as ML in my region. Why? Because the NaNoWriMo Headquarters sent out an email to a portion of the MLs with an updated agreement. I didn't see it, but others did. They forwarded me the information. The agreement would put the burden of barring minors from NaNoWriMo online communities on the MLs, most of whom were not involved in this scandal. In the same paragraph, in-person communities and events would also be adults-only, though I can't confirm or deny if this part has been changed since. Different clauses showed contradictions, and an actual lawyer went through the document.

Business school had a class on law. It is advised always to read and understand a contract before signing. This principle applies to volunteer and commercial positions. You need to understand what you are committing to before agreeing to this statement.

Normally, I would have asked questions about the agreement and about modifying it. Other MLs had, however, according to social media, most who asked questions were encouraged not to return, if not outright fired. The email also said we had to sign it by March 15. Such arbitrary responses and a tight deadline cemented my decision. While NaNoWriMo extended the deadline, it was only after multiple MLs pointed out the issues and the HQ managers organized a Zoom session that was meant to answer questions. That whole session has become a can of worms as a recording was uploaded to YouTube, which HQ did not like.

I felt confused, betrayed, and cheated when reading a draft of the agreement. While there are plenty of NaNoWriMo scandals, the changes to the ML agreement did not make rectifications or put in practical measures to prevent the alleged abuse from happening. Instead, it scapegoated the MLs for wanting to stay and lead writer communities. I have been very lucky to work with a good local community and avoided most of the fireworks. As a result, my resentment grows when hearing about the lack of answers.

The Backstory

While it's sordid, the long and short of it is that on the NaNoWriMo website forums, a moderator was accused of grooming minors. The moderator, nicknamed X, was allegedly linking them to at least one NSFW RP site. Other moderators and concerned members tried reporting it, but management did not take action. The situation went on for months until it reached a head in November 2023 , and people blew the whistle, right when the National Novel Writing Month challenge was underway. NaNoWriMo's HQ and administration kept hearing the allegations and took action: to ban minors from using the forums and website. Moderator X received a ban from NaNoWriMo on the grounds of making "threats".

That moderator is dead now; I found out from a verified source that in late 2023, they passed due to a long-term illness. Their Tumblr posts show no remorse, only anger, and insist they were the victim. From the accounts I read and corroboration from people who were on the forums at the time, the opposite was true.

Reddit has also listed other cases where the main NaNoWriMo organization has failed to address allegations. I would need to do further research to verify those claims, but given the large amount, a pattern emerges. And with it, the question: how did a fun challenge end up here?

What Does It Mean Now

This means that during April Camp April NaNoWriMo, there were plenty of MLs who were unable to help run the various regions. I was upfront with my local Discord server about what happened. If we do any challenges, it will be independent of NaNoWriMo. Other MLs have done the same, notifying their regions and making necessary changes.

The fun is now gone; even if I did another April challenge, it wouldn't be the same. There'd be the memory of what I thought NaNoWriMo was: a chance to grow and find a community. While I'm keeping the friends I made and shutting out the one creep who asked me out despite looking like my dad, I'm still grieving. Other MLs are as well.

My community was okay with my decision to separate my Discord from Nanowrimo. I was very fortunate in that regard when I shared the ML agreement with them. From what I've seen from the participants who weren't volunteers, the ones that have stayed are having functionality issues with the website, unable to log in their words accurately or receive medals.

Writing is a lonely business, I often joke, and we do better when we have friends. Taking the fun away means that a person has to find those friends in other places and find the joy somewhere else. It means moving forward and feeling every emotion to experience a necessary catharsis.

A GRUESOME GATEWAY: THE ENDURING VALUE OF *SCARY STORIES TO TELL IN THE DARK*: THE MOST FREQUENTLY CHALLENGED BOOKS OF THE 90S

CHRIS CAMPEAU

"Don't you ever laugh as the hearse goes by,
For you may be the next to die."

So starts "The Hearse Song," one of the many dark fables found in the pages of Scholastic's infamous *Scary Stories to Tell in the Dark* books. If you grew up in the 80s or early 90s, then there's a good chance you're familiar with the series—if not for author Alvin Schwartz's grisly retelling of campfire folklore, then undoubtedly for Stephen Gammell's haunting illustrations.

Most of us recall Gammell's work in detail because the illustrations *are* so detailed. At the time, our pre-adolescent eyes had never seen such disturbing works: an inky apparition with hollow eyes and rotting flesh, a pair of gangly limbs hanging from a blackened mantle. Only by giving the Blair Witch a hit of acid and a stick of charcoal could you truly rival Gammell's caliber of dark artistry.

But while most of us attributed our childhood insomnia to the series' nightmare-inducing pictures, the stories scared us just as bad, equal contributors to the ALA having cited the paperbacks as the most frequently challenged books of the '90s.

Unlike other concerned citizens, my parents never attended a PTA meeting in the books' opposition, but my mother did sell my copies at a garage sale a few years back; fortunately, after I expressed interest in reading them again, she managed to track down an original set on eBay (thanks, Mom!).

Having read them anew, I can better appreciate why I, like others, fell in love with the books in the first place. At an age where bigger texts were becoming more appealing than the picture books we'd grown up with, kids like me were drawn to the *Scary Stories* paperbacks for their transitional worth: Schwartz's bite-sized narratives were easy, digestible reads, but they still challenged our literacy.

More notably, they were imaginative and viscerally descriptive, and they significantly expanded our understanding of the horror story, not to mention the story in general. Schwartz drew on the sound structure of folklore to teach children the fundamentals of narrative, igniting in many of us a newfound passion for the written word. For some, *Scary Stories* became the foundation of a literary obsession, building us up toward bigger beasts like *Goosebumps, Fear Street,* King, Koontz, and more.

For those of us who managed to get past the jarring drawings, to read the stories themselves, there's no doubt we were fascinated. Ghosts, ghouls, bloody fingers, and decapitated heads—Schwartz delivered all the cheap thrills. At times, however, he dove deeper, giving us passages that added depth to our idea of death and mortality and left our vulnerable imaginations festering with fear.

"As Jim Brand lay dying, his wife left him with his nurse and went into the next room to rest. She sat in the dark staring into the night."—*"Like Cat's Eyes"*

We often identified with the characters, too. Though most of the protagonists are ghost-story staples (old men and women, husbands, wives, and widows), many are just children doing childlike things (at first): a boy playing in his garden discovers a toe sticking out of the soil; later, his parents cook it for dinner; a young girl goes to bed to find a ghost on her dresser; the next night, it's moved to her ceiling.

A portion of the stories also center on high-schoolers—no doubt of similar age to many readers' siblings: in "Hello, Kate!" a teenage boy is accompanied to the school dance by a dead girl; in "High Beams," a teenage girl is preyed upon by a knife-wielding maniac hiding in the backseat of her car.

But it wasn't just the stories that opened our minds to the macabre. In *More Scary Stories to Tell in the Dark,* the series' second volume, Schwartz introduced us to a "game that young people sometimes play . . . for the fun and the excitement." In hindsight, I can say with certainty that trying to summon Bloody Mary from the dead in my best friend's bathroom mirror was far from fun; hell, I still have a hard time facing mirrors in the dark. Thanks, Al.

Aside from stories, poems, and the odd song or game, Schwartz found another means of baffling our brains: his notes and sources. In *More Scary Stories,* he details the origins of a tale titled "Buried Alive," prefacing his citation with some unsettling exposition:

"When a dead person is embalmed, a fluid commonly containing formaldehyde is pumped into the blood and lymph systems. It preserves the body for a long time."

For many kids, particularly those who haven't yet attended a funeral, the cadaver-prepping process is a new topic. Schwartz didn't sugar-coat his research, and while some parents were put off by his bluntness, we youngsters, with our infinite curiosity being directly addressed, felt a little more academic for it and, therefore, more appreciated (despite being completely horrified).

In the series' final volume, Schwartz thanks the many boys and girls who asked for yet another book of scary stories, noting that he "hopes it pleases them." Having passed away shortly after its publication, the author likely didn't get a chance to gauge just how much enjoyment that third installment, and the series on the whole, brought his audience; though, if his book sales to date were any indication, I'm sure he had a good idea.

Despite ill-advising parents and elementary schools pulling the paperbacks from library shelves, demand for the books couldn't be silenced, partly because of their taboo status, sure, but more likely for their gripping content. Whether ordered directly through Scholastic or passed on to a friend at a sleepover, the books continued (and continue) to be read and shared long after Schwartz's death. Having been a fanatic of folklore, I'm sure he would have appreciated their continuity.

Schwartz's passion for researching and retelling tales of terror offered children something they hadn't yet been exposed to: the timelessness of urban legends and the resulting fun of collective fear. Reading *Scary Stories to Tell in the Dark*, even with one's friends, was like being led alone into a forest at night. With each story finished, one moved farther along a path built on centuries of age-old legend and littered with scraps of flesh. By the last tale, you were so deep in the woods that even upon emerging, the entire world seemed a little darker. And for us kids that found some solace in the dead of night, a little more thrilling, too.

WHAT WRITERS CAN LEARN FROM THEATER PRACTITIONERS: "WHAT'S MY MOTIVATION?"

ALEX KINGSLEY

"What's my motivation?"

This is probably the line that most people think of when they imagine the cliche of a pretentious actor, maybe wearing horn-rimmed sunglasses and a long silk scarf. As a kid, I knew this was "the thing actors say" before I understood it. Now that I'm a director, I find I'm always asking actors to ask themselves this very question. "*Why* do you move over there? *Why* do you say that to him? *Why* do you respond that way? What's your *motivation*?"

Strangely, I often ask the same thing during workshops with my writers' group. "I would believe this scene more if I understood *why* she did it." The connection made me realize that writing and directing are essentially one and the same—the only difference is that in the former, the actors live in your brain. The writer still has to do all the same work with them, though: ask them what they want, give them blocking, and, most importantly, make the audience believe that they are fully realized people. In fact, I believe my writing improved dramatically when I was able to layer my director goggles on top of my writer lenses.

So, if you're a writer who's never set foot in a rehearsal room—well, first of all, I really recommend it, but assuming you don't have the time—here's a quick and dirty guide to all the ways theater practices can inform and assist prose writers.

1. Character Work

When writing prose, characters are just one of the many aspects of the story we are juggling. Sure, we know they're important, but we've also got plot and setting and form and style . . . the list goes on. An actor, however, *only* focuses on character, and since a director's primary function is to guide and support the actors, they do a lot of character work together. Applying the same kind of character analysis to prose characters that actors do to stage characters can help breathe life into characters that were otherwise lacking.

I do a variety of character exercises with the actors I collaborate with. First comes **tablework**. "Tablework" is exactly what it sounds like—the work that is done not on the stage but at the table, in the form of a group discussion. I start with what I call the Character Web. Any story has at its core a complex network of relationships. In order to portray those relationships onstage (and, by extension, in order to express those relationships on the page), we must first intimately understand them. We go around the table and discuss every single character pairing in the play, asking questions like:

- Have these two met before the start of the play?
- What do they think of each other?
- What do they mean to each other?
- What do they want from each other?

Next, we do our **character dossiers**. This is a set of questions I've refined over the years that I believe best cut to the essence of the character. The questions range from core personality questions like "What is their biggest fear?" to mundane things, like "What do they like to eat?" In order to understand a character fully, it's important to know not just their underlying psychology but the ins and outs of their day-to-day life.

Lastly, we work on the various ways the characters interact with the world. We experiment with different voices before we find how our characters speak, play with different walks until we figure out how our character moves. We work on simple actions, like sitting in a chair. I even have actors improvise monologues so they have a sense of how the character's voice sounds and the peculiarities of their speech and word choice. Knowing these specificities about a character is often more useful to the actor than knowing, say, their deep, dark subconscious secrets.

Famed theater practitioner Stanislavsky, creator of the "Method" involved in the increasingly popular "method acting" * technique, started by having actors attack their characters' psychology—and found that these actors became so preoccupied with their thoughts that they didn't actually *act.* When Stanislavsky had his actors focus on manifesting the character in their body, their performances improved dramatically.

In any kind of fiction, whether it's a play, a novel, a game, or something else entirely, I call these little details "grounding granules." They are the little specificities that give a character life. Other elements of a story can contain grounding granules as well—a setting, for instance, or even a scene. A small, enticing detail can have a powerful effect.

When writing a character, you can do all the same work that I have actors do. Write a monologue from their perspective. Figure out how they speak, how they move, and even what their favorite food is. It's these grounding granules that make the character feel real.

2. Blocking

When writing the physical action of a scene, I often think of it as akin to blocking a scene in a play. "Blocking" means determining the movement of a scene—where the actors go, where they stand, what they do with the props, etc. A scene with no movement is boring. A scene full of meaningless movement, however, is confusing. Every action onstage must be motivated (which, again, is why actors are often asking for that motivation to be given to them). The same is true of action on the page. If a character adjusts their glasses and shuffles their feet while speaking, that means something. There's a reason they did it, even if the character themself wasn't consciously aware.

Given my background in playwriting, I often find that when I'm writing a novel that I have written a scene that is almost entirely dialogue. I need to add some kind of action, lest my reader come away feeling like they're reading a screenplay, not a finished work. I tell myself, "Alright, I've already approached this scene as a playwright. How would I approach it as a director? These characters are my actors, and they already have their lines. Now I need to give them their blocking." I go back through the scene and imagine I am directing it like a play. Where would I tell an actor to move? Why? What motivates the action? The result is a scene full of purposeful, interesting movement that enhances the scene instead of distracting from it.

3. Do and Being

The dichotomy of "doing vs being" in acting is akin to "show vs tell" in writing. "Show vs tell," however, was a difficult concept for me to grasp as a young writer. If I'm using words, isn't that telling inherently? It wasn't until I got involved in theater that I understood.

It doesn't get you very far to give an actor an adjective. If you tell an actor, "be sad" or "be bored," you're not really giving them much to work with. The best direction comes in the form of active verbs—the more vivid, the better. I get the most exciting and surprising performances when I say things like, "beg her," or "play with him," or "pull an answer out of them." These bold action verbs often manifest in bold choices from the characters as well. For example, if I tell an actor to "plead," they may fall to their knees in supplication, lacing their fingers together, their voice on the edge of sobbing. If I had just said, "Be desperate," then I wouldn't have gotten a performance nearly as interesting.

Treat your characters like your actors. Instead of focusing on what they are—contrite, joyful, bored, etc.—focus on what they're *doing* about it. In this respect, you are both director and actor. Choose the action verbs for your characters, and then make bold acting choices on their behalf.

Bonus—Tabletop Roleplaying Games

If you want to microdose on practicing theater, I recommend tabletop roleplaying games. When you play a character in a TTRPG, you do all the same character prep that you would need to perform a role. The major difference is that, just as in writing a novel, *there is no script*. You are tasked with not only performing your character but writing all that character's dialogue and action *on the spot.* It's essentially the practice of writing a novel collectively, and your only responsibility is to play this one character and take care of your fellow players as you do.

Does this sound fun or terrifying to you? If you answered the latter, let me give you the ultimate TTRPG hack: if you know your character inside and out, if you've done all the character preparation listed above, playing a tabletop character is not only easy—it is delightful. When you get to know a character that well, their dialogue flows seamlessly because *you know how they think.* With ample tabletop experience, you will never struggle with dialogue again.

At their roots, writing and acting are essentially the same activity: storytelling. Therefore, the same basic principles can be applied to both. However, sometimes reframing those principles from a new perspective helps you to better apply them. It is my hope that this new lens on writing prose can provide a fresh new look at storytelling conventions to those who are unacquainted with theater. And if the lens wasn't helpful, well, at least you are now a little more acquainted with theater than you were before.

Notes

*I include a footnote here because "the method" is something very commonly misunderstood. When most people refer to method acting, they are not referring to Stanislavsky's teaching but rather the work of Lee Strasberg, who claimed to use Stanislavsky's "method" despite never actually consulting with him about it. Irene Adler criticized Strasburg's interpretation of Stanislavsky, and when Adler traveled to Russia to study Stanislavsky, he agreed that Strasburg's teachings were not in line with his own. Ironically, thanks to Strasberg's reputation as an acting coach for famous movie stars, it is his interpretation of the Method that people often remember and not that of Stanislavsky, the originator.

THE RPGS THAT SPAWNED FROM ALIEN: FROM FREE LEAGUE PUBLISHING TO MOTHERSHIP TO CHRIS BISSETTE'S THE WRETCHED

A. A. VOIGT

Alien, Ridley Scott's 1979 sci-fi horror classic, turned forty-five this year. The legacy of the original film casts a long shadow over both the genre of space horror and filmmaking generally—I saw the chest-burster parodied in *Shrek 2* long before I watched its source material. But as *Alien* infected the imaginations of creatives throughout the years, it has jumped mediums.

Alien explores subjects such as corporate greed and the hazards of space travel while showcasing its iconic monster. While video games were an obvious next step, I'm interested in how *Alien* inspired tabletop games, and in particular, how much the spirit of the first movie is present in roleplaying games (RPGs) that draw from its themes and ambiance.

Alien's officially licensed RPG was released in 2019 by *Free League*, but games such as *Tuesday Knight Games' Mothership* and Chris Bissette's solo journaling RPG, *The Wretched*, also claim direct lineage from the film. The following is an analysis of how these three tabletop games work with those motifs and implement them in their text.

The Company

Part of *Alien's* charm is its framing as "space truckers" caught up in a scheme far beyond their pay grade, but inherent in that conceit is the exploitation of the crew's labor. From the film's opening, where Parker and Brett complain they're not being paid the same as the rest of the crew, to the final, corporate-mandated betrayal by Ash, *Alien* cares deeply about how organizations use financial incentives and legal contracts to extract value from workers, often at the cost of their lives. While Weyland-Yutani, the corporation known as "The Company," is never directly referenced in the first movie, its presence is keenly felt, an invisible hand pushing the USCSS Nostromo to its demise.

Free League Publishing's Alien RPG

The *Free League Alien RPG* directly references the history of the Weyland-Yutani company, drawing from the franchise's sequels and spinoffs to develop a lore-accurate timeline of the history of Earth and how humanity came to be dominated by corporations. But beyond deploying in-universe explanations for the company's greed, the *Alien RPG* also explicitly calls out the horror of late-stage capitalism as a thematic touchstone. "*Alien* focuses on blue-collar workers at the bottom of the economic ladder" (*Alien RPG Core Rulebook*).

While the Free League game doesn't place as much emphasis on worker exploitation as it does on combat, it makes a sincere attempt to mechanically integrate this theme into its rules. Two of the main player classes are "Company Agent" and "Roughneck," drawing a clear line between white and blue collar workers in the game world. The Company Agent's personal agenda, a narrative device tied to level-up incentives, ranges from pure self-interest to a desire to find out what your employer is keeping from you. As far as Starting Gear is concerned, *Free League* missed an easy layup, giving the Company Agent the same cash-on-hand roll as the majority of other classes.

However, this misstep is remedied by the inclusion of a table of weekly salary ranges, which vary based on occupation. Commercial employees earn a weekly rate of $400 to $960, whereas corporate workers earn $540 to $1200, while those in "elite occupations" rake in as much as $20,000. This salary table seems unlikely to be used often—what's the point of playing an *Alien* game if you're not going to be slaughtered by an alien?—but its inclusion is a smart way to demonstrate the worker versus employer divide at the heart of the first movie.

Tuesday Knight Games' Mothership RPG

Mothership expounds on this financial friction with an elegant debt system. Spaceships are expensive—a mere escape module will run you 200 million credits. If players want to be captains of their own ship, the rules ask them to simply put 10% of their earnings away toward paying off their loan and even allow for 6d10% of the debt to have already been cleared at the start of play. That sense that players are constantly working off a massive sum is a compelling way to frame characters' motivations.

If, at the start of a session, your Game Master (GM) reminds you that you only owe 140 million more credits on your sci-fi car loan, you're going to be especially motivated when a shady message offering a too-good-to-be-true payday comes across your inbox. Furthermore, the *Mothership Warden's Operation Manual* lays out additional rules governing salary, hazard pay, expenses, and contract negotiation. While these procedures are lightweight and straightforward like the rest of the base game, they suggest that Tuesday Knight Games wanted to provide GMs a narrative scaffold to more acutely target their players' pocketbooks, pushing them toward lucrative but ultimately deadly missions.

Chris Bissette's The Wretched RPG

Of the three games, *The Wretched* has the least direct connection to corporate exploitation, with no mention of a company or shares throughout the text. Bissette's take is the most structurally distinct from the *Free League Alien RPG* and *Mothership*, being a journaling game played with a Jenga tower, contrasted with the other texts' more traditional design. However, *The Wretched*'s ending is more in the spirit of *Alien* than any of the rules and mechanics laid out in the previous two games. It opens with a sliver of hope that players may escape the alien vessel they're trapped upon. But its end pulls back the curtain: "You were doomed from the start." *The Wretched* is not a game intended to be won. Just like the expendable crew of the Nostromo, the text of *The Wretched* does not care if its players live or die and, in fact, expects it.

The Void

Alien's famous tagline, "In space, no one can hear you scream," has more to do with its horror elements than the vast expanse of vacuum, but it highlights an element of the film that gets overshadowed by its iconic monster. Much of the movie's first act is spent navigating an unfamiliar region, landing on a strange planet, and attempting to survive a cold, uncaring atmosphere that human minds can barely comprehend. From the fossilized Space Jockey to mundane quarantine procedures, *Alien* wants its audience to understand that the universe is full of inexplicable and dangerous phenomena, and those who do not take pains to protect themselves from the unknown will soon become intimately familiar with its most destructive facets.

Mothership is more concerned with the goings-on inside various derelict space stations but acknowledges that stepping outside them will kill you more thoroughly than any alien creature. Players are expected to make panic checks whenever their ship is damaged, and occasionally a critical hit will result in a hull breach, which can result in characters being flung into the void if they're unlucky. This parallels directly with the scene in *Alien* when the crew realizes the facehugger's blood is made of acid, which is slowly trickling through their vessel's floors. Similarly, at the very end of the movie, Ripley is careful to first don a vacuum suit before ejecting the xenomorph into the void, an act which would, in the *Mothership* ruleset, prevent her from taking Disadvantage to her roll.

The *Free League Alien* RPG provides a little more support to simulate the difficulty of space survival. Two of its core character skills include Piloting and Survival, both of which would prove immensely helpful out on the galactic frontier. The Nostromo's rough landing on the unknown planet could be easily modeled in the Free League game, though the RPG's Stunt system gives players an advantage over a ruleset that would use a simple pass/fail check. The Survival skill's rules make clear that its expected use is for dealing with atmospheric or environmental hazards, such as the gnarly gale that constantly blows across the unknown planet's surface. *Alien* RPG also lays out a list of conditions that could conceivably impact players while trying to make it through hostile environments. Starving, Dehydrated, and Exhausted conditions may reduce a character's effectiveness in play, simulating the necessity of having adequate food, water, and sleep, but the text also includes a Vacuum condition to be applied when a character is in space without adequate equipment. In contrast with the relatively forgiving ruleset of the *Alien RPG* system, the Vacuum rule demands a Stamina check every round, with increasing penalties, with any failure reducing a character's health to zero and initiating Death saves. Unless players have specialized space suits, there is no salvation to be found on the outside of a ship.

Of the three games, *The Wretched* pays the most attention to the difficult work of staying alive in space. *The Wretched* takes place in something of an alternate ending of *Alien*, where instead of blasting the xenomorph into the darkness, Ripley remained trapped aboard the shuttle, conscious as the monster clung to the outside of its hull. As a journaling game, *The Wretched* differs drastically from *Mothership* and *Alien RPG* in that it is not concerned with the minutiae of dealing damage and suffering conditions but instead gives players prompts to structure their miserable days aboard the dead vessel. Many of these prompts involve ship maintenance: investigating strange noises in the air vents, unjamming broken doors, and frantically repairing a malfunctioning oxygen dispenser. Because the gameplay of *The Wretched* is more interested in description than simulation, the text allows greater flexibility for players to encounter and struggle with the numerous problems that would come with managing a damaged spaceship. In this sense, I feel *The Wretched* succeeds at creating a sense of dread that the other two games cannot adequately match. When paired with its block tower countdown, players of *The Wretched* will be able to physically see their ship falling apart, with increasingly flimsy bits of metal separating them from a frozen grave.

The Creature

Game designers of all three texts are presented with the daunting task of showcasing a monster as deadly and strange as the xenomorph while working within the constraints of their medium. While the Free League RPG has all the licensing and art required to portray the actual, trademarked "alien," game masters do not have the advantage of slow, tense camera pans and lovingly molded practical effects to force players to confront a sleek, black killing machine. What the *Alien RPG* does provide to help build a sense of dread is a system for pacing.

The *Alien RPG* encourages game masters to utilize maps to plan their adventures and then split map areas into "zones," units of distance that can range from twenty-five meters to "a few steps across." Unlike many tactical RPGs, these zones do not have to be of uniform sizes, which allows for time dilation when traversing them. Free League gives GMs a lot of freedom to control the speed at which players move through a location, which helps recreate climactic moments from *Alien*, the charged frames before the monster strikes from the shadows. You can get scenes like Dallas creeping through the ship's air ducts, cognizant of an increasingly close xenomorph, because player characters typically only move one zone during stealth gameplay, whereas the aliens can move as many zones as they have Speed points. When combined with hidden checks and concealed NPC movement, the GM can create situations in which players can be preyed upon by a xenomorph quickly and quietly, unaware of the danger until it's too late.

Where I feel the Free League game stumbles, unfortunately, is the moment after the jump-scare. Because *Alien RPG* uses a dice pool system, combat rolls can have GMs rolling a huge number of d6, only finding success when a die comes up 6. While the game wisely includes a probability table showing exactly how likely a particular number of dice are to succeed, I feel the die pool approach may slow down what would otherwise be a climactic moment, especially when working with the xenomorph's high stats (an adult soldier xenomorph can roll up to 12 dice in one attack). Even with the game's branded d6, it's hard to capture the sudden flash of teeth and claws that made the first film's death scenes so frightening when you're picking through a double handful of dice. Furthermore, properly equipped players can block the strike of a xenomorph and, if lucky, deliver a counterblow or reduce damage taken. While these rules allow players to remain in the game longer, the fact that they have a fighting chance at all feels more aligned with the sequel films. Perhaps James Cameron's space marines could splatter bugs all day, but it's unthinkable that a mere human could have so much as scratched the original Alien.

Mothership's combat rules are much more in line with the unstoppable killing machine from the first movie. While still an opposed check like the Free League game, *Mothership*'s dueling d100 rolls are a faster way to resolve the question of a character's continued existence. Health seems to have been adjusted between *Mothership* editions, with the newer version of the game only giving 1d10+10, much lower than the previous x2 Strength calculation. The Free League game, too, starts players with precious little Health. These more fragile incarnations of a first-level space adventurer feel perfect for the universe of *Alien*, where one false step could lead to a grisly end.

The most likely outcome of *The Wretched* is a sudden and horrific death by way of Creature, but the game also devotes a quarter of its prompts to the psychological pressure of having the monster skittering around the outside of your ship. Though much of the horror of *Alien* comes from the knowledge that some nightmarish thing is already loose within the Nostromo, much of that tension comes from anticipatory fear. In the same way, *The Wretched*'s Creature prompts ask players to consider what it would feel like to live in constant vigilance. Smears of blood and half-remembered fragments create a picture in your mind, inaccurate but worse than seeing the alien in broad daylight. Players might catch a snippet of its voice and hear its ragged breathing but never quite fully understand what it is that's hunting them. Bissette's brief but effective prompts channel the cinematography of *Alien* by leaning into impressions and emotions rather than graphic description. The precarity of the situation is reinforced as play goes on, with the block tower disintegrating after each turn. Like Ripley, they are forced to contend with fewer and fewer resources, slowly driven toward an inevitable confrontation that they are unlikely to survive.

Across these three games, it's easy to pick out big themes and ideas. Despite dramatic differences in design and intention between *Alien RPG* and *The Wretched,* both texts are still invested in creating an atmosphere of dread, of showing how absolutely terrifying the unknown of space could be. And though *Mothership* prioritizes playability above all else, it's easy to extrapolate its economic system from *Alien*'s concerns about shares and corporate exploitation. That one movie inspired such strong yet differing takes on space horror in the medium of role-playing games is a testament to the movie's quality. As tabletop games continue to evolve, I hope we will see further iterations of *Alien*'s themes, especially those that are as strange and upsetting as the creature itself.

FIGHTING WITHOUT FIGHTING: OPTIMIZE YOUR D&D COMBAT USING DE-ESCALATION

ALEX KINGSLEY

A Fantasy RPG that Discourages Violence

I've been playing Dungeon & Dragons (and DMing it) for years now, and there's one consistent complaint I hear from players: Combat is boring. Unfortunately, D&D is structured such that combat often takes up a large portion of the game. This means players sometimes spend the majority of the session just waiting their turn—and all they get to do on that turn is swing a sword or cast fire bolt, and then the turn is over.

This is part of the reason why I wrote the game *De-escalation*—a tabletop role-playing game that satirizes D&D, in which the players are not permitted to use violence. I was running a D&D campaign in which the players always avoided combat, opting for other, more creative options for moving the story forward. I wrote the game so those players could work with a ruleset that was better tailored to their gameplay style. While *De-escalation* serves the needs of players who prefer to avoid combat altogether, there are people who feel attached to the mechanics of D&D, even if combat rules bog them down. This raises a question: how can you use the scaffolding of D&D mechanics to make a dynamic and interesting combat?

This is a challenge I am facing as I craft a homebrew campaign for my current D&D party. I wanted to provide a guide for others who are interested in either crafting an interesting homebrew adventure or adding some spice to a pre-written module.

To begin with, I believe there is a common misconception about gameplay combat: the objective of combat is not to defeat the enemy. The objective of combat is to get out of combat. The key to making any fight interesting is to give your players a variety of opportunities to end the fight that do *not* involve besting their opponent. Consider some of these options:

1. A Skills Challenge

A skills challenge mitigates the need for combat entirely. It is faster, simpler, and asks players to get creative with their solutions. In a skills challenge, the players are presented with a combat, and each player proposes the way they would choose to contribute to solving the conflict. This setup encourages players to play to their character's strengths, instead of just making an attack. The DM sets a DC, and each player attempts their contribution. If there are more successes than failures, then the team succeeds, but if there are more failures, they fail the challenge. For example, in the campaign I'm running, my players have stowed away on a ship pretending to be chefs. We did a diner-dash-style skills challenge, in which the players had to prepare food for the crew of the ship. A high-intelligence character might be the one to read the recipe, a high-dexterity player might choose to chop vegetables, a high-charisma character might flirt with the crew in hopes it will distract them from the terrible food, and so on. A skills challenge serves the same purpose as combat, but it allows players to approach the situation in a more inventive way and explore their character while doing it.

2. A Time Challenge

One of the major issues with combat is that it can take forever. This issue is solved if you have a time cap on the combat—and if you've added a ticking time bomb to battle, that adds a lot of tension. This makes the most sense if the players have some other objective they must complete within the given time allotment. For example, I gave my players a challenge in which they had to load illegal cargo onto a ship while under attack from the city watch. They had to get all the cargo on and board the ship before it left, so I gave them a total of six rounds to complete the challenge. This meant players had more options on their turn—they could choose between fighting the watch, carrying or healing fallen party members, moving cargo, or boarding the ship. Another example of a time challenge is the Iron Throne in Baldur's Gate 3, in which your party must free hostages from a sinking underwater prison. Though your party is under attack, the main challenge is not fighting but freeing all the prisoners before everyone drowns. If you focus all your energy on fighting the enemy, you *will* fail. You are forced to strategize, not just fight.

3. Environmental Stakes

In a previous article, I discussed how fake writing advice from a ClickHole article is actually excellent advice. The advice is: "Every time you write, ask yourself: Could this scene take place in a hot-air balloon? If the answer is yes, then it probably should." Why is this good advice? Because it emphasizes the importance of setting. How can the location of your combat become a character in and of itself? Perhaps there is no enemy other than hostile terrain. A few examples of environmental stakes are:

- Your characters cannot see. How is combat different when they don't know where the enemy is?
- The environment is moving. How does the fight change when everyone's position changes each turn? Now, they can't anticipate where they'll be next or how close to the enemy they'll find themself.
- The terrain is dangerous. How does it impact the combat if there are swinging axes, lava, or falling rocks?
- The terrain is a puzzle. What if the fight takes place in a labyrinth? What if you must use your turn to solve a riddle to open a door that leads you to the next room?
- The combat takes place in an enclosed area, and the players must figure out how to get out. What does a battle look like if it takes place in an escape room?

4. A MacGuffin

A fight is most interesting when it's really not about the fight at all. Instead of fighting to the death, what if your players are fighting because there's a *thing* they want? What if you have to use your turn not to fight but instead to swipe the coveted object that brought you here in the first place? A fight is much more exciting with the added tension of a MacGuffin bouncing between the hands of the enemies and the heroes. Think of Frodo and Gollum fighting over the ring in Mount Doom. If there was no ring, we would just be watching two little guys goin' at it for no reason, which would be totally boring and also really confusing.

5. A Secret Third Thing

You can fight. You can flee. But what if there's a secret third thing? Every time I introduce a potential battle, I like to come up with a secret way the players could de-escalate the situation without fighting. Maybe they could make this all go away with a bribe. Maybe the enemy is actually really insecure, and if they give him a compliment, then he'll calm down.

Do my players always find the secret third thing? No. But just knowing that it's there, that combat isn't inevitable, makes the interaction more exciting. It turns pre-combat into a puzzle—the players ask themselves: is there a way to get out of this? How? And then, if they want to pursue combat, then they can!

6. Limitations

Putting limitations on the enemy AND/OR the party adds an extra puzzle element to the fight. For example:

- The enemy is only vulnerable to one kind of damage
- The players have no weapons and have to improvise
- The enemy can't see but has amazing hearing

Extra points if it takes a while to figure out the limitation. This, too, is a kind of puzzle.

7. One Piece of the Whole

Combat is best when it's short and sweet. It makes most sense when it's a small part of a larger dungeon. A series of small battles is not very interesting, but if they're sprinkled throughout a larger challenge, they become just a few of the many obstacles in that particular dungeon.

8. Logistics

Lastly, one of the major reasons combat gets so boring is that it takes forever. One of the most common critiques of D&D is that there are too many rules, and they're difficult to understand. The solution? Streamline combat but getting all the pesky rule issues out of the way. You can do this by:

- Level up with your players. That way, they have a full understanding of all their abilities before you get back into play, and they won't end up asking, "Wait, how does this spell work?" in the middle of combat.
- Spell cards. You don't need to buy these; I hand-write them on index cards. If you have tangible cards that you can play during battle, and those cards tell you exactly how the spell works and what dice to use, things move a lot faster. You don't have to limit yourself to spells. I use color-coded cards, with different colors for abilities and non-magical attacks, as well as a card for quick stats, so I can avoid having to pull up my character sheet all the time.
- A dice organizer. A surprising amount of time is lost just choosing the right die. I lay out my dice at the beginning of each session on a labeled index card, so when I see "d8" on my spell card, I don't need to dredge up my middle school 3D geometry knowledge and think, "Wait, which one of these shapes has eight sides?"
- Limit the number of NPCs. Combat is boring during other people's turns, but it's especially boring when the DM has to roll for 100 rats.
- Plan your NPC attacks in advance. This way, your players aren't waiting for you to finish your turn.
- Overall, ensure your players have a solid understanding of the rules before you start, so you don't have to spend time pausing to explain. This has the added benefit of making your players feel more confident! Players often feel guilty and embarrassed when they have to pause the game for a rule clarification. They will feel better if you help them understand what they're doing before the game starts.

With all these strategies, you can craft an entire campaign that avoids traditional combat altogether. Remember, the point of a TTRPG is to have fun. If it starts to feel like a chore (which combat often does), then you're missing out on the joy of role-playing games.

Chill out. Get creative. Be a lover, not a fighter. Specifically, a lover of innovative and interesting gameplay.

TWENTY YEARS AFTER THE RING: A HORROR MOVIE ABOUT PARENTING THAT'S JUST AS TERRIFYING AS AN ADULT

E. N. DÍAZ

I had not rewatched *The Ring (Dreamworks Pictures, 2002),* the US version directed by Gore Verbinski with script by Ehren Kruger and starring Naomi Watts and Martin Henderson, since I first watched it when I was about seven or eight years old. I had to go to therapy for the first time after watching the film. Then I stopped going after two sessions because I'd heard somewhere that serial killers disguised themselves as people kids trusted to get close to them and kill them. It was a relief to my parents when I quit. It meant I was normal, or normal enough to pretend that I was fine.

A few nights ago, I decided to rewatch. I've always been curious about what it was about that film that so deeply affected me beyond any other horror movie I've watched since.

When I began researching the film for this essay, I realized twenty years had passed since it came out. It is not really shocking to find out I'm closer in age to the protagonist, Rachel Keller (Naomi Watts), than I am to any of the kids in the film. Time passes. That's the way it is. What did shock me was to realize that Rachel and my mom were the same age when I watched the film.

For those unfamiliar with the film, *The Ring* tells the story of Rachel Keller (Naomi Watts), a young journalist and single mother who must solve the mystery of a VHS tape that kills anyone who watches it from a heart attack after seven days. What starts off as simple journalistic curiosity soon develops into desperation as Racher discovers her son Aidan (David Dorfman) watching the tape. Rachel teams up with her estranged partner, Noah Clay (Martin Henderson), to solve the mystery and break the curse.

I watch Rachel struggle to balance her career as a journalist and the relationship with her only son, Aidan (David Dorfman), as a single mother, and I think of my own parents as Rachel tries and fails to close the chasm between the two, choosing to maintain a kind of distance with her kid not born out of resentment or hatred, but that frustrating gap that cracks open in the silence after each attempt to understand someone who doesn't have the language you need to understand them.

My parents were excellent parents. And they were also extremely young when they had me and my siblings. My mom was nineteen, and my dad was twenty-three when they had my older brother, who died shortly after birth. They had my sister about two years later. Then, they had my middle sister two years after her. And, five years later, they had me. My mom was only twenty-seven. My dad was thirty-one. As with anything in life, dates might vary.

My parents have admitted—multiple times—that I was a challenging child. They said that the way I thought and behaved was very peculiar. I mimicked a lot of the voices and facial expressions of people I saw on TV. I copied speech almost word for word. I said things that, to me, were very obviously a joke or harmless but, to them, were either hilarious or completely horrifying. I could be very kind and well-behaved, but I could turn cold and cruel in a second without any apparent explanation. I saw things nobody else did, and I was punished for it.

Now, it is easier to put into words because I have the language, but back then, all these things were just shapes and sensations I couldn't comprehend that deeply affected me. I knew that certain things *felt* right, and others didn't. I couldn't explain why, and it frustrated me, and it frustrated them because neither of us knew how to breach that gap that was growing between us, a gap oozing with silence.

I know how it felt for me to feel trapped inside my head with all these overwhelming thoughts and sensations and have no language to express them. I was afraid all the time and didn't really know why. Now I know that I was afraid of my own mind, my own imagination, after being told for so long that what went on inside my head was wrong and could harm me or others somehow. If I hadn't discovered reading and writing as outlets, I sincerely doubt I would be here right now. Even with those tools, I barely made it.

But now I keep wondering how it was for them, and I can't imagine how profoundly lonely they must have felt, as I did.

In *The Ring*, we see Rachel's flawed but honest and loving attempts to clumsily connect with her son, but hers—I'm saddened to say—is the extraordinary exception. People can be so cruel when their kid doesn't turn out how they wanted them to be, when they think their kid is *broken*.

Mr. and Mrs. Morgan, owners of a horse breeding ranch, are unable to have children, so a depressed Mrs. Morgan leaves the island for a time and returns with an adopted daughter, Samara (Daveigh Chase). But, as Rachel discovers, Samara was a peculiar child. She had psychic abilities that allowed her to telepathically etch horrifying images in other people's mind.

Samara's usual targets were her parents and their horses. The relentless torment at the hands of their daughter became so unbearable that her parents had to banish her to the barn, building a tiny loft for her above where the horses slept. They had no other choice. Yet, when Rachel sees the video of Samara explaining her abilities to one of her doctors, what you see is not an evil child enjoying her role as tormentor, but a quiet little girl who sits helplessly while trying to explain in an exhausted voice that she doesn't mean to hurt anybody, she just can't help it.

No one—not her parents nor her doctors—is able to help her, for they can't get over their own prejudice. They don't really listen as she asks for help; they don't want to admit she looks visibly distraught and consumed by her own involuntary actions, for they have already decided that she is lying, that she is evil, that she can help it, but she chooses not to.

In what she is certain is a last act of love, Anna Morgan suffocates her daughter with a bag before throwing her down a well, uttering the words *All I ever wanted was you*. Her sweet words have the rotten smell of blame—*it is your fault you weren't what I wished for*. But Samara is not dead yet. She watches helplessly as her mother seals the well because she knows there is nothing she can do. She knows her screams will go unanswered.

So, all alone in the darkness of the well, she attempts to climb to her freedom, clawing at the walls until her nails snap off. After falling into Samara's well and being able to hold her body with the understanding she deserved in life, finally freeing her spirit, a horrified Rachel remarks that it takes *seven days for you to die inside a well*. Thus, explaining the origin of the now iconic line Samara's victims hear when they pick up the phone after watching her tape: *Seven days*.

Rachel returns to her son, and that gap between them seems to be finally healing. There's even the rekindling of a relationship with Noah (Martin Henderson), Rachel's ex and father of her child. Rachel shares the news of Samara's liberation with her kid, who can only ask with pure terror why she would do such a thing. In a scene that still fills me with dread every time I see a TV screen, Samara's rotten corpse crawls out of the TV of Noah's studio and mercilessly murders him.

A desperate Rachel finds the body and screams for Samara to tell her what she wants from her. But it isn't hard to figure out what Samara wants. In one of the most satisfying twists, it is revealed that Samara forgave Rachel's life not because she had opened her well and lovingly held onto her corpse but because she had made a copy of her murderous tape, a copy of her rage, and shared it with others.

Samara wants what any other vengeful ghost wants—for the injustice that made her to be unmade, the tape rewound, the tapestry unwoven. And the well-intentioned actions of a flawed but kindhearted journalist will never be able to give her the justice she wants, the justice she deserves. So, it falls on Rachel, with all her good intentions, to spread Samara's rage at the end if she wants to save her own son. What other choice is there?

After all these years, the movie more than holds up. The script, the acting, and the cinematography are all excellent. The exploration of the relationship between violence, trauma, and guilt as creatures endlessly feeding off of one another and preventing anyone from moving on, neutralizing any attempts for peace for anyone involved, is much more terrifying as an adult. An excellent rewatch of early 2000s horror.

SCIENCE FICTION AND THE POWER OF ITERATIVE REVOLUTION: SOCIAL CHANGE AND THE WORKS OF ANNALEE NEWITZ, BECKY CHAMBERS, AND NNEDI OKORAFOR

ALEX KINGSLEY

"Why are you young people so obsessed with communism?"

The man at the bar asked me in earnest, but with a grin that said, *Oh, this is gonna be good*. I've been asked the same thing with different words countless times, usually by a man confident that because he is significantly older, he is also significantly wiser. I answer that many of my generation are hopeful about humanity, that we believe in the inherent goodness that people possess, and that one day, we can live in a society that prizes taking care of one another. The conversation went the way it often does: He listed a series of "failed communist states" to prove that communism could never—would never—work, and I contented myself to move on to other topics of conversation, knowing I would get nowhere trying to argue. I left the conversation wondering if there was anything I could have possibly said that would have made him stop and think. Not change his mind, necessarily, just rethink the viewpoint that seemed to have calcified in his mind years ago. I didn't even identify as a communist, so I wasn't sure why his obstinacy had bothered me.

Perhaps it was because I'd heard the same pessimistic viewpoint time and time again. "Communism goes against human nature," and "If we get rid of the police, who will protect us?" It always landed on the same conclusion: there's no point in advocating for change because the change you seek will never happen.

An Anarchist Community in which All Are Welcome

Then I read *The Terraformers* by Annalee Newitz (*Tor Books,* 2023). *The Terraformers* takes place sixty thousand years in the future, an era so distant that I find it difficult to imagine. But Newitz does imagine it, and they imagine it with rich clarity and character. *The Terraformers* follows different members of the Environmental Rescue Team, a collectivist organization committed to maintaining the ecological balance of Sask-E, a planet that was built to resemble the long-abandoned Earth. While certain familiar struggles exist in Newitz's future—gentrification, resource scarcity, exploitation—many of our current challenges have faded from memory. Racism as we know it, homophobia and transphobia, and disease are essentially all relegated to the past. Most importantly, the ERT members have learned how to build an anarchist community in which all are welcome and everyone is cared for. It is a society that lives up to the Marxist maxim: "From each according to his abilities, to each according to their need."

The Terraformers made me realize the key aspect of my desire for social change that I had not been able to articulate to the man in the bar that night: *time*. I agree with him that I don't think we'll see a successful communist state in my lifetime, nor do I think we'll be able to abolish the police, nor do I think we'll be able to do a large number of revolutionary overhauls. But in sixty thousand years? Things will be radically different in ways we cannot even comprehend. That change, however, is only going to happen if we set ourselves on that path *now*. Revolution does not often happen in one decisive moment. It happens piecemeal, step after painful step, in iterations.

I don't believe iterative revolution would be possible without science fiction, especially the genre of solar punk. Solar punk is a subset of science fiction predicated on the idea that in a day and age in which cynicism has become the norm, imagining a hopeful future is inherently counterculture. It's important to note that there is a difference between a *perfect* future and a hopeful one. Solar punk authors are not writing utopias but rather painting a realistic picture of what a good future *may* look like.

Cozy Scifi: Humanity's Future Is Bright

For example, Becky Chambers' Wayfarers series (*Harper Voyager*) imagines a future for the human race after it has left Earth and has been accepted into an interplanetary organization called the Galactic Commons. The characters in the *Wayfarers* series face hardship, tragedy, and personal challenges, but on the whole, humanity's future is bright. I have often referred to Chambers' work as "cozy sci-fi" because it often focuses on the ways that different imagined cultures come to understand each other. The conflict is usually not violent but made up of subtle tension between peoples learning how to coexist.

Solarpunk and Africanfuturism

Nnedi Okorafor writes in a vein of solarpunk called African Futurism. While Afrofuturism is often defined as a genre that usually speculates what African culture may have looked like without colonialism, Africanfuturism is "less concerned with 'what could have been' and more concerned with 'what is and can/will be.'" For instance, Okorafor's middle-grade novel *Zahrah the Windseeker* (*Clarion Books*, 2008) takes place in a futuristic African city built on nature-based technology. Literature often puts nature at odds with science and progress, whereas Okorafor's world puts the two in harmony. In many of her novels, Okorafor imagines a world not only where humanity thrives but specifically where individuals of African descent or other marginalized groups lead prosperous lives.

Solar punk novels serve as a blueprint for the world we are trying to build. That world may be impossibly distant right now, but does that necessarily mean we should give up altogether or dismiss these dreams as impossible? I already see the principles of these seemingly impossible worlds put into practice every week when I attend service at the Unitarian Universalist Church. Each week, I enter a community of people who share their resources with each other, fight for environmental justice, advocate for equality, and welcome all who seek refuge with open arms. The UU congregation makes me feel as though my wildest dreams of communal living are truly achievable. Perhaps one day, we will have fully automated luxury gay space communism after all.

I understand why those like the men in the bar are so defeatist. They've seen a lot of turmoil in their lives, at least twice as much as I have, and they believe my optimism is merely a side-effect of youth. In actuality, my optimism is an active choice, and one that I make because I do believe that hope for a brighter future is the ultimate act of rebellion. To say something will "never" happen is an impressive claim, given that we have the entire future of humanity to sort things out. Just because you cannot see us moving forward does not mean we are not moving. After immersing myself in the imagined futures of solar punk, I know how to answer skeptics. In order to make a better world, we only need three things: faith in ourselves, imagination, and time.

GONE TO TEXAS: 50 YEARS OF CHAIN SAW MASSACRE: TOBE HOOPER'S LEGENDARY MASTERPIECE CELEBRATES HALF A CENTURY OF UNSETTLING HORROR

PATRICK BARB

To my mind, there are two essential versions of the 1974 horror classic *The Texas Chain Saw Massacre* (also styled as *The Texas Chainsaw Massacre/TCM*): 1) the version you're told about, the slumber party retelling, the "a friend's brother's girlfriend saw it and they got grossed-out" game of telephone reinvention, the version that captures morbid imaginations, imbuing the movie with urban-legend-level mystique and then, there's also 2) the movie itself.

It's remarkable how that latter version defies established expectations, especially when you consider the enduring power of the *TCM* that many of us imagine we're going to see before we hit play, and John Laroquette's baritone voice signals the start of a truly one-of-a-kind, never again replicated cinematic experience. The imagined buckets of gore and bloodshed aren't found in the "real" movie—at least not to the degree we're led to expect. And yet, it's the suggestive, surreal, nightmarish quality of Hooper's filmmaking that creates a liminal cinematic space in which each viewer crafts their own bespoke chainsaw-fueled, cannibal-crazed experience.

Like the cliché about jazz being about the notes the musicians *don't* play, much of *Texas Chain Saw Massacre*'s enduring appeal stems from what individual watchers bring to their viewings. To celebrate *TCM* at 50, I want to showcase how my original vision of the movie stacked up against the film as it was first presented to drive-in/grindhouse audiences and then spread regionally across the United States and as it's endured on streaming, 4K, and future formats across the world. Let's start with the chainsaw-wielder himself, good ol' Leatherface.

Leatherface, the franchise's Ed Gein-inspired, human-skin-wearing man-mountain of a man-child, is the character intrinsically linked to the *Chainsaw* movies. He's often grouped with infamous horror film slashers of the late 70s and 80s. You've got Jason, Michael, Freddy, Chucky, all of these killers with whom horror-loving audiences were on a first-name basis back in the g(l)ory days of slasher cinema. Yet, Leatherface, played in the original movie by Gunnar Hansen as equal parts menacing fairy-tale giant prepared to grind bones to make his bread and as naïve abused whipping boy to family members whose cruelties are more practiced, more refined, is known only by his nickname, a dehumanizing sobriquet that refuses to allow the audience or the on-screen victims to get to know the "real" Leatherface.

Nevertheless, my first exposure to Leatherface came second- and third-hand through conversations about slashers with my friends who had more lenient parents and/or siblings willing to drop a few gory nuggets of info to the younger generation. At an age when I was collecting G.I. Joes, Ninja Turtles, and any other number of action figure toys paired with plastic accessory weapons and gear, the inclusion of Leatherface with the slashers made all the sense in the world. Michael had his knives. Jason had his machete. Freddy had his claws. And Leatherface? He had *the* chainsaw.

Growing up out in the country, with an acre or two of forest between my family's home and that of our nearest neighbor, I had more than my fair share of exposure to the sounds and smells produced by revving chainsaws. Even just being around someone using smaller saws for clearing away brush, one is struck by the crescendo of the whirling blade, the grinding chain rotating, and the smell of gasoline and exhaust. There's no subtlety to the chainsaw. Hearing that revving sound and watching chunks of wood spew from the point of contact with the blade, it's impossible to imagine a chainsaw-wielding masked man as ever having the element of surprise. There's an aggressively masculine connotation to the chainsaw. It's easy to imagine it as an in-your-face.

The same can be said for "Texas"—both as a place on the map and as a state of mind. Even today, the cowboy, anti-regulatory bravado of the Lone Star State, even if it's primarily a self-perpetuated stereotype, is hard to shake from the national and even global consciousness. Ask someone about Texas, and you're likely to encounter visions of big trucks, big guns, big Stetsons, all of its pieces larger than life, so large that the context is stripped away, leaving only the symbols as signifiers. A chainsaw is something masculine, something menacing, but a *TEXAS* chainsaw? Forget it. There can be no chainsaw massacre more menacing than one from Texas.

Before the terror attacks on American soil and the mainstreaming of mass gun violence in our classrooms, workplaces, and halls of worship, the concept of a "massacre" was not something as easily fathomable as it might be today. In this time of "innocence," from the 1970s to the late 1990s, massacres were what happened to small groups you didn't know, or that took place in other countries, inside so-called enemy territory. Hearing about what "happened" in the *Texas Chain Saw Massacre* was akin to getting reports from an older brother or uncle who'd served in 'Nam or reading the lurid details of the Manson Murders in a true-crime paperback.

"Dude, this girl gets put onto a meathook. You see it and everything."

"Leatherface chainsaws people, and he wears a mask made of human flesh."

"They eat human flesh on camera! Did you know it was real?! Like it actually happened to some folks. Dude, I swear!"

Growing up in the 80s and 90s, *Texas Chain Saw Massacre* took on an urban legend quality for younger horror fans like myself. There was almost enough to fear just from listening to others talk about the movie. The effect at the time was similar for the *Faces of Death* (*MPI Media Group, Aquarius Releasing*, 1978) movies and, later, at the turn of the millennium for *The Blair Witch Project (Summit Entertainment*, 1999). And while *BWP* remains a worthy horror entry and the *Faces of Death* films . . . not so much, it is Hooper's masterpiece whose legend remains as vital as ever.

I believe this is because, quite simply, the movie lives up to and even surpasses the hype and expectations. However, it does this in surprising and oftentimes unexpected ways. Yes, there's a hulking monster in a flesh mask, wielding a chainsaw. You do get to see that. However, there is much in Hansen's performance reminiscent of Boris Karloff's original turn as the Monster in *Frankenstein*. Leatherface commits violent, inexcusable acts against innocents, but there is a sense of the pitiable about him as well. In many ways, Leatherface is, to reference the cliché, a "product of his environment."

At the macro level, place and time are major contributing factors to the development of menace and terror in the film. The Texas of *Texas Chain Saw Massacre* is a sun-bleached hellscape. The opening shots of corpses and cattle skulls, all of which are threaded into the latter narrative, along with the whine of news photographer cameras set up Hooper's Texas as a foreign, hostile land filled with symbolic dread. The characters traveling to and through this particular part of Texas may claim some connection to the land, as wheelchair-bound, perpetually whining Franklin (Paul A. Partain) does. But their approach to the people and the landscape, especially on the farm, is more exploratory in fashion. The house—in which Leatherface and his family ply their killing craft—is a landmark that our protagonists simply cannot pass up or leave alone. It must be visited, it must be examined, and it must be conquered. *Though, good luck with that last part!*

Much has been said previously about the film's connection to the Vietnam War era, with its depiction of youths as fodder for an enemy they don't understand in a land in which the enemies' familiarity provides a distinct upper hand. It is a compelling comparison. Just as Romero's *Dawn of the Dead* (*Universal Pictures*, 1978) puts the mirror up to consumerism and capitalism, so too does Hooper's *TCM* crystallize some of the cultural rejection of or warning against interventionism and colonialism. While perhaps more subtly handled than *Dead*'s use of the shopping mall setting to make Romero's thematic points, the impact of the issues of the time is no less evident in *TCM*.

In the world that Hooper and Company present, truly evil, cruel, and sadistic villains are introduced in shocking, in-your-face fashion. We are not spoon-fed the background but forced to journey inside it. We're kept close to the characters, good and evil. Almost disturbingly close at times. In doing so, Hooper forces the audience to bear witness, becoming active participants in these interactions with the "other."

Indeed, the sequence in the van with the Hitchhiker provides the first example of the claustrophobic, unsettling style of filmmaking and storytelling that is a keystone element in the movie. The manic, unhinged performance by Edwin Neal—cutting himself, burning the photograph of the group, attacking Franklin, all before finally being thrown out to mark the van for his family—is presented and consumed in breathless, breakneck fashion. A masked monster like Leatherface is something that even audiences of the late 70s had some conception of, with accepted literary motifs to draw from for processing. Someone like the Hitchhiker is a different, disturbing kind of evil. It is more human, and yet, because of that, it seems more alien to the horror film watcher's palate.

Jim Siedow's Old Man strikes a similar upsetting note with his performance. While the Hitchhiker manages to disturb almost from the first moment he appears on screen, the gas station attendant Old Man begins as a folksy, seemingly helpful figure. Thus, he becomes all the more frightening when the rug is pulled out from under Sally (Marilyn Burns, as one of the all-time Final Girls) and the audience. There's a torturous quality to the scene of him beating Sally with his broom before returning her to the family farm. Trust is violated. Just as Leatherface pulls the screaming, struggling Pam (Teri McMinn) back into the dark confines of the house and an appointment with a meat hook after she runs into the daylight, the message is broadcast loud and clear: nowhere is safe, no one can be trusted.

Torture is one of the key factors in the enduringly morbid appeal of this movie. I don't mean the bodily mutilation of the early 2000s so-called "torture porn" films. Rather, *TCM* deals more in psychological torture. It's present in the moments mentioned above and in the movie's infamous centerpiece of a dinner sequence. With Sally tied to a chair at the family's table, surrounded by the hooting, hollering members of the cannibal clan, as the camera catches the spittle-flecked, contorted faces of her tormentors, we see her broken mentally.

Her hysterical screaming is unrelenting. Like Sideshow Bob repeatedly stepping on the rakes on *The Simpsons* to diminishing and then increasing comic returns, the dinner scene moves from horrific to ridiculous and back to horrific by the end. Just as the script puts Sally through this claustrophobic torture, so too does the audience suffer from the point of view with which we're presented.

The mockery of Sally's pain by the family is never presented as slick or smooth. There are no clever one-liners to be lingered over. There is only raw, inhuman dismissal, a teasing in which we are made a part. By the time we see Grandpa dropping the mallet from his corpse-like hands, we are just as much unsettled by the experience as Sally. The relief from her escape is palpable, and yet, Hooper and his cast/crew never make it seem as if we're watching a triumphant egress from the nightmare. Sally is put through the paces physically in a way that matches the mental torment shown before. Jumping through a window and limping away from the house, Sally is left blood-splattered and laughing hysterically in the back of the pick-up truck, watching Leatherface and his chainsaw grow smaller and smaller as she heads toward the horizon.

But we, the audience, are not so lucky. We are not given the chance to escape. Instead, we return to an up-close and personal look at the monster man, swinging his chainsaw in these balletic, almost beautiful arcs. It is this final bit of beauty in a story that has, to that point, been relentlessly grim, bleak, and disturbing that has aided the film's enduring appeal. The stark contrast of the sublime with terror adds that further fantastical gleam to the proceedings.

And then, the movie ends. We go out into the world to share our version of *The Texas Chain Saw Massacre* with potential audience members like ourselves—the curious, the open-minded, and the soon-to-be obsessed. We extend the invitation to them to see how the movie they imagine compares to what they'll find on-screen. Like cows lined up for the slaughter, we know there's something devastating ahead, but we cannot escape it. We cannot turn away. Fifty years on, and the end of the line isn't even close to being in sight.

HOW THE VICTORIANS INVENTED SPECULATIVE FICTION AS WE KNOW IT: FROM DICKENS TO CONRAD TO STOKER AND BEYOND

GRANT BUTLER

Tales of fantastic beings, ghosts, monsters, and imaginary societies have existed since the beginning of civilization. Whether it's the legend of countless ancient Greek heroes or the numerous Middle Eastern folk tales in *One Thousand and One Nights*, these storytelling elements have long since transcended individual groups and have defined storytelling. But it wasn't until the Victorian era that these elements morphed into the stories most people know today.

Whether it's the legend of Count Dracula, Ebenezer Scrooge encountering three ghosts on Christmas Eve, a mummy's curse, or the well-known storytelling trope of the mad scientist, Victorian writers did much to define speculative fiction as we know it in the twenty-first century. These Victorian writers include H.G. Wells, Algernon Blackwood, Charles Dickens, Arthur Conan Doyle, Bram Stoker, Wilkie Collins, Sheridan Le Fanu, Lewis Carroll, Robert Louis Stevenson, Oscar Wilde, Rudyard Kipling, and W.W. Jacobs.

So why did Victorian-era writers have such a unique perspective that had a massive influence on genre fiction? In many ways, the Victorians were simply following the principle of "write what you know". The Victorians were able to define modern speculative fiction in part because they were interested in shocking and bizarre things.

One way that interest took literary form was in vivid stories of monsters and grisly crimes in what were then called penny dreadfuls. Published serial style, it was cheap genre fiction intended as reading material for the average citizen, which Victorian Britain couldn't get enough of. One of the most famous ones was the story of Sweeney Todd, a barber who kills his own clients with a razor before his associate, Mrs. Lovett, bakes what's left into pies. Over a century later, the story would be turned into an acclaimed Broadway musical.

However, Victorian interest in fantastic and grim things was well documented elsewhere in the era's literature. One of the most enduring literary legacies of the era is the modern image of the vampire, and two of the Victorian writers at the center of this are Sheridan Le Fanu and Bram Stoker. The fact that they both wrote about monsters with an insatiable appetite is significant because, aside from the similarity in subject matter, both men were Irish, and one of the most horrifying and significant events of the Victorian era was when Ireland was devastated by The Great Famine from 1845 to 1852 that's estimated to have cost one million lives due to starvation and disease.

H.G. Wells was writing *The War of the Worlds* (1897) and *The Island of Doctor Moreau* (1896) at the same time when Charles Darwin's theories of evolution and natural selection were becoming a powerful force in scientific and academic circles, so the concept of the survival of the human race was very much a matter of public discussion. The latter in particular is about a scientist whose theories and experiments make him a pariah in London circles, so he has to flee to an island.

Arthur Conan Doyle, who is most famous for his fictional detective Sherlock Holmes, also wrote about a mummy coming to life in the short story "Lot №249" (1892). The story, which would become widely influential, particularly because of its uniquely ominous take on a mummy coming to life, came about in no small part because spiritualism was a huge interest of Doyle's, and he lived in an era where fascination with ancient Egypt was a huge topic of national conversation in Victorian Britain.

In 1878, Cleopatra's Needle was brought to London from Alexandra. A massive granite obelisk that had existed for thousands of years, it was given to Britain in 1819 in honor of their victories against French forces in the Battle of the Nile and the Battle of Alexandria, but it wasn't until almost sixty years later that a proper ship for the massive stone monument had been paid for. But on the journey, the ship encountered a nasty storm, and when a rescue boat was dispatched, six men died in the effort. Once it was safely in London, Cleopatra's Needle took its place on the Victoria Embankment overlooking the River Thames.

Robert Louis Stevenson's *Strange Case of Dr. Jekyll and Mr. Hyde* (1886) was published over two years before the crimes of Jack the Ripper shocked the nation, and the story of a man who appears respectable while having a dark side that can take over without warning and express itself in horrifying ways would've hit close to home for the British public. Especially since the character in question is a doctor, and the grisly crimes of Jack the Ripper have often included discussion over whether or not the killer had medical training.

The story is also irrevocably connected to the idea of Victorian morals and morality. One of the most enduring images of the Victorian era is its connection to the image of morality and public propriety, typically that of a very prudish and repressive nature. But having a moral image is very different from actually being a moral person, and the story of Dr. Jekyll is just one example of how those appearances were a key part of the era's stories.

If something is a façade, then something else has to be lurking behind it. And typically, whatever is lurking beyond a façade tends to be surprising, disturbing, and generally unpleasant. One of the defining characteristics of Victorian writers was their eager puncturing of that moralistic façade to show what was going on often in plain sight, and a huge component of why the Victorian writers defined speculative fiction as we know it is that unprecedentedly unflinching look at what was going on in their own backyard, which was at the time the center of the largest empire in the world. They had the biggest storytelling canvas that had ever existed and an unprecedented abundance of rich material for storytelling to shock, frighten, absorb, unnerve, captivate, and even inspire.

One of the most famous examples of this is *A Christmas Carol* (1843) by Charles Dickens. The tale of Ebenezer Scrooge isn't just a defining Christmas story, if not the definitive fictional Christmas story, it was a defining story even during the lifetime of its author. Dickens became not just the most famous author of his age but one of the most famous authors in history, not by trying to minimize or conceal the grim conditions of the city and era in which he lived but by putting them front and center. And many of his fellow authors would do the same thing.

Because if the setting is an essential part of any good story, it's hard to find a bigger feast for the imagination than Victorian London. With cobblestone streets lined with gas lamps and appalling poverty and disease coexisting alongside equally gigantic wealth and status, it was the center of the largest empire to have ever existed, which would come to take up approximately a quarter of the Earth.

Regardless of whether there was a speculative element involved or not, Victorian literature lacked for nothing when it came to vivid inspiration for the horrors and wonders of the mind. The term "Dickensian" came to represent the crushing squalor in which the poor of London lived and worked. It's the era that's synonymous with workhouses for the poor, a famine that devastated Ireland, and the brutal murders of women working as prostitutes in the crime-ridden East End of London. Victorian women were known to wear makeup that had mercury and arsenic as ingredients, while opium dens are immortalized in many of the era's stories, including those by Charles Dickens and Arthur Conan Doyle.

The Victorians didn't just write about fantastic and horrific things, they lived it. Because, despite being an empire the sun allegedly never set on, there was no shortage of darkness. And the people who lived under it not only didn't try to ignore it or hide it, they were interested in it and gave it their full attention. And the rest of the world took notice. Regardless of whether it was considered literary or popular fiction, or if there was a speculative element or not, Victorian literature is full of shocking and horrific things. One of the most famous works of the era is literally called *Heart of Darkness* (Joseph Conrad, 1899), and it's one of the most intensely discussed and debated pieces of fiction not just from the Victorian era, but in all of literature.

Victorian literature can feel bizarre, unsettling, and disorienting because it's the result of an era that was often bizarre and unsettling, as it was a society that had never existed before, and it was all on a truly unprecedented scale. It was a heady, shocking time where things that had not seemed possible, both good and bad, now seemed all too real. Speculative stories had existed before, but the Victorians set them against this backdrop and often connected that setting to those storytelling elements. The speculative fiction element was and is merely a tool to explore their world, and a huge reason these genre stories, in particular, have endured so long and have had such a significant cultural impact is because not only are we interested in stories about Victorian ghosts, vampires, monsters, murderers, and mad scientists, we are interested in the Victorian era that created them. The speculative element is simply a tool to focus on what the heart of the stories is, which is the true nature of the age and the good and bad that uneasily coexist.

As Dickens himself famously said in *A Tale of Two Cities* (1859), "It was the best of times, it was the worst of times, it was the age of wisdom, it was the age of foolishness, it was the epoch of belief, it was the epoch of incredulity, it was the season of light, it was the season of darkness, it was the spring of hope, it was the winter of despair."

It was only a question of whether the individual writer saw the potential for light in the darkness or thought the darkness conquered all.

REVISITING ROSEMARY'S BABY AND ITS THEMES SURROUNDING BODILY AUTONOMY: A RETROSPECTIVE ON THE 1960S FILM OVER 50 YEARS LATER

VANESSA MAKI

There's something deeply unsettling about a book and its film adaptation from the '60s still having relevancy in 2024. *Rosemary's Baby (1968)* is based on Ira Levin's hit novel *Rosemary's Baby* from 1967, which touches upon themes about bodily autonomy that are still relevant. Before I dig any further, it's important to address the fact that Roman Polanski wrote and directed this film. And considering sexual violence does occur in *Rosemary's Baby,* it's ironic in a very disturbing way that he adapted the film. It goes to show that sometimes foul people are attached to projects that reflect back on them (take Scream 3, for instance, and how it has a #MeToo component).

Rosemary's Baby follows a woman named Rosemary (Mia Farrow) who becomes pregnant and is convinced that the elderly people in her life are part of a Satanic cult. Rosemary's increasing paranoia is cast off as nonsensical, and she is gaslit to the extreme, isolated, and controlled by nearly everyone around her. The atmosphere of the film, aside from when she's around her good friend Hutch (Maurice Evans) and her women friends, is so uncomfortable to experience. The fact that her pregnancy wasn't spousal rape but sexual violence by way of the actual devil is one of the most disturbing parts of the film.

Currently, in America, there are many states in which abortion is restricted, banned, or nearly banned. It's unsettling that rights have been taken away from folks who are capable of getting pregnant. *Rosemary's Baby* isn't about Rosemary being forced to carry a child she never wanted. It's partially about her husband helping orchestrate the sexual violence that results in her pregnancy for his shot at fame and success. The lack of choice in her own conception and the fact that spousal rape (Guy tries to trick her into believing that he got her pregnant when she was unconscious) was still legal up until 1983 are also factors. Rosemary isn't even allowed to be concerned about her own pain. In fact, even her doctors conspire against her.

The film shows Rosemary being controlled in practically every way imaginable. Even in the moments when she tries to escape, she's hindered somehow. As soon as her friend Hutch is murdered by way of the cult's magic, Rosemary is utterly alone. The idea of that lends to how Rosemary is being gaslit, and the effects of the abuse and the influence of the cult make her look "crazy" to people. There's nobody around to validate her valid concerns that people have brought harm or are bringing harm to her or her body. And the ending only solidifies how horrifying the situation really is.

Unfortunately, Rosemary's struggle to be believed and offered the proper support is what femme folks, in particular, have experienced time and time again. And that's only amplified the more marginalized you are. If Rosemary were a woman of color or queer, for instance, she would be taken even less seriously. Not to mention, have even less access to services in the first place. Bodily autonomy is a discussion that pertains to many folks, and ignoring the discussion of intersectionality does nobody any good. It doesn't delegitimize what Rosemary experienced in the film, but there are naturally several layers to this discussion.

The end of the film is when things reach a point of no ideal resolution. Rosemary's suffering is seemingly never-ending because her husband offered her body up, her child is the son of the devil, a cult used her to fulfill their desires to bring forth the antichrist, and nobody cares how she feels. Horror doesn't always have a victory moment, and there are uncomfortable endings throughout horror history. Rosemary's loss of choice in the conception and birth of her own child falls into that category.

Rosemary giving in and being a mother to her child isn't what everyone would expect. Earlier in the film, a woman she had befriended was being groomed to be in her position. And she died violently by way of what's considered to be a suicide (it can be interpreted that way or that it was the cult's doing). Rosemary's decision to stay and embrace motherhood, despite it all, can be frustrating to modern viewers upon first watch.

Of course, with it being a choice she makes, one might think it's her taking back her power. However, the fact of the matter is that Rosemary was living in a time when she had virtually no rights. She didn't have a bank account of her own and had to beg her husband to get their new apartment. The idea of the cult that watched her be violated, in hopes of it resulting in the birth of the antichrist, raising her child was certainly not appealing to her. Despite how horrified she was upon seeing her child because of his appearance.

The last interaction between her and her husband in the film is her spitting in his face, though. And it's about the only time Rosemary is allowed to properly respond to what has happened to her and her body. Reclaiming what is yours is crucial for empowerment. Considering we're yet again in a time where folks have to fight back against abortion bans. The film remains a startling reminder of what life is like for some right now in various American states. Where there's no such thing as a choice, much like in Rosemary's situation in the film, and that shouldn't be a reality in 2024.

REVIEWS

THE GHOST WITH THE MOST . . . D?: BEETLEJUICE IS A THIRST TRAP ON TIKTOK, AND I'M HERE FOR IT

HOLLY LYN WALRATH

"He beetle on my juice till show time"—TikTok, I Shit You Not

In 1988, depressed that Warner Brothers wouldn't greenlight his Batman project, Tim Burton began working on an even less likely-to-succeed film called *Beetlejuice* with Larry Wilson, who would go on to write *Addams Family* and this year's anticipated hit, *Beetlejuice Beetlejuice* (2024). Wilson went to a Cure concert and realized that teenage girls loved goth. "It felt to me that there were 50,000 teenage girls in black!" (Film Courage). He then wrote the original *Beetlejuice* screenplay with teenage girls in mind.

Beetlejuice 1 featured a 17-year-old Winona Ryder one year after her film debut. It launched her career as the Manic Pixie Dream Girl of the late 80s–90s, a new scream queen who starred in iconic goth-girl angsty roles like *Edward Scissorhands, Girl Interrupted, Bram Stoker's Dracula,* and *Alien Resurrection*. She was only to be rivaled by Christina Ricci, and together, the two set a new precedent for what girls liked.

Suddenly, goth was cool. It was in. Goth was girlhood.

All of this probably happened because of the energy of these actresses, who captured the existential dread of growing up femme in the 90s in a way that made teenage girls want to be them or be with them. They weren't Cher in *Clueless* or, god forbid, Julia Roberts in *Pretty Woman*. The wave of 90s goth girls was counterculture femininity in a way that hasn't ever been celebrated, even to this day.

And it represented feminine desire in entirely new ways. In Edward Scissorhands, Winona Ryder's character cares about the knife-handed, awkward, soft-boi Johnny Depp because he's different than anything she's ever encountered. Her boyfriend is a football jock, while Edward is monstrous but sweet, kind even. Across the board, these films, while being counterculture iconography in the way they represent femininity, are also often low on the totem pole in terms of sexuality. The girls represented by 90s goth films are often shown as being uninterested in sex or above it in some way.

The sex didn't quite matter. For young teenage audiences (like myself at the time), we were drawn to monstrous boys because they were othered like ourselves and somehow less dangerous than the men reality presented. Goth male leads were a dystopian vision of men—in order to be kind, the men had to be broken. Dracula was bound to try and eat you. Edward was sure to cut you up in bed. But at least they were *kind*.

Romance as a genre works because it manages divides—it creates a conflict without much external plot needed. Something has to keep the characters apart, and in the case of 90s goth films, it was usually that the character was a monster.

In the OG *Beetlejuice*, the titular "evil" character is represented as a crass, sexist disaster. His desire to wed Lydia is pretty much out of left field and as a result of his character's demeaning of women. He's trying to find a way into the world of the living—for what, we don't know. His ex-wife is a throw-away joke line as he takes her finger out of his pocket to steal the wedding ring. In many ways, the romantic spark could be seen as between Beetlejuice and Barbara Maitland, not Winona Ryder's character Lydia.

But even I can admit that I have fallen down the TikTok rabbit hole of Beetlejuice-as-heartthrob memes, overtaking social media since the release of the latest Beetlejuice movie.

If you haven't seen them yet, take a scroll through the app and you'll see a similar pattern. Clips of Beetlejuice are strung together with a contemporary song, often in amber or sepia tones, the results meant to encourage you to fall even more in love with the character—kink-shaming bedamned.

How Did We Get Here? To, You Know, Beetlejuice Crotch Shots?

As far as remakes go, *Beetlejuice Beetlejuice* is pretty standard. We meet Lydia Deetz as an adult who now has a talk show, Ghost House. Lydia is hallucinating, thinking she sees Betelgeuse in the audience—a bad omen. Then we learn her father, Charles, has died in an accident while traveling, so Lydia must make the journey back to Winter River, Connecticut, for the funeral, bringing along her estranged daughter, Astrid (Jenna Ortega), who very strictly Doesn't Believe in Ghosts.

The film builds on the lore of the first by casting Lydia in a speculative role. It's not that she grew up in a haunted house—it's that she is one of the few people who can actually see ghosts. However, this ability creates a rift between Lydia and her daughter, Astrid because Astrid is angry that Lydia can't see her father, who died when she was younger.

One major difference between the two movies is that now, Lydia is an adult with a kid and a job and a fiance and a dead husband. Ryder does a fantastic job, in her characteristically spotty way, of showing that Lydia is struggling with these average problems. Not only does she have to deal with seeing ghosts every day, but she also can't seem to connect emotionally with anyone.

When she needs help to save Astrid from the afterlife, who does she call? Of course, Beetlejuice. He represents a fascinating contrast with her fiancé, Rory, who is clearly just interested in Lydia for her money and fame. Beetlejuice, on the other hand, has been pining for Lydia since he got banished back to the afterlife in the first film.

The film puts Beetlejuice in the role of protector and helper. He quickly dispatches Astrid's toxic new crush to hell, forces Rory to admit he's only after Lydia for her money, and tries to marry her again. But this time, the audience can't help but appreciate the romantic aspects of the scene, in particular, Lydia and Beetlejuice dancing together as they rise up in the air, reminiscent of the Casper (1995) dance scene.

The film entirely passes over the previously icky concept of Beetlejuice wanting a teenager and instead recasts Beetlejuice as a potential undead mate. The film ends with a scene where Lydia is still dreaming about Beetlejuice—and their potential spooky Beetle-baby. But it doesn't feel like a nightmare anymore, does it?

So What Changed?

One thing that might have bridged the gulf between the two movies was the *Beetlejuice* animated series (1989–1991).

The series follows up on the movie's popularity by putting Lydia and Beetlejuice on the same level for the first time. In the series, Lydia and Beetlejuice are active partners in their adventures. In many episodes, Lydia becomes the voice of morality for Beetlejuice and the watcher. In *Drop Dead Fred* fashion, Beetlejuice goes on bad-behavior rampages and has to be reeled back in by Lydia. His animated character may look older than Lydia, but he basically has the mindset of someone who never grew up. In flashbacks, he's presented as a teenager or a baby, and the series also introduces us to Beetlejuice's family.

It's the animated series that first shows Lydia calling Beetlejuice's name three times to have him save her. By placing the two on the same level, the audience is primed for friendship, if not romance.

Another piece of media that may have an impact on the character is *Beetlejuice The Musical* (2018).

Like the animated series, the musical also features Lydia and Beetlejuice as the two main characters, but still follows the plot (somewhat) of the original Beetlejuice. In the musical, Emily Deetz dies, and Lydia feels like her father doesn't see her. This gives Lydia more of a reason for her goth sad girl vibes, using the trope of killing off the mother to give Lydia "issues", something which wasn't terribly clear in the original film.

A major difference between the original movie and the musical is that the end scene reveals Juno (the caseworker) as Beetlejuice's mother. She becomes the de facto villain, and because of his interactions with Lydia, Beetlejuice is able to appreciate the world of the living and defeat his mother with a sandworm.

By the end of the musical, we get the song "Creepy Old Guy", where Lydia sings about wanting to marry Beetlejuice:

> "Way back when I was just ten
> Simple and sweet
> Everywhere, fellas would stare
> Out on the street
> And I felt used, kinda confused
> I would refuse to look in their eyes
> But now I really love creepy old guys!"

The song pokes fun at the fact that the original movie's age difference was inappropriate ("Have you guys seen Lolita? This is just like that but fine!"), but it also kind of acknowledges the weirdness of why women are in love with Beetlejuice. Lydia is acting in the scene to trick Beetlejuice, but is she?

It's these two pieces of media—Beetlejuice the animated series and Beetlejuice the musical—that likely contributed to today's viewers seeing Beetlejuice as a more sympathetic character than the original movie intended.

Goth Girl Reclaimed

To go back to the goth girl stereotype, one thing I've always loved about Winona Ryder and that thrills me about the Ryder Renaissance is that she GOT the character of Lydia. Being a teenager, she understood that Lydia was a girl who hated the world's sappy-sweet facade and thus wanted out of it. She played Lydia honestly and with vulnerability. Winona Ryder's position on the character has been explained in many interviews. She often talks about how she saw Lydia as someone who would never get married—that she would be living alone. But when she met Jenna Ortega—the new goth girl for the 2020s—she began to see a world where Lydia, as a character, had a child. In many ways, it's not so much about the character becoming a mom but passing the proverbial goth torch.

Oh yeah—and Winona Ryder has admitted in interviews that she always saw Lydia as ending up with Beetlejuice.

"He's like endgame for me . . . I totally want them to be truly together." (Interview with ComicBook.com).

Perhaps the appeal of Beetlejuice IS his crassness, but in *Beetlejuice, Beetlejuice,* it's also the actions he takes for Lydia. *If he wanted to marry you from beyond the grave, he would.* The reality is that the world loves to treat anything teenage girls like as cringe. Sexuality, particularly at puberty, is a strange thing, and I kind of love how TikTok, like its predecessor Tumblr, is a safe space for that.

Of course, I have to give credit where credit is due. Michael Keaton is also a huge part of the enduring sexiness of Beetlejuice. From the moment he put on that leather bodysuit in *Batman* (1989), he became utterly crushable for not just goth girls but everyone else. Were our brains just mixing the two? Maybe. Whether it's in full leather bat ears or wormy, moldy wigs, Keaton will always be a major heartthrob.

Here's my advice: If you find yourself crushing on a dead, creepy old guy, just go with it. After all, it's 2024. TikTok's got you, bestie.

THE SKELETON KEY GIRL: A REVIEW OF THE WAYWARD CHILDREN SERIES BY SEANAN MCGUIRE

PRIYA SRIDHAR

Welcome Home . . . or Welcome Back

Portal fantasy dates back to stories like *Alice in Wonderland* or *The Wizard of Oz*. Children, mainly girls, end up in fantastic places and go on strange adventures. They get to be the heroes in colorful places after living in dull places like the English countryside or Kansas between civil wars and skirmishes.

The *Wayward Children* (2016–2025, *Tordotcom)* Series by Seanan McGuire shows the consequences of what happens when those kids return. They went through the Doors and came back because something in their adventures that they had on Earth was missing or because they had broken some rules. Some are changed irrevocably after having gone missing for months, if not years, and their parents cannot understand. Even those who understand cannot help since some doors call to families and generations.

That's where Eleanor West comes in; she runs a school for these Wayward Children, having been a wealthy child who went through a Door multiple times. Some came from standard fantasy worlds with rainbows and swords. Others came from underworlds with skeleton mermaids, Nonsense countries made of sweets, and horror tales with vampires and Drowned Gods. They also returned to Earth for a reason, and Eleanor hopes her school provides them the space to either recover from their traumas or find the way back to their Doors.

A Tangible Price

Wayward Children has taken its time building a dark take on multiverse theory and portal fantasy. We got some pretty game-changing information about the price each traveler has to pay when finding or losing their doors, and not just the trauma of returning to normal life.

The most recent books, *Lost in the Moment and Found* (2023) and *Misplaced in Parts Half-Known* (2024), focus on Antsy, a girl who worked in a shop of lost things for two years after running away from an abusive stepfather. Like the other students at Eleanor West's Finishing School for Wayward Children, she got ejected just as she had found a reason to stay and fight for this world. Unlike the others, she has a unique ability that, in the right hands, can save lives or, in the wrong hands, can waste time.

This will cover spoilers for both books, so you are warned.

Antsy discovers that opening a Door has a price: two days of the opener's life. For most Wayward Children, at most, they'll enter three times if going between Earth and their world, so they'll lose a week or a month at worst if their Door stays open. But for Antsy, who's opened at least five doors a day for two years? She loses half a lifetime, so she looks like a teenager while still being a nine-year-old.

Why Did Antsy Go Through A Door?

That's the big question. Antsy was running away from an abusive stepfather, but she had a plan: to call her paternal grandparents. All she needed was a phone, since it was a time period before cellphones, and she didn't know where to find a payphone or how to use one. (And this is a real issue since I've tried using payphones, and it's not as simple as putting in a coin and dialing a number.)

Antsy needed stability and adult figures that she could trust. Her mother failed to provide either of those aspects after her father died. And her stepfather? The fact that he was gaslighting and grooming her should say enough about what kind of person he was, to the point that when Antsy vanished, he was arrested for murdering her. That her mother still feels guilty about the monster she let into her children's lives and believes that it's her fault Antsy vanished doesn't erase the fact that she failed her older daughter. They both know it, even if Antsy's rapid aging means that her mother doesn't recognize her by the time Antsy returns to Earth.

Despite that, the adults in the Shop also fail Antsy. Vineta exploits her newest apprentice by not telling her about the price and lying that only children can open Doors. Hudson, one of many talking ravens, falls in line reluctantly because one previous shop owner didn't want anyone to know the price: If you open a Door, you give up two days of your life. Open too many doors, and you will age rapidly. So the previous shopkeepers started exploiting their apprentices, making them open the Doors instead and lying about why the adults didn't.

Rather than Antsy needing the shop, the shop needed Antsy. She finds out that the shop only works if a humanoid can run the front desk and open multiple doors. Vineta was getting older and had been exploiting many others. Antsy was the first child that the shop founder's ghost could reach. Vineta, like her predecessors, had disrupted the balance. Antsy was brought to restore it.

The question then becomes why the shop ejected Antsy as soon as she insisted other children like her had to know the price, and she wouldn't let Vineta exploit anyone else. We find out why, in *Mislaid in Parts Half-Known*: the shop's raven population needed to turn on Vineta. They were the realm's original residents and the ones who kept order. Antsy had to travel to find friends and rescue Hudson when Vineta sent him through a door in a cage to get eaten by the creatures on the other side or starve. As soon as Hudson's back in the shop? He agrees that Vineta needs to be taken down. Antsy won't kill or force Vineta out of the shop, but the ravens sure will. And they chase her through a door to suffer the same fate as Hudson. Once they do that, Antsy takes charge and strives to make sure no one suffers like that again.

A Changing Goal for Eleanor West's Finishing School

As *Every Heart A Doorway* (2016) notes, Eleanor West doesn't expect she'll help everyone find their Doors, but she will try. Different worlds change in their rules, from logic to nonsense. Trying to create a Compass, or a map to plot out the different worlds, is meant to help all the children. And sometimes, the kids were booted out of their different genres for a reason.

There's also the other addendum: Doors don't necessarily provide what you want or need. They come up when a child is trying to find something their world does not have. It's satisfying an innate desire, whether for safety, adventure, validation, or more. And they're completely random.

Eleanor cannot guarantee that the kids will return to their Doors. She can't even keep them forever; most graduate, and they have to decide what comes after. Whether it means pretending to be the normal kid their parents want or to risk searching for their Doors solo, neither is a good option. Some, like Kade, have neither choice since both their families and the world cast them out for being something they're not.

Nancy finding her door in the first book changed things. Up to that point, few had accomplished that at Eleanor's school. Heck, Jill was so desperate that she tried to create a skeleton key of a girl using body parts. But Nancy found her door, and the kids realized they could go to where they thought was home as long as they were sure. Nancy was sure that she wanted to go back to the Halls of the Dead. So she did, and that departure gave everyone hope. They could find their Doors without resorting to underhanded means. Sure, it was a random and desperate chance, but it was a chance. The students become empowered to help others with their trauma and various quests that appear.

They even defy the rules of life and death to bring back one of their own. And if that is possible, returning home is as well.

The Actual Skeleton Key

When Kade, Cora, and Sumi learn about Antsy's powers after rescuing her from Seraphina, a student who uses her beauty to get others to do what she wants, they realize that Antsy is a skeleton key for doors. She can find and open any, regardless of whether it's made for her. That means all the students could go home with that power. And that is precisely why she can't stay.

Mind, a skeleton key girl would have solved a lot of problems in the first book. Sumi remarks, without a hint of bitterness, that Jill didn't need to cut off her hands and leave her to die from shock and blood loss; if Jill had waited a few months, she could have used Antsy to return to the Moors, and no one would have died. Jill's impatience cost her life and the bond with her sister, twice!

The irony, however, is that Antsy doesn't want to open more Doors unless it is actually necessary. She found out about the two-day rule after giving up several years of her life and is lamenting how her ability has become a curse. Antsy grew up too quickly, in body and mind, and she is no longer a child in more ways than one. She doesn't want anyone to pay that price again unless they know. And she would have to pay it over and over again to help others until Eleanor's school no longer had students, and she'd be a withered husk. That would mean letting others exploit her, like her stepfather and Vineta did.

Another Price to Pay

Antsy escaping doesn't let anyone off the hook. Eleanor reads Seraphina and her friend Angela the riot act for scaring Antsy away, in layman's terms, and trying to use her to get home. Not helping is that Chris, Cora, Kade, and Sumi had to travel through dangerous worlds to help Antsy find her way back to the shop and rescue Hudson. Seraphina and Angela are on probation, and everyone else has lost their only skeleton key. Kade also forfeited his door and what once felt like home, not realizing it was in his room the whole time and that the goblins had long forgiven him for killing their king. He may not ever get that chance again, especially since he will inherit the school after Aunt Eleanor dies or enters her door one last time. Cora does find her door, but it means letting go of all the friends she made at Eleanor's school. And no one can ever tell Antsy's mother the truth about what happened to her elder daughter since it's too fantastical to believe.

The question is where the main series can go from here. It's confirmed that Antsy can open doors from the shop to the school, which is how Sumi was able to return after staying with Antsy for a few months to regain the aging that she lost while dead. The students now know that any arrival can be a Finder and potentially get them home. Kade realizes he has to keep a closer eye on the new and current students to improve the Compass and prevent a repeat of what happened to Antsy. There are so many places we can go with the rotating protagonists, and not even death can stop them.

Eleanor and Kade both have a disruptive status quo on their hands. They must figure out how to handle it when the next twist ends their normal world.

BEYOND GREEN AND BLACK: HBO'S HOUSE OF THE DRAGON: WHAT DOES IT MEAN TO FIGHT FOR THE IRON THRONE IN 2024?

DR. KAVITA MUDAN FINN

If you were out and about in a major city in the Western Hemisphere (I'm honestly not sure about elsewhere—do let me know) in May and June 2024, you probably came across posters featuring two determined-looking women—one wearing green, one wearing black—and the tagline "All Must Choose." You may have seen the AI-generated images of black and green banners flying on various famous landmarks. If you're a millennial, you may have experienced flashbacks—for good or ill—to conversations on Monday mornings in April improbably peppered with the word "Targaryen."

HBO's *House of the Dragon* (2022–2024) does not simply ask—it *demands* that we choose a side in the fictional civil war over the Iron Throne: Team Green or Team Black. It was a very clever marketing campaign that ramped up in the weeks leading up to the premiere of the show's second season on June 16, 2024. The cleverest part, however, wasn't clear until the season itself started airing, as the show proceeded to completely undermine that black-and-green premise, showing each side growing more militant, more willing to commit atrocities, and more eager to justify them. Some fans delighted in that subversion; others dug in their heels for one side or the other, taking to social media to spout vitriol at showrunners Ryan Condal and Sara Hess, and even at some of the actors, for failing to live up to their expectations.

What all of this discourse is missing is the much larger point the show is trying to make. Maybe it's because they put it into the mouth of the most punchable man in the fictional kingdom of Westeros, Ser Criston Cole (Fabien Frankel), who, in the Season 2 finale, bleakly observes that "the dragons dance, and we are all as dust beneath their feet."[1] It's like the meme—the worst person you know just made a good point. Which is that, when faced with the modern capitalist state, most of us are just dust under the feet of interests far more powerful than we as individuals can take on. It's a terrifying thought to know just how small you are.

But that isn't the conclusion, merely the parameters of the problem. And the show is constantly working to both complicate and subvert our expectations as the characters go about grasping for control in a situation that threatens to fly apart. As Yeats said more than a century ago, "The blood-dimmed tide is loosed upon the world, / The ceremony of innocence is drowned: / The best lack all conviction, while the worst / Are full of passionate intensity."[2] He wrote at the end of the First World War, a conflict so cataclysmic, so destructive, that it was, at least briefly, called the war to end all wars. How optimistic a thought that was.

One of the most interesting subversions in *House of the Dragon* is the inclusion and amplification of minor characters outside the main corridors of power. Chief among these is a former sex worker turned information broker named Mysaria, who, in this season, became the confidante of one of the two main claimants to the throne. Season 2, however, has added several more of these characters—normal people, part of the normally undifferentiated masses, like most of us would be if we turned up in a fantasy realm.

By happenstance, my partner and I rewatched the *Lord of the Rings* trilogy (2001–2003) about midway through *House of the Dragon*'s second season, and it occurred to me that anyone who wasn't a Named Person of Importance, or a ruler, was just . . . moved about. Part of that is the story J.R.R. Tolkien was telling, in which he was busy subverting other heroic archetypes through the cinnamon roll that is Samwise Gamgee. But even the source material for *House of the Dragon*—written by George R.R. Martin while mimicking the style and content of a chronicle compiled after the fact and based on multiple, contradictory accounts—has little to say about those who aren't kings, queens, or princes. Even the queens, truth be told, are given short shrift in comparison to the men surrounding them. Many readers found this narrative conceit to be off-putting, and I can completely understand why (even if my own reaction was nerdy glee), so it didn't surprise me in the least when the first season made several significant divergences from the book from the very beginning. One of the joys of this kind of palimpsestic storytelling is how much room it gives you for interpretation.

Those divergences have continued through the second season (some more favorably received than others), stretching out what in the books covered several paragraphs, maybe a few pages, into a simmering, sometimes unbearably tense, story about how otherwise decent people become complicit in horrific war crimes. And it planted the seeds for a growing awareness among the non-aristocratic members of the show's increasingly large cast that they might have more power than they realized.

In the meantime, those in power have never been more constrained. The show's two protagonists, Rhaenyra Targaryen (Emma d'Arcy) and Alicent Hightower (Olivia Cooke), spend the entire season being doubted, questioned, and talked over by the men around them. At different points in the season, both characters make desperate bids for peace, those attempts framing a climactic and destructive battle between dragons in Episode 4. By the end, Alicent has offered to give up her crown, her power, and two of her sons to save herself, her daughter Helaena, and her granddaughter. "I am, at last, myself," she tells her former best friend Rhaenyra, for whom the show implies she may also have romantic feelings, "with no ambition greater than to walk where I please, and to breathe the open air; to die unremarked and unnoticed . . . and be free." Rhaenyra, conversely, admits that "My part is here, whether I will or no. It was decided for me long ago." The episode and season end with wide-angle shots of, respectively, Alicent against an open sky and Rhaenyra beneath a latticework frame filled with ancient scrolls, the literal weight of history trapping her like a fly in amber.

It is not a coincidence, say I as a Shakespeare scholar, that Rhaenyra's concluding lines are a couplet in iambic pentameter.

I have written elsewhere that *House of the Dragon* is a fascinating analog to early modern historical drama, so I won't go into that here. But the reactions to the show have formed an additional layer of reception and interpretation that can, I believe, tell us a great deal about the present historical moment. Speaking as a South Asian woman in the United States in late 2024, I find myself begrudgingly agreeing with Criston Cole that I feel very much like dust beneath the feet of two old, creaky, and structurally unsound political parties, both in service of corporations and billionaires. But while *House of the Dragon* goes dormant for two years, having left us with a cliffhanger ending, it is at least within our power—as we have seen in India, South Korea, and elsewhere—to move beyond the binaristic marketing ploys that tell us we must choose one side or the other, full stop, and that is where our power ends. And those who fall into arguing over which of the two sides is better run the risk of missing the larger and more crucial point—that if we don't come together, we lose everything.

[1] *House of the Dragon*, Season 2, Episode 8, 'The Queen Who Ever Was'.

[2] William Butler Yeats, 'The Second Coming' (1919), ll. 5–8.

HAYAO MIYAZAKI'S THE BOY AND THE HERON: PORTAL FANTASY, MAGICAL REALISM, AND THE HUMAN UNCONSCIOUS

ARCHITA MITTRA

> "And in its own way, the film allowed me to inhabit my own grief and bitterness—losing my grandparents, several beloved pets, objects of sentimental value and other missed opportunities, all within a span of two-three years, post-pandemic. Perhaps all that was lost may be found again, briefly in a dream-like secret realm elsewhere, but to relentlessly pursue that thread is to lose touch with the living—with the things that truly matter."

The Boy and the Heron (Hayao Miyazaki/Studio Ghibli, 2023)—Hayao Miyazaki's latest (but hopefully not the last) film is a work of slow and sublime beauty. It unfolds a complex coming-of-age narrative in the guise of portal fantasy, delicately preoccupied with grief and wonder, laced with leitmotifs from his earlier works. It strives to be both a legacy to the Studio Ghibli brand of emotional storytelling as well as a love letter to genre, transforming the trappings of genre into crucial metaphors to understand the world. Told in the magic realist vein, the film resonates with poetic and oneiric vastness, a testament to the intricate interlinkage between the imaginative potential of art and the dream logic of the human unconscious.

The film's English title, *The Boy and the Heron*—bipartite, two singular nouns, conjoined—hints at the confluence of the human and spirit worlds, both plagued by wars within and without, represented by Mahito, our twelve-year-old protagonist grieving his mother's untimely passing, and the peculiar grey heron who leads him to the secret magical realm, acting as an obnoxious spirit guide of sorts. Though far away from the battlefield, the looming threat of the Pacific War is a constant presence in Mahito's life—his mother perished in a hospital fire, and his father is the owner of an ammunition factory. Mahito's hands are thus bloody, though we do not see it until he bashes a rock to his head, an act of self-harm that becomes a visible marker of his grief and guilt. Even when he is seemingly safe and secluded in his granduncle's countryside estate, the horrors of war are inescapable—and so is the alienation and isolation it engenders.

So much so that Mahito refuses the call of magic and adventure, not once but repeatedly—much to the heron's frustration. After his father marries his late wife's sister and moves the family to a manor in the wilderness, Mahito finds himself surrounded by traces of his mother's younger self, as well as the enticement that she might still be alive "somewhere".

Yet he is unable to escape the real world till he watches his kindly aunt/step-mother being taken into the forest. When he finally embarks on a quest to rescue her, he is accompanied by Kiriko, one of the old maids in the estate—a small reminder that magical quests are not just for the Chosen Ones but open to everyone, including those without any noble lineage or direct familial ties.

In his frantic search for his step-mother, Mahito encounters an assortment of fantastical creatures and objects—ancient dolmens, a giant fish, cutesy bubble-like spirits called the "Warawara" (symbolizing the cycle of birth, death, and rebirth), fierce pelicans, man-eating parakeets, and Himi, a young woman with pyrokinetic abilities. Miyazaki paints this pocket world in darkly surreal overtones, and yet, for all its beauty and wonder, this realm's ecosystem is as poisoned as our own. While Himi struggles to protect the innocent bubble-spirits from enemies, a dying pelican informs Mahito that without the Warawara, they have no other source of food.

The tower wherein the Creator (and Mahito's long-lost granduncle) resides is similarly taken over by cannibalistic parakeets that have proliferated unchecked, perhaps at the cost of other species. Thus, the ecosystem, ravaged by greed and desperation, hearkens back to the question of ecological balance posed in *Princess Mononoke* (1997). But while *Princess Mononoke's* ending suggests that a compromise between the natural world and human enterprise may be reached, *The Boy and the Heron* hints at a grimmer conclusion—Mahito chooses to let go of his family's legacy and leaves the magic realm (already rotting and unstable) to crumble into dust.

Unlike some of the Pevensie children who somehow find their way back to Narnia, the portal world depicted here is neither an afterlife of sorts (that waits in earnest to welcome characters at the end of their adventures) nor a parallel realm that exists independently of our own, but a limbo-like place (with doors to other worlds and timelines) that has, as a result of isolation, callous decision-making and entropy, decayed to the point where salvation is impossible—which perhaps can be read as an eerie metaphor for the future of our own planet, doomed by the irreversible forces of climate change. Thus, Mahito's choice of turning his back on the poisoned portal realm to embrace the present (which is no less poisoned and filled with horror and heartbreak) to be reunited with his loved ones becomes the only choice "worth" making—a willingness to say goodbye to escapism to confront one's guilt-ridden present.

Yet, while the emotional core of the story is deceptively simple, *The Boy and the Heron* eschews attempts to extract a singular moral or message from it. Unlike films made by American animation studios such as Disney, Pixar, and DreamWorks, which frequently utilize feel-good, family-friendly storylines that preachily aim for universal appeal, Studio Ghibli movies tend to favor ambiguity over specificity, allowing the audience to experience art as is. Their works, though accessible, are often complex and layered with symbolism, speaking to each viewer in a deeply personal way.

This is particularly relevant given their growing popularity among Western audiences, which has led to other films, books, and associated media co-opting the studio's aesthetics (just look at the gifs/film clips depicting Ghibli characters enjoying slow-cooked meals or going about their day, doing the rounds on social media) while blatantly disregarding their artistic manifesto and underlying political themes. One may argue that perhaps there isn't any "harm" in indulging in a little escapism every now and then, à la reading a cozy fantasy novel, but optimism without awareness of the socio-political realities dictating our lives isn't optimism at all, but delusion.

And it seems that populist media increasingly prefers to engage with cultures, genres, and modes of any kind only on the shallow basis of aesthetics that can be visually commodified and marketed towards the algorithm-mediated audience, without any interrogation of the core philosophies or tenets originally responsible for it. This, in turn, leads to assembly-line artistic projects that look pretty but feel empty, propped up only by formulaic plots, tropes, and tags, paying mere lip service to the works that inspired it or the issues it ostensibly claims to tackle.

Meanwhile, *The Boy and the Heron* narrates an utterly unique story, even while echoing the studio's past efforts. Mahito's familial relationship with the female characters, be it Himi or his step-mom, is reminiscent of the fated connection between the two main characters in *When Marnie Was There* (2014). The charming inner life of nature spirits (like the Warawaras here) and the idyllic beauty of the countryside—both under threat thanks to the engines of corporate capitalism—were explored earlier in *My Neighbor Totoro* (1988). Mahito faces several trials before he can save his aunt, much like Chihiro in *Spirited Away* (2001), who has to complete menial tasks and help the dragon boy, Haku, before she can rediscover her true name—in both instances, a rescue quest becomes a catalyst for self-discovery.

A close reading of *Studio Ghibli's* entire corpus can undoubtedly reveal more such similarities. Indeed, devoted fans have read meaning into almost every frame of the film, including the significance of the precariously balanced stack of thirteen stones representing the portal world (and how elements of the film faithfully reflect details from Miyazaki's own life), which bears little discussion here, as most (if not all) art is personal. But I'm more fascinated with how *The Boy and the Heron's* careful synthesis of the works that preceded it leads up to this question that reflects the film's Japanese title (*How Do You Live?*) that in turn references Genzaburō Yoshino's 1937 novel of the same name (that Mahito is seen reading—a bequest from his mother): **How does one live in a world that's inherently unstable and build something better?**

It's a question that definitely haunted Miyazaki when he came out of retirement and announced this film. In his project proposal for *The Boy and the Heron,* written in 2016, he contemplated how, in his old age, it would take "at least three years" to complete a feature-length film—and in those three years, the world we know could change inevitably. He remarks:

> *What state will the world and minds of viewers be in when they greet our film? Surely our current age, indistinctly drifting, indefinable, and indiscernible, is reaching its end? Isn't the world as a whole in a state of flux? We could be heading for war or disaster, or perhaps even both.*

Mahito, haunted by war and trauma, doesn't quite have an answer, but his decision to confront the malice within him and be there for his loved ones may provide a clue (or a consolation). It is, thus, a powerful commitment (to echo Miyazaki's own words) to "see with eyes unclouded by hate". Fantasy is thus rendered a space that one might visit only briefly and then face the real world with all its horrors—a choice that both Mahito and his mother finally end up making. The longer one tarries in the portal realm, the more it stagnates, and the illusory freedom offered by the loophole of time travel is only that—an illusion. And so this is where the film leaves us, with Mahito clutching a souvenir from his adventure and reunited with his remaining family—a "happy-for-now" ending contingent on the choices he has made and must keep making, for helping others and healing from grief and harm (be it self-inflicted or otherwise) is neither linear nor simple.

Indeed, there are moments when *The Boy and the Heron* can feel overwhelming. After all, it straddles so many disparate yet wondrous elements—time travel, pocket dimensions, a mysterious asteroid, strange ecology, a remote Gothic mansion with secrets, the Pacific War, the struggles of boyhood and loneliness —and seamlessly weaves all of it into this work of unmatched maturity, a tapestry that cannot be unraveled but witnessed. And in its own way, the film allowed me to inhabit my own grief and bitterness—losing my grandparents, several beloved pets, objects of sentimental value and other missed opportunities, all within a span of two-three years, post-pandemic. Perhaps all that was lost may be found again, briefly in a dream-like secret realm elsewhere, but to relentlessly pursue that thread is to lose touch with the living—with the things that truly matter. And in a dark, cavernous cinema hall full of strangers, that realization is enough to make you weep—weep because the world is sad but so full of wonder.

SPY ADVENTURE FLICK ARGYLLE IS GOOD, ACTUALLY? LET ME EXPLAIN . . . THE DIFFERENCE A FEMALE PROTAGONIST MAKES

LAUREN C. TEFFEAU

"You still want to go?" I asked my friend Laura. "It's getting panned *everywhere*."

A couple of times a year, we do dinner and a movie to catch up with each other. We'd seen the trailer for *Argylle* (2024, Apple TV+/Universal) during our viewing of *The Holdovers* (2023, Focus Features) last fall, and in those few seconds before the next trailer started, we looked at each other and agreed that would be the next movie we'd see. What was not to like? We'd seen the *Kingsman* films already and enjoyed Matthew Vaughn's signature take on humorous gun-fu. The trailer heavily featured Henry Cavill, who we both lamented being pushed out of the *Witcher* franchise. Throw in an introverted bookworm getting out of her comfort zone as the lead; we were hooked.

On paper, the movie should work—*if* you ignored the February release date, signaling the studio's lack of confidence in the flick. But they'd been wrong before with gems that bucked projections and found their way into audiences' hearts. We were willing to risk it. Then, the reviews came in. I started to waffle, but Laura insisted we still go. Said she could use a laugh regardless of whether it was intentional or not. So, we jettisoned all expectations and ended up enjoying the movie. Really!

Don't get me wrong. There are problems with the film. But I don't think I've watched anything else that comes close to capturing feminine hopes and dreams with such honesty on the big screen.

SPY ADVENTURE FLICK ARGYLLE IS GOOD, ACTUALLY? LET ME EXPLAIN . . . ...

Directed and produced by Matthew Vaughn and written by Jason Fuchs, *Argylle* is a cross-genre mashup with obvious parallels to the Melissa McCarthy vehicle *Spy* (2015, 20th Century Studios) and the Sandra Bullock romcom *The Lost City* (2022, Paramount), topped off with all the "Yeah, baby" glitz of *Austin Powers* (1997, Warner Bros). There's *a lot* going on with the film before we even get to the twisty plot. What follows is a discussion of *Argylle* positioned against these media properties, as well as the movies' different reception with audiences.

In both *Argylle* and *Spy*, our heroines must use skills they've only researched as a spy novelist (*Argylle*) or CIA analyst (*Spy*). It's slightly more complicated than that in each film, but their journey from the sidelines to the main stage and the self-actualization that follows is what serves as their character arc. By tapping into their true identities by the film's end, they're fully empowered and seen as a desirable romantic and sexual partner opposite their male co-stars. What's so interesting about these films is that both leading ladies exhibit body types that are traditionally not showcased in Hollywood despite push-back for more inclusive beauty standards. In *Spy*, it's played for laughs, while in *Argylle*, it's celebrated in a way I suspect audiences still aren't used to.

There's so much internalized fatphobia in *Spy* that parts of the movie are deeply uncomfortable to watch, despite the script's subversive attempt at humor and the enthusiastic range an actress like McCarthy brings to it. The messaging gets significantly muddied, seeming to indicate the only reason they could get away with making a movie centering a woman of size was if they constantly make fun of her and let the audience in on the joke for the entire runtime.

In comparison, while the camera never lies in *Argylle*, Bryce Dallas Howard's fuller figure, schlubby appearance, and wallflower status is never the butt of a joke or sight gag. I kept watching Howard on screen to figure out if that was her real live body or if she'd donned a fat suit. But it's clearly *her*, and in the media rounds, she talked candidly about how good she felt doing stunts because her body was *allowed* to be strong and dynamic without having to deprive herself to hit some arbitrary number on the scale during filming. The camera always treats her like a leading lady, allowing an actress of her caliber to perform in such a way that her inner beauty always shines through, even before her third-act glow-up.

Argylle also doesn't fall into the same trap *The Lost City* does with how both protagonists relate to their work. While both women have built their lives around their writer identities, Bullock's character spends way too much screentime slamming the books she writes as if the filmmakers themselves couldn't understand why anyone would love writing romance or take it seriously. Her character's self-loathing and minimization of her work send a constant message to the audience that romance is silly, juvenile, and unrealistic. Things romance fans are sadly used to hearing, but they still show up for anything that gets close to including the love, longing, and happily-ever-afters they adore—including me and my friend Laura, who made a point to see *The Lost City* together when it was in theaters. As much as I liked the movie, I was angry at how the attitude of Bullock's character undercut *all* the good work in the film that celebrated the romance genre and the tropes that make it tick. Including the fact that it's the hero who keeps pushing back on her negative self-talk (in a nice reversal of the education hero Jack needed about such things in *The Lost City* predecessor *Romancing the Stone*, 1984).

A Realistic Female Protagonist

In *Argylle*, our heroine deploys her book research to solve the mystery and get the guy at the same time, just like Bullock, but the difference is Howard's character loves *everything* about writing, embracing both the highs and the lows of the writing life and her deep, abiding love for her cat, something the film also honors and takes seriously at both the beginning and the end of the film. The only difference? She's writing spy thrillers instead of romance, and those male-coded stories are somehow ridicule-proof, no matter their lack of plausibility and racy storylines for which romance novels are so often maligned.

I believe much of the confusion and criticism lobbed at *Argylle* is because the marketing team didn't understand or was afraid to embrace the fact that the movie is essentially a gender-flipped version of *Austin Powers*, and the trailer suggested it would be more male-centered than it ended up being. In both films, we have highly imaginative main characters, one dreaming of adventure/romance, the other of grandeur/sex (a dichotomy that encapsulates so much of the battle of the sexes, I wish I was back in grad school with a thesis to write). But the script, the camera lens, and the filmic sensibility in *Austin Powers* are male-coded, while *Argylle* is female-coded.

That's why one was celebrated, spawning two sequels and rumors of a third (which sadly still haven't come together), and the other lampooned, derided, widely panned fodder for gleeful takedowns and reviews complaining of all the icky girl cooties contained therein. I have *never* seen more film reviewers actively encourage people to stay home from a movie before *Argylle*.

Why is it Austin Powers can be his ridiculous shagadelic self, but an equally mousy writer can't let her imagination take her wherever she wants without garnering extreme ridicule? Sure, it eventually turns out Howard's character has amazing Mary Sue spy skills, and sure, she gets the guy. When the hero does it, it's expected. But when it's a woman? That's wish fulfillment, and all the terrible things Bullock's character says about romance in *The Lost City* , then enter the chat. *Argylle's* reception baffled even director Matthew Vaughn, though it sounds like things have rebounded a bit since the movie hit streaming services.

Honoring Female Dreams and Desires

So that day, when Laura and I settled into our reclined seats and the lights in the theater dimmed, I was shocked by the film we saw. One that celebrates female authors, one that lets the female form exist without scrutiny, one that honors female dreams and desires. And did all this with a great cast and an ambitious but solid plot centering Howard's character.

Anne Hathaway said something during her promo tour for *The Idea of You*, a movie that also generated strong (gendered) reactions, that has stayed with me: **"We have limited ideas of appropriate ways for women to be happy. And we react harshly and punitively when we feel that women have stepped outside those boundaries."**

We ridicule what we don't understand. And I get it. It's so rare to see the female experience centered and celebrated. It's so rare to see female dreams rendered in stereo sound and twelve-bit color and given the budget and star power *Argylle* had. But if Austin Powers can sing and dance and shag without condemnation from the masses, why can't our heroine turn gunfu into a loving moment of connection? Why can't she rollerblade over an oil slick and save the day? Too silly or too female? *Argylle* is a movie I would have unabashedly loved as a young woman, one where it didn't matter what I looked like but what was in my brain and heart. Where the discovery of one's self is more important than anything else.

One movie cannot undo generations of cultural programming, but when one tries so hard to give us something different, one that looks more like *Argylle,* I hope there's a better understanding next time of what we're seeing on the screen and why.

PISTOL-WHIP ME, KRISTEN STEWART, A REVIEW OF LOVE LIES BLEEDING'S QUEER SURREALISM AND THE VALUE OF HOPE

HOLLY LYN WALRATH

Love Lies Bleeding (*A24*, 2024) is a bodacious exploration of queer sexuality that mixes 80s Hulk Hogan aesthetics with southern small-town terror. The film stars Kristen Stewart in Her Gayest Role Yet as Lou, a gym manager who falls for Jackie (Katy O'Brien—The Mandalorian, Agents of S.H.I.E.L.D.), a body-builder who wants to compete in Vegas but gets stuck in the politics of border-town murder.

Lou is dealing with the reality that her family, quite frankly, sucks ass. Her father is a crime lord smuggling weapons to Mexico, and her sister is married to an abusive macho-mullet. She's immediately drawn to the charismatic and criminally hot Jackie, a bodybuilder who is new to town and the gym Lou works at.

For any queer person who has grown up in a small town in the South, the dark realities of that life feel desperately authentic in this film. Lou is trapped at a dead-end job, dating the only other queer girl in town, a stringy-haired blonde with bad teeth who is constantly giving Lou puppy-dog eyes and following her around as she mops up other people's messes (played with beautiful empathy & humor by Anna Baryshnikov).

The lonely Lou manages to intrigue the stunning Jackie with the lure of steroids and some frankly delightful-looking cunnilingus. But as Jackie consumes more steroids, her body and personality start to go into roid-rage mode. Here, the writing fantastically aligns feminine anger with its appropriate vengeance on terrible men. The film's tagline is "Revenge gets ripped."

Jackie kills Lou's brother-in-law after he puts Lou's sister in the hospital. Katy O'Brien makes us sympathetic to Jackie while leaning into the chaos.

As Lou has to clean up more and more of Jackie's murders, the narrative goes sideways into bonkers territory, but it's a thrill ride the audience can't help but enjoy. Discomfort and cringe spiral into desire and daydreams.

This film is not for everyone. Some viewers online have questioned its appropriateness—accusing the film of pandering to cis straight men. It was interesting to look around in my theatre here in Houston, TX, and see who attended. It was mostly couples on dates and young women. Like last year's queer-coded breakout *Saltburn,* I got the sense that the film might generate unease for the straight members of the audience while creating a kind of buzzy energy for queer viewers. It's the kind of film I would've snuck out to see as a teen if such a thing existed. Queer rep means that films like this might end up reaching the wrong audience, but the audience they need to hit is right there, eagerly waiting, and shouldn't they take precedence, no matter what side effects might ensue? This argument feels like people are simply uncomfortable with the film, and so they choose to center cis straight people, even in critiquing the film.

The queer dynamics of the film are interesting. While Jackie is femme-presenting, her personality mirrors butch macho camp; Lou is butch-presenting with femme-nurturing habits—you quickly realize that any stereotypes you might expect degenerate when put in a queer lens. These characters are well-rounded and defy binary stereotypes in purposeful ways.

I was entranced by the film's cinematography, which pairs lonely shots of the New Mexico desert with slow-burn fades into Katy O'Brien's beauty. The film oozes queer femme gaze. The sex scenes are phenomenal. It's fantastic to see Kristen Stewart stepping into her queer icon era—a natural metamorphosis for an actress who has been historically panned by critics. Stewart's roles have been mostly queer-coded up till this point (See *Adventureland, Underwater, Spencer, Twilight,* according to the actress), so to see her fill such an audacious role is frankly magic.

My favorite scene in the movie is the end shot when Lou's just dragged another body out to the desert to bury it, and she stands with her hands on her hips in clear exasperation. The film's message is that queer love can overcome anything, even murder and the morally gray questions abiding therein.

What's most exciting is how the surreal aspects of the film were necessary to make the ending *happy*. Jackie's body literally becomes larger than life, just as we're beginning to worry that Lou and Jackie may never escape. In a beautiful metaphor for the power of the queer body, Jackie becomes a fifty-foot woman, saving Lou from her father. (Side note: When I saw the cast for the film, I wondered why the heck Ed Harris was in it, until I realized he was the villain.)

The power of this surrealism is that without it, the film would end in death for both queer characters. It reminded me of how often I fantasized about getting out of my small town as a queer kid growing up in the South. What queer kid hasn't dreamed of being powerful—and escaping the terror that is super-conservative society? Of squashing abusers like bugs? This necessary acknowledgment of the power of hope sets the film apart from what would otherwise be a straightforward yet depressing story.

This one is a must-see.

THE JUNJI ITO TOUCH: THE LIMINAL ZONE: A REVIEW OF THE POPULAR MANGA ARTIST'S LATEST SHORT STORY COLLECTION

PRIYA SRIDHAR

Junji Ito has become the most renowned horror manga artist in the 2010s and 2020s. From the visceral claustrophobia of "The Enigma of Amigara Fault" to the situational twists in "Uzamaki," Ito can make anything terrifying. He understands what visuals can make a person freeze, but they keep turning the page.

Ito's 2022 collection, *The Liminal Zone,* takes more time to set up its scares. Since Junji Ito didn't have as short a deadline and as many pages as he wished to tell his tale, he focused on the art and pacing. We get time to see him build up on atmospheric uneasiness, leading to a greater impact.

"Weeping Woman Way" And Fundamental Sadness

In the story "Weeping Woman Way," Junji Ito tells a story that looks at depression and how it depicts sadness as a parasite that defines your way. Antidepressants don't work to deal with this inner sadness because it comes from a root of oppression.

Yuzuru cannot explain why she is sad all the time after traveling with her boyfriend, Mako, through the countryside. A Weeping Woman, a woman who cries at funerals as a professional mourner, walked past them, and Yuzuru's tears started. She just starts crying randomly, even in her sleep, to the point that the bedsheets are soaked. Mako offers to break the engagement if they are unhappy, driving her to doctors' appointments and making sure she's eating right. A fortuneteller thinks that they need to go back and find the Weeping Woman who inspired Yuzuru to cry that much. Since they have no other options, Mako and Yuzuru make the trek, with Yuzuru wearing sunglasses to hide her red-rimmed eyes. Though they get answers, the Weeping Women try to force Yuzuru to stay and cry for all the spirits of the world. Yuzuru considers staying, but Mako nopes on that.

The story brings up questions about the agency. Can we make decisions when our emotions overwhelm us? Mako believes that Yuzuru's sadness makes her susceptible to creepy cult behavior. She doesn't resist when he pulls her away from the women and the spirits that need people to mourn for them, so that they can move on to the next world. Mako thinks that the women want to kidnap his girlfriend and change her life fundamentally.

One could ask why Yuzuru doesn't see a therapist while getting antidepressants and medical treatment. Therapy doesn't always help, but having that safe space can make a huge difference when dealing with a sense of loss or grief. We do find out later that her family felt guilty for alleged abuse and neglect, saying that Yuzuru didn't have a happy childhood. They mourn at her funeral as Mako weeps quietly, but aren't exactly sorry. Mako received blame and spite from Yuzuru's father when her health worsened, when his worst fault was making decisions for Yuzuru in the name of her safety. Yuzuru, talking about these feelings in a safe space, may have helped her deal with these sudden tears.

Mako's attempts to save Yuzuru from her sadness prove futile despite their best efforts. He has to let Yuzuru go and hope that in death, she can find peace. Her body disappearing at her funeral denies him closure, as does his inability to find the Weeping Women again. Yuzuru lost her agency the minute she encountered the first Weeping Woman.

Grooming The Virgin Mary

Maria's "Madonna" story shows this horror regarding agency much more blatantly. At her Catholic school, the principal systematically isolates her from the new friends she made by transferring her to a new class meant for students with intellect and "beautiful features." After that selling point, he moves her to another dorm. While she does make new friends, he constantly calls her after class for different rituals, saying that she is the Virgin Mary reborn.

His words activate Maria's creep instincts, especially when learning that the principal had several lovers while married twice and claims that his stepson Kirihito, his first wife Haruyo's son, went missing. One lover, Satomi Kiyokawa, is still teaching at the school and reveals that she is pregnant with the principal's child. She also manages the new dorms, but the teacher seems oblivious to how all the students languish with salt pouring out of their ears.

The principal does not understand the meaning of boundaries. Maria tries bringing up the salt problem and the blasphemy, but he responds by trying to say that she's the Virgin Mary. He goes as far as trying to kiss Maria and proposing marriage. Maria points out to the reader that she's only a teen, and none of this is appropriate. She also doesn't know how to leave.

Maria tries to keep her distance from him and not cross his current wife, Misuzu Tenzo, as she is very strict and the vice-principal. People also have salt falling out of their ears after talking to said woman, which only activates more creep flags for Maria. She wonders what's up with the weird services and being in a new dorm since worshipping the Virgin Mary rather than God is super odd for a Catholic school. Yet she can't escape; it's boarding school, after all, and who would believe her? She only hopes to endure and take the principal's words with a grain of salt before salt starts pouring out of her ears.

What's fitting is that when we learn that Hirohito, the principal's first victim, and his own son, is the salt figure on a large crucifix. Hirohito, from what we know, was an ordinary boy born into terrible circumstances. He tried to survive with a father who didn't see him as a person. He saves Maria in death when he couldn't save himself in life.

To add insult to injury, though Maria survives the story, she can't make anyone believe her. She tells the police what happened, but they don't find it possible that a woman could turn a horde of people into crumbling pillars of salt. At the least, they believe that the principal's wife did try to kill her, but that's about it. They also find the body of the first wife within the Virgin Mary statue. Everything else literally went up in flames.

This feels like a deliberate decision that Maria tries to tell her story. She feels that while the real world will find out the plausible crimes that the principal committed, they need to know about the woman who would turn others to salt out of pure jealousy. All she can do is know her truth and take caution in the case that another person takes advantage of this power dynamic.

Junji Ito isn't making pseudo-feminist statements like "all men are bad" and so forth; he shows the complicity that happens regardless of gender. As a result, these issues become more terrifying on a reread.

Condescension and Mansplaining Comes With Supernatural Healing

"The Spirit Flow of Aokigahara" is a story about martyrdom. A couple makes a pact to go to Mount Fuji, a sacred spot, before one partner dies of a terminal illness. The other wishes to stay with their partner to the end, dying with him. Much to their surprise, a strange spirit flows through the forest at night and heals him.

Mika is worried about Norio refusing to come home. If he's better, doesn't that mean he wants to seize the day, start a new life, and rebuild their relationship? Norio believes otherwise; he believes he needs to remain by the spirit flow and allow it to consume him. Sure, Mika can go home, but he's not returning with her. Norio bonds with another man who comes to heal, and they become obsessed with the flow. They both make fun of Mika for wanting to be sensible and figure out what's going on.

For me, the condescending tones hit hard. When you care for someone, especially one having a permanent condition, it drains a person. Then, when they throw your kindness in your face, like it was nothing? That hurts a lot.

Thanks to his sudden recovery, Norio goes from a sweet boyfriend to a selfish jerk who only cares about the flow and not the people in his life. Mika was worried, but she agreed to stay with Norio until his end came.

The YouTuber who serves as a caricature for Logan Paul is the only sane person he runs to when he sees what's in the cave. No one else does because Mika doesn't want to leave Norio. Eventually, she joins the spirit flow to understand and gain a reason for her boyfriend to want her to stay. Her choice to surrender gives her the power and ability to stay with Norio in a form where he won't shut her out and ignore her. It's a questionable decision where she gives up her humanity, but she is content with the choice.

Dangerous Dreams in "Slumber"

"Slumber" ends the collection, returning to traditional Junji Ito terrors. A man named Takuya Terada fears that he is a killer. Over a few weeks, he dreams of going to the streets and committing murder. The dreams match the details found at the scene of the crime, according to news broadcasts.

Takuya feels he has no power in his life. He's failed the bar exam three times and lives off his parents' financial support. When the nightmares start, all he can do is watch the news broadcasts and consider if he is the killer. He surrenders his agency at the start of the story because he considers if his mind is broken.

His girlfriend Kanami brings Takuya to his senses. She points out that there is a logical solution to figuring out if he is or isn't the killer: set up a camera to record him while he's sleeping. And unlike the other victims, Kanami carries pepper spray when the real killer attacks her. She knows how to use it in a dangerous situation. As a result, she survives and identifies the man who tried to murder her. It ends up not being her boyfriend but rather a neighbor gaslighting him and invading his dreams.

What's interesting is how Kanami's proactive nature contradicts Takuya's passivity; she brings him food when he's studying, tucks him into bed, and suggests the camera idea. She heads home despite the long hours to handle another errand.

The killer being caught is a mixed blessing; Kanami maintains physical and emotional trauma. If Kanami had stayed at Takuya's apartment rather than taking the train home, she would have been fine and proven to Takuya that he's not the killer. The killer also haunts Takuya in his dreams after incarceration, drawing pictures of a disfigured Kanami. He stops trying to pass the bar exam and goes to live back with his parents. Once again, Takuya surrenders his agency. When he and Kanami meet many years later, it's implied that the killer succeeded in hijacking his body and is going to finish the job on her. Takuya bears the same wide-eyed, haunted look, ending the story with horrific implications. A final surrender dooms him and Kanami.

Unequal Power Dynamics

Ito's work lasts because it talks about an important facet of horror: a protagonist's agency. Some protagonists can think their way out of a terrible situation, while others have to endure it until the end. With some of these stories, we get paranoia when authority figures, loved ones, and our own minds betray us.

In addition to the supernatural horrors that plague the protagonists (and they're lucky if they make it to the end of the story unscathed), there are also mundane ones. Namely, we see unequal power dynamics in most of the stories. Power dynamics remain unequal between men and women, as well as between authority figures and their charges. It's when a character challenges the dynamic that they live in, albeit changed for the worse. That agency makes all the difference.

A CLASSIC HORROR STORY (2021): HOW CLASSIC IS IT, REALLY?

CHRISTINA SNG

Fascinated by the idea of watching an Italian version of what a classic horror story was, I originally watched the first third of *A Classic Horror Story* before switching it off, the early part channeling *The Texas Chainsaw Massacre* and the later night scenes too hard on a day with a sinus headache.

Today, I decided to try watching it again, the premise no less intriguing, and found it to be a mash-up of familiar horror movies. Sometimes this works well. Other times, less so. How did *A Classic Horror Story* fare? Let's find out.

To start, most of the characters were likable, a quality that helps smooth any movie journey along. They are:

- Elisa (Matilda Lutz), the pregnant protagonist on her way to an abortion she was conflicted about, was empathetic, kind, and courageous.
- Entrepreneur Sofia (Yuliia Sobol), traveling with her unfortunately annoying boyfriend Mark (William Merrick), brightened the scenes she was in with her carefree spirit. Mark, less so.
- Riccardo (Peppino Mazzotta) offered gravitas as the oldest person in the group and a doctor with secrets.
- Their rideshare driver and enthusiastic travel blogger Fabrizio (Francesco Russo) came across as lighthearted and pleasant.

The story begins with Elisa joining a rideshare to Calabria. She is welcomed by the others on the RV camper while their driver Fabrizio, films them all for his travel blog and offers them beer in his cooler. They cheer each other and drink up.

There is a good amount of foreshadowing when you watch it the second time, as I did for this piece, such as the final question posed by a guessing game

Sofia plays on her phone in the camper: Who was "The apostle who betrayed Jesus"?

The landscape they drive through is absolutely stunning, filled with nothing but a blanket of lush green trees split only by the narrow, winding road where the group drives. Then, they pass a billboard with a family promoting milk, where their eyes and mouths are blackened away.

These two foreshadow what is soon to come.

Mark reads a local newspaper and sees an article about a missing mother and child and another feature on the mayor, a blonde woman with short hair dressed in red, whose appearance he insults.

Elisa needs to throw up, and they stop for her to disembark. Afterward, an intoxicated Mark forces Fabrizio to let him drive. Fabrizio reluctantly complies.

While the others sleep, Mark and Fabrizio talk about Fabrizio's ambitions as a filmmaker. Fabrizio tells Mark it is complicated to be one in Italy. Mark confesses he was an asshole in school, but then he hurt someone. The pair bond over good movies before Fabrizio spots a dead animal on the road and grabs hold of the steering wheel, crashing into a tree.

Mark has broken his leg. Riccardo splints it while Elisa tries to call emergency services, but there is no signal. She looks outside and tells the others that the road is gone.

The group exits the camper and find themselves in a clearing with a strange house with a roof like the top of a star. Nearby, there are loudspeakers on poles. No one answers the door, and when Sofia peers in, she sees that the house is empty.

Riccardo and Fabrizio try to find the road. Fabrizio talks about an American film he watched before about a group of people in a sort of a trap—a limbo where they are doomed to repeat the same things. Part of this feels like foreshadowing.

They come across three straw men with severed pig heads set up in a display. Fabrizio tells Riccardo that they should leave as the blood is still fresh, which means the decapitations just happened.

Elisa explores the house and finds a wall filled with old photographs of people wearing animal masks carved out of wood and a mural of three creatures: the first with no eyes, the second with no ears, and the third with no mouth, and a winged horse by their side.

The legend of Osso, Mastrosso, and Carcagnosso, Fabrizio says to the rest, a story his grandmother told him when he was a child. Three brothers from another world promised to save people from starvation if only they would make a sacrifice, whose eyes, ears, and mouth would be cut from him or her. The villagers continued the sacrifices and became a flock.

The group sleeps in the camper. Riccardo stays up to watch videos of his young daughter. The rest are woken up by screams from the house. Sofia and Elisa run there to find a girl (Alida Baldari Calabria) in the attic, tongue cut off and caged in a straw cocoon. Fabrizio tells Riccardo there is someone outside the camper, and the pair rushes to the house to join the two women.

The sirens sound. People in robes start gathering outside. They take Mark and place him inside the house. Fabrizio quickly pulls up the ladder leading to the attic to keep them safe. The strangers do not seem to know the others are upstairs. They start torturing Mark with a device that drills out his eyes. Then, they drag his body outside.

Sofia sits in shock while Riccardo rescues the girl in the straw cocoon. She races to hug Elisa, weeping. The group leaves the house and run into the forest. They arrive at a clearing filled with empty vehicles. The group rests in the empty cars for a reprieve, and Elisa bonds with the girl who shows Elisa in a notebook that her name is Chiara.

Elisa asks Chiara if there is a way out of the forest. Chiara writes, "This is not a forest."

Before she can ask Chiara what she means, the siren sounds. The group leaves and tries to find a way out again, but ends up back at the house. This time, the camper is missing. This reminds me of Fabrizio's earlier conversation with Riccardo about the American film he watched about people in limbo repeating their day.

Riccardo finds a beer bottle on the ground and returns to the house. They all drink from it except Fabrizio, who says he needs to be on watch. The group shares their personal stories before they go to sleep. Sofia gives Elisa the first 3D ring she made as a gift.

Sirens sound, waking Elisa and Fabrizio up. The other three were taken while they slept.

Elisa walks out of the house to see a huge crowd in masks, Sofia and Riccardo tied up on poles, and Chiara back in the straw cocoon. Fabrizio drags Elisa back into the house. They watch as the masked men gouge out Sofia's eyes and cut off Riccardo's ears. Their eyes and ears are placed in Chiara's cocoon-like an effigy. Then, they cut Sofia and Riccardo's throats.

Elisa realizes they never woke up during the kidnappings, and Fabrizio has never drunk the beer. When they hug, she grabs an earpiece from him. This explains the scenes where he seemed to wince and grab his ear to a high-pitched sound, only apparent to me during a second viewing.

Elisa puts the earpiece to her ear and hears a woman telling Fabrizio to take Elisa to the deer (error in subtitling?). Fabrizio starts calling her names and says she's ruined it all. Cult members enter and take Elisa.

Elisa awakens in daylight. She is seated at a long table with many strangers having a luncheon. Her hands are nailed to the arms of the chair. At the head of the table is a woman with short blonde hair dressed in red. She looks suspiciously like the woman in the newspaper Mark was insulting.

A young boy sings about "three wise knights" who brought "honorable laws," and they were all devoted to them. The story of Osso, Mastrosso, and Carcagnosso? Yes. The woman in red stands and gives thanks to the "Three Knights of Honor" and drinks to them.

Elisa begins to weep, and the people at the table mimic her. Not like how the women in *Midsommar* wept with Dani when she grieved, but in mockery.

The woman stops them and walks to Elisa. She tells Elisa she looks after the people, and they are content. She admits they mocked Elisa because they know she is "the most precious out of everyone," a statement that seems to mean nothing. The people bow their heads as if ashamed.

The woman goes on to tell Elisa that if she doesn't die, how will she look after everyone? But, she adds, the Mafia isn't what it used to be, and even it has to adapt. Is she the Mafia head, I wonder.

A car arrives. Elisa cries to the driver for help, but he does not respond. The woman tells everyone to eat, and they eat. She leaves in the car. One of the men pushes Elisa into a room and takes the ring Sofia gave her. Why? It is never revealed.

Here's the twist.

Elisa looks up to see nine huge video screens in front of her. The whole area has been observed and recorded all this time. Fabrizio's face fills the screens. Elisa realizes he's been filming everything. He tells her he is making a horror movie. She laughs hysterically, lamenting that she is going to die in some loser's fake movie.

Fabrizio complains that in Italy, no one wants to be scared by horror movies, and they are instead grossed out by them. But they love real-life horror on TV. In fact, they are the most requested shows, Fabrizio says to her before turning off his video.

Alone, Elisa agonizingly pulls her hands out of the nails and raises her hands in a *Poltergeist*-like shot in front of the white screens. She leaves the house, dazed, at the sight of many trailers outside.

Searching for Chiara, she peers inside a window to see dead animals. On the side of another trailer is a row of guns. Finally, she sees Chiara's dirty dress washed and hanging with other laundry outside an enclosure.

The penny drops for me here.

Elisa enters and sees all the grotesque masks that the people have been wearing. And video cameras.

She hears Fabrizio cursing about her and goes to investigate. Fabrizio is talking loudly about a brainwave he has about editing his film. We see Chiara clean, speaking, and playing a video game. She is in on it, too, and says, "Mom was clear about that. The client wants her to be aware."

They are siblings! And are doing this for commercial reasons!

Chiara and Fabrizio complain to each other about the distasteful part of their roles. The quarrel ends when Chiara slaps Fabrizio and tells him to shut up. He calls her a dwarf. Outside, Elisa cries.

As Chiara gets ready for their next scene in a new dress, Fabrizio continues to bicker with her. A woman calls them to get on set in fifteen minutes. I wonder at this point, how much of this is theater and how much is it ritual? My money is on it being theater for money.

Chiara opens the door, and her eyes widen. Elisa stands masked, pointing a shotgun at her. And shoots. Chiara flies backward with a loud thump. Fabrizio stares at her dead body in horror.

He rushes outside, and Elisa shoots him in the leg. She turns the camera to him and records herself shooting him in the face. Staggering back to the camera, she pulls off her mask (while I silently scream, *Why tell the world you killed two people*) and says to the lens, "There, you have your ending."

Elisa struggles to find her way out of the forest. A crack of a branch makes her turn around to see a young boy with floaties around his arms. He runs from her. She follows him through a hole in a fence with a sign above saying, "Military Area—No Trespassing. Armed Surveillance."

Elisa ends up on a crowded beach, face, and clothing covered in dry blood. Her phone notifies her of multiple messages from her mother, reminding her of her upcoming abortion. She drops her phone in the sand.

The sunbathers—regular, non-murderous cult people—stare at her. Many start recording her on their phones. (Why, though? A satire on our citizen surveillance culture?) She submerges herself and washes away the blood, holding her stomach, suggesting she may keep her baby after all.

In a post-credits scene clearly sometime in the future, viewers of the movie on Bloodflix (!!), apparently edited and posted without Fabrizio, offer largely negative comments, asking for more blood, or they will cancel their membership.

A man clicks to watch the movie, skimming to the end, where Elisa shoots Fabrizio. His daughter calls him to dinner, and he clicks a thumbs down to the movie. The end.

I felt the latter half of the movie turned really camp after the twin reveals. What felt like a folk horror story turned up to be a satire about amateur snuff films being sold to streaming platforms, although with such a huge cast, I do wonder about how amateur the budget is.

How could the entire cast participate in actual murders? For food, as hinted by the woman when she said she takes care of them? Was the scheme: make snuff films and sell them to Bloodflix for income and feed the cast with food?

Back to my original question: how classic a horror story is this?

The movie adopts many tropes from *Texas Chainsaw Massacre, The Ritual, Midsommar, The Descent, The Cabin in the Woods,* and others, namely:

- A group that will be slowly killed one by one
- The cabin in the woods
- The walking in circles and ending up where you started
- Ritual sacrifice with the removal of body parts
- Cult members with masks
- The Judas (remember the early mention)
- The Final Girl
- The twists in the tale

Still, it did not feel like a classic horror story to me, particularly the reveal that this was an amateur film to be sold on alternative streaming platforms, a rather modern invention. Perhaps the director meant it to subvert the viewer's expectations, but the combination of all the elements did not work for me as a whole.

Now, many parts worked for me.

- I really liked Elisa and cheered for her all the way. Her final scene was fantastic, but for the illogical part of her recording herself committing murder.
- The movie fleshed out the characters well, so much so that their terrible deaths hurt, except justifiably, Fabrizio and Chiara's.
- The twist that Chiara was in on it, and the further reveal of the extent, was a surprise.
- I wanted to know who Mom was. Was it the woman in red or a yet unseen character?
- I loved the foreshadowing, which was very well done. I enjoyed my second viewing much more because I picked up on the clever details that were included.

But for this jaded horror fan, I wish there were more than what felt like a collage of scenes I'd already seen in too many other movies. Still, I am glad our Final Girl Elisa got away. Regretfully, though, the Bloodflix enterprise continues, ripe for a sequel. With Elisa returning, of course.

WELHAMIN: THOMAS HA'S SHORT STORY "GROTMATTA": UNDERCURRENTS OF THE COLONIAL PLIGHT OF THE PHILIPPINES

KYLE TAM

"Ne, Grottmata."

There is a shared history of colonialism that exists the world over. Networks and spider webs that crisscross the globe, binding together countries across oceans, seas, and continents. A bridge forged in blood, such as it were. It's something that we as Filipinos are taught about in our schools, its impact felt as we approach life and the world. I remember finding myself in conversation with a Spanish man and a Portuguese man, as they realized that I was from a country their own had worked together to conquer. They laughed at this delightful realization, forging a strange pact of friendship. I did not.

The short story Grottmata by Thomas Ha (*Nightmare Magazine*, July 2024) is, by the author's own admission, a short story about imperialism and colonialism that does not specifically draw from any one former colony. He himself is a third culture child—of Korean and Irish descent, raised in the USA, product of both the colonizers and the colonized. And in Grottmata, he speaks on the universal truths and horrors inflicted by the conqueror and the hauntings of the conquered. And yet there are still echoes of specificity in the reading of his work. An echo with the Philippine colonial experience, among others, but specifically in its strange symbiosis and shared plight with other colonies under the Spanish reign.

The story of Grottmata begins with the death of soldiers guarding a factory and the interrogation of those who work within it by representatives of their colonial overlords. We are introduced to Gemma, one of the factory girls, and to the nameless inspector who accompanies the military forces. The inspector is not just interested in the soldiers, but in the people under their thumb, more so as the bodies begin to pile up. Gemma and the people of her planet are connected to the Grottmata—one part infectious and deadly spore, one part hive mind between inhabitants, one part goddess of a damned land. It is the Grottmata who is infecting soldiers and representatives of the colonialists, turning them against themselves as retaliation for the indignities and death suffered by the factory workers at their hands. And when the inspector himself is infected, after confessing his own past as a child almost killed in an accident at another worksite, another colony, Gemma takes part of his consciousness into herself.

It was my sister who first told me that a number of the Spaniards who had come to the Philippines during the height of our colonial period, a span of time exceeding four hundred years, had originated from Mexico. They, too, had been oppressed—but here, they were not at the bottom of the order. More Spanish than we were Spanish. More trusted than we were trusted. They sailed the galleons, they taught the *indios*, they reported to Mother Spain. Apparently, over a third of the Philippines can trace their ancestry back to Latin America, blood intermingling with sisters and brothers from a country most Filipinos will never have the time, inclination, or opportunity to see. Even so, they still weren't trusted /enough/. The Spaniards still needed to send "pure" Spaniards because they feared what would happen if we savage lesser beings conspired amongst ourselves. If we realized that we were not so different, that they could not cage or kill us fast enough. Eventually, there was a revolution. Eventually. But it is impossible not to wonder what could have happened if they had united sooner.

But let's go back even further. Once upon a time, the islands that would come to be known as the Philippines were wealthy in physical goods, in resources, in culture and faith. We had gold, you see. Gold traded for silk, crops aplenty. And we had spirits, too. Our ancestors, our world, the natural and the divine. The gods of the sky and the earth and the rain. They stood by us, they protected us, and so we venerated and celebrated them. Until the Spaniards came.

The Spaniards wanted what they believed to be the spoils of India, which is why we were labeled *indios*—the label assigned to those they assumed to be from India, the indigenous people of Austronesia and Oceania, which they knew as the West Indies, and the native people of the Americas. All of them lumped under one assumed India, one assumed indigenous population not worth learning the terms and culture of. In doing so, they tried to take our body and soul from us. Oh, they tried. Named this disparate group of islands after their king and conspired with turncoats and snakes to take the land over. Stripped and sanitized those sons and daughters until they were spouting prayers and teachings in Latin, their brains metaphorically rewritten as the inspector's brain quite literally is. The better to be tools of their rulers. Or else the colonizers beat and broke and shot the ones that were too clever to be tricked, too angry to be fooled. But the old spirits and their worship are still intermingled in the tangled, bastardized Roman Catholicism now practiced on these shores. We venerate saints as if they were spirits and old gods, sleeping gods, speak to them as Gemma speaks to the Grottmata in Ha's story. Hearing their calling in our blood.

The Spanish occupation was not the last of the atrocities visited upon us. Possibly not even the worst. Everyone knows someone who lived through World War 2. Most as babes or small children. I remember being told the story of someone's old, old father who hid beneath a bed while his family was slaughtered. He survived because they did not stab deep enough. Because they couldn't be bothered to check for his body. Mother, father, sisters, and brothers, and he was the only one to live.

Perhaps the well, the boat, the chemically burnt skin, the brain transplants of "Grottmata" are not real. But this is real. Those deaths were real. The scars across this archipelago are real. Wounds that refuse to clot properly and close crooked because it was not so long ago that death swept across the Philippines like a tidal wave.

There is the language, as well. Old languages, dying languages, mother tongues that are already fading from the public consciousness. Even the words I speak now are a pidgin stew derived from every country that has touched my own. Friends and slavers alike. And I have so very few of these because it is almost shameful in this civilized, modern world to be fully fluent in Tagalog. Tagalog becomes Taglish becomes English, a loss that you see in "Grottmata", in the cutaways between Gemma in conversation with the Grottmata itself and the conqueror's tongue she and the other workers are forced to predominantly speak.

As I read Mr. Ha's work, I could not help but see the Filipina in Gemma, and the Mexican overseers and travelers in the character of the inspector. In the same way that factory workers and former victims of the colonial powers in "Grottmata" were thrown down wells, subjected to dehumanizing experiments, or killed without mercy, occupants of the islands that came to be known as the Philippines were burned and bled and changed by Spanish occupation. Tools but still with tongues to speak and ears to hear, to understand that they are not alone. That their spirits are bound by that chain which is called oppression. And the Grotmatta, too, is one of ours. A spirit of the wounded earth, of a chained, oppressed people. She belongs to the islands of yesteryear, back when the datu of Mactan stood atop the sandy beaches and killed the first wave of those who would return to conquer the land. She is the curse intoned by the dying, the dead. The ones slain upon the sandy shores. The ones starved of their own culture. The ones who walked to Bataan to their uncertain demise.

That is not to say that it is a work that doesn't stand on its own merits. "Grottmatta" is beautiful, painful, haunting. But it means something because colonialism is a shared story, and its aftereffects echo from centuries ago up until today. It is a horror story because it speaks to a true horror that once existed and still exists today. Palestine, Haiti, Sudan, the Congo, Ukraine, to name the obvious ones on every lip, but every former colony must still contend with the shadow of its conqueror. This is at once a work of fiction and a short story that is painfully true, but I cannot help but wish that it were truly only a fiction.

TRIZOMBIE: DOWN SYNDROME IN THE APOCALYPSE: BELGIAN FILM SHOWS PEOPLE WITH DOWN SYNDROME CAN SURVIVE

HOLLY LYN WALRATH

Director Bob Colaers has created a conversation piece in the new Belgian film *Trizombie* (2024), premiering at Fantastic Fest this week in Austin, Texas. The film follows a group of people with Down Syndrome as they survive a zombie apocalypse where only people with trisomy 21, an extra twenty-first chromosome, are immune to the virus.

The film was originally a TV miniseries and has been cut together into a film with surprising success: It never feels as if you are watching a shortened version of a TV show. The story follows Luka (Jelle Palmaerts), Kelly (Gitte Wens), and George, aka The Slasher (Jason Van Laere), as they battle zombies to save Robin (Tineke Van Haute), who has recently left the care center to live in assisted living (essentially, independent living).

Robin is a huge fan of invented-for-the-film popstar Will Murray, who sings catchy pop Oktoberfest rhymes in the genre of "Schlager" songs. (The soundtrack is available on Spotify.) After saving Robin, the crew decides to head out to the singer's theme park as a safe haven.

With excellent humor and a hilarious soundtrack, Trizombie hits all of the expected zombie tropes. I was struck by how the film pairs these obstacles as a metaphor for the obstacles people with Down Syndrome face when learning to live on their own. For example, the characters have to learn to get out of the care center safely by bypassing the security gate. They learn to drive a car, figure out that one should probably lock the front door, and seek out shelter and food. These are all things that can be tricky for people with mental disabilities, let alone in a disaster where survival is key.

Survival is not a given for people with Down Syndrome. In Belgium, where the film was made, 94% of doctors support after-birth abortion for children with disabilities. The rate of pregnancies terminated for Down Syndrome is around 90% there. Down Syndrome babies often have other health conditions, including congenital heart disease, conditions of the eye like cataracts, hearing loss, and hypothyroidism, to name a few (NIH).

Despite these facts, the film doesn't sugar-coat the experiences of its characters, nor does it expect them to be perfect. It allows the characters to fail, to make mistakes, to curse, and to be flippant. Zombie films are not cutesy, and this film, while being heart-warming, is no different. Diehard zombie film fans will find a lot to enjoy here.

The performances in *Trizombie* are a lot of fun to watch. I particularly enjoyed Jason Van Laere, who plays the tropey, macho-machismo sledgehammer-wielding Slasher, who reminds me of a mix between *Shaun of the Dead* and *Rambo*. The cast is part of the Turnhout-based Theater Stap, a theatre company that serves the disabled community and that does not shy away from putting its actors in sometimes controversial productions. According to its website, the goal is "putting first the actors' authenticity, increasing the visibility of disabled people and livening up broad discussions about theatre."

All these positives aside, I wonder about the film's premise. Does it fall into the "mystical disability" trope, where characters with disabilities are often magical plot devices? The characters here are "safe" because of their disability, inherently making them special. The film would, in my opinion, be just as successful without this status. Audiences would still be interested in seeing how people with a disability survive a zombie apocalypse. Does it diminish the stakes of the film if we know the characters can't be killed? I, for one, think it would be cool to see zombies with disabilities—but perhaps the filmmakers thought it would be a step too far.

Nevertheless, Trizombie brings disability representation to a wider, zombie-loving audience, and that makes it worth a watch and worth talking about.

MAYBE THE REAL MONSTER WAS THE INCOMPETENCE ALONG THE WAY: REVIEW OF MONARCH: LEGACY OF MONSTERS ON APPLE TV+

R. THURSDAY

John Goodman dodges between the segmented legs of a spider and crab of giant proportions, a classic, almost Harryhausen-esque scene beautifully translated with modern effects, and I think: "Strong opening."

Monarch: Legacy of Monsters follows the web of lives impacted by the rise of giant, city-walloping monsters. It jumps around in time from just after World War 2, to Goodman's Skull Island 70s, to 'G Day' in 2014, to the present (2015). The story pivots around Cate and Kentaro Randa, half siblings that just found out the other exists. Monarch is *their* legacy: their grandparents started it in the 40s, their dad disappeared while working for it, and now they are searching for him despite it. Joining them is Kentaro's . . . kind of girlfriend(?), May, who (as a Washingtonian) has one of my favorite backstory lines: "I'm from Tacoma. Tacoma sucks. I moved to Japan." Finally, there is Colonel Shaw, portrayed in flashbacks by Wyatt Russel, and in the present by Kurt, bringing a pretty trademark 'unhinged dad' energy (see: Stuntman Mike, Ego, The Commander) despite being, as everyone points out, at least 90 years old.

There's a lot to like about AppleTV's new kaiju—sorry, *Titan*—show. I wasn't sure what to expect since AppleTV is a bit off the beaten streamer path; this was my first experience with their catalog since I'm not a subscriber, and I was ready to be converted. Every time Godzilla (the only recognizable Titan from Legendary's canon) shows up, it's colossal, impactful, and even frightening.

The other Titans on display in the first five episodes are new—the show taking place before the events of *King of Monsters*. Still, the fresh (and fleshy) faces are visually interesting, the special effects are polished, and the characters' reactions to their destructive immensity make them even more effective.

The contrast in how America (specifically San Francisco) and Japan (Tokyo) rebuild and adapt to living in a monster-attacked world is an intriguing background consideration, which felt organic and meaningful. It was genuinely fascinating to see how these spectacular cinematic events affect the street-level lives of regular people over time.

The handling of trauma is often (though not always) nuanced and complicated, the dialogue is frequently funny, tragic, and realistic (often at the same time), and there are many characters you genuinely cheer for (the moms) or at least find compelling.

I love Godzilla movies (someone pay me to write an essay on how *Godzilla: Final Wars* was the singularity, and we all got dumped in the bad timeline after it), but I'm aware that they carry an inherent dissonance. The kaiju are forces of destruction; they cause the death and suffering of hundreds to thousands of people, and they are intended to be terrifying. But they are also . . . the main characters, the protagonists, amoral if not the loosest interpretation of 'chaotic good.' On the other hand, we have Monarch-as-stand-in-for-authority, another concept people are frequently divided about. We want *someone* to know what they are doing, but we are also wary of overreach. In the original *Gojira* movies, the government was usually made up of bumbling bureaucrats whom the intrepid heroes had to maneuver around. This attitude reflected a not-uncommon one in post-WWII Japan, and I'm sure there are essays on how reinforcing the idea of weak collectivist rule contributed to the rise of Strong Men(TM) leaders in more recent times, and if not, someone should pay me to write that, too. I was truly hoping that *Legacy of Monsters* was going to explore or even deconstruct that dissonance. Instead, it paid homage to that history by seeming to have two minds about every aspect of the story it was telling. Monarch, the organization is both manipulative and yet clearly doing more than any government. The characters are earnest and likable except when they're betraying each other. The scientists are headstrong and confident but also have no idea how to interface with the forces (human or otherwise) that they are dependent on.

Most of all, everyone, from the protagonists to the government to the shadowy not-quite-government monster trackers, *everyone*, is inconsistently but often wildly and inexplicably *incompetent*. The scientists make foolish and dangerous decisions and then are shocked at the consequences. The main team just barely sneaks away from soldiers and then *breaks into commercial jingle singing* while creeping to their destination. The eggheads at Monarch do enough research to find a single person on the street in *Tokyo* , but not enough to know she has intense PTSD and will respond violently to having a bag put over her head after they don't restrain her in any way. Colonel Shaw has terrible trigger discipline and no discernable plan. In the old films, this could be fun in a campy way, but with the much more serious tone the show works hard to develop, I found many of the script choices baffling. There were so many great moments: May talking Cate through a panic attack was one of the best representations of trauma-informed care I've seen on screen; both Cate and Kentaro's respective moms are MVPs of Women-Having-Complicated-Feelings-But-Doing-Their-Best and I genuinely cheered for both of them; the flashback sort-of flirting between May and Kentaro didn't make me want to die, and on and on. Unfortunately, this only served to make the weaker/more opaque directions more frustrating.

I kept hoping that many of these issues and other mysteries (why hasn't Shaw aged as expected? Why is May doing *that*? What happened to the girlfriend Cate clearly didn't deserve?) would be resolved in later episodes—and while some were, I can't say the payoff was worth the wait for all of them. Like *Monarch*'s writers, I find myself also of two minds: there are interesting and valuable bits . . . but I don't know if paying for AppleTV is worth it.

WHEN THE ORDINARY IS EXTRAORDINARY: A REVIEW OF UNDER THE MOON, A SHORT STORY COLLECTION BY E.M. FAULDS

TAYLOR JONES

E. M. Faulds' debut short-story collection *Under the Moon* explicitly features female or female-coded protagonists from many walks of life, in many and varied situations. Some stories ("Women of Sparta," "Goewin & Hydwn," "Wight-Song") draw heavily on mythology, putting new spins on old tales. Some explore situations likely familiar to many readers: working in a clinic for drug overdose patients; trying to prop up a failing restaurant; having to carry on with your daily business while facing the imminent annihilation of your planet. Others feature situations that are more fantastical: tricking demons, time-traveling, or being called by a ghost to solve a murder (you know, #just-girlythings).

The author notes in the afterword that she didn't have a particularly feminist agenda for writing about women. "To be honest," she says, "I just wanted to see women centre stage because I am one." As a female reader, I loved seeing the ordinary, multi-faceted, and complex humanity of women—so often erased when we are objectified, pilloried, worshiped, or exploited—showcased and celebrated as Faulds gives us windows into the lives of diverse female characters.

I particularly enjoyed "The Amelioration of Existence in Spite of Truth and Reconciliation," an affecting story that turns the trope of the logical—and therefore uncaring—AI on its head. Here, logic doesn't lead to heartlessness. The main character, a warship AI, is demoted to running an isolated desert convenience store when it refuses to carry out its planet-annihilation duties. It decided to stand down because it concluded that "[t]here is no tactical advantage to killing. You cannot renegotiate with the dead. You cannot find growth or mutual benefit. Only endings." Its new convenience-store life is monotonous but in line with its values. And it may find a new kind of meaning in the relationship it starts to build with a regular customer.

I was also blown away by "Contemplation," a brutal gem of a story. The main characters—two courtesans who have been forced to lie all their lives to please the people who use them as playthings—turn their powers of deception into a desperate, suicidal plan to topple a corrupt empire. It left me shaken long after I finished it. Indeed, many of the stories in this collection are difficult to read, dealing as they do with themes of violence against women and femmes. I appreciated that each one was prefaced with a brief content warning to prepare the reader for what was ahead. The collection ends with the thought-provoking "The First Ever Tapestry on Station 17," in which the tapestry artist poses the question, "What is art if it cannot inspire you to save the world?"

E. M. Faulds inspires by reminding us that even when a bad situation seems impossible to change, seemingly ordinary people and seemingly small acts can have world-saving impacts.

About the Author

E.M. Faulds is a science fiction and fantasy author who lives in Scotland. She knew she was a writer for as long as she could write and, early on, decided speculative fiction would be her weapon of choice. Her first novel, Ada King, came out in 2016, and since then she has had short stories published in various SFF magazines, including Shoreline of Infinity and Strange Horizons. She loves how speculative fiction can be a mirror for our own lives or an escape from them. They can show us the best and worst of ourselves, or help us to exceed the boundaries of our own experiences. At their heart, the best speculative fiction stories are about people, the choices they make, and how they live with them.

AN INCLUSIVE FUTURE FOR SPACE OPERA: REVIEW OF SEASON ONE: IRIS AND THE CREW TEAR THROUGH SPACE BY CAIT GORDON

LISA TIMPF

In the book *Season One: Iris and the Crew Tear Through Space*, Cait Gordon offers an intriguing view of an inclusive future. With chapters positioned as "episodes," reading *Iris and the Crew Tear Through Space* reminded me of watching a TV series. Gordon's book combines the camaraderie of *Star Trek: The Original Series* and the offbeat humor of *The Orville*.

In some episodes, the crew of the *Science Ship SpoonZ* tackles typical space opera threats, such as enemy agents trying to infiltrate the vessel or a pack of nasty space pirates — in this case, the Piranha Brigade. But it's not always phasers and blasting the heck out of things that win the day. Often, the crew's ability to work together and leverage their combined capabilities is just as important as more traditional weaponry.

Iris and the Crew Tear Through Space is inclusive on a number of levels. Many of the crew members operate using assist devices. Chief of Security Leanna Lartha has high-tech, sentient prosthetic legs that can double as props during musical performances. A tech named Fran utilizes a "candy-pink rollator-wheelchair" to get around. Iris, the communications officer, employs assistive tech to enhance her vision, but when it's not working or being uploaded, she can call upon a retractable cane or her guide-bot Clarence. Lieutenant Commander Horatio Herbert, the head of Engineering, resolves his anxiety in social situations by retreating into a privacy box that "calms him so he can focus while in a larger group." On the bridge, crew members use ISGL, or

Intragalactic Sign Language, with information also transmitted to their heads-up displays.

Crew members can access accessible technology at Assistive-Tech Stripes. By asking a series of questions, the AI can determine the user's need and then provide the tech, whether it be a hover chair, transport chair, or other device.

Even in the world of *Iris and the Crew Tear Through Space,* there are people who don't get it. Nobody said the future was perfect. But Gordon deals with this as well. Security officer Lieutenant Junior Grade "Beachfront" Bronwryck, whose privileged upbringing didn't include much exposure to empathy training, needs to learn respect, and that's dealt with in one of the episodes.

Gordon's novel depicts a relationship between two men and portrays an accepting future society when it comes to sexual preference.

All in all, there is an air of optimism to *Iris and the Crew Tear Through Space.* In one episode, the crew of the *S.S. SpoonZ* encounters a new species whose prime motivators are "empathizing with those we share the universe with and offering compassion." In one of my favorite episodes, a lively shoreleave ends with some of the crew members performing onstage. Another episode told from the viewpoint of Iris's guide-bot Clarence, who finds the therapist's power chair more helpful in addressing his needs than the human therapist, was also entertaining.

Gordon writes from a position of authenticity when it comes to depicting characters with disabilities. The book's "About the Author" section notes that Gordon is an "autistic, disabled, and queer Canadian writer of speculative fiction that celebrates diversity." Gordon, along with Talia C. Johnson, co-edited *Nothing Without Us* and *Nothing Without Us Too.* These anthologies feature authors and protagonists who are disabled, Deaf, neurodiverse, Spoonie, and/or manage mental illness.

In the acknowledgments for *Iris and the Crew Tear Through Space,* Gordon notes that the Pandemic was a difficult time for her and states that she "plunged into Iris's galaxy because I needed to exist in a space where Universal Design and the Social Model of Disability had gone next level."

As a fan of *Star Trek: The Original Series,* I have often marveled at the fact that devices that may have seemed far-fetched at the time they were introduced on the show have, in many cases, become reality. The ability to make video calls is now commonplace with apps like *Zoom* and *FaceTime.* I even had a flip phone once that bore a resemblance to the *Star Trek* communicators. And, as I learned while reading *Dinner on Mars,* the capability for making synthetic food is continually expanding. In other words, imagine it, and there's a good chance that it will be developed (although we don't have the transporter . . . yet . . .)

Perhaps books like *Iris and the Crew Tear Through Space* will set the foundation for broader thinking about assistive technology — or better still, help us get to the point where, as is the case with the crew of the *S.S. SpoonZ*, the word "disability" will have no relevance.

At the end of *Iris and the Crew Tear Through Space,* Gordon suggests that there may be more in store for Iris and her companions. We can only hope that's true. Gordon's view of the future is something we could use more of.

About the Author

Cait Gordon is an autistic, disabled, and queer Canadian writer of speculative fiction that celebrates diversity. She is the author of *Life in the 'Cosm* and its prequel, *The Stealth Lovers*. Her latest novel (available September 2023) is the first in her new disability hopepunk space opera series—*Season One: Iris and the Crew Tear Through Space!*

Cait's short fiction appears in *Alice Unbound: Beyond Wonderland, We Shall Be Monsters, Mighty: An Anthology of Disabled Superheroes,* and *There's No Place*. She also founded the Spoonie Authors Network and joined Talia C. Johnson to co-edit the multi-genre disability fiction anthologies, *Nothing Without Us* (a 2020 Prix Aurora Award finalist) and *Nothing Without Us Too* (a 2023 Prix Aurora Award winner for Best Related Work).

QUEER HORROR AND THE POWER OF FEELING SEEN: FEAR STREET, I SAW THE TV GLOW, AND FROM

CHLOE SMITH

When you watch a horror film or TV series, the last thing you might expect to feel during the film and when the credits roll is hopeful—or even seen. But given recent horror films and shows, members of the queer community might just feel all that and more.

Of course, there are several common tropes within the horror genre that are damaging to the queer community as a whole—such as the "bury your gay" trope, where queer characters in a horror film are murdered with no real rhyme or reason, sometimes even just for the shock value. Queer characters are likely not only to be more at risk of being murdered due to this trope, but they are likely to face more toil and terrors simply for being queer—traumas like homophobia, bullying, and discrimination for who they are.

Fear Street (2021)

Deena, Sam, and Sarah are examples of this in Netflix's *Fear Street* (2021) trilogy of films. The difference is that the Fear Street trilogy is still an affirming series that allows the queer community to be seen while still being in horror films. While the lesbian protagonists—Deena, Sam, and Sarah—do face homophobia, and in Sarah's case, persecution for being queer, ultimately, the film sends a positive message to its queer audience.

Fear Street utilizes the homophobia that the characters face within the films by not just making it a part of the film but by making it the horror and evil that the queer characters in the films face. An example of this is how Sarah, as a character, is remembered as a horror villain—an idea that is reinforced when characters feel as if Sarah and her "curse" are haunting and killing others.

However, if you watch the entire trilogy, particularly *Fear Street 1666*, you will find that instead of facing a vengeful monster, both in the sense that Sarah never really was the vengeful controller of the past killers that she was made out to be and that the real controller of them was the furthest thing from a lesbian—a straight white man—the true horror that our protagonists are trying to survive is homophobia.

Sarah is presented as the big bad villain when she was simply painted as such due to homophobia and a fear of queerness—the very thing that got her killed in the first place after her kissing another woman led to her being accused of witchcraft and hanged. While this is a sad fate for the character, the fact that she ultimately gets her truth revealed, and justice done by a lesbian in the future is not only cathartic for her, but also to the film's queer audience as they are able to see both Deena and Sam live and overcome homophobia. Sam embraces her relationship with her girlfriend, and Sarah finally gets the peace and justice she deserves, even though she couldn't overcome the homophobia of the past.

I Saw the TV Glow (2024)

Likewise, in *I Saw the TV Glow (A24,* 2024), the film allows a queer audience—particularly a transgender audience—to be seen as Owen battles the horror not of external homophobia or transphobia (unless you count his father pulling him out and away from the TV an example of him being faced with homophobia and transphobia from others) but internalized transphobia. The film showcases the horror of denying who you really are and what it can do to you—all you have to do is watch as Owen looks considerably sicker and sicker throughout the film as his internalised transphobia is literally killing him; you can even hear it as his asthma worsens, his breathing becoming more labored and shallow.

Owen may not be running from a masked murderer in *I Saw The TV Glow,* but the horror of rejecting his true identity is very much out to get him throughout the film and almost succeeds in killing him. This allows for a moment of catharsis and a feeling of being seen by members of the audience who are struggling with their own identity—particularly those like Owen, who are struggling with their gender identity.

However, the film also allows its transgender audience—and its queer audience at large—something else beyond this incredible power of feeling seen and heard. Feeling their feelings, no matter how terrifying, validates that terror—allowing for hope.

While the ending of *I Saw The TV Glow* as ambiguous, it can be argued that Owen is walking out of the arcade away from his old life, away from his old self, and towards his true self, of Isabel. With this ending in mind, the film is telling its audience—particularly its members who are transgender—that it is never too late. As one scene of the film illustrates in pink chalk, "there is still time," both for Owen and for viewers. No matter what, even if, like Owen, the horror nearly catches up to you, you can still outlive it. You can become who you really are and, in Owen's case, literally become a final girl.

There is also power in queerness continuing to exist despite horror characters end up facing. While love triumphing over evil is powerful no matter what, being able to see queer love conquering various terrors in horror as a genre is particularly powerful.

From (2022)

The horror/drama TV series *From* (2022) has people randomly transported to "Township"—a town that traps anyone that enters it—only for them to try and survive the nights there without being murdered by the ghostly human-like monsters that appear, without any ability to return home. One of the pivotal characters both in Township and the show is Kristi, a third-year medical student who cares for the inhabitants of the town and is engaged to someone back home. While she does care deeply for Kenny, the Sheriff's deputy, she remains loyal to Marielle, who we learn in Season Two is her fiancée. Despite the terrors that they face, Marielle believes Kristi has abandoned her, and Marielle's addiction puts a strain on the couple. At the end of the third season, both Kristi and Marielle are devoted to each other. The ability to see their queer love existing and conquering everything thrown at them in the series is incredibly powerful, and a joy to see amidst the horrors of the show.

These films represent a new frontier for queer horror cinema that focuses on hope. For a queer audience, in queer films and TV like the *Fear Street* trilogy, *I Saw The TV Glow*, and *From*, the horrors presented are very familiar, even if they are presented in a unique way. From homophobia to death, these shows allow the queer audience to process fear alongside the queer characters as they fight to survive, to love openly, and to be themselves openly, just as the queer audiences have done and still do.

Survival takes on new meaning in this context. As the queer audience cheers along for the protagonist to defeat this homophobia or continue to survive and love proudly in the process, they strengthen their own ability to fight, too. After all, if a character like them can outlive and defeat evil, or even continue to try and live and love despite everything—why can't they? And there's nothing more hopeful than that.

WHAT WE TALK ABOUT WHEN WE TALK ABOUT WITCHES: A REVIEW OF "THE SHADOW CABINET" BY JUNO DAWSON

TAYLOR JONES

The Shadow Cabinet, the second installment in the *Her Majesty's Royal Coven* (HMRC) Trilogy, delivers on what the first book promises. Author Juno Dawson brings twists, turns, and fresh ideas into the narrative, keeping it rocketing forward.

To set the scene: four friends—fiery Leonie, timid Elle, kind-hearted Niamh, and stubborn Helena—fought in and lived through this universe's version of a "wizarding war," during which the opposition was led by disgruntled warlock Dabney Hale. The four friends' vastly different ways of recovering from the trauma of the war don't break the bonds between them in the years following. But in the first book, conflict over Theo, a young trans witch, tears them apart catastrophically. The institution at the heart of the book, Her Majesty's Royal Coven, must grapple with the consequences of its staid and traditional approach to witchhood.

When the second book opens, HMRC High Priestess Helena has been executed for the unforgivable crime of consorting with demons as part of her reckless plan to kill Theo, whom she was convinced was the prophesied "Sullied Child" primed to usher in the apocalypse. Theo's gender, the crux of most of the conflict in the first book, is less of an issue in the second as HMRC seeks to put the scandal behind them and install Niamh as the new High Priestess in order to usher in what most witches hope will be a more progressive era.

There's only one problem: Niamh is dead.

The shocking cliffhanger that ended the first book pays huge dividends in the second. Ciara, Niamh's damaged and self-absorbed twin sister, takes over from Niamh as narrator after springing back to life from a years-long coma, stealing her sister's body with the help of demon magic gifted to her by Helena, and then dispatching Niamh, now trapped in Ciara's comatose body. Ciara is a well-written unreliable narrator, seeking to piece together lost memories of what she did during the war and why Dabney Hale (still alive and on the lam after escaping prison with Helena's help) and a multitude of demons have taken a close personal interest in her.

And, as she commits egregious acts along the way, she never lets the reader forget that it was perfect, kind-hearted Niamh who unraveled her memories and put her in that coma in the first place.

As Ciara uncovers more about her life before and during the war, though, she starts to realize that her excuses for her crimes might not hold as much water as she thought. Her returning memories are rarely pleasant and force her to confront truths about herself that she's not entirely comfortable with. The book opens with a prophecy; Ciara and Niamh's mother, Miranda, is given the unwelcome news that one of her expected twins "will be kind, generous and loving, [while] the other will consort with the devils." The prophecy becomes self-fulfilling as suspicion drives a wedge between Miranda and the still-innocent Ciara. Relentlessly compared unfavorably to her seemingly perfect sibling and blamed for everything wrong in the family unit, Ciara grows up understandably bitter. But rather than trying to overcome this admittedly painful upbringing, she uses her hurt and grief as excuses for bad decisions that cause further suffering and lets the long string of slights, grievances, and tragedies in her life lead her down a very dark path. Ciara's awakening to her own culpability is a painful and necessary exploration of what it means to realize you've caused harm and need to seek forgiveness, even if you may not find it.

There are a multitude of other plotlines—Elle's sudden realization of how shockingly powerful her own magic is after discovering her husband's affair; Leonie's search for her missing brother, who is himself searching for Dabney Hale, who in turn seeks a dangerous and powerful artifact so he can finish the war he started; Theo's uncertainty and confusion about the magical transformation of her body and where she stands with "Niamh," who she sees as the closest thing she has to family; the discovery of a utopian island of witches reminiscent of fantasies of Atlantis; tension between the mundane government's titular "Shadow Cabinet" and HRMC, which comes to a head with the help of a cartoonishly horrible secret society of misogynistic witch hunters—but Ciara steals the show, and is ultimately the lynchpin that ties all the subplots together in another shocking conclusion that leaves the reader hungry for more.

The end of "The Shadow Cabinet" promises further revelations about demons and their motivations; answers to lingering questions about the "Sullied Child" prophesy; and a potentially explosive confrontation between Ciara and the person she loves and hates most in the world. I can't wait to see what the third book delivers.

About the Author

Juno Dawson is a #1 Sunday Times best-selling novelist, screenwriter, journalist, and a columnist for Attitude Magazine. Juno's books include the global bestsellers, *This Book Is Gay* and *Clean*. She won the 2020 YA Book Prize for *Meat Market*. Her first adult fantasy trilogy, *Her Majesty's Royal Coven,* launched in 2022, becoming an instant best-seller.

She also writes for television and has multiple shows in development, both in the UK and US. Her debut short film was *The Birth of Venus* (*BBC* 2020), and she created the first official Doctor Who scripted podcast, Doctor Who: Redacted (*BBC Sounds* 2022). An occasional actress and model, Juno had a cameo in the BBC's *I May Destroy You* (2020), a recurring role in *Holby City* (BBC 2021), and was the face of Jecca Cosmetics Play Pots campaign.

Juno grew up in West Yorkshire, writing imaginary episodes of Doctor Who. She later turned her talent to journalism, interviewing luminaries such as Steps and Atomic Kitten, before writing a weekly serial in a Brighton newspaper. Her writing has appeared in *Glamour, The Pool, Dazed,* and the *Guardian*. She has appeared on Pointless Celebrities, BBC Women's Hour, Front Row, ITV News, Channel 5 News, This Morning, and Newsnight.

Juno lives in Brighton. She is a part of the queer cabaret collective known as Club Silencio. In 2014, Juno became a School Role Model for the charity Stonewall.

THE DOCTOR WHO SPECIALS ARE A WIN FOR DISABILITY REPRESENTATION: THE IMPORTANCE OF PROVIDING AN ACCESSIBLE ALTERNATIVE IN AN INACCESSIBLE WORLD

CHLOE SMITH

> "How can you help save the world if the protagonist's time machine shuts you out?"

"Welcome to the twenty-first century!" cries Shirley Bingham, a new character on *Doctor Who* who happens to be a wheelchair user, when the TARDIS is shown to have a ramp—and be wheelchair accessible—for the very first time in the show's sixty-year history in the episode "The Star Beast."

She sounds overjoyed, almost tearful—with the actress' own elation shared on her Instagram. As a disabled fan of *Doctor Who*, who is also a wheelchair user, I can relate to all of those emotions and more.

I started watching *Doctor Who* in 2005 when I was eight years old. The show quickly captured both my imagination and a steadfast place in my heart—as an undiagnosed autistic and physically disabled child, I often felt alien and alone, and right there on the screen was an alien who too felt the same loneliness, but still strived to seek out fun and whimsy, make connections, and create more hope and joy in the universe then there was before, all while saving it from various villains and foes.

How could I not love it? It has brought me a lot of joy and comfort over the years; I grew up with it, but in many ways, the show did not change with me. In an inaccessible world, *Doctor Who* never really offered an accessible alternative for its disabled fans. You might imagine yourself as a companion of the Doctor, like I did, but those fun daydreams quickly stopped for me as soon as I realized that I couldn't even get into the TARDIS in my wheelchair. **How can you help save the world if the protagonist's time machine shuts you out?**

Nevertheless, the TARDIS remained that way for decades, almost as if the idea of a companion or even a Doctor in the future who used a wheelchair was impossible or never even considered. While we don't yet have a disabled Doctor or companion per se, a series of *Doctor Who* specials aired in 2023 introduced the character of Shirley Bingham, played by Ruth Madeley—who uses a wheelchair herself—and who is also the Head Scientific Advisor for UNIT, making her a very powerful and important guest character within the universe of the show. She quickly establishes herself as a smart and larger-than-life character and helps assist The Doctor in many ways during the three specials she has appeared in so far. Not only that, but one of her appearances in the specials even allowed *Doctor Who* to touch on the ableism that the character, and many others like her, face.

In "The Giggle" the third of the show's recent sixtieth-anniversary specials, Shirley's boss, Kate, is affected by a negative energy spread across the world by the villain that makes everyone full of rage and anger, and when spewing hatred at everyone in the room, she looks at Shirley and claims that she can walk—that she's even seen her doing it—thereby implying that she doesn't need her wheelchair. You only need to see the hurt on Shirley's face to see the impact this has on her, and the pure sorrow and regret on Kate's face when she's cured of the rage when she apologies to Shirley to know how well, and realistically, that this was handled by the writers and actors. Honestly, I really appreciate this element of realism; that even in a show where the universe could end thanks to a trickster who loves to make toys and play games, an alien can avoid dying by regenerating a new body, and people can time travel —that ableism still exists.

Of course, it would be amazing if ableism didn't exist at all, but to move forward with that idea and not show ableism when there is a disabled character present wouldn't be authentic. It wouldn't allow disabled people and their experiences to feel seen, and even for those who aren't disabled to realize just the kind of vitriol we have to deal with. *Doctor Who* definitely dealt with it the right way—making it a small but impactful moment and nothing too drawn out or devastating, but just having that moment to show an element of a disabled person's experience.

Shirley, like the actress who plays her, is also an ambulant wheelchair user—something else that hardly ever gets represented in the media. As an ambulant wheelchair user myself, it was incredibly meaningful to see this represented, and it just shows how much Doctor Who is listening to either its actors, or writers, or even advisors—and I hope those behind the show know how impactful it all is, and continue disability representation like this throughout the future run of the show. I'm sure they will, if their casting of Rwandan-Scottish actor Ncuti Gatwa, who is also queer, to play the first black male Doctor Who in history, and their casting of Yasmin Finney as Rose Noble, the first openly transgender character in *Doctor Who* history, are anything to go by. Doctor Who is definitely making great strides in terms of representation simply by finally allowing so many audience members to be seen on the screen, and not just their disabled audience members.

However, in terms of their disabled representation—while Shirley is fantastic both as a character and for representation, she is only a guest character. Now that the TARDIS has a ramp to get inside and throughout, why can't she travel with The Doctor every so often? I'm so grateful that this positive step forward has been made within the show, but wouldn't it be great to have this representation in every episode?

I might never be a companion now, but since the TARDIS can finally let people like me in, it's time to see a wheelchair user like Shirley make good, regular use of that ramp in Doctor Who. And not just in daydreams.

THE GAY KISS MIGHT NOT HAVE BEEN DOCTOR WHO'S FIRST, BUT HERE'S WHY IT'S STILL IMPORTANT: THE POWER OF INTERSECTIONAL REPRESENTATION

CHLOE SMITH

Doctor Who, the infamous British sci-fi show, has been on air for over sixty years, so there's quite a bit that the show has covered or portrayed in that time. However, it certainly can be said that the show could be more diverse—given that Ncuti Gatwa, the fifteenth incarnation of the alien time-traveling Doctor, is only the second person of color to portray the main character of the show, beyond a brief appearance by actress Jo Martin as what appears to be a future incarnation of the character (which has yet to be confirmed within the canon of the show itself).

However, you can say that *Doctor Who* is trying to become more representative of the world around it in 2024, whether that's by finally having a black man play the protagonist beyond a few episodes, finally including disability representation beyond a single episode appearance, and also in terms of its LGBTQIA+ representation.

The show is currently in its fourteenth series of the modern run (or the first of its second modern run, but that depends on who you ask). In this most recent series, in episode six, titled "Rogue," the Doctor and his companion Ruby travel to what appears to be a grand ball, which is referred to multiple times in the Netflix show *Bridgerton*, to give you an idea of the flair. Amidst the dancing and drama, Ncuti's doctor meets the mysterious Rogue, who is brooding on a balcony and watching the dancing below. Played by Jonathan Groff, the elusive character soon reveals himself to be a bounty hunter, and he then tries to kill the Doctor when he believes he's the shape-shifting entity he'd been sent there to destroy.

After the Doctor is able to convince Rogue that he isn't the killer alien that he's looking for, the pair team up in an attempt to find them before they kill anyone else. In an effort to not spoil the entire episode, I'll just say that in their attempt to find and stop the shapeshifter, the pair bond over their mutual losses and grow closer due to their shared experiences—and some not-so-subtle flirting. They manage to trap the evil alien, but the Doctor is devastated at the prospect of losing his traveling companion, Ruby. At the same time, given that she gets caught in the immovable trap that is set to send the aliens—and unfortunately Ruby—to a barren parallel world. In order to help the Doctor and save Ruby, Rogue then takes Ruby's place in the trap and is sent to the alternate universe instead. But before he steps forward to take Ruby's place, Rogue kisses the Doctor and asks him to find him before he disappears alongside the aliens he was sent to hunt down.

While this kiss may seem like nothing out of the ordinary—thankfully—in 2024, it is a particularly pivotal moment when you consider the show's history.

It has been incorrectly reported as the show's first-ever gay kiss - there has been a number throughout the show, beginning with a kiss between the Doctor and Jack in "The Parting of the Ways" in 2005. However, this was more of a platonic kiss—but even so, there have been a number of romantic gay kisses in the show after this point, even if they were between companions and guest characters, and not The Doctor themselves kissing anyone, they still matter, and provide well-written romantic queer representation within the show (although personally I'll never forgive the show from killing the hilarious lesbian companion Bill, even if her spirit did live on forever in space alongside her girlfriend's spirit—but I digress).

Despite this queer representation, before this episode, The Doctor had yet to share a romantic kiss with someone of the same sex they presented as (the Eleventh Doctor's quick kiss with Rory doesn't count as it was both improvised and not intentional and also not romantic if anyone is wondering!) It was, in fact, the Fifteenth Doctor's kiss with Rogue in this episode that—finally—shows the Doctor kissing someone of the same sex they are presenting as—a man, in this case—in a romantic sense.

This is incredibly impactful within the history of the show, particularly for long-time queer fans and queer fans who have just started the show. To finally have the protagonist share a same-sex kiss allows the show to finally step into the modern world—and embrace queer representation fully.

While it isn't the show's first same-sex kiss in its sixty-year history, it is monumental in itself as the show—and the Doctor—finally embraces its queer identity fully by allowing its protagonist to share a same-sex kiss on screen. Sure, it may not seem impactful to some, but to others like me, it means an awful lot—

as a queer fan of the show since I was eight years old who has always admired and seen parts of themselves in the character, who has always gotten lost in their stories and dreamed of being part of them myself, to see that character share my identity, to feel even more seen in them, means the world. And, since it's Doctor Who... you could even say that it means the entire universe.

I can only hope that in a future series of the show, Rogue is able to return somehow, maybe even as a companion to the Doctor, and we can see more of their romance on-screen and allow the queer representation to flourish and develop further under the guidance of gay showrunner Russell T Davies.

But until then, there's always reruns of the episode itself, and the kiss, which is a reminder that Doctor Who is both for everyone and queer as hell—and that the show has a queer history beyond it, and hopefully an even queerer future ahead of it.

REALITY TV, GHOSTS, AND TEAMWORK: REVIEW OF HAUNT SWEET HOME BY SARAH PINSKER

WILLIAM SHAW

Sarah Pinsker, like many of us, is haunted. Several of her acclaimed novels and short stories feature ghosts, though the focus is usually less on the spirits themselves than on their medium. I don't use the term 'medium' here to mean a psychic, but rather as the singular form of *media*; Pinsker's ghosts arrive via old music recordings, obscure internet postings, or forgotten TV shows. In her short story, "Where Oaken Hearts Do Gather" (*Uncanny Magazine,* Issue 39, 2021), a series of forum posts gradually reveals a chilling, predatory secret. In "Two Truths and a Lie" (*Tor.com/Reactor,* 2020), an unreliable narrator is ensnared by a spectral children's show. And in her debut novel, *A Song for a New Day (Berkely,* 2019), the world is captivated by holographic recordings of musical performances, the ghosts in the machine repackaged and sold back to us as streaming entertainment.

Her latest novella, *Haunt Sweet Home (Macmillan,* 2024), is a straightforward continuation of these themes. It centers on the titular TV program, a combined home renovation and supernatural reality show, in an efficient combination of Pinsker's usual obsessions. The result is clever and charming, an amusing romp through the tropes of horror literature and the mundane work of television production. But the efficiency of its conceit betrays an overall neatness to the project; its very straightforwardness marks a comparative lack of depth versus Pinsker's previous portrayals of mediated hauntings.

Our protagonist, Mara, is a chronic underachiever. After several failed attempts at community college, she's drifting through her twenties with little sense of purpose, unable to assert herself within her large and raucous family. When her cousin, Jeremy, offers her a Production Assistant job on his "kitschy basic-cable show," *Haunt Sweet Home,* she abandons her educational plans once again and jumps into the world of reality TV production. As a lowly (and non-union) PA, her job is to help stage the show's elaborately faked hauntings, finding places to hide and set off fog machines or make household objects go bump in the night. But after she strikes up a friendship with production "floater" Jo, the hauntings start to become a bit too convincing, and Mara soon finds herself at the heart of some genuine paranormal activity.

Haunt Sweet Home has a lot of fun with the mechanics of reality TV. The main narrative is interleaved with transcripts of the TV show, and Pinsker does a good job capturing the genre's trashy appeal. Jeremy is a classic reality host, all superficial smarm and circuitous overstatement ("Wow. In all my time on this show, I have to say without a doubt that's the eeriest thing I've ever experienced"), and the featured fixer-uppers provide plenty of laughs, too. At one point, Mara helps fake a haunted pasture, and one of the homeowners laments: "We've been vegan for fourteen years. I don't wear leather. I don't deserve to be haunted by cows."

Pinsker is also savvy about the ways reality TV distorts events. After reading the transcripts of the broadcast episode, we get to see how the presenter and guests reacted in the moment. Jeremy's objection that he can't risk getting injured by a poltergeist because "My face is my money" unsurprisingly hits the cutting room floor, and his arguments with the production crew are a canny reminder of how little power the ostensible stars of such shows can have. The production crew's conversations about how to stage the show's hauntings are especially good value. Mara finds herself swept up, not just in practical matters of how to achieve in-camera effects, but in more philosophical discussions about what makes a good haunting:

> *"Maybe he was a hobo they'd taken in, and everyone liked him, and something tragic happened, like he was allergic to bee stings, and after he died they realized nobody even knew his last name. Or a traveling salesman? Those dudes in the house would relate."*
> *"Melancholy!" Felix was ecstatic. "Melancholy is so much more interesting than evil."*
> *"I like melancholy better too," said Andi. "They have to live in the house after we're done shooting, so I'd always rather leave them feeling sorry for their ghost than scared of it."*
> *"I'm okay with either and both, so long as it keeps people watching." Ms. Tran had the final word on the subject.*

This exchange is Pinsker at her best: witty, metafictional, but equally aware of the hard, pragmatic realities of the media she is commenting on.

Once an actual ghost shows up, however, things get a bit less exciting. While the description of Jo as "a floater" is cute, it's painfully obvious that she is the source of the supernatural goings-on, even before Mara starts declaring that "you're better at being me than I am." Jo is transparently here to facilitate Mara's character arc as she develops from a timid, awkward loner into a more self-actualized, mature character. The trouble is that this arc is communicated so bluntly that it's hard to get invested. When Mara declares in chapter one that her family "always seemed to fit together like a machine . . . I was just a spare part," it's moving. But by the third or fourth declaration of Mara's lonely outsider status, it starts to feel wearisome, and the unsubtle telegraphing of her eventual growth drains the story of any tension. The result is that the novella's turn into explicit supernatural territory is one of the least scary stretches of the book.

That said, the novella's ultimate resolution is delightful. Having learned of Jo's true nature in a compelling psychedelic sequence, Mara and the ghost decide to work together "with Jo as a not-so-silent partner" on further TV hauntings. It's a clever story beat, emphasizing the teamwork and social connectedness Mara has learned over the course of the book while still allowing her to retain her unique personality. This sweet and carefully nuanced end to Mara's journey helps make up for some of the awkwardness in getting there. *Haunt Sweet Home* feels like a minor work from Sarah Pinsker, which is to say it's still charming, fun, and thoughtfully assembled, but ironically, it's less likely to haunt you once you've turned the final page.

TAROT (2024): WITH FINAL DESTINATION AND SLASHER VIBES ABOUND, TAROT IS A TAUT WATCH IN A COMFORTINGLY FAMILIAR GENRE.

CHRISTINA SNG

We have all seen this movie before. In different skins, in different settings. Most stories in the world have been retold in multiple ways, so it's hard to find an original story anymore. But as similar as our life stories are, how we lived them and how these stories are told—the journey matters.

In *Tarot*, a group of friends find themselves in a similar situation to many similar teens in horror movies. What happens to them? How do they die? How do they live? What evils do they encounter? And what do they learn? Those are the questions that matter.

Join me as I walk this journey with a group of teenagers, innocently celebrating their friend's birthday, only to uncover a darkness they never asked for, as many of us do. This is their story.

It is Elise's (Larsen Thompson) birthday, and her friends have booked a house in the middle of nowhere to celebrate her special day with her.

While rummaging for beer in a clearly stated Private area of the house, they find a really creepy hand-painted tarot deck in a wooden box. The art features horrific characters with grotesquely enlarged teeth.

Their friend Haley (Harriet Slater) is a tarot card reader. She tells them it is bad luck to use someone else's cards, but they are all keen to get their fortunes read. Since it is Elise's birthday and Haley does not want to spoil her day, she relents and gives them all a reading.

The readings possess an ominous tinge of danger, almost like a foreshadowing of how each of them will die . . . which the movie considerately does play out with a flashback and a distorted voiceover of Haley's reading before each death.

I'd imagined most of the action would happen in the house, but the group leaves the next day without incident, in high spirits, in the sunlight, even listening to a murder podcast on the 4+ hours drive home.

The birthday girl, Elise, is dropped off at her dorm, alone for the night, and unwisely investigates a disturbance in the attic. Standing at the top of the attic ladder, she is shocked by a hideous creature and falls backward onto the ground, her phone flung far from her. Peering down at Elise, it repeatedly drops the ladder onto the girl's body, crushing her to death.

The group gathers at Haley and Paige's (Avantika Vandanapu) flat after hearing the news of Elise's death. Paige is asleep, inconsolable and guilt-ridden that she left Elise alone at the dorm. Unable to help, Lucas (Wolfgang Novogratz) walks Madeline (Humberly González) home. The pair embraces before he leaves.

After Paige wakes up from a nightmare, Haley tells her about her mother dying of cancer and, subsequently, how she embarked on her tarot journey and discovering that every reading told her her mother would die, and she did. She reminds Paige she can't change fate.

At the train station, Lucas encounters the same creature that killed Elise. It seems to be able to literally press the darkness onto him, like a wall. A terrified Lucas flees into a restricted area, a place where it seems old trains are retired.

Inexplicably, he calls out "Hello?" at a time when he should be hiding, and finds a newspaper on the ground with his face on it and a headline that says, "You Die Today".

Haley's distorted voiceover recites his reading again, and it is literal: "The Hermit's light could lead you down the wrong track". Lucas is abruptly shocked by the creature in a jump scare and runs into another train car to escape. The Hermit's light pushes him yet into another cabin, then suddenly out the door, where he is slammed by an oncoming train.

Daylight. The police interview the group. There are no insights, and they say there are no signs of foul play.

The group sits together and tries to figure things out.

Haley thinks it is fate, piecing together that her readings are coming true.

In a familiar turn (haunted friends look for experts to help them, as seen in

Phantoms, *Poltergeist*, and more), they find a diviner, Alma Astrom (Olwen Fouéré), online and take a road trip to ask her for help.

Alma recognizes the description of the tarot set Haley describes: cards in a wooden box with a zodiac wheel in front of it.

She tells them about a case in Mexico City back in 1951, where there were six mysterious deaths in under 48 hours. The victims all had their horoscopes read by the same tarot set at a wedding.

A similar incident happened in Woodstock in 1969, all in freak accidents, as it did in London in 1988, where only one walked away alive: Alma. She did everyone's reading but her own. Alma has been searching for the tarot set since.

She says divination has been around for thousands of years and, for the longest time, the only way to predict a dark and unpredictable world. Combining horoscopes and tarot was one of the most powerful forms of divination known to man.

Now, she tells them the origin story of the tarot box.

In Hungary in 1798, there was a powerful diviner known as The Astrologer. She worked for a Count. One day, she foretold that the Count's wife and their infant son would die in childbirth. Enraged, he demanded she change their fates. She tried, but each time, the cards gave the same result. And in the end, they died.

The Astrologer fled with her daughter, but the Count hunted them down and killed her daughter.

Her grief led her to create a death curse through a dark ritual. She read the fortunes of the Count and those closest to him, then killed herself and bound her soul to the tarot cards. Soon after, the Count and his closest kin died horrible deaths.

Alma warns that anyone who uses the cards will face the dark side of fate, and the only way to change their fates is to destroy the deck.

The group drives off, skeptical but scared.

Their car stalls in the middle of a bridge while they are replaying Haley's reading on Elise's phone. Panicked, Madeline runs off as Haley saw in her reading. Haley chases after her.

The creature returns, terrorizing the others in the locked car. Unable to get in, it goes after Madeline and Haley. Out of nowhere, Madeline finds a rope around her neck. Haley watches her being yanked up by the creature before being dropped. To her horror, Madeline becomes The Hanged Man, as she predicted.

The rest run for their lives and decide to return to the house to destroy the deck. But Paxton (Jacob Batalon) leaves, deciding his dorm is safer.

Paige books the house online, and she, Haley, and Grant (Adain Bradley) head there.

Back at the dorm, Paxton finds himself followed by a laughing creature in a costume resembling The Fool. He realizes he is "boxed in" an elevator as predicted. The Fool taunts him outside the lift. Paxton does not dare leave it, but it finds its way inside.

The other three reach the house. Paige says they need blessed objects and holy objects to do the ritual, or else they can store the tarot set in a cursed box. But they have neither. The third option is incineration, the best way to destroy a cursed object. They throw the cards into the fireplace, but the cards do not burn.

Alma arrives to help. She tells them The Astrologer embodies the cards, which means The Magician, The Devil, and Death will be coming for them.

Alma attempts a ritual to speak to The Astrologer. And she appears.

The Astrologer does a reading for Alma—the six of swords—and she seizes her, flinging Alma back at the trio with six swords in her.

The three run.

Paige, separated from the other two, becomes locked in the basement, lured by Haley's voice asking for help. She wanders onto a stage where The Magician awaits. Running from him, she climbs into a trunk to hide. The trunk is wheeled out onto the stage, and a terrified, weeping Paige is painfully sawed in half.

As Haley and Grant talk, Haley realizes that if she reads The Astrologer's cards, perhaps she can change their fate. She remembers her mother's fight right to the end and resolves to do the same.

The Astrologer snatches Grant out the window, while as Death, chases Haley and catches her. Grant hits Death over the head and frees Haley. He tells her to do the reading while Grant faces "his demons" with the visage of The Devil. It pulls him toward a fiery landscape in the wall that looks like hell.

Haley does a reading for The Astrologer. The Astrologer appears in front of Haley and holds her up by the neck. Nearby, demons from hell try to pull Grant in to finish what The Devil started.

Haley tells The Astrologer she has read her cards and it is over. In her case, Death just means death. The Astrologer looks at her cards and sees the Death card in the center. A powerful wind blasts through the room.

Haley says her fate doesn't have to be a curse, and she can choose to let go. The Astrologer thinks of her daughter, and Haley, of her mother. And The Astrologer lets go, vanishing into the tarot circle on the ground. Grant breaks free and rushes to Haley's side.

When the wind stops, all is still.

The Astrologer is last seen walking away hand-in-hand with her daughter as leaves slowly drift to the ground.

Haley and Grant embrace. The Death card burns, signaling the curse is lifted. They walk back to town, hand-in-hand.

A car stops in front of them. It is Paxton, as predicted that he would come through for his friends in unexpected ways.

Paxton asks how they know it is over. Grant says Haley broke the curse, and it is over. Haley, who believed in fate before, replies, "F*** fate."

Haley questions Paxton about how he got out of the elevator. His catlike reflexes, he replies. Grant asks how he unfoxed The Fool. Paxton admits that his roommate, Todd, had opened the elevator, making The Fool disappear. All Todd saw was Paxton lying there on the ground, looking awkward.

I got the sense the story was not over. But the end credits rolled. An odd note to end the movie with. I felt it would have been stronger if they ended the story with The Astrologer and her daughter walking away or with Haley and Grant embracing. Paxton surviving felt like a loose end unresolved.

Still, I liked it overall. The movie was genuinely suspenseful, with the occasional jump scare. It was well-paced, with few slumps in the middle. Each death was drawn out and lengthier than it had to be but always evocative and heartrending, especially Paige's.

The characters were generally sympathetic. Haley carried the show, while Paige and Elise brought much emotional depth to the story. Lucas shone for the brief time he appeared, and Alma brought so much to the table with her presence.

Even The Astrologer evoked much grief, weeping for her hanged daughter. I felt so much for her then, but she got her revenge, and her subsequent killings of innocents for decades after were unjustified.

Tarot was predictable and familiar, but it makes for a great weekend watch with a bowl of potato chips. It's always about how the story is told, isn't it?

THE HAUNTING AND ALLURING SEA IN EMMA HAMM'S WHISPERS OF THE DEEP: FANTASY MERMAN ROMANCE DEFIES GENRE

LAURA DÍAZ DE ARCE

In a distant future where humans are forced to reside under the sea due to climate change, an engineer named Mira finds herself at odds and ultimately kidnapped by Arges. Her kidnapper is an undine, or merman, who is a sworn enemy of the humans that have populated the ocean floor. Slowly but surely, their hatred for one another shifts to understanding, to attraction, to love. *Whispers of the Deep* by Emma Hamm (Self-Published, 2024) is a merman-themed enemies-to-lovers, somewhat fantasy, somewhat science-fiction, and somewhat monster romance. When we swim away from some of the core tropes, we see that Hamm has played with genre and setting to push the stakes and inject tension into the plot. She leans into the abject terror of the ocean, which makes for an interesting intersection for the characters to explore.

Baby, You're a Fish Man

I often refer to horror and romance as sister genres—both have a focus on sensation, on an embodied experience, and, ultimately, are inherently concerned with sensuality. What an intriguing parallel, then, that the ocean in *Whispers of the Deep* is a setting of both wonder and terror. Abject mutilation and danger are intertwined with natural beauty and mysticism that sutures these twin themes of horror and romance.

To Hamm's credit, she does a good job of utilizing the setting as a viable character within *Whispers*, weaving scenes of temptation and discomfort within one another. Perhaps I'm biased about the horror element in the book, as I have a very real fear of deep water and the ocean*. Consequently, this book gave me both the *heebies* and the *jeebies*. But Hamm leans into this dichotomy. The ocean is a source of danger and beauty for Mira.

Mira is part of a colony of humans that have been forced to live at the bottom of the ocean due to climate change. In the beginning, when the tube Mira is in begins to flood, and she is pressed out into the bottom of the ocean, held by Arges in an uneasy bargain, Hamm writes:

> *"The cold started settling into her fingers and feet. She couldn't move them. Couldn't even hold onto him as he swam toward the glass elevators she'd indicated. And somehow, even though she was almost blacking out, she saw the depths flash before her eyes. So vast and dark. Never ending space that was both overwhelming and so freeing."*

Despite the fact that humans have made a "viable" living situation for themselves beneath the waves, it is an uneasy compromise. Mira resides in the Beta, a mostly engineering and utilitarian colony. They reside in tubes and glass, peppered with blast doors that are there should any of their structures fail. And it looks as if it was not too uncommon for those structures to fail, especially with the hostile forces ready to swim up and break glass when possible. It is all the more dangerous as they are constantly at odds with the undines, who see the technologically advanced humans as an interloper, poisoning their oceans**.

Hamm does pick and choose which sets of dangers to highlight with varying degrees of accuracy (she says so in her forward), but there are still a number of alarming sacrifices that people have to make to adapt to their newfound watery existence. Outside of the constant threat of their colony's structures collapsing, there is the potential for lost oxygen when tubes are damaged, the water pressure of the deep ocean, the freezing temperatures, etc.

And Mira's inability to adapt fully to the environment is highlighted even more after she is kidnapped. Arges moves her from undersea cave to undersea cave. In one instance, he settles her in what I will affectionately refer to as an octopus's garden, which, while a beautiful and fascinating place, isn't sustainable for her long term. Being out in the open ocean also leaves her vulnerable to enemies and other predators that she is ill-equipped to defend herself against.

Therefore, she goes back to being shuttered from cave to cave as a means of hiding and survival. And in all of these, she is cold, becomes waterlogged, and malnourished. She cannot subsist on fish alone, and the subsequent vitamin D deficiency threatens her life as well.

Between the Devil and the Deep Blue Sea

Arges functions as both an extension and a representation of the sea and also Mira's foil. He inhabits that dichotomy in the text. As an undine, or People of the Water as they refer to themselves, he is a creature of the depths. He is described as dark and dangerous. A predator like any other sea creature, but one defined by a sinister sentience from Mira's point of view at the start. But he is always tinged with this natural and mystical beauty.

> *"A monster hovered in front of the glass. His black tail, so long it tangles in the kelp, was at least ten feet long. Blue slashes of fins, so deep they blended in with the water, undulated all along the black scales. It stretched up to his waist, seamlessly turning into that pale, almost gray skin. His body was all the rumors claimed. So handsome it was painful to look at, and eerily like the god sculptures that surrounded her."*
>
> *"Dark claws on his hands were intimidating enough, but it was his black eyes that felt like they'd somehow captured her soul. Black, entirely. Inky and dark, they stared straight through her as though she was nothing. Just a maggot wriggling beneath him . . . ."*
>
> *"And is the rumors were true, his plush mouth was full of razor-sharp teeth. He tore through his prey like a shark, but so much more intelligent. So much more dangerous."*

Readers of monster romance are intimately familiar with descriptors like these, which use beastly accoutrements to remind the reader of the monstrosity of their visage. You have to remember, in monster romance, that the appeal is inverse to the proximity of human-ness. The fear these images are meant to conjure up is a feature, not a bug, in this subgenre.

But Arges isn't just the love interest, he is also a representation of the very environment that Mira is inhabiting, and should have a healthy fear of. His appearance reflects the uneasy balance between the beauty of the ocean and its creatures, as well as the real and present dangers that Mira experiences.

Surf n' Turf

The descriptions of Arges and Mira, therefore, make for an interesting study in contrasts. Arges is dark, dangerous, and mysterious. Mira is lightly colored with red hair. Weak in that environment, and so on.

But there are also aspects of their characters that enhance this tension in more subversive ways. Mira represents the science fiction bent of the text. Her home is a sort of steampunk, undersea technical marvel. She is an inventor and engineer who develops an underwater breathing device. She even ends up with a robot sidekick.

Arges comes to represent the fantasy portion of the book. He has a religious experience with pseudo-ancient-fish gods who grant him visions of the future.

The matriarch of his people is a somewhat-immortal-half-dead jellyfish undine. He regularly refers to the ocean and sea as living, mystical entities that communicate through currents. There are pieces of the text that support that vision, as the current often pushes Arges and Mira together in moments of intimacy.

But for all these surface-level contrasts, the differences fit seamlessly with one another, and it does not result in a disjointed experience. Part of this is the dual perspectives that help the reader to adapt to the worldview of each character and, therefore, adopt their readings of the settings and actions within a context that is understandable to them.

The contrasting technologies and features of their individual universes become the mechanisms by which they get together. Mira's robot sidekick creates translators so they can speak to each other. It's the magical vision Arges experiences that emboldens him to be with her. And it is the strange magic or biology that ultimately creates the possibility by which they can be unified in the water. Their mating results in Mira having a tentacle appendage that allows her to breathe underwater as long as she is attached to an undine.

In many ways, this is a body horror situation. A hapless, in-love woman comes to find her body changes without her consent to evolve for a new environment. While Mira appreciates the change, as it makes her fitter for the undersea life, it does strike me as another way that the horror and grotesque manifest differently in a romance context. Sudden alterations of the flesh are not to be feared—but embraced for the advantages that they are.

Ocean Eyes

> *"Brightly colored glowing plants brushed against her sides, trailing along her skin as she struggled to reach the mouth of the cave. Once there, she held onto the side of the wall and stared out into the abyss.*
>
> *"There was nothing out there. She knew it was because her eyes hadn't adjusted, and the bright light behind her made it even more difficult to see into the distance. But it looked like she stared out into a black wall of nothing. There could be anything out there. A hundred sharks. Killer whales. Monsters from the depths that she couldn't imagine or even dream up."*

Mira and Arges share one commonality—an innate curiosity and fascination with the *other*. At times, that draws them into the danger of one another's realms. The temptation of playing along the borders of a human colony and the deep sea that allows them to connect, or in this case, abscond. And though the places they swim through are fearful, aggressive, and full of peril, they are nonetheless victims of that curiosity. One which transforms to desire tinged with the ever-present danger of what darkness lurks beneath. It is a distinctive and intriguing representation of love in duress played out in the open sea.

I'm looking forward to the sequel.

Notes:

**When I tell you that I live in Florida and it has been literal years since I have been to the beach . . .*

**In all fairness to the undines, this is kind of an accurate assessment.*

EVIL SPACE SPAWN AS SATIRE, OR HOW I LEARNED TO STOP WORRYING AND LOVE THE GRUB: REVIEW OF GRUB: THE MISADVENTURES OF A MISCREANT AND HIS ASSOCIATES ON ALT-EARTH BY KATE BOYES

JOSHUA GAGE

> "Kate Boyes has a strong moral code and layered understanding of the issues at hand and how they affect our country. She is not content to just target one major politician, or one type of politician, but creates a world in which these people are so corrupted with alien spores that their toxic influence spreads and infects everything, right down to the literary organizations that she and her readers are a part of and hold dear."

Satire and parody, by their very definition, are tools of dismantlement. The entire purpose of these genres, stretching back to Quintillian, is to ridicule, embarrass, and hopefully, humble and change the targets of its derision. Poetry and satire have always gone hand-in-hand, so speculative poetry is a clever and unique take on these literary tropes. *GRUB: The Misadventures of a Miscreant and His Associates on Alt-Earth* (Self-Published, 2024) by Kate Boyes is an outstanding satirical commentary on current U.S. and World politics, but also serves to poke fun at her audience itself, and even herself as a reader and writer of speculative poetry.

The premise of the book, established in the prologue, is that in 1946, an event called "The Switch" occurred, but nobody knows who or what caused it. The best guess of scientists and historians is that repeated atomic bombings in Bikini Atoll caused a temporary rift in space and time that forever altered the history of the Earth. As the prologue states, "However, almost everyone who lived in or has studied our world as it was before 1946 agrees on two points: 1) our trajectory changed for the worse that year, and 2) The Switch also led in some way to the bizarre arrival on this planet of the alien being called G. U. Bouffant, who most of us refer to as GRUB." Thus, the setting for our satire is set. Earth is on a disastrous trajectory, and our country is being led by an alien grub who poisons his followers with infectious spores.

The satire in this book is as angry and vitriolic as anything Swift could conjure. Boyes uses the technique of parody, specifically nursery rhymes and children's folk songs, to emphasize the childishness of her targets. For example, the poem "TUCKER CARLSON, FORMER FAUX-FOXY VILLAGE FOOL" is set to the tune of Old Dan Tucker and begins:

Bowtie Tucker is a cunning man,
lies to our face when e'er he can;
defends the dregs of the human race —
he'll end his days in deep disgrace.
Oh, get out the way, Bowtie Tucker,
you must think that we're all suckers.
The jig is up, your hands are grimmy —
cuddling GRUB has made you slimy.

To add to the effect, and to continue the idea of "book as historical artifact," Boyes adds a footnote about the creation of this song, which resulted from an interview with Tucker Carlson, in which he insulted Dolly Parton and kicked his dog repeatedly. Part of the footnote reads: "Negative responses to his actions were swift and intense. This song reached the top of the country music charts two days later, where it remained for several months, and it could be heard blaring from truck stops across the country for many years." This is the level of creativity and world-building that Boyes is crafting in this book.

The poems themselves are parodies and satire, to be sure, but the creative footnotes and history, in which alien spores turn conservative politicians into hybrid beasts, each with their own unique talents and curses. The layers of satire in this book are, as rhetorician Dustin Griffin argues, "designed to win the admiration and applause of a reading audience not for the ardor or acuteness of its moral concern but for the brilliant wit and force of the satirist as rhetorician." It is Boyes' wit and cleverness that permeates this book, and the ways she synthesizes classical myth with science fiction and political satire that really drive the brilliance home.

What makes Boyes' satire so striking is that she doesn't just poke fun at obvious targets but also at the institutions that serve to prop up those targets. For example, targeting Boomers and older Xers who refuse to adapt to Gen Z slang, understand how the internet functions, how to use information literacy to distinguish between truth and fiction, Boyes writes the poem: "LEAKED GOVERNMENT DOCUMENTS CONFIRM TIME TRAVELER VISITED U.S. IN 2015, REVEAL HIS DIRE WARNING" which begins with lines like:

Gas & ^5!
Obo evr1 still aak in 2209, I'm hts: omg, ppl, wtf?
Srsly, ru totes derps? I'm smhid!
GRUB—aka 'hwsnbn'—is a ng pita, an iwiam, dal.
Icymi, he's a wkd soab w/ Z 🩶 & a veg.
Waj! Wal!

The satire is that this is a confirmed message from a time traveler from 2209. Fortunately, Boyles provides a "translation," and the opening stanza reads:

Greetings and salutations & high five!
On behalf of everyone still alive and kicking in
2209, I'm here to say: Oh my god,
people, what the flick? Seriously,
are you totally foolish? I'm scratching my
head in disbelief!
GRUB—also known as "he who shall not be named" —
is a no good pain in the ass, an idiot
wrapped in a moron, dumb and lazy.
In case you missed it, he's a wicked son
of a bitch with zero heart & a very evil grin.
What a jerk! What a loser!

Clearly, this is a poke at everything from TurningPointUSA to politicians and pundits who say we should ignore Greta Thunberg and Nupol Kiazolu because they're too young, inexperienced, etc.

Elsewhere, Boyes turns her pen towards other institutions, including those within the speculative genre. The footnote to the poem "BOUFFANT'S LAMENT" explains that the poem, as well as an award-winning sonnet crown, were written by a poetry instructor who was blackmailed. The footnote explains, "We assume the instructor also penned GRUB's *These Cell Walls Weep and Whisper "Sir"*, a chilling heroic crown of crowns sonnet collection that won both the Elgin and Bram Stoker awards (after judges and other finalists suffered mishaps, including Novichuk poisoning)," so even the Elgins and Stokers aren't safe from Boyes' biting pen! This is very meta jab at the institutions to which the book in question would be promoted and awarded, especially considering Boyes herself has won an award from the SFPA itself. Readers will be aware of controversies like Sad Puppies and Rabid Puppies to vocal public attacks about various minority Dwarf Star and Rhysling winners, and will know that even in smaller literary communities, misogynists, racists, anti-Semites still exist. Boyes, as a member of those communities, is using her book to challenge and shame those toxic voices in her and her books' immediate community.

Literary satire is difficult to pull off successfully. It must be timely, but it can't be so time-specific as to not have lasting longevity, lest it deteriorate into propaganda. It has to not only be artistic but also clever and biting. If we accept that satire pushes or challenges the clear boundaries and guidelines accepted by the bulk of society, then the satirist must see themselves as a moral champion of sorts, a knight armed with wit and scorn ready to battle the dragons that represent the evil in their community. Juvenile, one of the most revered classical political satirists, is often championed as having a strong moral code and tight understanding of the moral issues involved. In the same vein as Juvenile, Kate Boyes has a strong moral code and layered understanding of the issues at hand and how they affect our country. She is not content to just target one major politician, or one type of politician, but creates a world in which these people are so corrupted with alien spores that their toxic influence spreads and infects everything, right down to the literary organizations that she and her readers are a part of and hold dear. This is Boyes' skill as a satirist, making the grand and political personal and immediate, making the immoral but abstract and ethereal very tangible, direct, and important in the life of a reader. *GRUB: The Misadventures of a Miscreant and His Associates on Alt-Earth* by Kate Boyes is an important book for 2024 and the current election year, but it is also an important artifact in the legacy of satire and satirical poetry, and is strongly recommended for every reader of speculative fiction and poetry.

GO WEST, YOUNG MA'AM: MIA GOTH'S MANIFESTING DESTINY IN THE X TRILOGY: A REVIEW OF A24'S AND TI WEST'S TRIO OF HORROR FILMS

PATRICK BARB

> "The film serves as an effective capstone to a trilogy where the concept of Manifest Destiny, the driving Eurocentric colonizing force behind the westward expansion of the United States, is given an individual (well, two individuals) avatar(s)—while being no less bloody and murderous."

In the opening of Ti West's *Maxxxine (A24, 2024),* the recently released final chapter in his horror trilogy starring muse and collaborator Mia Goth, Goth's titular antiheroine walks through a barndoor-like opening onto a studio soundstage, moving with supreme confidence as she prepares to audition for a role in a horror movie sequel. The metafiction nods come fast and furious in this film (and its predecessors). So, if it's not your thing, the trilogy may not be for you.

Additionally, opening shots of barn doors are a repeated element throughout the trilogy (with *X* and *Pearl* preceding this concluding chapter). Whereas the prior installments showcased actual barn doors on a farm, the final chapter reserves them for an in-world backlot. Here again, West reminds us that we're watching a movie, one of a trilogy, focused on the paths to stardom taken by two ambitious young women from Texas drawn by the allure of Hollywood glamor and fame, sin, and sex. And while Maxine opens *Maxxxine* closer to that dream than ever before (certainly closer than her darker, older counterpart

Pearl, also played by Goth), there's something empty, superficial, and false about her arrival at this dreamed-for destination. In a sense, it is as hollow as the soundstage where she auditions.

The film serves as an effective capstone to a trilogy where the concept of Manifest Destiny, the driving Eurocentric colonizing force behind the westward expansion of the United States, is given an individual (well, two individuals) avatar(s)—while being no less bloody and murderous.

Odd as it may sound to compare a gory, often schlocky (in the best way possible to this reviewer's mind) horror trilogy to the westward expansion of settlers across the land to the Pacific Ocean, it becomes easier to buy into when one acknowledges that West and Goth's collaboration is, at its blood-soaked heart, a tribute to film and filmmaking. Hollywood is that final destination, the signpost marking one's arrival in the West.

X Marks the Spot (Where Things Begin)

However, before we look at the end of this film journey, let's return to its beginning (or at least the beginning for Maxine Minx). Released in 2022, *X* is a cover version of *Texas Chain Saw Massacre*, *Eaten Alive*, and other films from the Tobe Hooper catalog. (Indeed, you can even draw a line between *X*'s focus on sex and sexuality and Hooper's alien vampire flick *Lifeforce*.) Goth plays Minx, a stripper with dreams of star status as a sex symbol. Her strip-club owner boyfriend, Wayne (Martin Henderson), dreams of making money as a producer in the emerging XXX film industry. He's recruited another dancer (Brittany Snow), her well-endowed boyfriend (Kid Cudi), a dorkily pretentious, long-haired wannabe filmmaker (Owen Campbell), and his accompanying mousy, reserved girlfriend, played by Jenna Ortega, to make his smutty money-making dreams come true.

Leaving the stark industrialized landscape of Houston behind and clambering into a van straight out of *Texas Chain Saw*, this ragtag crew travels to a run-down, out-of-the-way farm whose near-senile elderly owner, Howard, agreed to provide lodging (though he hasn't been informed about the exact nature of the work taking place on his land).

Hinting at the violence to come, a dead cow, run over in the middle of the road with its insides exposed graphically, delays the journey. Maxine, gagging at the sight, is quick to note: "I hate blood and guts." These *nudge-nudge wink-wink* asides to the true nature of the film serve as West's opening volleys into the world of metafiction and film/film history commentary. He goes a step further with the rag-tag filmmaking crew's arrival at the farm, which one character declares to be: "Our own studio backlot."

The shot of the van's arrival on the farm is reminiscent of Hooper's *TCM*, with this comparison carrying through to Wayne's initial knock on the farmhouse's door. Knowledgeable horror fans might well expect Leatherface to yank the outsider into his home, sledgehammer ready to fall. Instead, we're introduced to curmudgeonly Howard (played by Stephen Ure in old-age make-up). His equally aged wife Pearl watches from a window upstairs, with Maxine catching sight of the frail-looking woman in white via her passenger-side window. In a sense, both characters (played by Goth in a dual performance) get their first looks at each other through the glass, just as we, the audience, see them on-screen, filtered. This initial cameo of the film's eventual antagonist is also the beginning of the motif of "Pearl as a voyeur," which will carry throughout the film and whose origins will later be explored in the prequel *Pearl.*

For a voyeur like Pearl, the cast and crew of the in-movie porno film *The Farmer's Daughters* sure give her quite the show. She eventually spies on Maxine during a sex scene filmed in the barn, finding herself drawn to her younger counterpart's beauty, confidence, and unchecked sexuality. There is a moment during this filming scene when Maxine looks directly into the camera, locking eyes with the viewer/Owen the director. The moment serves as a reminder that *we* are voyeurs, like Pearl, not only watching the unfolding sex scene but also watching with the knowledge of what we're *really* seeing. We know we're watching a horror film, even if the characters don't yet know it. We are complicit, staring, waiting for the (blood)money shot.

The contrast between Pearl and Maxine is one of the driving elements behind X. The choice to have Mia Goth play both roles is an interesting one, even though there may rightfully be some argument against the old age make-up worn by Goth and Ure, and the presented fear of aging/the elderly that seems on display here. In *X*, West presents growing old at its absolute nadir. Wrinkles, liver spots, sexual inadequacy, *more* wrinkles.

That said, one can argue that the monstrousness of the aged aligns with the worldview of both antagonist *and* protagonist. Pearl is saddened by her aged state and that of her husband, jealous of the younger women in their prime who've come into her domain. Likewise, Maxine views Pearl's aged body and mind as a type of warning, presenting the dark future she doesn't wish for herself. Neither woman, young or old, is "right" here. The horror of Pearl and Howard's appearance is a by-product, an external expression of the character's fears.

While Pearl's trapped, eventually lashing out in murderous fashion at those she believes think of themselves as her betters because their dreams (sleazy as they are) remain intact, Maxine is still defiant in her dream of a better life, even in the face of a total nightmare. As she says, in one of the movie's (and trilogy's) most famous and informative lines: "I will not accept a life I do not deserve." This mantra is at the heart of the trilogy. Both Pearl and Maxine want something better for themselves, and that something is largely informed by the glitz and glamour of being a "star." It's just that by the time they cross paths, Pearl has seemingly abandoned her ambitions, settling for rage and revenge. As Pearl says to Howard about Maxine, once their killing of the younger, fitter, more confident interlopers begins: "She has something special. Like I did."

While we, as viewers, don't yet know about Pearl's "something special," we are given glimpses of it—in photographs of her younger self displayed around the house and in the Norma Desmond-esque dance she performs following her initial kill, her body lit up in high contrast by the van's headlights.

At *X*'s conclusion, we find Maxine Minx moving on from the horror show farm in a way that her counterpart Pearl never could and never can. As the words of a televangelist preacher heard at the beginning of the film and repeated in the conclusion echo Maxine's mantra, "I will not accept a life I do not deserve," we bear witness to her journey continuing, the life she "deserves" still out there to the West.

Pearl Before Swine

However, before reaching the end of Maxine's journey, West and Goth teamed up to pen a look at the road not taken. Released later in 2022, *Pearl* marks a departure from the sleazy, 70s, exploitation horror vibes of *X* and instead presents a character study/origin for the former film's antagonist with stylistic flourishes more commonly associated with Technicolor, musical, big-screen blockbuster epics. Just as West and Goth take viewers back in time to show how Pearl became the murderous old lady on a farm, so too does West and crew return the audience to an earlier style of film and filmmaking.

The picture begins with a film reel whirring life, a darkened image of the barn doors, reminiscent of what was seen in *X*. However, as the doors open, viewers encounter an expansive, brightly-colored landscape. This is not the farm of *X*, but more like the sets of *The Wizard of Oz* or *Oklahoma!* We're conditioned to expect song and spectacle here rather than bloodshed and shadows.

The year is 1918—the year of the Spanish Flu. The recently married Pearl lives on her family's farm while her husband, Howard, is overseas fighting in the First World War. It is a lonely, isolated existence for Pearl, with only her overbearing, strict German mother, mute, invalid father, and the farm animals (some of which she slaughters and feeds to the alligators in their pond) for company. And yet, Pearl manages to find some less murderous means of entertaining herself, performing and dancing on haybales with the livestock as her audience stand-ins.

The script and Goth's performance go a long way to evoking sympathy for the lead character. It's amplified by the accompanying performance of Tandi Wright as Pearl's mother. The mother's hinted-upon German nationalism causes her to tamp down Pearl's support of husband Howard off at war, and she generally stands in opposition to all of Pearl's dreams of stardom. It is this character's actions primarily by which we see Pearl stifled and driven to inevitable violence. On a metatextual level, it is perhaps apropos that a German character would serve as the impetus for horror in the film. After all, it was the work of German Expressionist filmmakers that had such an impact on the development of American horror cinema in the 20s and 30s. One can't help but wonder if this isn't another clever nod on West and Co.'s part to film history.

It's also vital to note the connection between the 1918 of *Pearl* and the not-so-long-ago impact of the COVID-19 pandemic and various lockdowns during the early part of the 2020s. Scenes with Pearl masked up on her bicycle or her mother refusing to allow guests (and food, pig from Pearl's in-laws) inside her home still resonate today, but they certainly did at the time of the film's release. Just as there was a push at the end of the lockdown year(s) to get people out and about, taking in entertainment, and consuming as normal, so too do we find Pearl drawn to her local movie theater.

The big-picture spectacles of films like *Palace Follies* and Theda Bara-starring *Cleopatra* present goals that seem impossible to Pearl, even early on at her most optimistic. And yet the Projectionist (David Corenswet) emerges from a back alley (a not-so-subtle hint at the true nature of his character) as a tempting Lothario, an Errol Flynn/Clark Gable/Douglas Fairbanks, taking Pearl behind the scenes of the movies she loves (or to the projection booth at least), and promising her that, *yes, she is worthy and yes, she could be a star.*

Of course, the "stardom" he has in mind for her is more akin to that of Maxine in X. As part of his rather unsophisticated seduction, he shows her stag films, and—similar to Maxine's porn-making boyfriend Wayne—declares (re: his plans to make his own risqué films): "I for one plan on capitalizing early." Pearl is reduced to a sex object in the eyes of the Projectionist. While her counterpart, Maxine, will see her dreams go from XXX to mainstream Hollywood, Pearl suffers for taking that journey in reverse. Rather than striving for more, she's forced to accept a life that is less and less than what she believes she deserves.

Indeed, Pearl's big dreams of stardom are shut down one after the other, as her body count escalates. The rotting maggot-covered roast pig left on the farmhouse porch hints at the infection of horror overtaking the bright, Technicolor world of illusions that Pearl had established for herself at the film's opening. The bright reds grow darker, inside the house, on the barn, and in Pearl's final dress, speaking to the bloodshed to come.

Her fate is sealed during her audition for a church dance troupe that will tour the state (not unlike the traveling preacher revealed to be Maxine's father in X). This last-ditch effort at escape ends as a spectacular failure. While Pearl imagines herself in a Busby Berkeley-style chorus line complete with silent film star exaggerated facial expressions, the judges (and ultimately the audience) see, instead, a manic, desperate, and ultimately unfulfilling performance.

Much has already been said and written about Goth's performance in the role of Pearl, especially this earlier incarnation of the character. All praise and kudos are well-deserved and quite earned. No more so than in the climactic monologue that Pearl delivers to her sister-in-law (Emma Jenkins-Purro). Here, we find the troubled protagonist, bearing her soul, talking about the loss of a child, her loneliness, and her murderous inclinations. It is a speech that's simultaneously heartbreaking and horrifying. The final turn, with Pearl acknowledging her sister-in-law got the coveted dance troupe role because she's blonde, will resonate later in *Maxxxine,* where Goth's Maxine has switched from the brunette of X to a towheaded hair color.

Perhaps even more symbolically powerful is the film's final shot. Howard returns from the war to the farm where Pearl waits for him, smiling wider and wider until tears run from her eyes, standing before a table of rotten meat and decaying corpses. The camera zooms tighter and tighter, Pearl's world and our view on-screen both becoming smaller and smaller. We leave her trapped in a nightmare existence. The same nightmarish existence that Maxine rejects in *X,* fleeing the farm and the dead bodies of her friends and loved ones in search of the better life, the life of a star, which she believes she deserves.

Hollywood or Bust

While *X* plays as a cover-band version of 70s exploitation horror and *Pearl* blends the disparate elements of the Golden Age of Hollywood, the final installment of the trilogy, *Maxxxine,* is a return to a more direct horror subgenre/style tribute. In this case, West and Co. offer a note-perfect take on 80s horror, particularly the *Giallo*—the Italian mystery-thriller subgenre noted for its sex, graphic violence, and "whodunit" plotting that served as a precursor to the slasher. In addition, West sprinkles in more distinctly 80s flavors of horror, including nods to the Satanic Panic, the rise of serial killers (in this case, Richard Ramirez, aka The Night Stalker), the sequelization of horror films, and killer cults.

Importantly, *Maxxxine* is a film that opens with our heroine, featured in the opening and concluding chapters of the trilogy, having already arrived at her destination (at least physically). We see Maxine in California, in Hollywood. We watch her nail her horror film audition, no doubt drawing from the very real, very bloody experience she endured in X. With these conditions already set, the final installment becomes less about the character's journey and more about her struggles to firmly plant her metaphorical flag in the ground and make it impossible for the past (personified here by a mysterious stalker, wearing the stereotypical *giallo* killer's black leather gloves and trenchcoat, who seems to know all about Maxine's pastor's daughter past *and* her early forays into porn) to drag her back to where she came from.

The rejection of the past is firmly and gorily established in an early scene where a Hollywood Boulevard panhandler dressed as Buster Keaton threatens Maxine, only to suffer a *crushing* defeat at (under) her heels, one that leaves him and his manhood in less than working conditions. There's a rejection here of the male influence on Maxine, as seen in X. It plays out throughout the film. As she wraps up her commitments in porn, stripping, and peep show performances, Maxine establishes herself as an independent woman—someone still very much cognizant of the future she wants for herself and unafraid to reject the words of the men surrounding her, especially when they go against her vision of the future. This is a confident, more world-weary version of the character, and Goth does a fantastic job of showing how the subsequent years in porn and Hollywood have impacted Maxine Minx.

It is interesting to note that her male companions in the film are limited but much improved in terms of protecting and nurturing her development. There's gay Black male video clerk Leon (Moses Sumney), Maxine's roommate, and her agent Teddy Knight (masterfully essayed by Giancarlo Esposito). Both characters serve as protectors to Maxine, not viewing her in a sexual manner (at least so far as we see onscreen) and also providing her with the necessary information and tools to deal with the increasingly murderous mysterious stalker who picks off the women in Maxine's life one by one, setting up the crime scenes to suggest a connection to Satanic cults. While the killer is left genderless until the final bombastic sequence, they employ a blatant male avatar in the form of Kevin Bacon's sleazy private detective, John Labat.

Bacon is the evil Mirror Universe version of Jack Nicholson's Jake Gittes in *Chinatown*, down to the suit, hat, and nose bandage. His scenery-chewing is second only to the eventually revealed killer's. He is a looming, lurking presence, providing daylight intimidation in conjunction with the killer's night-time slaying. It is a credit to Bacon's performance and West's writing/directing that this villainous homage to one of the most famous films about California (Los Angeles in particular) is included in the DNA of *Maxxxine*.

While the male figures in the film are either protectors or menaces, it is a new woman in Maxine's life who seems to best comprehend her goals and provide her with the tools and opportunities to achieve them. In both *X* and *Pearl*, the filmmaker characters (Wayne, the porn producer-boyfriend, and Pearl's Projectionist) are masculine-coded and focused solely on their gratification, both sexually and monetarily. In contrast, Elizabeth Debicki's androgyne-coded female horror director, Elizabeth Bender, recognizes Maxine's talent and works to give it the spotlight and platform necessary for a breakthrough success. Neither protector nor exploiter, she is instead presented as an equal partner to the dynamo that is Maxine Minx.

It is an interesting choice, given the male/female director/actor binary presented throughout the trilogy with West and Goth. West seems fully aware of this feature of the relationship, giving nods that are subtle and not-so-subtle throughout the trilogy, particularly in *Maxxxine*. The inclusion of the Bates Motel and *Psycho* House on the studio lot both provide a direct connection between West and Goth's trilogy and the work of filmmaker Alfred Hitchcock, a man known for his complex relationship with his leading ladies. Indeed, Maxine's transition from brunette in *X* to the blonde of *Maxxxine* also recalls the transformation of Kim Novak's character in Hitchcock's most psychologically intriguing film *Vertigo*, where Jimmy Stewart's obsessed character can potentially be read as a stand-in for Mr. Hitchcock himself. The bold choice to confront these stereotypes of the leading lady/male director relationship head-on is an admirable one.

Indeed, *Maxxxine* is a film that is in conversation with film and film history, similar to his predecessors, but is also one that looks back at those same antecedents in a like fashion. There are newspaper headlines taken from Texas, referring to the events of X as "Texas Porn Star Massacre," making the same connection to Hooper's classic as many critics of X had. The studio backlot features one shot of actors dressed as soldiers off to film a period war piece, their costumes reminiscent of those featured in *Pearl*. Through this self-referencing, West and Co. create a sort of feedback loop, the trilogy's components coming together as a cohesive whole but also existing as all films do, individual but still very much part of a greater tapestry.

This is the promise of filmmaking, particularly Hollywood filmmaking, with its emphasis on star-making and stardom. The trilogy ending in the 80s, which saw the rise of the blockbuster (where the seeds were sown for the fall of the actor/performer and the rise of the "property" as the driving force behind what is made and screened), is an apropos choice. Maxine Minx is left to continue refusing a life she does not deserve, and the world/time in which we leave her is one where that goal is still very much possible.

BRING THEM DOWN REVIEW: IRISH HORROR ON A SHEEP FARM WITH BARRY KEOGHAN

HOLLY LYN WALRATH

In Fantastic Fest 2024 feature *Bring Them Down*, Christopher Abbott plays Michael (Mikey) might-as-well-call-him-Danny-boy, a shepherd with a dark past forced into violence in this gripping domestic thriller. The film opens with one of the most heart-wrenching introductions to a character I've ever seen, taking the popular horror movie trope of opening a film with a car accident (*Get Out, Final Destination, The Descent*, etc., etc., etc.) and turning it on its head. Barry Keoghan is an Irish teenager with a chip on his shoulder. Colm Meaney (Star Trek's Chief O'Brien) is a disabled father who speaks only in Gaelic out of stubbornness, rounding out this cast of talented male actors in a film on the perils of toxic masculinity.

Michael is a shepherd in rural Ireland who is down on his luck after an accident results in the death of his mother and injury to his girlfriend, Caroline (Nora-Jane Noone). What he hasn't told his bearish father is that his mother meant to leave his father. When a feud breaks out between neighboring sheep farmers, the wife of which is his former girlfriend, Michael is forced to take matters into his own, somewhat unhinged hands.

Christopher Abbott is fantastically riveting as what the director calls a "stoic, mythical character" (The Wrap) despite not being Irish. While the role would be somewhat more convincing with an Irish actor, Abbott's performance is convincing and, for me, reminiscent of Ryan Gosling's darker roles. The audience yearns for Mikey to act out his revenge after the death of his flock of sheep.

Meanwhile, Barry Keoghan is satisfyingly annoying and yet timelessly soft as Jack, the son of Caroline. Halfway through the film, we flip to his point of view, and the empathy he brings to the character is nuanced and delightful.

HOLLY LYN WALRATH

One of my favorite storytelling structures, and one particularly effective in horror, is the "slippery slope"—where a situation is played out to its absolute worst and inevitable end. *Bring Them Down* does just that, answering the question of what happens when you push a man to his breaking point, and an Irish man at that.

Loosely based on a true story, the film is rife with animal violence. It calls to mind the parable of the good shepherd, where Jesus likens his role as a savior to the shepherd: The good shepherd is willing to die for his sheep. But for those who can't endure animal violence, this film should have a trigger warning. Be warned. Several traumatic scenes of animal death are almost too difficult to watch.

Against this violence, the cinematography, writing, and aesthetic from debut director Christopher Andrews are spot-on, showcasing the dark closeness of the Irish countryside painted in swaths of misty greens and blues—which serve as a beautiful contrast for the touches of blood as the film descends into a dark look at the human soul. Resentment, miscommunication, and domestic abuse drape the story in emotion.

The theme here is toxic masculinity. Who it hurts, who it kills, and who it destroys. The stereotypes of Irish masculinity—alcoholism, domestic violence, and closed-off emotions, are explored with empathy. As always, as inevitable as it is, toxic masculinity hurts men as much as it does women.

It is a difficult but nuanced film that will capture the audience's hearts. Far from funny and a gripping watch. Let's hope this gets wider distribution, STAT.

WHY OWEN IN *I SAW THE TV GLOW* COULD ALSO BE AUTISTIC: THE FREEDOM IN ACCEPTING YOUR TRUE SELF

CHLOE SMITH

> "I know the harm not knowing your true self can cause, and likewise, know the freedom in knowing and accepting your true self."

I *Saw The TV Glow* (A24, 2024) is an incredibly impactful film in a number of ways, but one that is yet to really be discussed is that, alongside being transgender and being affected by internalized transphobia, Owen as a character can also be said to be autistic.

I Saw The TV Glow follows Owen, a lonely child who loses his mother and is left to be cared for by an uncaring father. He finally finds kinship in Maddie, an older girl who is also a fan of his favorite show, "The Pink Opaque." Owen sneaks over to Maddie's to watch it in secret, and she burns episodes on tape for him. But then Maddie goes missing . . . only to return years later, telling Owen that "The Pink Opaque" is actually reality, and they must return to that reality or die. The film itself is an allegory for being trans and the harm not accepting your true self can cause, but also that there's always time to embrace who you truly are.

However, as an autistic person myself, after watching the film, I could definitely see parts of myself and my autism in Owen, making the film all the more meaningful to me. As someone who was diagnosed later in my life, I know the harm not knowing your true self can cause, and likewise, know the freedom in knowing and accepting your true self.

Why is Owen autistic, to me, then? Well, throughout the film, Owen's monotone tone of voice is obvious—and while it can be a sign of his inner struggles in terms of accepting his true self and gender, it is also a clear sign of autism, and one that is clear from the start of the film. While autistic people can sometimes have monotone tones of voice, in Owen's case, the particular inflection of his voice could also showcase how drained he is of life—that denying his gender identity is impacting him, but also that his constant need for reassurance (even his only friend Maddie tells him to stop apologizing to her) and the fact that he is forced to mask and ignore his own needs as an autistic person—such as not watching the show that he enjoys as his dad disapproves of a "boy" watching what he calls "a show for girls."

Speaking of that TV show, "The Pink Opaque" is another reason why Owen can be read as autistic is that he clearly has a special interest—a term that essentially means a highly focused interest in a particular topic, of which autistic people can have a variety—in television, but specifically the TV show "The Pink Opaque." While the show is also a window into his true identity, it also serves as a special interest that brings him joy and friendship in allowing him to meet Maddie. (I myself have found friends and immense happiness via my own special interests as an autistic person).

Owen is learning to 'mask' his true self throughout the film. Masking is a term that essentially means when an autistic person hides their autistic traits—their own selves—and tries to perform what is expected of a non-autistic or neurotypical person, in that scenario, to "fit in" to societal standards and what is expected. We learn that his own family can sense his difference—his own mother expresses her worry about Owen and her hope that he finds the right path in life.

Then, despite being encouraged by Maddie to embrace his true self and follow the path that leads to his true identity, Owen runs away and gets a job and a family—all of the things expected of him, even if they don't appear to make him all that happy. Essentially, Owen starts to employ a type of masking that further represses his true identity and true self as an autistic individual—what he feels is the right path for him, even if it takes away all the joy in his life, even his viewing and appreciation of "The Pink Opaque"—until it all becomes too much, and he has an autistic meltdown—breaking down and becoming overwhelmed while at work.

Statistics also show that a number of autistic individuals also belong to the LGBTQIA+ community in some way. For instance, information published and a study highlighted by the University of Cambridge state that transgender and non-binary people are 3 to 6 times more likely to also be autistic when compared to cisgender people. Therefore, given that *I Saw The TV Glow* paints Owen going through the journey of initially resisting and finally starting to accept his gender identity, given that he isn't cisgender, he is also far more likely to also be autistic, supporting the reading that he is both transgender—and autistic—whether it was subconsciously intended within the film or not.

Lastly, at the end of the film, after what can be interpreted as a moment of terrifying realization that denying his true self is killing him and an autistic meltdown and sensory overload while a crowd sings around him (or indeed, the terror of denying his true disabled and transgender self is affecting him)

Owen leaves, apologizing to everyone he passes for what just happened. As an autistic person, you feel so different from others and are often shamed and isolated for being so—just look at Owen, who only has Maddie as a friend—that when you feel you've let the mask slip and have done something wrong socially or broken some unknown neurological rule, you feel shame and apologetic, as Owen does in this scene, despite his own enlightenment in terms of his identity.

While the ending of *I Saw The TV Glow* itself is ambiguous, the final scene is Owen walking out of the arcade, and I hope, away from the repressive life of masking and hiding both his gender identity and neurodiversity. He may apologize to those around him for his meltdown, but he is opting to leave the situation that led to that instance—the best thing you can arguably do in that situation as an autistic individual, so you can regulate and take care of yourself after a meltdown.

Throughout the film, we see Owen slowly start to accept his true self, and while there is no concrete ending for Owen beyond him leaving the arcade, in the final moments, we hear rain and a gasp as the credits start to roll. Maddie herself said it was raining as she became Tara—her true self in "The Pink Opaque" universe—so we can only hope that Owen does the same—finally accepting and embracing his true self as Isabel, a transgender and autistic person, free of the mask he had been forced to wear up to that point.

Jane Schoeburn, the trans creator of the film, said "[Being Trans], it's about hiding from this thing inside you for half your life, and then the dual horror and catharsis of finally letting those walls down and seeing it for the first time, and being left with this sort of double-edged sword of two bad options: to put your authentic self you've been hiding from back inside and just pretend like you never saw it and go on half living half a life, or face the unknown, which will almost certainly mean complete social death, essentially the end of reality as you know it. The film's genre elements and central metaphor grew out of a desire to talk about what I, and I think many other trans people have experienced, which is trying to figure out a way to be yourself in a world that has done a really good job of trying to convince you that you're someone else."

In a sense, I also believe the same sentiments apply to someone who has to accept and embrace their neurodiversity, particularly autism, and being disabled—especially if it's your first or only diagnosis.

Everyone deserves to fully, truly be themselves, after all—especially those who have struggled to fit in their entire lives and hide their true selves, as Owen and many undiagnosed autistic people did and still do. But as the film states, written out on the road in pink chalk—whether you are repressing or rejecting your true self in terms of your gender or neurodiversity, "there is still time" to free yourself and finally accept and become your true self. No one deserves to feel as if they're dying just so everyone else thinks they're on the right path—no matter what, there is still time.

THE NIGHT IN THE WOODS TEAM HAD TO CANCEL REVENANT HILL: WHY CREATORS SHOULD PRIORITIZE THEIR HEALTH AND FANS SHOULD SUPPORT THEM

PRIYA SRIDHAR

I love *Night in the Woods* (2017), an adventure puzzle game about a college dropout who discovers a dark secret in her hometown while reconciling with her high school friends. The game was funded via Kickstarter, and prior to its release, a companion game, *Longest Night,* was released in 2013. It was a game that I discovered by chance, thanks to Irish YouTuber Jacksepticeye playing it and realizing that the price was not that bad on Steam. After a few stressful business school weeks, I would go to my gaming desktop and boot up a stream. I played the Gregg and Angus route since Gregg is the best character, and I wanted to go down the story arc that would help him work through the relationship issues that he shares with his boyfriend, Angus.

It was a delight to find out that the *Night in the Woods* worker-owned cooperative studio, consisting of Scott Benson, Bethany Hockenberry, and Wren Farren, The Glory Society, was coming out with a new game called *Revenant Hill,* and a prequel to the established story, no less. It would feature an immortal cat traveling through different time periods, the trademark animation that shows an eerie Pennsylvania fraught with economic disparity and systematic biases, and a different story.

The trailer caught my attention, with a non-anthropomorphic cat wandering through the centuries and observing how the land's inhabitants change, along with the technology and fashions. Yet the attitudes and psychologies don't. We human beings are predictable and fragile, engaging in healthy or destructive patterns. The latter rebound in negative ways across generations, something *Revenant Hill* implied it would cover.

Just one problem: game development has been canceled. The Glory Society may also have gone on hiatus.

November 2023 Announcement

According to The Mary Sue and The Verge, the developers had to pull the plug on *Revenant Hill* because two key team members have sustained serious health issues. Scott Benson developed heart failure in 2023 and realized he had to focus on his health. I agree this was the right decision, but it still hurts on an emotional level. Please send all your best wishes to Scott for a speedy recovery, and may he have a peaceful holiday.

What Darkness Lies Beneath The Cheery Surface of Possum Springs And Its Creators

The game is personal to me because I was able to do one thing I haven't been able to do since I was a kid: say goodnight to my dad. Mae Borowski, our player character, can opt to watch television with her father every night. I did so, and I would read aloud the story text. As a result, I could say "Good night, Dad" and remember the times that my dad comforted me from a nightmare using hot chocolate and reassuring words about whether the house would flood with water like it did in my subconscious.

Unfortunately, *Night in the Woods* came from a place of pain. Not my pain but that of the developers Scott Benson and Bethany Hockenberry. They put their all-in toward the story, which you can see, but one has to question if their trauma was worth the final result for their sake. I believe that if one is forced to choose between a creator's health and their work, health should come first. Otherwise, burnout and long-term chronic injuries will ensue.

After game composer Alec Holowka died by suicide following allegations of abuse and harassment, Scott posted a long article on Medium. He described how Alec emotionally abused him and Bethany after they came together for this collaboration, and that Alec always put on an aura of authority. To add insult to injury, he ghosted them and forced them to miss important deadlines. The story was Scott and Bethany's creation, based on Scott's experience in rural Pennsylvania and the legacy of generational trauma and abuse. Scott details how he took many financial risks to bring this dream project to life, and Alec couldn't seem to understand that or the stakes if they had to pull the plug. It took Bethany accidentally shaming Alec on Twitter for his unprofessional behavior for him to clean up his act and agree to finish the game.

Hearing all of this makes a person sad. *Night in the Woods* provided and still provides comfort to me. I was hoping that *Revenant Hill* would be the second chance to play a game born out of love rather than stress in a familiar setting. Alec would not be involved for obvious reasons, and the fanbase would have ample time to provide the necessary funds for Kickstarters, love and support. Now that second chance is on hold, perhaps indefinitely, and we are left with the pain that Scott and Bethany suffered. They gave us a beautiful, comforting project, and it's not fair that Scott has developed heart failure at such a young age.

Players and media critics have learned how fraught and debilitating game development can be, thanks to creators and developers speaking about their experiences. Whether it's corporations laying off loyal teams while claiming the copyright to their original projects or indie developers running into obstacles while raising funds or doing a Kickstarter, the effects become clear.

My biggest wish is for the Glory Society to take care of their health and recover nicely. They gave me a story that comforted me over the years.

THE RULE OF JENNY PEN: AGING AND ITS HORRORS EXPLORED IN NEW SHUDDER FLICK WITH JOHN LITHGOW AND GEOFFREY RUSH

HOLLY LYN WALRATH

> "Life is precarious, happiness is fragile, triumph and disaster are only a random incident apart." — Owen Marshall

Real-life Horror Is Often Overlooked

It may seem slightly out of character for IFP to review a film about old men in a care home, but stick with me. In its world premiere at Fantastic Fest, *The Rule of Jenny Pen* is a psychological thriller that follows Stefan Mortensen (Geoffrey Rush), a respected judge who begins a new life in a residential care center when he has a stroke. There, he meets what seems to be an oddball group of elderly residents, each with their own strange quirks. The strangest of all is Dave Crealy, who, as one resident remarks, is one of those who has been given a doll (in this case, a terrifyingly eyeless puppet named Jenny Pen) as a comfort, like a child.

With exacting empathy, the film showcases the loss of humanity—both psychologically and physically—that often occurs when people are cared for by the thinnest margins. Set in New Zealand, the film fictionalizes a real-life horror for those shunted into under-resourced aged care centers, where oversight is small and accidents are ignored. We forget that the aged are often one of the largest populations of marginalized people today, and Indigenous elderly are often at the highest risk for abuse. Like many countries, New Zealand struggles to care for its aged, who make up 20% of its population. 38% of people over 65 die in care centers, and the situation has been called a human rights crisis, with several high-profile incidents gaining national attention. The film is set during the height of the COVID-19 pandemic, which feels like a fitting choice given how many people in aged care were particularly at risk.

As someone who has watched a loved one go through the stress of entering a nursing facility, I was struck by how carefully the film addresses the specific horrors that can occur. Horror is uniquely situated to comment on the realities of our world with empathy. The film does a fantastic job exploring the terror of dementia and illness: Loss of bodily autonomy, memory gaps, and, most importantly, the infantilization and disbelief people who cannot control their bodies often face. It quickly becomes clear that the residents are not strange because they are strange—they are doing everything they can to survive.

In the case of *The Rule of Jenny Pen,* this horror is exacerbated as the puppet-handed Crealy terrorizes the residents. Lithgow's performance here is delightfully creepy, heightened by the interjection of surrealist elements. At times, the doll becomes larger than life, looming in the background, forcing the audience to look into her eyeless sockets and fall under her judging gaze.

This sounds quite bleak, but the film does a good job of pairing humor with pain while still not making fun of the characters. It is Māori actor George Henare who steals the show as Garfield, Mortensen's friend and roommate. A former football player, he has, in his mind, lost his honor by submitting to Crealy's abuse. The absolute best scene of the film shows Garfield attempting to perform the Haka, a traditional war dance, but struggling as his voice and body fail him.

Based on a Short Story

The Rule of Jenny Pen is based on a short story by New Zealand author Owen Marshall, who also worked with director James Ashcroft on Coming *Home in the Dark (Light in the Dark Productions,* 2021). In Marshall's story, Crealy is the main point of view character, telling the story in his voice versus in the voice of Stefan Mortensen. The film follows the story faithfully, the only exception being that it gives Crealy a sketched backstory that verges on surrealism.

The best horror looks terror in its face and does not judge it; it merely provides an awareness of it. *The Rule of Jenny,* which does have a scene of sexual assault, is not for everyone. However, it is worth a watch for its stellar performances and fascinating cinematography. The film will be streaming on Shudder soon.

INTERVIEWS

HORROR'S REAL-LIFE FINAL GIRLS: WOMEN IN HORROR ON SURVIVING PUBLISHING

LEE MURRAY

> "Given that the odds are against us, how exactly do we become that 'final girl' who survives to tell her story, to borrow film scholar Carol J. Clover's iconic term? What strategies will help women writers prevail and thrive in their writing careers?"

More than once, I've considered giving up writing. I wouldn't be the first woman to fall by the wayside. Writing is a tough gig, as brutal as any slasher movie, full of sinister villains hellbent on eviscerating you and leaving you to bleed out while they move on to their next victim. The assault is relentless. There are new platforms, publishing models, and literary trends to follow. Writing techniques to learn. Deadlines to meet. So you achieve your daily word count? You still need to write a blog, update your website, and maintain your subscriber list. It's exhausting.

Even when we succeed and get our work out into the world, women writers typically receive less media coverage and lower earnings on average than our male counterparts. "The difficulties [women] face in receiving review coverage within the flood of fiction hitting the market makes it harder for them to sustain an income, and ultimately a career, as a professional writer," writes Danuta Kean, author of The Emilia Report, a British study examining the gender gap in literature. Inspired by a stage play on the life and work of England's first published female poet, Emilia Bassano, the report found that four hundred years on, "women still aren't provided with an equal platform to men upon which their work can be judged." However, the study's author rejects the myth of the "pram in the hallway being the enemy of promise." Instead, Kean says, "It's about structures being created in a way that militates against women being able to be recognized for their creativity."

It's enough to make anyone throw up their hands and surrender. So given that the odds are against us, how exactly do we become that 'final girl' who survives to tell her story, to borrow film scholar Carol J. Clover's iconic term? What strategies will help women writers prevail and thrive in their writing careers?

One answer might be to write horror. As a genre, horror is transgressive: subversive even. Horror demands that we ignore our better judgment and tread those dark alleys. Swallow your fears, it tells us. Step off the path and into the woods. It's a route we know well and the reason women have formed the backbone of the genre from its very inception. In their introduction to *Monster, She Wrote: The Women Who Pioneered Horror and Speculative Fiction*, Lisa Kröger and Melanie R. Anderson explain: "Women are accustomed to entering unfamiliar spaces, including territory they have been told not to enter. When writing is an off-limits act, writing one's story becomes a form of rebellion and taking back power."

Taking back power. Could it be that the genre itself lends strength to women writers? I asked some colleagues for their views.

Angela Yuriko Smith, double Bram Stoker Award® winner, author of *Bitter Suites*, and the publisher of *Space & Time Magazine*, leads by telling me she shouldn't be writing. "I was once told girls shouldn't write horror. 'Girls are for getting scared, not scaring,' a man said. I didn't believe it, but I did little to disprove it at the time.

"Up until my late thirties, I was often afraid. There were the usual fears—spiders, ghosts, serial killers, crowds—but I was also afraid of being an author. Since my first ghost story in second grade, I wanted to make a career of writing. If I failed, I was certain I failed as a person.

"I have been told all my life why being an author is a terrible idea. I think people meant well, but the advice was based on fear. Fear can be a healthy thing. It freezes us, hides us, and keeps us safe. I didn't want to be safe. I wanted to be published, but fear kept me immobilized.

"Everything changed when I learned that fear makes great fuel. It keeps us wide awake on watch, running long past our limits, and inspires hyper-awareness. I learned to convert my fear of failing into action. It drives me to hone my craft, produce more, and explore new ideas," Smith says.

Australian Shadows Award-winner and editor of Bram Stoker Award®-nominated essay collection *A Vindication of Monsters*, **Claire Fitzpatrick** maintains that writing body horror gives her the strength to "kick down the door" after a lifetime of rejection.

"Ever since I was diagnosed with epilepsy at twelve, I've been told I can't do things," she writes. "No going to Grade 8 camp. No going to discos. No playing sports. No getting a learner's license. No having baths. No using the iron if I'm in the house alone. No eating grapefruit. No being a pilot or joining the army. No. No. No. No. No.

"Epilepsy isn't just having seizures, it's being constantly rejected by your friends, rejected by your peers, rejected by society. Thankfully, the one area in which I'm not often rejected in is my writing. I grew up with so many doors shut in my face, I knew I had to kick down the door myself and throw myself in the deep end, otherwise, I'd end up failing, and failing in my writing career has never been an option for me.

"My tip for women—if it is a tip—is to use your struggles, your doors in faces, your fears, and turn them into strengths, and just write. Don't be afraid to do something just because the world thinks you can't. Life's too short. Just flippin' write."

Kröger and Anderson are clearly on to something when they say writing horror is an act of rebellion: Smith and Fitzpatrick not only brandish their fears as weapons to cut through what they've been told they can't but also to write themselves out of a place of unease, to take back their power.

"For me," says Fitzpatrick, "body horror is where it's at because it's how I deal with my epilepsy and the depression that comes along with it."

Smith agrees. "There are a million and one reasons to let fear freeze us," she says. "Here's my advice: give your muse a flamethrower and let her light up your fears. Create with those ashes. Repeat daily."

A slow learner, I came late to the horror genre myself. Drawn in by that "write what you know" adage, and having previously completed twenty-two marathons, I cut my writing teeth on a chick-lit novel incorporating running, romance, and reality TV. It was pure light-hearted escapism, the book's plot events involving wardrobe malfunctions, muddy tumbles, and cupcake deprivation. The book also served as an invaluable learning tool, teaching me about the craft, markets, how to botch a book cover. Most importantly, I learned I wasn't destined to be a chick-lit writer, and not out of any disdain for the genre, but because I didn't want to write escapist stories.

I realized that at my core, I wanted to address the things that terrified me, to confront those issues head on. Subjects like racism and post-colonialism, the impact of climate change, economic and technological uncertainty. Earthquakes. Ageism. Otherness. Anxiety. It's a long list. And in order to explore these complex themes, it made sense to me to turn to horror, a genre which my Australian colleague Deborah Sheldon, the award-winning author of *Perfect Little Stitches and Other Stories*, describes in a Kendall Reviews blogpost as "the most authentic type of fiction. It mirrors life as it really is—unfair, unjust, unpredictable, ultimately lethal—rather than the way we wish it could be . . . Horror fiction reminds us that, yes, we're all in this together, the only way this is going to end is in death, and it's okay to be frightened."

"Writing horror is a wonderful platform to elevate these problems and decimate them with words," says Fitzpatrick.

HWA Lifetime Achievement Award winner, the legendary **Linda D. Addison** agrees that to succeed, we need to feel that our work is relevant and authentic. "It's important to write from what speaks to you," insists the award-winning author of *How to Recognize a Demon has Become Your Friend.* "Don't feel driven by being a woman to avoid harsh storylines, be a human writing the story/poem that needs to be told."

Addison also offers advice about writing your best work and owning it. "Many years ago, I spoke with a well-known science fiction woman writer about using a pen name (L.D. Addison) instead of my full name (Linda D. Addison) because I was concerned that editors would assume my main character was female because of my first name. Her answer to me was to write well enough so that wouldn't be an issue. I took that answer to heart and have since concentrated on making sure my final manuscript is written as well as possible. This means increasing my edit skills, editing myself as much as I can, and then getting second editing eyes on my work before sending it out."

A five-time Bram Stoker Awards® winner, Addison needn't worry her work isn't up to scratch, and she isn't alone in that, as my compatriot, author **Marty Young**, observes: "There are a hell of a lot of female novelists out there writing kick-ass horror stories, the equal to anything a male has ever written. Anyone who thinks that women are not capable of writing horror with as much style and punch (both visceral and emotional) as male writers is sadly ignorant of the truth."

"It often feels like the rest of the world doesn't see us," says Fitzpatrick.

Acclaimed UK writer-editor **Marie O'Regan** agrees. "I think the most important thing for a woman in the horror genre is to make your voice heard, and not to let yourself get discouraged."

It's not so much that we're not heard, it's that when there are men in the vicinity, we're often erased from the conversation. I write a supernatural crime-noir series called The Path of Ra with my long-time friend and colleague Dan Rabarts. Equal partners in all our collaborations, Dan's name appears first on the book covers, a conscious decision on our part because the name Rabarts is more distinctive than Murray and therefore, we hope, easier for readers to remember. We also share the promotional tasks. However, when I am the one sending out emails, if a response comes from someone who doesn't know me personally, it is invariably addressed 'Dear Dan' even when my name is listed first as the correspondent, and my obviously female avatar appears at the top of the page. Since Lee is more commonly a man's name, it's as if they see my photo and decide they'll speak to the man instead. Dan does what he can to redress this within the bounds of politeness, but I'm no damsel in distress, and it isn't his role to defend me. Still, O'Regan is right: it's hard not to be discouraged.

I recently discovered an online site called worldometers.info, which provides real-time statistics based on UNESCO data. The figures for book titles published in just the first few weeks of 2024 are fascinating: 435,300 new titles when I accessed it on 26 February 2024. In the few minutes I was online, the number increased by a dozen titles. If making ourselves heard in this deluge of new books isn't daunting enough, there is a gender disparity in the media coverage received for those works. In the Emilie Report, for example, Kean notes that new books by men garnered 56% of review coverage—12% more than their female counterparts.

Moreover, Kean reports that "assumptions that an increase in the number of women reviewers would result in an increase in the number of women reviewed are based on a false correlation. Which means this bias is inherent and systematic. Does that same inequality apply to conference and panel invitations, and anthology invites? Selection panels for awards and stipends? What about the "best of" lists?

On Halloween 2019, bestselling author Jeff VanderMeer made a post on his social media: "*Annihilation* made another top 10 horror books of the decade list. But the list is all men, so I'm not going to link to it. The idea that no women wrote anything good enough to crack a top 10 of the decade is ridiculous."

A small gesture perhaps, but the response was resounding. Women especially were grateful for his solidarity. In our 'final girl' analogy, perhaps VanderMeer's stance is akin to a character not revealing the heroine's hiding place when the killer enters the room. While surrounding ourselves with people who acknowledge and support women's writing—sometimes at their own expense—doesn't fix the problem, it's a start. It makes us feel less alone.

A more effective strategy is to celebrate and showcase women's horror writing, as O'Regan attests: "When I edited *The Mammoth Book of Ghost Stories by Women,* it was because I kept seeing articles saying there were no female horror writers—and of course there were, there are, and there always have been. I wanted to address that and showcase what I thought were great examples in my favorite subgenre of ghost stories. There's a tendency for women to be quieter about their accomplishments, I think, although I have to believe it's improving, if slowly. We're brought up to 'be nice', to be supportive—where a man is determined and 'go-getting', those qualities haven't, historically, been encouraged in women or in young girls.

"As a woman, you have to keep putting your work out there, keep waving your hand to show you're there. Persist, in other words."

O'Regan's comment about the ghost stories subgenre is interesting. I wonder if it is easier to persist when we stick to the fringes where fewer writers dare to tread?

In Kean's study, when discussing the reviews, Susan Hill, author of the gothic thriller *The Woman in Black,* says, "My crime novels are only ever reviewed under genre, which is normal. But very often [they're] banded together with other women crime writers. The ghost stories are different as not so many people write them and they seem to be treated separately, reviewed by both men and women."

Kröger and Anderson make the point that "society doesn't always pay attention to what's happening on the edges."

In an example from my own work, before writing *Into the Mist*, there were few, if any, horror thrillers set in the New Zealand context. There was no local kaiju fiction and nothing incorporating our Māori mythology and culture. As a result, I was able to create a space for myself before anyone else moved in. The same applies in my Path of Ra collaboration with Dan Rabarts, where I write the rigorous Chinese scientific consult Penny Yee, and Dan writes her broody and impetuous little-brother-by-whangai with Māori and otherworldly parentage. As far as we could tell, nothing of its kind had been written before, so we were the first to the bleachers. In fact, in a letter written on our behalf, publisher Jennifer Barnes said: "The characters are loosely based on the cultural and work experience of the authors themselves. These are unique perspectives, and they are probably the only such writing team in existence." It seems that by writing in the fringes of what is already a transgressive genre, not only is there space for new subgenres and forms of writing, but we also open the door to a diversity of perspectives.

Larissa Glasser is the author of *F4*, a novella that stretches the realms of bizarro horror and which one reviewer claims "seamlessly integrate[s] a story about gender politics and a story about giant monsters and evil corporations into one damn impressive book." I asked her for her views.

Glasser replied: "The final girl triumphs at the end, bloodied and harried, but she stands alone. Her friends and family have all been iced. But she still triumphs. As a visible queer and trans woman facing a universe of bigotry, I write horror and its creative/destructive impulse as a coping mechanism, to channel trauma and embarrassments of my life into something I can try to understand. But I don't want to stand alone—I deal with exclusion and isolation enough in real life that I need other trans women like me to fight for and with. I don't want to be ahead of any of them, but I don't want to be left behind, either. Although writing is a solitary activity, it explodes into the world when we put ourselves out there, and we have to try and keep a balance between vulnerability and assertiveness. Fighting for the mere right to exist is a horrific concept in and of itself, but I really look to history rather than politics. I look to other trans writers who also put themselves out there, and that helps keep me alive and hold my own work to a higher standard. Sure, we write for an audience, but we start with ourselves. That impulse keeps us alive and fighting."

Glasser's comments about "not wanting to stand alone" and needing others "to fight for and with" are insightful since they highlight a problem I have with the 'final girl' concept where a plucky protagonist survives through her own resourcefulness but *at the expense of all the other characters*. In my experience, women like to work together, and in doing so, we amplify each other's voices.

In a Forbes article by Shelley Zilas, Sider CEO Jocelyn Greenky says: "Now that so many more women are entering the workplace, we're finding our voice. We're also building circles of trust with one another because we may be experiencing similar hurdles and have each other's backs."

This same phenomenon is apparent in the horror community. "Once you find yourself within the inner circle, you discover a horde of wonderful women writing terrifying things," says Fitzpatrick.

Author and screenwriter, **Rena Mason**, arguably one of the most hardworking and connected women in horror, recommends going a step further and rolling up our sleeves. "As a woman in any community, including the workplace, I've always felt that if I'm dissatisfied with discrepancies and want to see changes occur, I'm going to have to do what I can to make those changes happen," says the three-time Bram Stoker Award® winner. "One of the ways I've found that gives me a voice within a community is volunteering. Over the years, I've participated in, and have spearheaded several committees. In a couple of cases I was the 'final girl' in the sense that I was the only woman and/or the only minority among the chairs. It was difficult putting myself forward, but I felt so strongly about having that voice and seeing changes made, I overcame my fear and anxieties and spoke up. It hasn't been easy and there have been many controversies, but seeing some positive end results of all the hard work and time spent have made my efforts worthwhile.

"One of the quotes that keeps me going when I'm feeling defeated in my tasks is: 'When you are laboring for others, let it be with the same zeal as if it were for yourself.'—Confucius."

Whether by accident or design, all of the women I contacted while writing this essay are actively working to improve the situation for other women writers. Addison makes a point of telling me how proud she is to have devoted a large amount of her writing time to co-editing a horror anthology of fiction and poetry by thirty-three African American women titled *Sycorax's Daughters* with Kinitra Brooks PhD and Susana Morris PhD, a book which went on to become a Bram Stoker Award® finalist. "I needed the world to see that there were more than just a couple of Black women in horror," she says." In fact, all the women I spoke to have curated anthology projects in support of women authors. They've mentored emerging writers. They review, blurb, and signal boost work written by female colleagues. They invite other women to join them on panels (and do their best to let them get a word in edgewise). Several have convened major national and international conventions. Those who are publishers and editors actively advocate for representation of women at all levels. Writers like Kröger and Anderson have focussed their attention on celebrating the contribution of women to the horror genre, also pointing out contemporary horror writers we should be reading. And it is exactly the right approach, according to Zalis: "Raising each other up and channelling the power of collaboration is truly how we'll change the equation."

This collaborative model comes with a caveat to women to protect themselves from collaboration overload, since to save others, a 'final girl' must first save herself.

We need survivors.

"When it feels like the world is going to hell in a handbasket, there's catharsis to be found in a horror film where the final girl fights off the bogeyman," says film critic Katie Walsh.

Yes, there will be days when surviving to tell the story is enough, because as Maya Angelou reminds us, "Each time a woman stands up for herself, without knowing it possibly, without claiming it, she stands up for all women."

THE SONICS OF STORYTELLING: INTERVIEW WITH PREMEE MOHAMED, AUTHOR OF BENEATH THE RISING, THE SIEGE OF BURNING GRASS, THE BUTCHER OF THE FOREST, & MORE

R. THURSDAY

IFP writer R. Thursday has had the privilege of meeting and interviewing a range of nerd royalty from R.A. Salvatore, to Jane Yolen, to Seanan Maguire, and more, and we can say with confidence, Premee Mohamed may be the coolest one yet. If you're not familiar with her work, close whatever you're reading this on, go to your local bookstore (or library!), and get everything she's ever written. There is something for everyone: comedy, fantasy, horror, upsettingly plausible dystopias, and wildly fantastic adventures, and more than one story that manages to be all of these at once. Whether rooted in science or folklore, regardless of length, a Premee Mohamed story blooms with vibrant language, exquisitely described settings, and a deep understanding of what it means to make choices in imperfect worlds. And if you're still not convinced (how?!), let her brilliant responses to R. Thursday's overly-nested questions win you over.

INTERSTELLAR FLIGHT PRESS: I wanted to start with a collection of questions about your writing process because you've published all prose lengths, from flash to novels.

When you start developing a new story, do you already know roughly how long it will be?

PREMEE MOHAMED: Tough question! Or trick question, haha. These days, if I'm writing my own idea (very infrequently, unfortunately), I generally decide that right away. You can take literally any idea and cut it down to a flash or build it out to a novel, if you're careful about what you include and leave out. I ask myself what's the minimum I would need to illustrate the idea via characters and events, then I ask myself (much more seriously, sitting myself down) whether I want to explore any side-branches from that minimum and whether they would add to the story or take away from it.

But the short answer is "Yes, because I'm being solicited or I've already sold the idea." So 95% of the time right now, the 'how long will it be' question has been answered for me and is completely out of my hands. All I can do is be conscious of how much development I do with the idea, so I can try to keep it appropriate to the length without thinking afterward, "Ugh, I wish I had had more space."

IFP: Is there generally a point in the writing process where you feel confident something is more a novelette than a short story, for example? Does that affect the way you write or edit it?

PM: It's generally at the start—I used to have a problem with things getting out of control because my natural length is novel (I want everything to be a novel; ideally, I want everything to be a 400,000-word novel). Before I begin drafting, it's not so much that I have a sense of how long something will be, but more that I have a sense of how much leeway I'll give it. For many stories, if I start and I feel I want more room, I'll give it more room; for others, I'll be like, "Nope, no, stay in your box." But that almost always happens at the outline stage, not while I'm drafting.

IFP: Connected to the "how do you manage the length of a text," I wanted to ask about your worldbuilding, which is always one of my favorite aspects of reading your writing. I personally find your work very character-driven, but even in shorter works with less space to go into huge detail about the environment, I think you do an incredible job using economy of language to get across significant "vibes" of the setting.

PM: (Aww, thank you!)

IFP: What are your favorite elements of worldbuilding?

PM: I particularly love physical setting (as I think is evident from my books, haha). The geography, geology, weather, plants, animals, features like rivers and mountains. Those, to me, are the most fun to make up, and I think they add not . . . verisimilitude exactly but sort of a patina of authenticity. We see that in non-speculative fiction as well—the tense scene in a spy novel in Berlin where one of the men sitting on the bench notices a robin in a tree, a scene in a historical fiction novel with meticulously researched roses in a nobleman's garden, a boar hunting scene, things like that. It's local colour but it's also not, it helps ground the characters in where they are and what they're doing, and then that helps ground the reader too. We do notice the physical, biological world around us, and I love trying to show that in my fiction, even at shorter lengths. I'm very envious of authors who do great, detailed worldbuilding about clothing or food or language or things like that. For me, those are much harder than just making up like . . . a new bird.

IFP: In general, do you start with a strong idea for a character (or set of characters) and then create the situation they find themselves in, or does the premise or world/environment develop first, then the characters?

PM: Most of the time, I start with the idea! That can be sparked a variety of different ways, so the next steps often depend on what gave me the initial idea —something I've read, like a news article or something from another novel or book I'm reading, or an image or a song or another piece of media (or, as with *The Butcher of the Forest,* a brief moment of a dream!). But I almost always start with the idea and then ask myself, "Who do I want to help me illustrate this idea?" which then helps me decide the other parameters around the story, like length, pacing, worldbuilding, voice, tone, atmosphere, structure, etc. I imagine it's like casting a play (which I've never done). Do I think one or two people is enough to let me explore the idea as far as I want? Maybe that's a flash. Do I want more people, do I want scenery changes, maybe a chorus or a voice-of-God coming from the ceiling? How many people do I want to speak? Who do I want them to speak to, and for how long? How many to do something without speaking? How many just to appear and not say or do anything? I guess to mix metaphors, I view characters as the building blocks of a story, so I'll need as many as my blueprint has called for, arranged in the various ways that will make them into a useful and functional building. Too few isn't ideal, too many isn't ideal, and characters that aren't doing their jobs are also not ideal. But we don't have a story of any length without them.

IFP: What are some considerations you take in regarding word choice, language style, formal versus informal terms, etc?

PM: I'm generally not too conscious of those considerations until I'm done with the thing and am at the revisions stage! I tend to outline the actual "things happening" of the story (event A causes event B, B causes C, the characters panic, and event D results, etc), but as for the language, the voice, the vibes, that's something I tend to write into. So I guess I am a planner for things happening and a pantser for the voice? I will say I want the voice to fit the story (like, a lot a lot a lot), and it bothers me almost at once (like, during the drafting phase) if the voice feels wrong for what I'm writing—the examples of my work that I used the other day in a talk about dialogue were a cyberpunk bounty hunter story (from *The Reinvented Detective*) versus *The Apple-Tree Throne* (a novella set around 1899 in England). The voice and style, the language choices, the vocabulary, the slang, etc., etc., etc., even who speaks to whom and when they speak and what forms of address, etc., they use, they aren't interchangeable, and they shouldn't be. Both stories need their own distinct, unique, and appropriate voice. I'm weirded out by people who insist that writers need to find 'their voice' in their fiction—because surely, unless you're writing the same book again and again and again, your voice is different from book to book?? The individual story has a voice, not the writer. Maybe I'm way off-base there.

But anyway, what a story sounds like is far more important to me than whether it makes sense or not (SORRY EDITORS), and I'm pretty deliberate, at least in revisions, in trying to make sure that that sound is consistent from the start to the finish of the work, and that it fits the genre or sub-genre of story I'm trying to tell. And that's mostly intuitive, I'm going by ear rather than logic, so (for example, in *The Apple-Tree Throne*) I might go back in later and do things like correct vocabulary, slang, idioms, etc, to fit better with the story, because I can't distract myself with individual words while I'm drafting for sound. Often, in a first draft, I'll write three or four iterations of a similar sentence, then in revisions, I'll delete the extraneous ones or mush a few of them together so there's just one left. (This is partly why I don't worry about wordcount as a marker for progress; if I'm doing the 'similar sentence' thing a dozen times in a chapter, and all the unneeded sentences are getting deleted later, wordcount isn't a useful marker for me because there are going to be *so* many excess words.)

IFP: Who did you grow up reading, and how do you feel that has impacted your writing?

PM: A lot of Diane Duane, Lloyd Alexander, Terry Pratchett, Monica Hughes, Barbara Hambly, and stuff from the giant omnibuses (omnibi?) that I sometimes got from library book sales—Edgar Allan Poe, Edgar Rice Burroughs, and Robert E. Howard. As I got older, more Ursula K. Le Guin, William Faulkner, William S. Burroughs, Umberto Eco (as soon as I discovered him I started munching through his books like a woodchipper), Gene Wolfe, all the Russian authors I could find (poetry and fiction, so lots of Vasily Grossman, Tolstoy, Pushkin, Akhmatova, Mayakovsky, Dostoevsky, whoever was around), Robert Graves, China Mieville more recently, Christopher Priest, Ismail Kadare. Honestly, a lot of the reading I did as a kid, though, was reading the same book again and again and again, like taking it out of the library six or eight times in one year—*The Green Book* by Jill Paton Walsh was one I did that with literally until I moved out of my parents' house and bought my own copy, and same with *Watership Down* and *Dr. Zhivago* (which I now have in two different translations for some annoying reason) and a half-dozen or so other books where I've never read anything by the author except that one book.

I think the main influence of my reading while I was growing up was helping me to realize that imitating *one* writer, even if I really loved that writer, was actually an incredibly boring thing to do. (I was writing a lot as a kid, finished my first novel when I was twelve or thirteen, and of course, it was a blatant and terrible *Lord of the Rings* ripoff, as much of my previous work had been). The more I read, the more I realized there was more out there to read (I would hunt down books mentioned in the acknowledgments or indexes of books by authors I liked, so I could read who they had read), and it really broadened my horizons in terms of letting me see what fiction could do, what you could do in a story and still have it work. The stuff we were reading in my English classes in school, aside from being subject matter that usually didn't interest me (the actual content is usually the least interesting thing for me about a book), was always very standard in its structure and format. I get that they were trying to teach us writing rules so that we could use them appropriately, but I got bored easily. It was validating to know that you could literally just write *whatever you wanted*, use whatever shape, timeline, voice, point of view, structure, language, etc, that you wanted ('Naked Lunch,' anybody?), and it could still be a wonderful book. A novel didn't have to look like every other novel unless you wanted it to, and I found that very freeing.

IFP: What did you find yourself wanting to see more of in the stories you were consuming?

PM: No offense to Edgar Rice Burroughs (love you, buddy!), but better prose, generally. The number one thing that made me give up on a book was if the writing itself was boring. As a child I plugged through it even though I knew there was something dissatisfying about it, but as I got older, the dissatisfaction kind of turned to nails on a chalkboard. I would even take bad but vivid prose over very bland stuff. I wanted language that held my attention; I didn't care much what they were writing about. (I regret to report that this is still the case, and I put down something like 95% of books I start because the writing bores me.)

IFP: What characters did you find yourself drawn to, and how did that change over time?

PM: Definitely some kind of technical pro, I always loved those—witches, wizards, mages, scientists, academics, detectives. Anyone in a story that would say things like "Let's get to the bottom of this!" or "I'm going to try something here!" I mean, of course, we're all reading books to see how characters solve the problem that the plot presents them with, but I especially adored seeing people problem-solve by getting an ancient tome down from a shelf (or booting up a computer that had fried in the crash onto Mars or whatever). That hasn't changed much, I don't think? I still like a character who is a Knower Of Things, maybe a Holder Of Restricted Knowledge (or at least a Seeker of it). And I really love when we get very interior with those characters, get into their heads, explore their thought processes. So I guess I can add to my answer from above: one thing I wanted to see more of was what characters were thinking and feeling, rather than just doing. I can see what they're doing for myself! Let me into their heads! More roundedness, more dimension, more complexity in characters, that's always my jam. Fetter from Vajra Chandrasekera's recent novel 'The Saint of Bright Doors' comes to mind—he felt very real to me, every sentence in the book is by him or about him, and even at the end, I found myself thinking, "More! More Fetter!"

IFP: Speaking of characters, I'd love to hear about a few that absolutely live rent-free in my head. I especially love the character type that is 'A good person having to work for or within a bad system, absolutely terrified, but doing their best.' Jewel, from 'And What Can We Offer You Tonight', particularly resonated, but Veris Thorn from 'The Butcher of the Forest' and several others also have strands of this. What draws you to writing this kind of person?

PM: I wish I knew! (Maybe my therapist knows?) Genuinely, I think this is just who I keep coming up with as the most . . . I was about to say 'realistic,' but I think I mean to say 'relevant' character within the story ideas I keep having. (I don't think they're unrealistic, but we are discussing fiction, after all.) I think it's exactly like you said—if I want to write about a bad system, how useful is it for me to populate the story entirely with people saying, "The system is great!!"? Not very. But if I put people in the story who are able to say, "The system is actually not great," and can show us why, rather than just telling us, that's a story I'd rather write. I hope I'm not writing preachy, messagey stories or eighteenth-century morality plays; mainly I hope I'm writing stories where I'm presenting an unjust, inequitable, unworkable, calcified, or repressive society in an interesting way. I can't do that without characters who have something to push against, because it's the unequal application of force that makes for tension in a story.

I guess for me that's what's (a little bit) boring about old sword and sorcery stories—you know, there's a guy and he's got a problem, but he's also seven feet tall, he's a king, he knows how to use a sword, he's got an army, so we're reading the story to watch him succeed and there tends to not be a lot of uncertainty or tension in there. There's often a lot of violence and fighting, but there's no real conflict because we never doubt the outcome for our hero. I would like for people to doubt. And I want there to be some friction, some sparks, some pinch points, some grinding off of paint and squealing of metal as my characters navigate the world I've given them.

IFP: Is it a type you notice becoming more common, and if so, what do you think makes it appealing for current writers and readers?

PM: I do think so actually? And part of that is, now, authors are becoming not exactly more savvy but more, I guess, self-conscious about patterns and tropes and structures, and asking, "Can we do something other than the Hero's Journey?" It's not that there's anything wrong with the Hero's Journey, but if we've read 10,000 examples of it in our lives, we tend to feel hungry for something that pushes back against it or subverts it even a little bit. I'm seeing more characters acknowledging that they're not the full-autonomy-full-agency-full-driving-the-plot hero (which is a ridiculous idea anyway), that they're barely the main character of their own story (which is accurate), that the world is actually set up so that none of us have that much control over our lives (in fiction or in real life), and that there can be just as much interest and engagement and indeed dignity and nobility in acknowledging that and choosing to work within an imperfect system as there is in going on a quest and sticking a sword in it. (I want to shout out Vida Cruz's amazing essay in Fantasy here, "We Are The Mountain," which was life-changing for me in helping to articulate some very nebulous thoughts I had about this.)

I also enjoy the more complex situations we're seeing where not only is our main character succeeding or failing in community, but also highlighting the structures and institutions that allow or repress communities to form and continue. Simon Jimenez's book *The Vanished Birds* comes to mind at once, same with Claire North's *Ithaca*. I think the appeal for readers is improved emotional engagement, which I love—we have people to cheer for and suffer with because they seem more real to us, their problems seem more real to us, no matter what setting they're presented in.

IFP: How do you navigate presenting complicated, pragmatic, relatable characters without feeling tangled in the #tooreal of it?

PM: I don't mind the tangling! I guess for me it's just a matter of going back in revisions (and working with my editor) to make sure that I'm staying close to the heart of the story, that the story is allowed to continue on its path. I always *want* to go deeper into certain characters, but I have to consider whether or not it'll help the story keep moving or have effects on other characters and their decisions and limitations. Sometimes, the detangling happens at the end, when the final work is looking most like a final work, and I can (sometimes regretfully) be like, "Oops, too many knots here," and snip them out or comb them out.

Quickfire round!

IFP: Are there any questions you have always wanted to be asked?

PM: Too many! I guess I would say very vaguely I wish more interviewers asked about specific characters, scenes, works, and about process—which we've done here, YAY—*rather than* about me. I don't care about me! I am very boring and this is 99% of most people's questions! I care about the work! Ask about the work!

[Editorial Note: Hearing authors nerd about their own writing is one of my favorite things, but our fact-checkers looked into it, and Premee is not, in fact, boring.]

IFP: When you need to step away from writing, what kinds of activities do you find renewing?

PM: ?? Step away from writing ??

IFP: Finally, who are you reading right now that's inspiring you?

PM: Vajra Chandrasekera is a big one! Doing some great stuff with setting, structure, and prose. Simon Jimenez ditto (I really need more books from him).

Nick Harkaway, big inspiration. Claire North. Re-reading Mary Stewart for the pure elegance of her Arthurian stories (I wish I'd discovered those much earlier in life!). And a ton of short fiction in various anthologies (enjoying 'Never Whistle At Night' right now)!

Thanks so much to Premee Mohamed for responding so thoughtfully and authentically and for being an absolute delight.

About the Author

Premee Mohamed is a Nebula, World Fantasy, Ignyte, and Aurora award-winning Indo-Caribbean scientist and speculative fiction author based in Edmonton, Alberta. She has also been a finalist for the Hugo, Locus, British Fantasy, British Science Fiction, and Crawford awards. In 2024, she was the Edmonton Public Library writer-in-residence. She is the author of the Beneath the Rising series of novels as well as several novellas. Her short fiction has appeared in many venues and she can be found on her website at www.premeemohamed.com.

THE GULF OF LONELINESS: AN INTERVIEW WITH LYNDSIE MANUSOS, AUTHOR OF FROM THESE DARK ABODES

ANNIKA BARRANTI KLEIN

> "There is bloody body horror, there is fantasy, there is mythology, there's gothic, there's romance, but they all play off of each other. It really is a revelry of all the genres I love and adore, and I hope that shows for readers."

There is nothing I love quite so much as a story about a house. I love the nice houses like Bag End and Villa Villekulla, of course, but I can't resist a house that is maybe, perhaps, just a tiny bit haunted. Hill House, Starling House, Thornfield, Manderley . . . and now, St. Edah's.

In *From These Dark Abodes* by Lyndsie Manusos (*Psychopomp*, September 17, 2024), Lethe and Petunia are unwilling inhabitants of a house with no exit, forced to serve Erinyes and her crew of voluntary exiles, all of them looking for solace from something in their pasts—but Lethe can't remember anything before they were in St. Edah's, and Petunia's memories are slippery. Every night, Erinyes and the others unzip their skins and engage in revelry, free from bodies and history and everything else. During the day, Lethe and Petunia search for a way out as their captors sleep. But when one of the inhabitants disappears, leaving his skin behind, Lethe and Petunia must search for him, and what they find raises more questions than it answers.

Lyndsie and I have been friends since 2019 and frequently trade writing to give feedback or simply encouragement (as needed). I got to read the first few thousand words of this book early in its writing and have been utterly enchanted from the very first. Now, it's a real book, and I've read it in its final form, and I am still utterly enchanted. I have taken full advantage of my friendship with Lyndsie to demand that she let me interview her for IFP, and she graciously agreed. Our conversation, very lightly edited, is below.

INTERSTELLAR FLIGHT PRESS (ANNIKA BARRANTI KLEIN): Hi! Thanks so much for chatting with me about *From These Dark Abodes*. It feels like it's simultaneously been five minutes and one hundred years since you first sent me the early pages, way back when you started writing it. I'm so excited that it's out now as a real book!

LYNDSIE MANUSOS: Thank you so much for having me, Annika. Oh my goodness, that is so true. It feels like a hundred years ago when I began writing it, while my youngest child was still an infant. Now she's starting preschool and it's like, what is time?

IFP: This book does a lot in a small package! You explore many themes, but to me, more than anything else, it's about the enormous gulf of loneliness that can accompany becoming a parent, especially for the first time. Can you tell me a bit about how your experience of motherhood informed this story?

LM: The gulf of loneliness is the perfect way to describe it. Of course there is this overwhelming joy in becoming a parent, this unquenchable love. But parenting—even parenting with a village—can be extremely lonely. Your identity is filtered down to this single role as a caregiver, and as such, you set your identities aside to nurture life. It's a beautiful, worthwhile sacrifice, but absolutely a sacrifice.

I began writing the bones of this story while in the thick of that complexity. My youngest was not a great sleeper in her first months. She mostly slept when held or when in the baby carrier. And when you're sleep deprived, everything is magnified. Additionally, there was a sudden death in the family a few months after my youngest was born. So there's this juggling of life and death, joy and grief. I had a lot of health-related anxieties, and I needed an outlet. I needed a place to pour these emotions into to process it, which in a way was reclaiming my identity as a writer. From all of that, the story of *From These Dark Abodes* was born.

IFP: The *bones* of this story. Nice. (Sorry.) There's a lot of influence from mythology here, from character names to bigger concepts to, well, major spoilers. The Greek influences are the most obvious, and I'd love to know if you have a personal connection to any of those—but I'm also curious if you pulled from other myths and stories that might not be as obvious to a modern US reader.

LM: Yes, much of this story has nods to Greek mythology. I am part Greek on my Dad's side, so I have great respect and love for Greek mythology and culture. Regardless of what mythology anyone is inspired to write about, it's important that that inspiration is utilized with appreciation and nuance. Greek mythology is very "trendy" in fiction, and there's a lot of complications with that trend, which I wrote about in a Book Riot article that's very dear to me. I didn't want to write a trendy story.

From These Dark Abodes has lesser-known characters from Greek mythology that I wanted to explore, and these characters try to create an underworld for themselves because theirs misunderstood and exploited them. Layered with that, I wanted to create the idea that there are multiverses of gods and immortals, from underworlds we have not even fathomed. So, for some characters, I did not use direct mythology so much as delved into the etymology of their name and/or hinted at a possible mythology.

IFP: I adore that, and I think you absolutely succeeded. I want to talk about so many specifics, but they're all super spoiler-y! So let's talk about the house itself. You seem to be referencing not only mythology but the gothic tradition in St. Edah's, which is so ambitious, but you totally pull it off. My elevator definition of the gothic is "the past haunting the present," and you have somehow succeeded in creating a haunted house that is haunted by its occupants. How did you decide on the specific rooms and their distinct personalities? Did you build the house one room at a time as you wrote, or plan it out first?

LM: Oh, Annika, this is a brilliant question. You absolutely nailed it with the house—I wanted St. Edah's to be haunted by its occupants, who are haunted by their own pasts, and so the house feeds off of that. It'd be nice to say that I knew what I was doing when building this place, at first, but I discovered much of it along with the characters. Erinyes's rooms and the parlor are very much in her image, on what she believes a place of revelry and luxury should be. Her past was rigid and violent, so she wants luxury, she wants ease, and the gothic style is perfect because she still can't escape that violence.

I imagine the library and conservatory as places of refuge. St. Edah's as a whole is a refuge for immortals, but I wondered what rooms might appeal to mortals. The conservatory and library are examples of humanity and the organic.

We (I say we but also mean me) often use cellars/basements/attics as storage for the past, where we put items that we don't know what to do with. I wanted the cellar in St. Edah's to embody this to the most unsettling degree. It's a place of memories, items that immortals wouldn't know nor want to contend with. And what's something we always fear to find in the cellar? There's already monsters in the house, so I also used a rat to the most unsettling degree possible, too.

IFP: The *rat*, though. Oh my goodness. You somehow created a character who will automatically trigger a sense of unease, if not outright disgust, and then you gave him the role of . . . not quite mentor, but he delivers information/exposition, revealing a hint of what's really going on to Lethe, who can't remember. So good! Did you have other ideas for how she would begin to learn St. Edah's secrets, or was this another piece that just fell into place?

LM: These questions! Amazing! Writing the initial draft while postpartum with my second child (very sleep-deprived, very not demure), I was discovering a good portion of this story along with Lethe and Petunia. The first chapter was very clear to me, but then I had to peel back much of the stakes, the house, and what secrets Lethe was hiding. My rat of unusual size came about in my mind at the same time Lethe and Petunia discovered him. It was a delightful surprise, and it allowed me to play with the expectations of the house and its occupants. It also presented a way to impart information, which allowed the story to grow in a way I didn't expect.

IFP: I love this because it has so many layers of discovery—you as the writer, Lethe and Petunia as the characters, and now us as the readers. So perfect. For my last question about the book, I'm turning it around: what is something you wish I would ask, or something you'd like to talk about that we haven't covered?

LM: Ooo, this is a tough question because you already mentioned the things I find most important and/or enjoyable to talk about. One particular thread about this journey that might be fun to ponder is how to think of this story in terms of genre. After finishing this story, I was worried it was too in-between and across genres to fit anywhere. I had two horror editors look at this story, and they gave great feedback, but it wasn't quite horror *enough* for them, and billing it as a fantasy or dark fantasy—while totally true—also doesn't quite describe it in full. There is bloody body horror, there is fantasy, there is mythology, there's gothic, there's romance, but they all play off of each other. It really is a revelry of all the genres I love and adore, and I hope that shows for readers.

IFP: Revelry is the perfect word! For my last question, can you tell us a little bit about your experience of being published by a small press? Both the process and how it's felt for you as an author with your first book publication?

LM: Oh it's been a wonderful experience. Kind of going off of the previous question, this story is a mix of many genres, and what I love about Psychopomp is their unflinching support of genres. I was previously published in *The Deadlands* with a story titled "Immolatus," which, similar to *From These Dark Abodes*, I feared wouldn't fit in anywhere. Sean and Elise saw both of these works and embraced the weirdness without question. And during the editing process, Elise encouraged me to stay in the moment, to really push the emotion and sensory details. I never felt held back in any way. I always felt seen, heard, and accepted. This story really bloomed with Psychopomp's help, and I am very grateful for such a personal and encouraging experience.

About the Author

Lyndsie Manusos's work has appeared in LeVar Burton Reads, The Deadlands, Lightspeed Magazine, and other publications. Her debut novella, FROM THESE DARK ABODES, recently released from Psychopomp. She lives in Indianapolis with her family, works as an indie bookseller, and writes for Book Riot. You can read more at lyndsiemanusos.com.

POETRY AS ACTIVISM AND HEALING IN "SALT CHORUS": AN INTERVIEW WITH DOMINIQUE ROSSI

LESLIE ARCHIBALD

Dominique Rossi, Attorney, legislative assistant, and poet, resides in Oregon and spends her days serving the public as a legislative director in the Oregon Senate. Outside of her legislative duties, she writes meaningful poetry that lends itself to activism and awareness. Her debut poetry collection, *Salt Chorus (Self-published, 2022),* inspired Leslie Archibald to take a deeper dive into climate change and how poets have a responsibility to write out loud and make their voices heard. The themes Rossi weaves throughout the collection are an activist's manifesto, a call to action, and a road map to healing. Leslie reached out to her to ask her a few questions about the collection, poetry as activism, and balancing public service and the intimacy of writing poetry.

INTERSTELLAR FLIGHT PRESS: I am always interested to know where titles come from. Can you talk a bit about the collection's title, Salt Chorus, and the poem from which it came?

DOMINIQUE ROSSI: *Salt Chorus* is a reference to family and reckoning with the fragments of inheritance you can't outgrow; in this case, mental illness. The phrase comes from the poem "I Come from a Long Line of Brains Miswired." I envisioned ancestors speaking to you and through you as a chorus. Voices you can't outrun but hope to make peace with. Salt felt fitting on a few levels, not only does the poem start in Sicily, but it also speaks to a tarnished perseverance.

IFP: The first poem in the collection, "Everything on Earth is Recycled Space Particles," transports us immediately over the rainbow to another world of color and the newness of spring and connects it to our very life force. Can you comment on why you chose this poem as the jumping-off point for the collection?

DR: I didn't set the order of this book until I got to the end. "Everything on Earth is Recycled Space Particles" felt like it set a guidepost for the reader; a heads up we are going to a lot of places in these pages.

IFP: As a fellow poet and nature writer, I am drawn to the environmental theme throughout *Salt Chorus*. How important is it that we poets keep highlighting climate change's effects on our world? Do you think anyone is listening?

DR: I vividly remember the first time I had a panic attack over the climate crisis; I was working at the Alaska Sea Life Center, and our scientists were presenting on how ocean acidification was decimating keystone species. That was fourteen years ago, and since then, climate grief has been a constant in my life. As artists, I think we have an obligation to bear witness. Poetry has the power to make pain palatable. If we keep creating spaces where people can reflect on it, they may be more likely to speak and act.

IFP: The tender and thoughtful connection between the speaker and the helpless creatures in "Burial" and "Twin Rabbits" resonates with such meaning. Was this intentional? Does it come from your life experiences, a love of animals, or is it something you created through an empathy for this helplessness?

DR: "Burial" and "Twin Rabbits" are both based on experiences engraved in my memory. For me, wildlife rehab and poetry are both conduits for empathy, a means to channel it so I don't break from the weight.

IFP: You currently serve as legislative director for the Oregon Senate President. Is your poetry a product of your position in the government or did the poetry inspire you to seek out a position where you could do more to affect change?

DR: I would say the drive to work as a public servant comes from a similar place as my poetry. Both help me to move forward; to not be paralyzed by injustice.

IFP: Does a professional position in law and government stifle your creativity? How do you disconnect from the important objectives of legislation to seek out and put together beautiful words?

DR: There are certainly days, weeks, and sometimes months when the exhaustion or stress of work makes it hard to do any creative writing. When I'm going through a dry spell and can't disconnect, I try to focus on reading to store up inspiration. Sometimes that inspiration conjures only a few words or at best a sentence. I keep an email thread of those fragments and come back to them when I'm ready to start writing again.

IFP: In "Queen of the Prairie," the speaker bows and shows the creature respect as an offering or submission to its authority. Can you talk about the need for humans to respect natural habitats and what you do to coexist with the natural world?

DR: There is an illusion created by our daily lives that we exist separate and distinct from nature. We don't see our food production, we live in temperature-controlled homes, few have seen the fibers that become their clothes. That disconnect feels so dangerous to me. Not only does it lead us to devalue the natural world, it hides how truly interdependent all living things are on this planet. I try to honor and remind myself of that connection in whatever ways I can. I turned my urban quarter acre into a micro-farm that includes free-range chickens, fruit trees, and native plants for pollinators. Of course, I recognize that I'm privileged to be able to do these things. My recommendation is to connect with nature in whatever small ways you can. For instance, when I lived in an apartment, I kept a windowsill garden with a small bird feeder. It all matters and can really boost your mental health.

IFP: This collection touches on themes of the environment, domestic abuse, health issues and trauma, recovery, and resilience. My questions have focused on the environment, but I am interested to know why you chose to weave all these themes (beautifully, I might add) into this collection. Can you talk a bit about what moved you to include these threads?

DR: I wrote this book over the course of two years, but I've been searching for a way to tell these stories for most of my life. It was important to include the various themes to remind myself and the reader that beauty and trauma are not mutually exclusive. Both women's lives and the natural world straddle that duality.

IFP: Fun Question: What is the last picture on your Instagram feed? What do you think it tells us about you?

DR: At the time of writing this, it is a work-in-progress photo of an embroidery project. The embroidery is in the shape of the Giant Pacific Octopus.

IFP: Can we expect to see more poetry from Dominique Rossi? Are you working on anything now that you can tell us about?

DR: I am just now starting to write again after some unexpected life twists set me back last fall. My poetry group was patient enough to let me take a hiatus, but we are picking back up this summer. The good news is I can feel the beginnings of a book brewing; I have so many new experiences and themes I'd like to explore. Maybe in 2026?

About the Author

Dominique Rossi is an attorney and political advisor. She has previously worked as a journalist and a domestic violence survivor advocate. Her articles have appeared in magazines including Bitch, Adbusters, and Northwest Travel. Rossi's hobbies include international travel, reading and embroidery. Originally from Chicago, she now lives in the Pacific Northwest with her partner, dogs, and chickens.

Salt Chorus is now available in print and digital here.

ADDICTION, FAMILY, AND POLITICAL INTRIGUE: INTERVIEW WITH SUSAN FOREST, AUTHOR OF THE ADDICTED TO HEAVEN SERIES

LISA TIMPF

Susan Forest's *Addicted to Heaven* series (*Laksa Media Groups,* 2019-2023) is an epic fantasy set in a richly imagined world called Shangril. The three novels to date, *Bursts of Fire, Flights of Marigold,* and *Gathering of Ghosts,* feature individuals called magiels, who have the power to perform magic. However, the books also deal with matters closer to our own mundane world, such as addiction, discrimination, and other social issues. Susan Forest took the time to share some insights with Lisa Timpf about the series.

INTERSTELLAR FLIGHT PRESS: C.S. Lewis's Narnia series was said to be inspired by an image of a faun carrying an umbrella and parcels in a snowy world illuminated by a nearby lamp-post. Can you pinpoint how the idea of Shangril/or the Addicted to Heaven series began for you?

SUSAN FOREST: I have a distinct memory of waking up in my tent on a camping trip with the incredible smell of the woods, the sound of the leaves fluttering in the trees, and the dappled sun on the grass through the open tent flap, thinking: so much epic fantasy is dark; I want to write a really fun romp.

I envisioned a character you haven't met yet, Kireen, doing aerial gymnastics to sneak into a medieval tower as a thief, and later, flirting with a rogue con man (Raoul, who shows up as a child in *Marigolds*). Of course, although the series has breathless excitement and the cons I envisioned, it also has its dark moments. You don't deal with addictions (or, for that matter, write an epic fantasy with gripping stakes) without going into dark territory.

IFP: Some fantasy books show people performing magic without it taking a toll of any kind. In the world of Shangril, magiels perform magic by altering the state of items in time. After performing magic, magiels live snippets of their lives in a different time than their current one. This can be potentially dangerous if they have to perform magic while on the run, because they can find their consciousness plunged into a past or future event while their physical body might be exposed to danger in the present. Was it important to you that magic exert a toll of some sort rather than coming for "free"? If so, why?

SF: Absolutely. Magic is always better with limits because a magic-user who is too powerful doesn't face significant obstacles in getting what they want—which reduces the stakes and the drama. Bad for fiction.

My characters have to think twice about using magic for a number of reasons: Will it help get them what they want? Not always, because the magic can only do certain things, and needed ingredients may be in short supply. Will they be safe afterward when paying the cost? Sometimes it's a choice between an urgent situation now, and facing the consequences later. So one of the upsides to magical limits includes making the characters use their wits, which is fun.

But in this particular case, having characters flip back and forth through their lifetimes—for only a few minutes at a time—gave me a great tool to reveal backstory dramatically to new readers (or refresh the story for people who read earlier books) and to foreshadow clues to drive curiosity about the rest of the book.

IFP: In some books, the lead characters are a group of friends or allies. You've chosen to make the key characters three sisters, and there are also brother/sister relationships among the Delarcans, who, after a political upheaval, end up ruling various kingdoms in Shangril. What advantages did you see in leveraging family dynamics as you developed your characters and plot?

SF: Family dynamics are huge, both in the loving sense of being willing to die for someone who is kin, and in the painful sense of feeling stabbed in the back by someone you thought was in your corner. Sibling ties are formed when a person is young, at a time when kids don't have a full understanding of the world and of relationships, this emotion is carried into adult relationships. Grudges can last a long time, and trust can be hard to re-forge after what one interprets to be a betrayal—and yet blood is thicker than water, so when push comes to shove, you stand by your sister. And that can forge new understandings.

Until characters are willing (or forced by the events of the story) to examine childhood incidents from an adult perspective, they themselves might be uncertain about whether they will stand by or abandon a sibling, so the reader is uncertain, too. The question always is: *what will she do?* And the reader has to turn pages to find out. This gives the story high drama—and, it's fun to write!

IFP: In an article on John Scalzi's website, you note that *Bursts of Fire* and the other books in the Addicted to Heaven series are "many things: a political epic, a family saga, a heist romp, a magical fantasy" as well as "a garden of exploration for big ideas." As a writer, what are the challenges of managing so many different threads?

SF: I like a book that has some meat to it, and especially when you are inventing a world out of whole cloth, you really need to dig into the details and underpinnings, not only to create that richness, but because it is *from* that world that your characters spring. It's my belief that all secondary world fantasy is either based on eras in our history, or can be enriched by what we learn from history and geography. So, yeah, I wanted each of the seven nations in Shangril to have different foods and songs and social expectations based on similar but differing beliefs, so I have an extensive "bible" of reference material to fill in the details.

Epic fantasy is almost always highly political, with wars fought over economic and ideological differences. Because I didn't want my antagonists to be one-dimensional villains, they had to have reasons for believing they were right. High King Huwen seems to be a tyrant, but all he wants to do is be a good king for his subjects by unifying the seven nations. Some people in the books believe passionately that kings are chosen by the Gods, and it is blasphemy for men to believe they should have a hand in government, while others are trying to establish democracy. Fear of magic has led to genocide and enslavement of magiels. Importation of goods from distant lands—through one, taxed, port—has led to wealth inequity, as has the introduction of new ideas such as textile factories, which upends the entire medieval way of life. Each of these social pressures creates obstacles for the characters to overcome. In other words, plot!

But your question is: how do I manage it? Clearly, the bible of reference materials and research into our own, human, history is key, as well as imaginative *what if* thinking. Additionally, in the plotting stage I ask *why now?* for every action and scene in the book: why does Rennika say, think, or do that, and why does she do it *now*? How is she responding to her sisters in the moment, but also, how is her response shaped by the multiple forces in her world, both current and in her past? In the revision stage, I double check that the thread factory introduced in one chapter is influencing where and how the peasants, merchants, and aristocrats are living in each of the subsequent chapters where these show up—and of course, how all of this affects the story's central actors.

IFP: Addiction is a key issue in the Addicted to Heaven series, and this plays out in different ways in different characters. In *Flights of Marigold*, Janat struggles with substance addiction, and her sister Meg tries to support her, sacrificing some of her own ambitions and desires in the process. Some scenes show how Janat's addiction impacts Meg. Others portray Janat's diffi-

culty in balancing her desire to abstain against the power of her cravings. Was it important to you to show addiction from multiple viewpoints?

SF: Absolutely. Commercial fiction, full of adventure, romance, and intrigue, is a wonderful vehicle to delve into important issues because it is fun to read and can gain traction with an audience. But it is super-important *not* to trivialize such issues through a superficial, black-and-white, good-bad treatment. These are medical issues that cause tremendous trauma in people's lives.

Coming from a family where addictions are a complex and sometimes intractable plight, I can see how personal, family, social, medical, and political barriers intensify the issues. Sometimes I really wish I knew the answer—as if there was a single answer. There isn't, and sometimes, like Meg feeling unsure about how to manage Janat, I feel helpless and wonder if my actions are helping or hurting. Fiction is a way to explore multiple answers to complex questions.

In my life, I've seen devastating outcomes, hopeful outcomes—both short and long term—and in some situations the jury is still out. I think all of that complexity should be reflected in the series, which is why this multifaceted theme needs seven books. The experiences of different characters are needed to show these different attitudes, choices, and outcomes.

IFP: *Bursts of Fire, Flights of Marigold,* and *Gathering of Ghosts* include book group discussion questions and an extensive list of resources in the event readers can consult if they or their loved ones are struggling with addiction or discrimination issues. What sparked the inclusion of this material in the books?

SF: This was a decision between myself and my publisher, *Laksa Media Groups*. Laksa's mission is to raise awareness of social issues ("To change the world, one book at a time"), and has produced award-winning SFF anthologies on mental health and mental illness (*Strangers Among Us*), caregivers and caregiving (*The Sum of Us*), and migrations (*Shades Between Us*), among others. So that's why my series was a good fit for Laksa: we both want to use story to raise awareness and open conversations to reduce stigma around these issues. It only made sense to provide the resources as well.

IFP: At the end of the books, there's a section titled "Why Mental Health and Anti-Discrimination Resources?" Here, you make the observation that including issues like addiction in epic fantasy can be a way of opening the dialogue, because we can see that even characters living in different places and times might struggle with the same issues we see in our daily lives. Why is it important to open the dialogue?

SF: No one wants to believe they are a failure and disappointment to those closest to them, but when society takes a moral attitude toward addictions, we imply that the individual is at fault. The resulting stigma and shame can drive these issues underground, where the person who is suffering fails to receive the medical attention they need.

Addictions and mental illness are medical conditions, but with our current understanding of brain and mind functioning, they are very hard to treat. We don't need the further barriers of people trying to hide their illness. The more society can normalize mental illness through open dialogue as an illness like diabetes or myopia, the more we can encourage people to seek help and treatment before their situation becomes too overwhelming. Fiction can be one means to normalize this conversation.

IFP: Can you share any information about projected timing for the release of Book 4 in the series, *Rivers of Ivy*? Are there any tidbits of information you can give about *Rivers of Ivy* (for example, will we see more of Meg, Janat, and/or Rennika)?

SF: Yes! We are looking at a 2025 release date—possibly in time for When Words Collide (August) or Can*Con and World Fantasy (October). The book is written, but will undergo rewrites. *Rivers of Ivy* takes the story and the world several years into the characters' futures, where an influx of technology (textile factories) leads to migrations toward the cities. The resulting changes in economic, political, and social conditions affect the epidemiology of addictions. And . . . did you notice that Rennika's unborn child was cursed in *Gathering of Ghosts*? Be prepared to meet Kireen!

IFP: Your website notes that in addition to being an author and editor, you are also a visual artist, focusing on acrylic paintings on canvas, with Western Canadian landscapes as well as speculative fiction paintings. Have you ever painted landscapes or settings from Shangril? Why or why not?

SF: You know, I never have. I think this might partially be due to the fact that I have seen so many phenomenal fantasy landscape paintings at the World Fantasy Convention and other places that I just don't think I can do my world justice. However, here's a cool story: my daughter, an amazing visual artist, created the map of Shangril that you see in the books. But when she was creating it, she quizzed me about the cartographer—to whom I had given no thought whatsoever! But clearly, he had to have been commissioned by someone with money, who had a need for maps . . . likely the king of Arcan.

We noticed that some parts of the map, particularly the east and south, were much more detailed than the west and north. So we realized the map maker must have travelled south from Arcan and headed west . . . and then, likely, sat in a tavern and asked travelers about their homelands, to fill in the rest of the map.

Also, note how little detail shows up in the country of Oromon. Just a hint: this becomes a plot issue in later books . . .

IFP: Is there anything else you'd like to comment on in relation to the Addicted to Heaven series?

SF: Just that it has been a pure joy to work with *Laksa Media*. As owner of a small press, Lucas K. Law has really treated me well (as he does all his authors). There may not be as big a splash for books coming out from small press, but—I feel—the quality is there. Lucas has worked incredibly hard and challenged me to make the books better. His editorial input and vision has influenced the direction of the books for the better. I am very proud to be a *Laksa Media* author.

About the Author

Susan Forest is the author of dual Aurora Award-winners Bursts of Fire (2019) and Flights of Marigold (2020) as well as over 25 internationally published short stories (Analog, Asimov's, Beneath Ceaseless Skies). She edits an award-winning Laksa Anthology Series: Speculative Fiction anthologies for Laksa Media Groups, was Editor Guest of Honor at Keycon in 2022, and most recently co-edited Life Beyond Us: An Original Anthology of SF Stories and Science Essays (European Astrobiology Institute Presents). Susan loves travel and has been known to dictate novels from the back of her husband's motorcycle.

SURVIVING THE DARK AND RECLAIMING THE SELF THROUGH FICTION: INTERVIEW WITH CARINA BISSET, AUTHOR OF DEAD GIRL, DRIVING

ANDREA BLYTHE

> "Each time one of my characters discovers a way to break the cycle, a part of me is healed. It may have taken years to get out of my own abusive relationship, but the women I write are stronger than I was; they break that cycle. I hope that by exploring the complexities of abuse in fiction, I can let other victims and survivors know that they are not alone."

Content Warning for discussions of domestic violence, suicidal ideation, and drug abuse.

In her debut collection of short stories, *Dead Girl, Driving: And Other Devastations (Trepidatio Publishing,* March 8, 2024), Carina Bissett offers a stunning collection that blends horror and the fantastical to address issues of abuse, domestic violence, and self-harm. This collection delves down dark corridors to find the light, presenting stories in which women reclaim their own power and strive to carve a space for themselves in an unkind world.

INTERSTELLAR FLIGHT PRESS: Congrats on publishing *Dead Girl, Driving and Other Devastations,* your debut collection of short stories. What kicked off the process of writing the stories in this collection? And what was your journey in bringing it all together?

CARINA BISSETT: I became Carina Bissett in July 2013, when I was finally granted a new identity through confidential channels as a survivor of domestic violence. Two years earlier, my ex-husband was apprehended by Interpol and extradited to the United States, where he served time in prison for numerous felonies committed against me. When I was granted this new start, I made several major life decisions. The most pivotal was to dedicate myself to my lifelong dream of writing fiction.

My first publication as Carina Bissett was the poem "Wild Girl," which was published in the inaugural issue of *NonBinary Review* (Grimm's Fairy Tales, June 2014). This piece was based on Australian novelist Kate Forsyth's research on Dorothea Wild, the wife of Wilhelm Grimm. "Wild Girl" went on to earn nominations for the Sundress Publications Best of the Net Award and the Pushcart Prize, so I thought I was off to a good start. And then, a year later, my story "More Wings than the Wind Knows" was published by *Timeless Tales* in Issue #4: Perseus & Medusa.

I wrote a few other pieces along the way, but there was something missing. I simply didn't have the knowledge I needed to fulfill my dream. So, I researched MFA programs, settled on Stonecoast at the University in Maine, and sent a complicated request to admissions. You see, as part of my identity change, I lost everything I had accomplished before my disastrous marriage. It didn't matter that I had earned two associate degrees, a bachelor's degree, and a master's degree; they were all under my old name and social security number. And that meant, on paper, I didn't have the qualifications to apply to an MFA program. Luckily, the admissions department was able to link my identities, keeping my confidentiality intact. Finally, I was ready to take the next step in my journey. Or so I thought.

(Note: This story continues in the next question.)

IFP: Your title story, "Dead, Girl Driving," presents a young woman who is granted new life by her Godmother Death, but this gift goes devastatingly awry. Can you talk a bit about your inspiration and process for writing this particular story?

CB: This is a hard one, and in all honesty, I never thought this story would find publication, let alone be the title story of my debut collection. But, let me back up a bit. In 2016, I was accepted to the low-residency MFA program at Stonecoast in the Popular Fiction cohort—this area of focus in speculative fiction is the main reason I selected a school in Maine, even though I live in Colorado. In preparation, I was busy with required reading and workshop manuscripts. However, fate had another twist waiting for me.

Four weeks before heading to the East Coast, I was involved in a freak bicycle accident. I don't remember much, but when I finally woke up twelve hours later, I discovered that I'd nearly died. The doctors did the best they could to patch me up, but I was a mess. Four hours of surgeries put my face back together. The surgeons had debrided gravel from my chest, hands, and feet, and they'd repaired the damage on my left knee as best as they could. The physical damage was bad enough, but even worse was the traumatic brain injury. I couldn't read. I couldn't write. My brain was blank of everything but pain. When I was released a week later, I was broken in every way that mattered.

Determined, I decided to move forward with my plans to attend my first residency. This was a mistake. Unable to cope with the unmanageable pain and cognitive impairment, I failed on a spectacular level. When I returned home, I did so with the knowledge that I couldn't do the two fundamental tasks associated with being a writer. And this is when I approached the darkest time of my life. I counted all the medications I'd hoarded and contemplated my options. I'll never forget the moment when I realized I was one pill short of a fatal dose of morphine. Would I have taken them otherwise? I don't think so. But I kept that bottle for years before finally disposing of it.

It took several attempts before I was finally able to compose the first full draft of "Dead Girl, Driving." It is the most vulnerable story I've ever written, as it not only explores my struggles with suicidal ideation but also draws from my experiences with drug abuse and domestic violence. It was a hard story to write, and it is a hard story to read. But I believe it is an important story. I know I am not the only person who has faced this darkness, and there is something powerful in the knowledge that we are not alone in our struggles. I firmly believe that.

IFP: Many of the stories in your collection present portrayals of women who reclaim their own power after experiencing violence or abuse. What draws you to writing such characters? What do you hope to reveal in the process of writing them?

CB: As a survivor of domestic violence, it's a subject I often explore in my stories. To this day, I struggle with a sense of shame and embarrassment about the situation I was in. I look back and wonder how I could have done things differently. I question how I could have been so easily manipulated. I am not the only survivor who feels like this, and I know it.

As part of my attempt to understand the cycle of violence, I volunteered at TESSA, the local domestic violence shelter in Colorado Springs. I went through training on the subject, and then I shared my story with other volunteers in other training sessions. I hosted booths at festivals and tried to help educate others. It didn't take long before I learned how pervasive this problem is. It is not just adults who become victims of intimate partner violence, nor is it only women. So, when I went back to school for my Master's in Curriculum and Design, I wrote my thesis on dating violence in young adult populations.

That degree (along with all the rest) no longer belongs to me, yet I found that I wasn't done with the subject. So, I turned my musings into fodder for my fiction. Each time one of my characters discovers a way to break the cycle, a part of me is healed. It may have taken years to get out of my own abusive relationship, but the women I write are stronger than I was; they break that cycle. I hope that by exploring the complexities of abuse in fiction, I can let other victims and survivors know that they are not alone. I am also hopeful that this evolving discourse—both in my stories and others—will educate those who are not as well versed on the situation.

Victims of domestic abuse are not weak. We are not pathetic. We do not deserve to be abused and shamed. It is a complex situation that is *not* determined by class, race, religion, age, ability, gender, sexual orientation, or any other box a person might want to check. It can happen to anyone. But it isn't until people stop looking the other way that we can address the perpetuation of this global crisis and the continuing harm caused by such violence.

IFP: Another theme that often recurs in your collection is the exploration of fairy tales, folklore, or mythology through a new lens. What are the benefits of reimagining these kinds of stories? What can writers and readers alike get out of exploring new visions of old tales?

CB: Fairy tales have always been an important part of my life. As a young reader, they helped me to make sense of the world. I read the tales of the Brothers Grimm and Hans Christian Andersen over and over again until I could nearly recite them by heart. I also watched the Disney versions, which were often much different than the tales I knew. But it wasn't until I was in my twenties that I came across Angela Carter's reworkings of Charles Perrault's fairy tales in *The Bloody Chamber* (Harper & Row, 1979). This discovery—paired with the adult fairy tales collected in the *Snow White, Blood Red* series (*William & Morrow Company*, 1993) edited by Ellen Datlow and Terri Windling—helped me realize that I, too, could mine this material for stories of my own making.

I find that these core stories and themes offer a sense of familiarity for both writers and readers alike. There are cues and expectations that create a foundation of common understanding. For instance, familiar symbols—glass slippers, apples, keys, mirrors, and so forth—resonate on several different levels. And then, when writers push those anticipations in unexpected directions, readers can follow that bridge from the known to the unknown. We build on the past to reveal the present and to explore the future.

IFP: Your stories address the horrors of humanity, delving into challenging issues of abuse, manipulation, and suicide, among others. How do you separate yourself from the work? Or, how do you safely deal with the emotional impact of addressing such topics?

CB: *Dead Girl, Driving and Other Devastations* is a collection of hope—a definition that might seem at odds with the dark and dangerous moods that weave throughout the collection. Through the lens of fiction, I tend to explore subjects I've personally had to overcome, including suicidal ideation, post-traumatic stress disorder, disfigurement, disability, abandonment, poverty, and violence against women. And with each story I write, with each demon I dismember and dissect, I feel a little stronger.

That being said, I'm very deliberate in the stories I decide to share, especially in the form of short fiction. My novel-in-progress leans into similar themes, but the approach is different. Longer work offers more grace when it comes to unfolding difficult topics. There is space to let the reader—and the writer—breathe. But the most difficult stories are the ones I prefer to approach in the form of short fiction.

When I know that I only have a few thousand words at my disposal, I am protected by that knowledge. I have an idea of how long I will be intimately connected to the subject at hand. Armed with the predetermination of a story's shape, I am shielded—at least partially—against the emotional toll of whatever might be dredged up during the creative process. In my opinion, there is a reason the best horror is short. Too long in the darkness, and you might never find your way back.

IFP: Through The Storied Imaginarium, you run a series of workshops and courses to support writers in exploring the mythic and fantastical in their work. What is one of the key lessons you try to impart to the writers in your workshops? Conversely, what is a lesson that you have learned from them in turn?

CB: I have been running generative writing courses at The Storied Imaginarium since 2016, the same year I had my accident and started my MFA program. Some of the participants in my workshops today are the same people who took those first courses back in the fall of 2016. That means that I've been working with some writers for eight years now. How magical is that?

Until recently, my courses have *not* been about teaching the craft of writing. They have historically been generative in nature. For each module, I pair a fairy tale or myth with a scientific or cultural concept in hopes of offering multiple avenues to ignite creative inspiration. For instance, I paired "The Pied Piper" with viruses. In another module, we explored "Hansel and Gretel" with epigenetic memory. It's amazing how many different types of stories come out of these prompts. Even more incredible is the fact that most stories written in these classes end up bearing little resemblance (if any) to the source materials.

In my workshops, I am diligent in creating a safe space for writers to evolve, a community where participants have the freedom to explore their own experiences through the lens of fairy tale and myth. It brings me great joy to celebrate their successes. I'm proud to say that stories generated in my workshops have been published in a wide array of markets (*Apex Magazine, Beneath Ceaseless Skies, Clarkesworld, EscapePod, Fantasy Magazine, F&SF, Gamut, Interzone, Nightmare Magazine, Strange Horizons, Sunday Morning Transport,* and more). Not only that, but many of these publication credits were these writers' first sales. How amazing is that? They are much more accomplished than I will ever be, yet they keep returning to this space we've created together. There are times when my classes have filled up before they were even announced to the public. And that is the lesson I've learned: When we support each other, there is nothing we can't do.

IFP: Now that your collection is out in the world, what do you hope readers will take away from the experience of reading it?

CB: There was a time when I thought I'd never be like the writers I admire so very much, that I would never see a book with my name on the cover. After my accident, my hopes of being a fiction writer seemed more like a pipe dream than ever. But now that my dream has become a reality, I hope that my stories will resonate with the people who read them. I hope people will find a moment of connection or reflection or revelation, a glimmer of a shared experience in the ambiguous nature of the characters I tend to write.

But most of all, I hope my readers will know that they are not alone. We are allowed to talk about the things that have shaped our identities, and no topic is off-limits. Life is hard. Accidents happen. We all make mistakes. But it is the cumulation of these individual experiences that makes each of us unique. There is beauty in embracing the past while still working toward a better and brighter future. The possibilities are endless.

About the Author

Carina Bissett is a writer and poet working primarily in the fields of dark fiction and fabulism. She has written numerous short stories, many of which are featured in her debut collection *Dead Girl, Driving and Other Devastations* (2024), and she is also a co-editor of the award-winning anthology *Shadow Atlas: Dark Landscapes of the Americas* (2021). Her poetry has been nominated for the Rhysling Award, the Pushcart Prize, and Sundress Publications Best of the Net. Her nonfiction has been nominated for a Bram Stoker Award®. Links to her work can be found at http://carinabissett.com.

EXPLORING THE FUTURE, CLOSE TO HOME: INTERVIEW WITH TIMOTHY S. JOHNSTON, AUTHOR OF THE RISE OF OCEANIA SERIES

LISA TIMPF

> "Many people theorize that, in the future, resources will come from asteroids, the Moon, Mars, and so on, but the oceans are far more realistic within the next several decades or centuries. The underwater cities and habitats in my books are therefore based on this near-future certainty."

In his six-book *The Rise of Oceania* series, Canadian author Timothy S. Johnston blends science fiction, thriller, espionage, and climate fiction in action-packed, imaginative novels that largely take place underwater. Thoroughly imagined, and with supporting materials like timelines and schematics heightening the believability, Johnston's books provide a sneak peek into what life might be like if and when humanity opts to explore undersea living. Johnston took time to answer Lisa Timpf's questions about the series and the notion of underwater human habitations.

INTERSTELLAR FLIGHT PRESS: One thing that struck me in reading *The War Beneath*, the first book in the series, was the degree to which everything seemed to be thought out in terms of how the undersea colony of Trieste would function. How did you flesh out your ideas about what underwater living would be like? Was this based on research, your own logic based on your background and training, or a blend of the two?

TIMOTHY S. JOHNSTON: The important consideration in any fiction writing is that there has to be a reason for the characters to be involved. What is their motivation? Why are they part of the story? Why are they doing these things? If the writing doesn't answer these crucial elements, then readers will notice. In this series, therefore, there has to be a reason for undersea colonization. Oceans occupy 70% of the planet and the ocean floor is twice the area of Mars. It contains a vast amount of resources, including vegetation, marine life, and mineral wealth. The continental shelves are easily within reach. The deep abyssal plains will take more technology and effort, which my books delve into.

Many people theorize that, in the future, resources will come from asteroids, the Moon, Mars, and so on, but the oceans are far more realistic within the next several decades or centuries. The underwater cities and habitats in my books are, therefore, based on this near-future certainty. The cities are designed to raise crops underwater, to fish farm underwater, and to harvest mineral wealth. Families will accompany the workers. Tied into this is the ongoing climate change on the surface, and as cropland fails, governments fail, and refugees stream across the globe searching for safety and survival, many people will begin to migrate toward the source of new and reliable resources: the ocean floors. That is the reason for the ocean colonization in this series, and the cities, therefore, have to reflect this.

The designs came about from research and education. I first had the idea during my years at University in the late 1980s and early 1990s, when many professors were talking about climate change, global warming, rising waters, failing cropland, and more. I began researching and studying the issues at that time. I knew that there could be a gold rush to the ocean floors, and this could trigger a new Cold War. The idea of espionage, action, and adventure during this colonization intrigued me. It is shocking for me to think about, but it has been a thirty-five-year journey from the initial idea to my latest book, *A Blanket of Steel*.

IFP: On a scale of 1 to 10 (1 being not very likely, and 10 being you're absolutely convinced it will happen one day), how likely is the scenario of undersea cities being developed here on Earth? Why would you give it this rating?

TSJ: It is a 10. It is inevitable. We will need new resources as our populations increase. And it is not just inevitable, it's already started! We mine oil and gas underwater. We already have fish farms. We know there are fields of metallic nodules underwater, on the abyssal plains, that merely need to be scooped from the ocean floor. No digging necessary. The largest barrier is the enormous water pressure, but innovation and technology will overcome that in time.

Environmentalists have been warning us for decades. Many of them are doomsayers, predicting disaster and end-of-civilization events. I don't believe this. We are changing the Earth and the climate, that is certain, but we will change with it. We will adapt. We will create new jobs. We will find new resources on Earth before we migrate off it. People don't stay confined to continents and stagnate or die. We innovate, we change, we evolve. When it becomes cost-effective (meaning the resource extraction earns more money than it costs), it will happen.

The Earth's population was 3.6 billion when I was born. It's now 8 billion people, more than double in only five decades. Climate change will continue to affect our arable land, and meanwhile, there is an underwater crop that can grow a meter a day in optimal conditions. Kelp forests are currently exploding off the coast of Australia and in the Arctic Ocean. Our needs for minerals will continue to increase, and in the Clarion Clipperton Zone, there are fields of potato-sized mineral deposits. Their frequency has been observed at 15 kilograms per square meter! There are more than 500 billion tonnes of these in the oceans, but the number has been estimated as high as 1.5 trillion. In a world starved for resources, the oceans represent our survival.

IFP: On your blog, you note that the idea for *The War Beneath,* the first novel in the series, came to you when you were a university student, taking courses in environmental systems, geography, geophysics, and geography. Do you feel your technical and educational background was beneficial in writing The Rise of Oceania series?

TSJ: Absolutely. Good writing is grounded in reality. There has to be a reason for things to be happening in a book or movie, otherwise readers will lose interest. Motivations need to be realistic, especially in thrillers. Why are my characters living and working in the oceans? Why are they engaged in corporate and military espionage? Why are they risking death for this way of life? It's all tied into resource extraction, to provide for the exploding populations on the surface. To provide for families . . . this is the strongest human motivation. It is also historically accurate and makes sense in the grand scheme of economics and climate change.

Human beings adapt, and climate change is a real thing. We can't stop it. But we can change with it, and develop new economies, jobs, and ways of life. We can make a lot of money from climate change, actually. The best politicians and industrialists realize this. Green energy is fueled by climate change, pun intended.

IFP: Currently, there are "undersea habitats" like underwater hotels or research facilities. Have you ever been to an underwater facility like this (and if so, what was the experience like)? If you haven't been, why would you, or would you not, want to go?

TSJ: I would absolutely go to an underwater hotel or research facility. I'd love to. At the moment, I spend most of my time writing, reading, and contributing to the genres that I love. I want to leave a legacy to the genres. I want to help change other peoples' lives through my writing. When I was a teenager, works by people like Isaac Asimov, James Cameron, Agatha Christie, John Carpenter, and Michael Crichton got me through the toughest times. I want to provide escapism for people. Life is stressful, and people need escapism. It can be a perfect medicine, and safer than a drug. Books, movies, video games, etc. It worked for me. The type of escapism I provide is realistic, grounded in reality, but more importantly, I believe it is *fun*. It is everything I'd want to read, and that's why I'm writing it. That's what I spend most of my time doing. Don't get me wrong, though—if someone invited me, I'd go. If the US military invited me to tour a *Virginia* Class sub, I'd go in a heartbeat.

IFP: If humans do establish settlements on the continental shelves of the world's oceans, do you have some thoughts on how this can be done without negatively impacting existing marine life and the health of the ocean itself?

TSJ: Good question. The answer is that human beings are already having a massive impact on delicate marine ecosystems like the Great Barrier Reef. We have fished some species to near extinction. We're releasing dangerous pollutants into the ocean, and simply put, as environmentalists sometimes say, "Dilution is not the solution to pollution." Climate change is affecting the ocean as well. Kelp forests are exploding due to warming waters in some areas of the world. Migration patterns are changing. Oil spills have had devastating impacts on localized regions, like the Deepwater Horizon spill in the Gulf of Mexico or the famous Exxon Valdez disaster.

But when it comes to future ocean floor colonization, to be honest, I'm not too concerned about it . . . yet. At first, there will be very small numbers of people. We need to survive, grow, and prosper. We can mitigate our impact, like we do in developed nations after mining a resource or logging an area, replanting and remediating an ecosystem to "nature" again. We can do this underwater too.

IFP: Your website includes an article titled "Why Underwater? Ten Important Reasons I Wrote The Rise of Oceania, and a Message for the Future." In this article, you suggest that there are many important resources under the ocean surface, and establishing undersea colonies is "far, far easier (and cheaper) than going to outer space." We hear a lot in the media about steps being taken to travel to the moon and Mars, or to explore space, but we don't hear much about steps taken toward establishing underwater habitats. Why do you think this is?

TSJ: There have been writers investigating this, like Frederik Pohl, Jack Williamson, Nick Cutter, Jules Verne, and others. But you are correct—many writers focus on outer space because it is exciting and new and perhaps seems more futuristic than the oceans. However, the oceans are more realistic at present. They are easily accessible. The resources there are vast . . . almost incomprehensible, in fact. Mars's surface area is 144 million km2. Our oceans are 361 million km2. In strict terms of economics, as our need for resources increases, it will come down to cost. It will be cheaper to extract from our oceans than from outer space. It is currently far more expensive to get to space, and the oceans are right next to our coastlines. In fact, a country's Exclusive Economic Zone (EEZ) extends 200 nautical miles out *into* the ocean, and includes all resources in the ocean and on the ocean floors. As I mentioned earlier, our movement out into these areas (and beyond) is inevitable. Writers today seem to focus on outer space, you're correct, and many readers do enjoy this because of an innate need for escapism. I'm tapping into something that has been largely neglected, and I think readers are noticing it. Fingers crossed.

IFP: *A Blanket of Steel* is noted as the sixth and final book in The Rise of Oceania series. Do you have other writing projects on the go, or are you taking a break?

TSJ: I have other projects on the go. I will have some announcements soon. I am always working. Contributing to the genre and providing escapism to those who need it most is a driving force for me. Leaving a legacy is another. The creative people who made an impact on me while growing up—Carpenter, Spielberg, Asimov, Heinlein, Pohl, Christie, Hitchcock, and more—changed my life. I want to have an impact on others, to help them the way those people helped me.

IFP: You sponsor the "Timothy S. Johnston Future Writer Award" at London South Collegiate Institute in London, Ontario, which I think is a pretty cool thing to do. What prompted you to do this? Have you had a chance to chat with some of the recipients, and if so, how have they responded to receiving the award?

TSJ: I want to give back to aspiring writers. I want to inspire and encourage them with an award early on, to give them a little push. For me, the journey took over twenty-five years before I got my first publication deal for *The Furnace*. During that time, I received hundreds of rejections. It was crushing but normal (and necessary), and I want to give others some encouragement during the process.

Before I was published, I had the incredible fortune of developing communications with David Feintuch, who wrote *The Seafort Saga*. He encouraged me, read some of my work, and helped guide me through some writing issues I was having. I take his lessons with me every day, in everything I write. I never got to meet him in person; he passed away before that could happen. I have been in touch with his family, though, to thank them for his selfless act of helping me, at the time a totally unknown and unpublished writer. This happened more than twenty years ago, and I plan on one day telling the complete story. In the meantime, I created the Timothy S. Johnston Future Writer Award at a local high school, which a graduating student receives each year. I run writing sessions for aspiring creative writers in the Board of Education, and I try to give back the best I can.

IFP: Your website bio notes that you'd like to see one of your books in film or on television. Just for fun, which actor(s), (present or past) do you think would be suited for the role of Truman McClusky, a key player in the series? Why would he/they be a good fit?

TSJ: I would go with Ryan Gosling as Mac. He has the characteristics that fit nicely, especially demonstrated in films like *Blade Runner 2049*. He can show the defining features of the character: someone who deals with past trauma, family issues, and his alpha abilities to gain the respect of others and lead people through incredibly dangerous social, political, and military/espionage events. Mac takes a tremendous amount of punishment, emotionally and physically, in these books. Gosling has demonstrated that he can believably show this. I think he really encapsulates all the elements of Truman McClusky. He can display Mac's nuances. He's an incredible actor. There are others who would also do a great job: Chris Pine, Jake Gyllenhaal, Tom Hardy.

IFP: Your most recent thriller, *A Blanket of Steel*, contains many schematics, diagrams, and maps. What is the purpose, and how do they add to the story?

TSJ: I do it to add 'texture' to the story. I want my books to be as immersive as possible, to pull readers in and make them feel totally involved in the story and, in fact, a part of the adventure. On the run, in danger, fighting for a purpose, with their lives on the line, and trying to protect others. I want readers to experience what it might really be like to be in a seacar, at great depths, involved in a torpedo battle with enemies. The maps and schematics add to the feeling, setting, mood, and they enhance the narrative. As you may have guessed from previous answers, one of the reasons I write is to provide escapism and help people. I will continue to work with graphic artists to add that important texture to my stories.

IFP: Horror author Nick Cutter, who wrote *The Deep*, provided a very nice blurb, comparing your writing to Clive Cussler's NUMA files and Mac to Dirk Pitt. Does this help define the genre you are writing?

TSJ: The blurb blew me away, frankly. He's an incredible talent, and I'm a fan of his, so it was thrilling to see it. Although my series takes place a hundred years from now, it's based on real technology and research and development. It's not fantasy or *too* futuristic—these books are technothrillers. I appreciated that he compared it to a popular modern-day thriller series by Clive Cussler.

About the Author

Timothy S. Johnston is the author of Science Fiction/Thrillers *The War Beneath, The Savage Deeps, Fatal Depth, The Shadow of War, A Blanket of Steel, The Furnace, The Freezer*, and *The Void*. He has won the GLOBAL THRILLER Award twice, the EPIC Award, the CYGNUS Science Fiction Award Grand Prize, as well as the CLUE Award. Visit www.timothysjohnston.com to register for news alerts, read his blog and reviews, and learn more about his current and upcoming thrillers.

SPIRIT POSSESSION, PARASITOIDS, AND FRIENDSHIP: INTERVIEW WITH SAM KYUNG YOO, AUTHOR OF SMALL GODS OF CALAMITY

CHLOE SMITH

> "I don't think I consciously applied a queer lens so much as I just wanted to write a supernatural detective story that also happened to be queer. Likewise, the processing of grief and unresolved trauma are just things I tend to write about in general, regardless of the genre. I took the "write what you know" advice to heart, so all of my stories are casually queer and a little bit sad."

Within a story that explores spirit possession, superstition, and East Asian folklore, there is an overarching theme of friendship and overcoming trauma; Chloe Smith spoke to author Sam Yoo about their debut novella *Small Gods of Calamity*, what inspired it, and their writing process.

INTERSTELLAR FLIGHT PRESS: You weave both the mundane and supernatural together effortlessly in Small Gods of Calamity. What inspired you to create a part mystery and part urban fantasy, or a supernatural noir novella?

SAM KYUNG YOO: I've enjoyed a lot of stories from the occult detective subgenre, so I wanted to try creating one of my own where the occult aspects were based in East Asian folklore and superstitions. I originally meant for this to be a short story, but I ended up having even more fun with it than I expected so I made it into a novella instead.

IFP: Small Gods of Calamity has such a rich and unique premise in Detec-

tive Han-gil searching for the deadly worm spirit, what inspired the story in particular?

SKY: Honestly, it was my childhood obsession with Animal Planet and love of nature documentaries that gave me the idea–specifically behavior-altering parasitoids. The way the horsehair worm grows inside of a cricket, hijacks the cricket's nervous system, forces it to drown itself, and then emerges from the cricket's body like a writhing, coiling nightmare, resonates with the concept of spirit possession in a very interesting way.

I was also inspired by the large-scale negative impact an invasive species can have on an unwitting ecosystem—I imagined a spirit that spiritualists and exorcists have never encountered before and thus have no established means of defending against.

IFP: I enjoyed your portrayal of spirits and how Detective Han-gil is able to communicate with them using incense. How much research did you do into Korean shamanism when writing *Small Gods of Calamity*? Are there elements of this research you wish you could have included in the story but didn't?

SKY: I'm one of those writers who constantly falls down research rabbit holes, for better or worse. In the case of Korean shamanism, I also make the habit of presenting panels on East Asian folklore at conventions alongside my sister, so I'd already done an amount of reading on the subject beforehand, which was helpful.

There were definitely some things that didn't make it into the book, but a majority of the time, the research is just for me and my thought process anyway. I like to keep my writing as ADHD-friendly (aka me-friendly) as possible and try to avoid including too much exposition.

IFP: Kelsea Yu called *Small Gods of Calamity* a "wonderfully queer exploration of grief, trauma and reckoning with the past." How did you find exploring grief and trauma through a queer lens within the supernatural noir genre?

SKY: I don't think I consciously applied a queer lens so much as I just wanted to write a supernatural detective story that also happened to be queer. Likewise, the processing of grief and unresolved trauma are just things I tend to write about in general, regardless of the genre. I took the "write what you know" advice to heart, so all of my stories are casually queer and a little bit sad.

IFP: *Small Gods of Calamity* is so captivating it's hard to put it down—what initially inspired the idea for the story, and how quickly did the story take shape?

SKY: After my initial phase of researching and writing equivalent of storyboarding, the first draft mostly came together in about a month. My approach to drafting and revising often involves just opening a blank new Word document and starting over multiple times, which takes a while. I stand by this approach, it's extremely freeing, but it does make it a little difficult for me to track my overall forward progress.

IFP: If you could sum up *Small Gods of Calamity* in three words, which would you choose?

SKY: Spirits, friendship, trauma.

Or alternatively, "Parasitoids are upsetting."

IFP: Detective Kim Han-gil is a great protagonist who leaps off the page—is there any chance we could see him again in another novel?

SKY: Absolutely! I have plans for a sequel and hopefully a third book as well, if possible. The second book is still very much in progress, but the working title is *Spirits in the Killing Jar*. I hope to be able to share it with people soon.

About the Author

Sam Kyung Yoo is a queer/ace author and third-degree black belt taekwondo instructor from Massachusetts. They graduated summa cum laude with a B.A. in English, creative writing, and film studies, but have since abandoned academia to write stories about ghosts, East Asian folklore, and sad robots. Their work has been published by *Fantasy*, *Neon Hemlock Press*, and *Strange Horizons*, among others. You can find them online at samkyungyoo.com.

CONTEMPLATING THE UNIVERSE THROUGH POETIC VERSE: AN INTERVIEW WITH EMILY HOCKADAY ABOUT THE HEARTBEAT OF THE UNIVERSE

ANDREA BLYTHE

> "I think of all poetry as speculative, because when we write poetry we are looking into the future, or perhaps reimagining a present or past differently. To me this tinkering or speculating with reality is the beauty of poetry—the joy of imaginative leaps that the reader just must accept."

Science fiction allows its readers to explore what it means to be human when faced with advanced technologies, extraterrestrial intelligence, alternative social structures, and other scientific explorations that provide an analogy for the world in which we live today. Similarly, poetry is a space to delve into the incomprehensible and give voice to emotional experiences that are otherwise indescribable. When the two come together, they create a space of deep resonance that opens up new insight into the nature and spirit of the universe around us.

The Heartbeat of the Universe (*Interstellar Flight Press*, 2024) is a perfect embodiment of this convergence, gathering together extraordinary poetry by poets from around the world—published in *Asimov's Science Fiction Magazine* and *Analog Science Fiction and Fact* over the past decade.

Interstellar Flight Press: Tell us a bit about yourself and your work as both

an editor and poet. Do you find that your experience with one informs the other? Or do they feel like separate creative processes?

Emily Hockaday: I've been with Dell Magazines for thirteen years, working on *Asimov's* and *Analog* in some capacity. I've been selecting poetry for the magazines for a little over a decade, which was the inspiration in many ways for this anthology. In terms of my own writing, I received an MFA from the NYU creative writing program and have published a number of poems, two full-length collections, and six chapbooks. I have a third full-length work coming out in 2025.

These two aspects of my literary life feel very separate. I tend to compartmentalize them, and since working on the magazines is my day job and profession (I know how lucky I am!!), it's easy to keep them discrete, as the hours don't overlap. All this said, they definitely inform each other. When looking at poems in the slush pile, I think I'm more likely to pick a poem that needs tweaks or sometimes more radical revisions than I would be if I wasn't a writer myself.

IFP: Both *Asimov's Science Fiction* and *Analog Science Fiction and Fact* have long legacies in the science fiction and literary communities. Can you talk a bit about these publications? How have they evolved in recent years? And what has been their relationship with poetry been in particular?

EH: Both magazines have a long history of publishing poetry, though both published less of it with less frequency in the early years. *Asimov's* had poetry in the third issue (Fall 1977), and *Analog*'s first poem was published just a few months prior in May 1977, despite having been running since January 1930 as *Astounding*. So it looks like poetry in the SF space was going more mainstream around the time both magazines started printing it—and indeed, SFPA (Science Fiction Poetry Association) formed in 1978.

By the time I took over poetry selection, *Asimov's* was using poetry in every issue; our quantity hasn't changed very much. *Analog*, however, was running a poem every year or two. Now we have two poems consistently appear in each issue. We saw the space for it in the layout without cutting into any fiction, and we saw readers responding to it, so it made sense to bulk that up a little.

Both *Analog* and *Asimov's* have evolved in the same way the industry and genre has—we're seeing so many more voices entering science fiction and fantasy, and it's wonderful! The stories are becoming more diverse as we get submissions from a wider variety of people and representation from different groups.

IFP: Can you talk a bit about your work at these two publications? What are you looking for when you're selecting poetry for each issue? What makes a poem well suited to either *Asimov's* or *Analog*?

EH: Most of my work for the magazines is under my Sr. Managing Editor hat, which involves copyediting fiction, laying out the magazines, proofreading and assembling the pages, and corresponding with authors and other departments.

When I do look at the poetry, the center of the *Analog/Asimov's* Venn Diagram is pretty large. Both magazines publish science fiction poetry. There are a few things that are unique to the magazines, though: *Asimov's* is also open to fantasy and horror poetry, while I love snapping up a science poem (no fiction necessary) for *Analog*.

IFP: In your introduction to *The Heartbeat of the Universe*, you mention that "all poetry is speculative." Can you talk about your thoughts on this? Why are poetry and science or science fiction such a good fit for each other?

EH: I think of all poetry as speculative, because when we write poetry we are looking into the future, or perhaps reimagining a present or past differently. To me, this tinkering or speculating with reality is the beauty of poetry—the joy of imaginative leaps that the reader just must accept. There's also the concept of metaphor, which in poetry is, of course, figurative language but also literally true despite the impossibility. A lot of science fiction uses metaphor in an extended way that harkens to poetry.

IFP: *The Heartbeat of the Universe* covers a decade of poetry published in *Asimov's* and *Analog*. How did you decide which poems would be included in the anthology? Did you often agonize about having to leave certain poems out?

EH: I decided on the poems by observing which poems spoke to each other. I gathered poems that, when collected in a book, would accumulate momentum and become a larger cohesive piece while also being lovely individual works. I did agonize! I could have made at least two more collections this length! The thing that helped keep me from agonizing too much was knowing that I wasn't deciding which poems were "good" (They all were!) but rather which poems created a story together without being redundant.

IFP: The poems in the anthology are beautifully organized around themes that evoke both scientific concepts and personal experiences. What was your process for arranging the poems? What effect were you trying to create with this arrangement?

EH: Thank you! Choosing the poems helped give me a kind of guiding structure to follow, because as I mention above, I selected poems that resonated with each other. So there were already little clumps of themes starting to form before I got into the real and messy work of ordering.

My process looked a lot like me on my floor surrounded by papers, like a nest. I read and re-read these poems countless times, taking notes on the pages by jotting down themes. I started shuffling these into piles by theme, and then eventually, I had to order the sections themselves and then the poems within the sections. In each round of ordering, I asked myself what I wanted the reader to experience. How did I want them to enter or leave each section?

Where did I want the poems to take them? I wanted the reader to have an emotional journey that included a beginning, middle, and end, as best a poetry collection can provide.

IFP: What do you hope readers will get out of their experience of reading *The Heartbeat of the Universe*?

EH: I hope that readers will have the chance to pause from daily life and consider our one incredible Universe! I really want a sense of wonder to transport our readers in a way that only science fiction and poetry can. I also hope readers will connect to all of the fascinating and specific science details these incredible poets have wrought.

IFP: What are you currently working on? Is there anything exciting in the works that you'd like to talk about?

EH: At any given time, I'm working on at least four magazine issues—two each of *Asimov's* and *Analog*—and we always have tons of incredible work stuffed into our pages. Trevor and Sheila choose phenomenal fiction, and I have a lot of fun picking out the poems.

On the personal writing side, I have a third collection coming out in 2025 that is somewhat of a narrative centering around a character whose father is ill and dying, a pregnancy the narrator is experiencing, and a sibling's struggle with addiction.

The Heartbeat of the Universe collects poems from the top writers in the science fiction and literary genres, including voices such as Jane Yolen, Bruce Boston, Robert Frazier, Jessy Randall, and many others. These poems, selected by editor Emily Hockaday from the pages of *Asimov's Science Fiction Magazine* and *Analog Science Fiction and Fact* over the past decade, examine the Universe's smallest particles and largest astral phenomena. These poems travel through time, speak to and from the dead, explore the body and quantum physics, all depicting the human condition and allowing readers to learn more about their universe and themselves.

Editor Biography:

Emily Hockaday is the senior managing editor for *Asimov's Science Fiction Magazine* and *Analog Science Fiction and Fact*. With Jackie Sherbow, she coedited the horror anthology *Terror at the Crossroads*. She is the author of the poetry collections *In a Body* (*Harbor Editions*, 2023) and *Naming the Ghost* (*Cornerstone Press*, 2022), along with six chapbooks. She can be found online at www.emily-hockaday.com.

INTERVIEW WITH DR. ANDREA KRIZ, PHD: AUTHOR OF LEARNING TO HATE YOURSELF AS A SELF-DEFENSE MECHANISM FROM INTERSTELLAR FLIGHT PRESS

PRIYA SRIDHAR

Dr. Andrea Kriz is taking the world by storm with both science and science fiction. With a PhD in Biological Studies and a new short story collection released this year, she demonstrates looking at our familiar world through unconventional lenses. Dr. Kriz sat down with Priya Sridhar for an interview about her collection *Learning to Hate Yourself as a Self-Defense Mechanism*.

INTERSTELLAR FLIGHT PRESS: What an amazing collection! I greatly enjoyed reading your science fiction and got immersed in each world. What led you to write about how technology, time, and perception can affect how we feel?

ANDREA KRIZ: Thank you. I'm really glad you enjoyed it! Most of the stories in the collection were written in 2020 and 2021. Like many writers at the time, I was influenced a lot by the pandemic. I was doing my PhD and had just gotten peer reviews back for my paper when the world shut down. Not being able to go to lab really messed with my perception of time, but in retrospect, I do think I needed a break and probably wouldn't have taken one if the world hadn't literally shut down. That led to me writing stories where the characters also found themselves grappling with a changing world (albeit through different mechanisms than a pandemic) or a post-COVID world. It became comforting to me to have the characters attempt to cope in those worlds rather than change them, which I think is a theme that runs through the stories in this collection.

IFP: I saw many of these stories were published before author sock puppet scandals (cough Cait Corrain cough), AI controversies with OpenAI and ChatGPT, and other tech dramas emerged. How did it feel to anticipate these many torment nexuses or nexi?

AK: It's interesting, when "There Are No Hot Topics on Whukai" was published, I was asked in an interview whether the story was inspired by the Rachel Dolezal incident, and I spoke about a sock-puppet episode that had recently occurred on science Twitter. At the time, I said that the story wasn't inspired by a particular incident but rather the cycle of internet anonymity in general. I'm not surprised that the cycle has continued, but do continue to be shocked by the audacity of certain types of 'creators', the personalities they invent, and their success.

IFP: Related to this, what torment nexus would you want to create, if only to see how it would play out in real life?

AK: Haha, I don't have to invent one—I'll point readers to *Yellowface* by R.F. Kuang. In the novel, an author literally steals the manuscript of her colleague/maybe-friend after the friend's untimely death/maybe-murder and passes off the manuscript as her own. It's an absolutely excruciating read involving culturally appropriating the dead author's background and even sock-puppeting the dead author, in a sense. I would say it exaggerates current trends to highlight them, except there was recently a similar real-life incident that played out on social media (minus the untimely death/murder), down to the way the author was 'caught'. So readers can read both the novel and read about the real incident and get the worst of both worlds *sobs*

IFP: The titular story in your collection touches on a fear many creators and friends of creators have that someone will take us and put us wholesale in a story devoid of context or consent. How do you feel about this fear, and how often it seems to happen?

AK: I think artists are often inspired by their own experiences, whether that manifests in a person they know being incorporated into a story or less obviously. This can be empowering, even cathartic, for a creator. However I think it can also turn negative when there are outside forces pressuring creators to use their experiences to make something that 'sells'. A big pressure mentioned in the titular story is marginalized artists being encouraged (directly or indirectly) to 'use' their trauma to market their stories or write stories that directly draw from their trauma.

IFP: Your time travel stories are unusual in that they have a sense of inevitability despite attempts to change the future. What inspired you to take this angle?

AK: I was inspired a lot by Puella Magi Madoka Magica, which is a magical girl anime that delves a lot into the inevitability of time travel and the concept of fate (and subverts a lot of magical girl tropes along the way), which was in itself inspired by Faust. I think it's rare for someone to time travel for purely altruistic reasons. Usually, there's a deeply personal reason for wanting to alter the past, and I became really interested in what kinds of factors could drive someone to take such an extreme action of living through the same period of time hundreds of thousands of times.

IFP: So I have to ask, if you could choose a superpower: time travel, rewriting reality, or flight?

AK: Flight!

IFP: Many of the stories published in this collection have been accepted into pro publications such as *Clarkesworld* and *Daily Science Fiction*. Can you tell us about your writing journey and what the submission process was like?

AK: I started seriously writing around the end of college when I took a writing class taught by Shariann Lewitt at MIT. That class also introduced me to the world of speculative short fiction. I became particularly inspired when I saw *Nature* journal published science fiction stories. Like many writers, I steadily submitted to the venues I enjoyed reading, including *Clarkesworld* and *Daily Science Fiction*. I often think about the similarities and differences between short fiction and academic paper submissions. There is a lot of rejection inherent to both, but of course, academic papers involve peer review and rebuttals, while short fiction submissions typically don't. Being involved in both kinds of submission processes often leads to interesting mental cross-talk (see "Rebuttal to Reviewers' Comments On Edits For 'Demonstration of a Novel Draconification Protocol in a Human Subject'" in the collection).

IFP: What future works can we expect, and where can readers find you?

AK: I have a story out in the June issue of *Lightspeed*, "Udo Gehler and the Virgin Bitch of the Resistance." It's a mecha-fighting story set in a future-fractured America. Readers can also find me online at https://andreakriz.wordpress.com/ or on Twitter @theworldshesaw

About the Author

Andrea Kriz writes from Massachusetts, where she does research as a molecular biologist. In addition to the stories in this collection, her short fiction has appeared in *Clarkesworld* and *Lightspeed Magazine*, among others, and been translated into French in *Galaxies SF*. She is also part of the Dartmouth Speculative Fiction Project, a collaboration between authors and Dartmouth faculty to create short stories exploring the future of humanity. You can find her online at https://andreakriz.wordpress.com/ or on Twitter @theworldshesaw.

FOUND POETRY, NARRATIVE, AND IDENTITY: INTERVIEW WITH ANDREA BLYTHE, AUTHOR OF NECESSARY POISONS

LESLIE ARCHIBALD

> "I was thinking about the way our lives are shaped by stories—both the ones we tell about ourselves and the ones others tell about us. As we go through our lives, we gather a collection of moments that coalesce into memories, and we share those memories with each other as stories. But we are also made up all those moments we don't remember but nevertheless have an impact on who we are."—Andrea Blythe

Andrea Blythe, author of *Twelve* (*Interstellar Flight Press,* 2020), has assembled a beautiful and tension-filled collection of found poetry in her new offering, *Necessary Poisons* (*Interstellar Flight Press,* 2024). Blythe selects texts from an unfinished Steven King novel and bends them to create pieces in a new and authentic voice, embracing the experimental form and creating a new and exciting experience for her reader. Interstellar Flight Press caught up with the poet to ask her a few questions about the form and her new collection.

Interstellar Flight Press: In "A Little Background Information," the writer is the work. Can you tell us a bit about your connection to the work?

Andrea Blythe: When I was writing "A Little Background Information," I was thinking about the way our lives are shaped by stories—both the ones we tell about ourselves and the ones others tell about us. As we go through our lives, we gather a collection of moments that coalesce into memories, and we share those memories with each other as stories. But we are also made up all those moments we don't remember but nevertheless have an impact on who we are.

In a way, this is the collection of moments and memories as manuscript that shapes us, as I write in the poem.

My work as a poet and a writer is a vital part of the manuscript of my life. I will be writing or creating stories and art as long as I am able. But I also think it's important to remember that writing is not my whole identity, to separate myself from the work enough so that, when things inevitably go wrong (failure to finish something, rejection, bad reviews, etc.), it doesn't shatter my sense of self. My writing is important, but it is not the whole of me because I am also made up of my relationships, adventures, and other experiences.

IFP: Also, that poem can be read in columns or across (I loved both readings). Can you talk about that structure, the caesura, and how it relates to the voice?

AB: The two-column structure is essentially what inspired this poem in the first place. I had seen a number of other poets use the two-column format in various unique ways, and I wanted to experiment with this kind of structure and how it could influence the meaning of the poem. When exploring a poem about identity and seeing oneself through text, it seemed fitting that there would be multiple ways to read the poem, multiple interpretations. The break in the middle could also represent the gaps, the parts of ourselves we forget or are not written and recorded. Every text can be read in many ways, and because a person is infinitely more complicated than a written text, the two-column structure really supported that layering.

IFP: "This Narrative" highlights the struggle between the writer and the words. Could you speak on the importance of finding the perfect word in poetry, the struggle, and how found poetry relates to it.

AB: Most of my struggles when first starting a piece come from trying to figure out the voice or tone to evoke the feeling at the core of the idea I have in mind. I will often phrase and rephrase sections of the poem, searching for the words that fit that voice. Once I find it—well, the act of writing doesn't necessarily become easy, but it does become easier to know which words are working and which are not, making it possible to find the flow while I'm writing.

With found poetry, this is still true, but the process is a bit reversed—because I begin with selecting words. I scan the page of the original text, looking for interesting words that jump out at me, and I begin bringing them together and see what ideas or poetic concepts lead me to. Because I'm limited to the words on the page (or within a few pages), I can't just pull any word out of the ether. The struggle is to discover the core meaning of the poem using the words available to me. And I love that challenge.

IFP: "The Intention of Being" focuses on inhibitions or limitations we place on ourselves (or are placed on us by others). Does the found form (using words that are written) lead one to push the limits or ignore those inhibitions?

AB: It's such an interesting question because I find that limitations in creative work can be freeing. The blank page with its infinite possibilities is often terrifying; if you can go for anything, then how do you know where to begin. Narrowing the scope even a little bit can create an opening for freedom and exploration because instead of vast emptiness, there's a starting point from which to kick things off.

Found poetry restricts things even further, but within that specific selection of words, there is room for self-expression and many ways for the poet to make those words their own. A great example of this is the found poetry collection *Obliterations* by Jessica Piazza and Heather Aimee O'Neill. Using news stories from *The New York Times*, each poet developed their own unique poem. Seeing these dual poems side-by-side, each pair created from the same article illustrates how the poet's individual perspective comes through despite only having access to the same limited set of words.

IFP: How important is authenticity and speaking self-truths, as reflected in "On Taboo Ground" (My tongue, of course, doesn't care, it has proceeded to unzip the world, the narrative undone without regret)? How do we get there?

AB: My mom is fond of this one quote (though I'm not sure where she originally heard it): "Tell the truth as fast as you can and have more fun doing it." The idea of taking joy in being more honest and sharing your true self is valuable and beautiful. It is also essential for building deeper and more meaningful connections with our fellow human beings—but such authenticity can be terrifying (and dangerous in certain circumstances). It takes a lot of courage to be authentic and speak one's truth in the world.

It can also be incredibly difficult to even really know our true self. Our minds are constantly churning out thoughts, some of which are wildly unhelpful at best. Sifting through these thoughts, personal biases, and other fallacies to dig out our personal truth requires a significant amount of introspection and personal work. And doing that work, getting to know ourselves more closely, can make it easier to be authentic and outwardly speak our truth.

All of this—working to understand myself and speaking my truth—is something that I'm continually learning. In general, I find it easier to explore my words and truth through text than I do through verbal speech. Something about the written word helps me to lower my walls and try to be more honest (even if that honesty is expressed through fictional characters and metaphor).

IFP: *Necessary Poisons* is a collection of found poetry. Can you talk a bit about how the original text informs or influences the found poem?

AB: Whenever I think about found poetry, I tend to compare it to visual art, specifically collage, because the poet is taking pieces of things that already exist and reconfiguring them into a new form, with new meaning. In the case of *Necessary Poisons*, I wasn't so much focused on having a conversation with the original text (Stephen King's unfinished novel, *The Plant*). Instead, I treated the text as a kind of limited palette (the way a painter might limit themselves to three colors), out of which to shape new poetry.

The original novel tells a horror story about a man who wants to get revenge against a publishing house by sending them a magical plant, so the available palette of words involves manuscripts, greenery, writing, bloodshed, magic, and violence. When I pull from this specific set of words to shape my poems, they are going to naturally color the tone and vibe of what I am able to create. Much of the same imagery comes through but is recontextualized through my own perspective and voice, which is what makes the words entirely new.

IFP: Reflecting on your last collection *Twelve*, a fairytale retelling, would you consider it a form of found poetry, and how did your process with *Necessary Poisons* differ from *Twelve*?

AB: I probably wouldn't have considered comparing retellings to found poetry until reading your question. Now that I'm thinking about it, I can definitely see some similarities. Both forms draw from an original source material to spin out something new—but at a core level, they *feel* fundamentally different to me.

With retellings, the author is generally drawing on the larger elements of the narrative, such as the overarching plot structures and/or the characters as archetypal concepts. The author can then take these elements and adhere to them closely or use them loosely, crafting a story with vastly different characters, settings, or plot structures with only the barest hint of the original.

Found poetry is more tightly situated within the specificity of the language itself. The author can choose to be in conversation with the source material, if they want, but they don't have to adhere to plot, setting, or character elements at all. They're free to use the words and shape them in a way that has little to no association to the original (except for the specific words), much as I did with *Necessary Poisons*.

IFP: Following up to the last question, *Twelve* and *Necessary Poisons* could be considered experimental forms. Why experimental forms, and where does the inspiration for experimental forms come from?

AB: I love exploring form and how it can add to the depth of emotion or narrative experience of the piece. In *Twelve*, I considered breaking each poem into lines, like traditional poetry, but the prose poem format felt more natural to what I was writing. It also helped to lean into the fairy tale tone of each poem, so that's what I went with. With *Necessary Poisons*, found poetry is inherently experimental, and I also played with how those words were laid out on the page to reflect the emotional state of each poem (for example, jagged, broken lines tend to reflect a feeling of being disjointed).

Experimenting with form is such a fun way to explore the potential of language and storytelling. And poetry is particularly great for experimentation since it inherently plays with language in a variety of ways (rhythm, rhyme, structure, and so on). I definitely recommend reading and playing around with experimental forms since it's a great way to stretch yourself as a writer.

IFP: Identity is reflected throughout *Necessary Poisons*. How have other works helped you discover your identity or your voice as a writer?

AB: I feel as though my identity as a writer is always shifting. There are commonalities that come through—feminism, identity, personal power—but my style is always adapting to suit each poem or story that I'm working on. For me, this is part of the fun and experimentation involved in writing.

Reading and consuming other works, whether it's poetry, fiction, film, theater, visual art, or video games, provides inspiration and ideas about how to play with narrative. I love having that moment of shock when experiencing a narrative that surprises me, when I get to think, "I had no idea you could do something like that." Just a few examples of this include *A Little White Shadow* by Mary Rueffle, which first introduced me to the concept of found poetry; *Run Lola Run*, a 1998 indie film directed by Tom Tykwer, that experiments with style and timelines to create a kinetic experience; and Disco Elysium, a video game developed by ZA/UM, which is an incredibly lyrical experience about a washed-out detective in a fictional post-revolution town.

The world is full of so many brilliant creatives out there, and I'm just so grateful that I get to experience their work and learn from them. I hope that someday I can create something as wonderful and surprising as some of the narratives I've experienced.

IFP: In "Sudden Botany," the writer becomes the plant. Can we talk about personification and what it lends to the poem?

AB: Personification a great device in the poet's toolbox, but I wasn't specifically thinking about it when writing "Sudden Botany." My intention with this poem was to explore the experience of an intimate relationship—the hidden gardens inside a person, the initial connection and exploration of each other, the cultivation of a relationship, and then unveiling the deeper, darker internal truths (which the other person may or may not be able to handle). Personification is something that came through naturally as part of that exploration, echoing the way the narrator seems to become more plant than human toward the end of the poem.

IFP: I see environmental and feminist themes in several pieces in this collection. I am going to ask you the same question I asked the last poet I interviewed. How important is it for poets to speak up and call out injustice? Is anyone listening?

AB: Art can be powerful, providing a space to explore intense emotions, helping people to feel seen and less alone, and evoking empathy for people different from ourselves. It allows for connection and understanding outside of ourselves, and that's incredibly valuable.

Art is also inherently political. As writers and creatives, we exist in a specific time and place, and whether we mean them to or not, our perspectives, beliefs, and biases are embedded in the work. And I believe, we have a responsibility to examine our internal biases and consider how they may influence our work to better understand the potential impact that work could have on other people in order to avoid doing harm (as much as possible).

At the same time, it's important to do work outside of the craft by participating in community events, supporting fellow writers and creatives from marginalized communities, and voting (particularly in local elections).

IFP: What can we expect to see next from Andrea Blythe?

AB: I always have more projects going than I can complete in a reasonable amount of time. Currently, I have two poetry collections that I'm in the process of drafting. The first is a set of poems imagining fictional characters as religious-esque icons as a way to explore the convergence of pop culture and the sacred. The second is a book-long series of ekphrastic poems in response to Hieronymus Bosch's The Garden of Earthly Delights.

I have also been doing some narrative work in video games, playing around with some small solo projects along with freelance work. For example, I've been providing narrative design and game writing work on *Monochrome Heights*, a game being developed by Patrick Knisely (solo developer at One Frog Games). The game is a challenging platformer, in which a robot named Happy is attempting to climb a hidden tower to confront a former ally turned enemy. A demo is currently available for anyone who wants to give it a shot.

About the Author

Andrea Blythe is an author, poet, and game writer. Necessary Poisons is her fourth collection of poetry. Her previous chapbooks include *Twelve: Poems Inspired by the Brothers Grimm Tale* (Interstellar Flight Press, 2020); *Your Molten Heart / A Seed to Hatch* (2018), a Kickstarter-funded collection of erasure poems; and *Every Girl Becomes the Wolf* (Finishing Line Press, 2018), a collaborative chapbook she coauthored with Laura Madeline Wiseman. She is a member of the Science Fiction and Fantasy Poetry Association and the Horror Writers Association. Find her on Twitter @AndreaBlythe or at www.andreablythe.com.

FLASH FICTION

What follows are the stories from Interstellar Flight Press' 2024 Flash Fiction Series, guest edited by Annika Barranti Klein. Each story was chosen for each month to be in time with its season. Here at IFP, we love celebrating non-standard forms in the speculative genres. Flash is one of those forms that gets so little love, but is vital to the genre and has been a part of SFF from the beginning. To that end, we published one flash fiction story a month in 2024, and then interviewed the authors on our Patreon. Now you can read those interviews here!

HONEY IN HER HANDS

DEVAN BARLOW

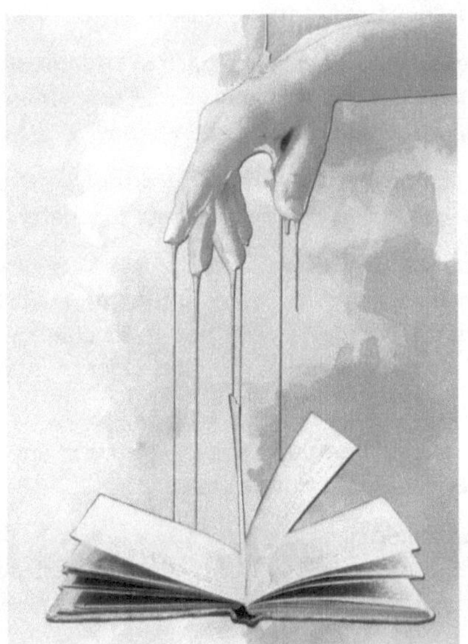

It had been years since Margot could read a book without it turning to honey in her hands. Like she was some sort of incorrectly shaped bee. She could at least still read books, though she had to be fast, and there was no turning back the pages to reread. No savoring the words for her. Despite reading widely, trying every genre she could find, honey always seeped up from the words, and the margins collapsed beneath the weight of sweetness.

She was an expert at nodding along when someone mentioned a plot point they had only noticed upon rereading. Almost as expert as she was at positioning herself with a jar placed *just so* beneath her book so that as she read, the honey dripped into the jar instead of onto the couch or the table or herself.

She had never intended to cultivate the swarm of book lovers who now gathered in her living room once a month. It had started as an invitation to a few friends, and somehow, it had spiraled ridiculously. Even though she wouldn't allow anyone to come who hadn't been vouched for by a trusted friend, she had gotten a few emails from total strangers asking to be informed if space ever opened up. It was wild.

They *did* have great discussions, as they literally consumed the book spread upon fresh bread. Margot always baked a loaf on book club day, and put it out alongside the honey that had resulted from her read of the month's book.

The random emails from strangers always mentioned the honey. Occasionally, a new guest would creep around her house, "lost on the way to the bathroom," but actually in search of the hives they were convinced Margot was hiding, no matter how often she insisted it came from a friend who kept bees. She never let someone return if they tried that nonsense.

The truth buzzed in her head, along the back of her throat and the skin of her lips. Like she was nothing more than a hive for bees who were desperate to go searching for pollen. But she had never told anyone.

Clara—a historical fiction devotee and one of the nicest people Margot had met through the book club—had invited Margot to a party.

But even now, as she stood on Clara's front stoop, Margot was conflicted as to whether she should have come. A strong argument against was Clara having followed up the invitation with, "I want you to meet a friend of mine! I'm not sure why, but you two have a similar . . . vibe." Her words had held a definite matchmaking edge.

Margot didn't date much. She couldn't read in front of anyone else, and it was unthinkable that she would just stop reading.

Clara, of course, had asked her to bring a jar of honey to the party, so Margot had chosen one of the many jars in her pantry. A small taste had confirmed that it was once a mystery novel, familiar suspects and clues rolling across her taste buds.

When Margot arrived, there was no trace of Clara or anyone else she knew. She placed her honey on a table among other mismatched containers and plates and thought once more that she probably shouldn't have come. But it had been nice of Clara to invite her, and there were already people trying the honey, and once Clara saw the jar she would know Margot had come, so she should at least stay to see her. To look busy, she put a few items of food on a small plate. Some pita and a scoop of an olive tapenade. She took a bite, enjoying the chewy, briny olives —

She was racing down the train platform, pulse pounding. She had to get the briefcase to her contact, but they were watching even now —

Margot started, nearly dropping her plate as she pulled herself out of what was so obviously a spy novel. She looked around, seeking a television playing, listening for someone else's conversation about a recent read . . .

Nothing even close.

She took another tentative bite and confirmed the impossible.

Someone else at this party could turn books into food.

"Clara!" She finally spotted the host and hurried toward her through the swarming guests. "Do you know who brought the tapenade?"

Clara looked briefly surprised, but then grinned triumphantly. "Oh, I think that was you, wasn't it?"

Margot realized Clara had her arm linked through that of another person, who she shoved toward Margot. Clara said, "Perfect! Ben, this is Margot, the one I've told you about from book club, with the honey!"

GOOD STORIES COME IN ALL LENGTHS: INTERVIEW WITH DEVAN BARLOW, FLASH FICTION WRITER

Here at IFP, we <3 flash because it's truly a genre of its own. It takes real talent and skill to pull off a good flash story that has a beginning, middle, and end in so few words. We love the twists and turns of a good flash story, and how it surprises the reader while delighting.

Devan Barlow's "Honey In Her Hands" is no exception! What we love about this story is that it starts off by introducing a speculative element that is reminiscent of the story of King Midas. But what could be a devastating tale becomes a sweet romance when two strangers with similar problems meet. A perfect hopeful start to the new year.

How did you get your start writing?

For me, it was a natural consequence of devouring books and having big feelings about them.

What is a favorite piece of flash fiction that you've read?

"Blood, Bone, and Water" by Ash Huang was gorgeous.

What do you like about writing flash fiction, and what do you think is its importance as a form?

I love how compact it is! I think it's important for both readers and writers to recognize that good stories come in all lengths.

What are your influences, both external and internal, for this piece and for your work in general?

I'm a huge fairytale/folklore/mythology nerd, and that underlays a lot of what I write, but I've always been an eclectic reader (as well as a musical theatre nerd), so there are all sorts of things bouncing around in my mind . . .

Golden Age murder mysteries, Sailor Moon, Dorothy Dunnett, Stephen Sondheim . . .

Regarding this particular story, I've always thought bees and honey are kind of magical (I may, in fact, have a trunked novel that might be resurrected one day that's a fairytale retelling featuring magical honey . . .). I don't remember where the spy novel tapenade came from, but once that had occurred to me, the rest of the story coalesced.

WOLVES

LISA SHORT

There's more than one kind of wolf out on the prairie. Everybody knows about the first kind—twice as big as any dog, usually gray but sometimes black or even white, melting in and out of the tall, thick grass like ghosts, if ghosts had fangs and claws. A pack can kill even a full-grown bull—I saw the remains once, back when Da used to take Mama and me into town.

I think people know about the second kind of wolf too, though they won't speak about it directly—not to me, anyway; I suppose because I'm just a girl. But even I overheard the whispered stories about them—first when Mama would drag me along to her Ladies' Aid Society meetings, then later when she and Mrs. Jenssen, our only real neighbor, would visit. That was before the Jenssens gave up on their homestead and moved away, and there was nobody left in visiting distance of us anymore.

And then there's a third kind of wolf, out in the deep dark grasses that grow taller than the top of my head, that go on for so many trackless miles in all directions. I don't think most people do know about that kind of wolf. I only know about them because of what happened to Da.

The townsfolk told Mama that Da was killed by wolves—the first kind, of course. Specifically, Mr. Stockton, the closest thing the town has to a sheriff, told her that. He rode all the way out to our shanty to bring us Da's *effects,* as he called them. Mama thanked him, in the voice she gets when visiting's over and it's time to go home. Since she and I already were home, I assumed that meant Mr. Stockton was leaving instead—but he lingered.

It's a hard thing for a woman, living alone out here so far from town. Especially such a young *woman, and with a child to think of, and winter already rolling in —*

We're fine, said Mama, even more firmly in her *visiting's over* voice.

This went on for several more minutes. I wasn't paying close attention because I wanted to see what Da's *effects* were, and I was trying to sidle along the cabin wall to catch a better glimpse. But when Mama said *Get out NOW,* the words and tone were enough to freeze me where I stood, jerking my gaze up from the tabletop in time to see Mr. Stockton stomp out the cabin door, slamming it hard enough behind him to rattle our shutters.

Da's *effects* turned out to be his belt, boots, and tobacco pouch, the last empty of anything but a few crumbs and its familiar sweet, sharp smell. The belt was stained an ugly reddish black along half its length. *Wolves,* I whispered, without really meaning to. Mama made a sudden sharp movement, startling a flinch out of me, but she was only reaching for the door's latch string.

She pulled it all the way inside, where nobody but us could reach it, then turned back to face me, startling a second flinch out of me with the bitter razor's edge of her smile. *Wolves,* she said.

Wolves finally did come for us one night, just a week or two later; that second kind of wolf. My first inkling of it was a scraping sound outside, muffled by our thick log walls, that woke me up abruptly from a deep sleep. Dazedly, I sat up, looking instinctively towards the door. The shutters were closed over our cabin's two small windows, but Mama had left the oven damper cracked open against the night's chill; in its sullen red glow, I couldn't see anything out of the ordinary. I glanced over at Mama, alone in the big bed across the room from my pallet; her eyes were wide open, gleaming in the dimness. The scraping sound came again, followed by a muffled *thump* and a low, sharp exclamation. Then, more scraping and a stronger, louder *thump!* followed by silence, as if whoever was making the sounds wanted to listen and see if they'd awakened anyone.

Then something slammed into the outside of the door hard enough to shake a shower of splinters loose from its frame. A scream shattered the horrid, pregnant stillness in the air, ending in a long, choking gurgle like nothing I'd ever heard before. And then—*STAY AWAY FROM THEM!* A bellowing voice, snarling, horrific and mangled, but somehow impossibly familiar —

No, DON'T! yelled Mama behind me, but I was already out of my pallet and at the door, fumbling with the latch string and shoving the door open, bare feet slipping on the frost-coated grass outside. Or not *frost*-coated, no—and just beyond my bare, now darkly smeared toes were the torn-out remains of Mr. Stockton's throat, barely attached to the jumble of sprawled limbs that was all that was left of the rest of him.

The crunch of dead grass underfoot wrenched my terrified gaze upward. The full moon glared down bright and merciless on the tall, rangy figure that was backing away from me towards the shadowy depths of the high prairie grass beyond our firebreak. Its shirt glittered in the bone-white light, its fine embroidery catching silver sparks . . . just like the fancy shirt Mama had made Da for trips to town, though it was considerably worse for wear now. The embroidery blurred and swam before my eyes; I opened my mouth to sob out, *Wait—!*

It shook its head, the wolf-thing that had once been my Da. The moonlight gleamed on its long silver claws and carved deep shadows in the distorted horror of its face, its muzzle lined with razor teeth. A ragged gasp behind me, then the sharp heat of Mama's arms clamping tight down over both of mine—and then my Da, that third kind of wolf, turned from us and loped away, vanishing into the infinite, grass-choked darkness of the prairie.

FROM A CUTTING BOARD PERSPECTIVE: INTERVIEW WITH FLASH FICTION WRITER LISA SHORT

Lisa Short is a fellow Texan and fantastic flash fiction storyist. Our guest editor, Annika Barranti Klein, is a sucker for Little House on the Prairie adjacent stories, as well as wolves. I have literally had to talk her off the "what if all the stories were about wolves?" cliff for this call. "Wolves" by Lisa Short embraces feminist ideas while managing to juggle complexity with a beautiful atmosphere. We thought "Wolves" was perfect for a chilly February.

How did you get your start writing?

As far as writing stories period goes, I don't remember why I thought it was something I could do, especially—I was only eight years old the first time I wrote one! I had been reading an old classic (Tarzan of the Apes, if you must know) that I'd dug out of my stepdad's closet, and the intensely imaginative worldbuilding snared me to the point where I thought I would like to write a story, a new story, in that fascinating, gorgeous, intense and fast-paced setting —so that was what I did. (Gender-swapped TotA fan-fic by an eight-year-old . . . I think we'll pass on ever letting that story see the light of day, though!)

What do you like about writing flash fiction, and what do you think is its importance as a form?

I have written stories ranging from 250 words to 10,000, and in my experience, flash fiction (usually maxing out at 1,000 words, though I've occasionally seen people define it as up to 1,500) is about as far down as you can whittle a story's wordcount while still retaining a recognizable, complete plot arc (there are a few exceptions to that that I've encountered, but they're rare!). I enjoy both the plotting challenge (some stories cannot be flash-length, and nothing you do to them from a cutting-board perspective is going to result in a genuinely complete and well-rounded story—the challenge there is choosing the right story to manifest as flash) and the wordsmithing challenge (every word needs to count in flash—there can't be any deadweight!). I think as a form, there is no other length that as effectively hones a writer's tight plotting and word choice skills.

If you write other lengths or formats, how is your approach to flash different?

As I mentioned in the above question, like most, if not all, other writers, I always have a massive backlog of story ideas—however, in no way are they all suited to become a flash piece. When I'm approaching any story idea, I always assess it as best I can for its likeliest finished length. Does it have more than five named characters and of those characters, how many of them are significant characters? Is the setting one that's familiar enough to most readers that they can fill in the worldbuilding blanks automatically, or not? What is the central conflict—is it something that can be resolved in just a few scenes, or will it require a more extensive plot arc? If I'm approaching writing a story in a different way—ie, I already know the story will be flash—I tend to start out with the assumption that I must minimize the number of characters, especially significant ones; that I need to choose a setting that won't require too much detailed explanation to make sense; that the introduction-conflict-climax-resolution arc must be resolvable in less than five pages.

What is a favorite piece of flash fiction that you've read?

The last three I read that I really loved were "Things You Should Be Aware of on Waking, Daniel Carter" by C.L. Holland, "Thing With Feathers" by Avra Margariti, and "View of the End of the World from the Holiday Inn Express-Salina" by Kara Oakleaf.

LILT AND LUSTER SPRING NEWSLETTER

SUSAN TAITEL

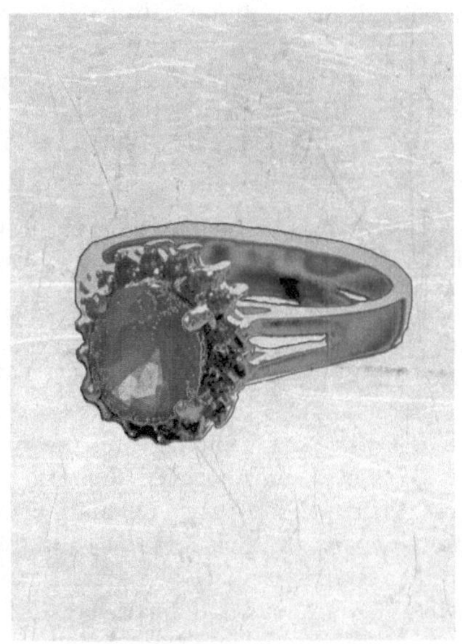

Welcome back, Glitterbugs! I'm thrilled to announce that Lilt and Luster will soon be reopening for in-person shopping.

What a few years it has been, huh? Between the Goblin strike shutting down our supply line and the Wyvern-pox outbreak forcing us to close the storefront indefinitely, we were beginning to doubt this moment would ever come. If I hadn't personally overseen the warding, I would have sworn our humble little jewelry store was cursed.

Honestly, the only thing keeping us going during these unprecedented times has been the unwavering support from you glitterbugs. We are deeply grateful that so many of you continued to place orders by troll-post, and we are raring to finally get started on filling them.

Even now, Wendy is training this year's clutch of salamanders in advance of lighting the forge. Meanwhile, Greg and Freya are testing their tools and arranging their workbenches. I, for one, am eagerly anticipating getting my hands on the next batch of raw gems.

You may have noticed a missing name. It is with mixed emotions that I announce that after fifteen years, my cofounder, partner in crime, the Lilt to my Luster, Eloise, is leaving the shop to get married. While we were all a bit shocked by the suddenness of her departure, we wish nothing but the best for our dear Eloise and her fiancé, the Duke of Nightingales.

El, if you're reading this, you will be sorely missed. You were the first person I met after I stumbled through the rift nearly two decades ago. I doubt I would have made it a day without you. You not only taught me to survive in this strange new reality, you also taught me to find beauty in the unexpected. In this world of wonders, you amazed me every day. Though there's no replacing your level of craftsmanship and unique point of view, I promise to keep our dream business going for both of us. Know that should you choose to return, you will be welcomed back with open arms.

In honor of Eloise's joyous, if unexpected, news, I'm dedicating this newsletter to a certain essential piece of jewelry. That's right, we are talking about the all-important engagement ring!

If you are subscribed, you are probably of the mindset that one can never have enough jewelry, and of course I agree, but consider this. For some, an engagement ring is the only piece of fine jewelry they own. Yet so many people wind up with interchangeable diamond solitaires. Cut, set, and boxed for the masses. From the start, Eloise and I believed that your ring should be as unique and beautiful as your love story. Each Lilt and Luster ring is a singular creation, with an origin to match. Designs for our spring collection are already in development (and they are spectacular), but we still have a few unclaimed treasures in our showroom. Read on to find the perfect ring for your intended.

The Miner's Delight, artist Greg

A perfect blend of materials and design. The gem is a 5-carat obsidian-shaded dragon heartstone (so rare!). Although it appears smoky at first glance, when brought to the light, you can see echoes of the flames that came perilously close to snuffing out the lives of the brave dwarves who discovered its source. But what is a little danger when it results in such a find! (I kid! We take the health and safety of our contractors very seriously. The dwarves were rigorously trained in safely exhuming dragon remains and were generously compensated.)

Before I could make the first cut on this beauty, it had to pass an eighteen-month cooling-off period in our deep-freeze, allowing it to be handled safely while retaining the appearance of fire. I cut the perfect facets to show off its shine and etched runes of binding along the rim. This is one heart that won't crack.

Once my work was finished, I handed it off to Greg, who set it in a braided band made of finely polished rose gold and blown glass. Greg has really outdone himself with this one.

This ring is perfect if your intended's emotions run deep until they explode to the surface.

Call for price. Serious inquiries only.

The Mermaid's Tear, artist Freya

At a diminutive 3 carats, this gem may not be right if your intended believes that size is the only thing that matters. But if they prioritize sparkle, this stunner packs a heck of a punch. As the name implies, it started life as a tear harvested from a lady of the deep. It was then pressurized into a diamond. With a clarity rating above IF, this gorgeous stone needed little cutting to dazzle to the fullest effect.

Displaying the elegance and delicacy we've come to expect from a Freya piece, this ring is truly special. She chose to surround the diamond with a halo of freshwater pearls and complemented it with a platinum band.

If your intended has an affinity for the sea and a penchant for melancholia, this is the ring you want! (You will get used to the constant knell of the pipes. I did.)

Call for price. Installment plan available.

The Suzanne, artist Dagmar (That's me!)

This piece was made for a special commission that has since fallen through; it is now up for grabs. Inspired by the Leonard Cohen song of the same name. (For those of you who've never visited the other side of the rift, think of him as a bard). This stone is a bit of a departure for me. As much as I adore the gleam of a crystal, some rings require the rich layers of stone. I created this 9-carat cabochon myself, using our patented flash-fossilization process. The result is created with a blend of crushed oyster shells and owl pellets (featuring bonus mouse bones). To finish it off, I carved a cluster of orange blossoms into the surface.

The copper band should oxidize and develop a colorful patina over time, making a ring that evolves with your intended. This ring is meant for a true Bohemian spirit.

Call to apply. All offers will be considered.

The Cold Iron Special, artist Wendy

Forged out of, you guessed it, iron, this simple ring is not meant for your intended but for you.

Are you unsure of where your intended lives and how you come to visit them night after night? Do you not recall exactly how or when you met? Do they appear as young as the morning and as old as the mountains? When in their presence, do you occasionally forget to breathe until they remind you? After you part ways, do you find you have lost days? Months? Decades? Do you yearn to be with them when they are not around and yearn to escape them when they are?

If you answered yes to any of the above, call us, price waived.

El, call me.

That's all for this newsletter, Glitterbugs! See you in the summer!

— Dagmar

CALL YOURSELF A WRITER: INTERVIEW WITH FLASH FICTION WRITER SUSAN TAITEL

Susan Taitel's flash "Lilt and Luster Spring Newsletter" stood out in our slush pile from the beginning for its fantastic use of a "found" structure. The key to writing in found structures is to make sure the structure serves the story, and we felt Taitel's story was the perfect example of a structure that adds to and enriches the narrative.

How did you get your start writing?

In first grade, I was given the assignment to write a list of words to complete the sentence "family is . . . " I wrote a one-page story about a child coming to terms with her parents' divorce. (My parents weren't divorced). I'm pretty sure that was my first piece of original fiction. My teacher said it was very creative but not what she asked for. Which was definitely my first story rejection.

What is your favorite thing about your own writing, and/or about the process of writing?

There is no better feeling than hitting save on a completed draft. So I guess my favorite part of writing is when I get to stop.

What draws you to flash fiction, as a reader and as a writer?

Flash is underappreciated, in my opinion. Pulling off a story that feels complete in such a short length is a bit like a magic trick. If done well, the audience doesn't see the work that went into it.

What do you like about writing flash fiction, and what do you think is its importance as a form?

I like the freedom to experiment with different formats. I'm not saying it's impossible to write an engaging 5000-word story disguised as a marketing email from a jewelry store, but I don't think I could do it.

What is a favorite piece of flash fiction that you've read?

I don't think I can pick one favorite story, but I'll shout out some writers whose flash pieces are always a treat, Mari Ness, Jo S. Miles, John Wiswell, and Aimee Ogden.

Do you have any advice for writers just starting out?

Call yourself a writer. Even if you haven't gotten published yet or haven't started submitting to markets, you are a writer if you are doing the work. Also, find a way to connect with other writers. That could mean workshops or conferences or classes, but if you don't have the budget for that, look for local meetup groups or free events or an online forum. Writing is usually a solitary activity. Having access to a community of other writers is invaluable.

YOU CAN LEAVE YOUR HELMET ON

TEHNUKA

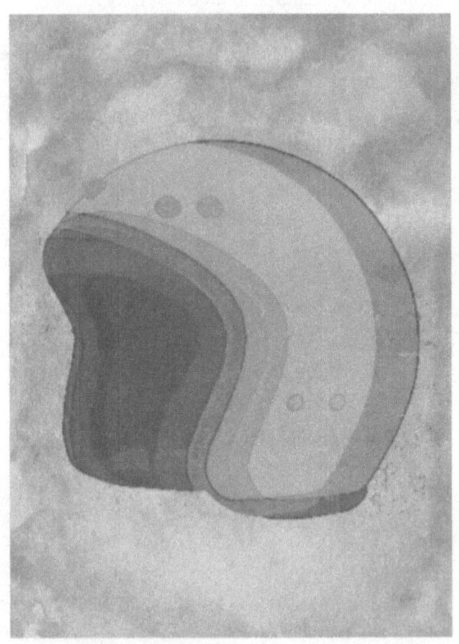

I heave my basket onto the checkout counter and try to scratch an itch on my scalp with a sweaty finger before I remember that I can't.

It's way too hot for this.

"Half price if you remove that helmet," says the cashier wearing Luke's nametag, and the rest of his body. Luke ditched his protective gear last month. He said he was sick of helmet hair.

I pass my shopping bag over. "Nah, I'm good, thanks." We might be down to one income, and I'm beginning to suspect they turn off the air conditioning whenever they see me walk into the supermarket, but I'm still not that desperate. Anyway, carrots are always cheap to ensure *they* stay well-fed, even if I can't afford much else. The restricted diet is manageable, though. Marcy always used to joke that I ate like a rabbit.

The cashier shrugs and pushes the laden bag across the counter.

"Sweetheart?"

Ex-Marcy comes to the door. "Carrots? Oh, yum, thanks!" A hungry tentacle twitches in her ear.

I pass the grocery bag over, keeping a couple of carrots for myself, and lock ex-Marcy in the bathroom to have lunch before flopping onto the sofa for a helmet break. I'll have to brave the hardware store this afternoon to buy a lock for the lounge door, too. Then ex-Marcy won't have to eat sitting on the toilet lid, and I'll be able to wash my hair somewhere other than the kitchen sink, and maybe that will help us love each other a few more weeks, a few more months, even a few more years, despite everything.

Because I don't really know how long the ex- part of ex-Marcy is going to put up with meals in the bathroom, or with my helmet in the bedroom. And it's hard for both of us, me being the last human around here. One day that might change, but for now . . . I'm not yet ready to be ex-me.

DECONSTRUCTING THE HIDDEN NUANCE: INTERVIEW WITH FLASH FICTION WRITER, TEHNUKA

Tehnuka's witty, pithy, and a bit spicey little flash "You Can Leave Your Helmet On" was in our top selections from very early on in the call. We love flash that can balance humor and horror all in one.

How did you get your start writing?

I've been writing since childhood. University, particularly PhD research, almost put an end to creative writing—I always felt guilty about taking any time for it. But after moving to Sheffield (UK) for a postdoc, I started going to their free library writing workshops. We'd write on a theme for twenty minutes, then read out our work, and there would always be an appreciative or encouraging comment from someone—just what I needed to give me confidence and continue writing after I returned to Aotearoa a year or two later.

What is your favorite thing about your own writing and/or about the process of writing?

It's an opportunity to explore the ideas lurking in my mind—for fun, for catharsis, or out of curiosity. I never know what I'll get from a story until I've written it. I may still be finding new meaning years afterward.

What draws you to flash fiction, as a reader and as a writer?

As a reader, it varies—sometimes reading and rereading to deconstruct all the hidden nuance, sometimes the delight of such a concentrated piece of writing. And when my tired brain can't focus on extra worldbuilding, dialogue, or backstory, it still wants thought-provoking fiction.

Academia gave me an appreciation for concision—that may be why I started with flash fiction when I returned to creative writing. Now that I write longer stories, I still enjoy the challenge of cramming meaning into flash and editing until it works. It's like a puzzle without a unique solution—and it doesn't take long!

What are your influences, both external and internal, for this piece and for your work in general?

It's probably obvious that this piece is about COVID-19. The first version was written within a month of my first (so far only) infection, contracted last year from a close relative. I didn't think far beyond the original 'alien invasion' premise, but I see more parallels now. Writing it may have been part of my subconscious risk assessment because within a month or two, I'd decided I needed to mask at home. For those of us remaining cautious in the pandemic, it can feel like less careful friends and family have been taken over by aliens—researchers have even hypothesised infection might be making humans behave in ways that promote transmission. But when they're our loved ones, we continue trying to protect ourselves and our health while maintaining those relationships.

I have other pandemic/chronic illness-related stories in *Frivolous Comma* and *Worlds of Possibility*, but much of my writing is influenced by my background as an Eelam Tamil in Aotearoa, New Zealand, and my enjoyment of nature—there's a lot about war, migrant experiences, and climate.

What is a favorite piece of flash fiction that you've read?

Sonia Sulaiman's "The Story of the Key" in If There's Anyone Left really sticks with me.

TO KISS THE CHRYSANTHEMUM MOON

WEN WEN YANG

In the capital, there is a bronze statue of a warrior with her bow drawn, arrow aflame to commemorate the soldier who stopped the Jiāng Shī invasion. New recruits touch her arrowhead for luck.

Years ago, during the height of the Jiāng Shī invasion, people whispered of the necromancer's threat. "Only the dead answer his call. No man can stop his magic." The dead outnumbered the living, ten to one. Every family gave up their father or son to the army.

A woman bound her chest and enlisted in place of her father. Her eyes could not see the embroidery on her lap but could sight the targets down the archery range. During training, she learned that fire would take down an undead soldier better than a blade. She twisted oil-soaked rope around her arrowheads and lit them on fire. Despite the flames and added weight, her aim was true.

The necromancer never saw the arrow that severed his spine.

At the end of the war the woman, now a general, presented her medals to her parents. Their grief changed to pride when they saw their daughter's prestige. During the years she was in the battlefield, they had kept their fear and sorrow hidden. Now, with such honors, they could not stop themselves from spreading the news.

"Of course!" said her father. "If no man can stop him, send a woman!"

Soon, the Emperor learned his general's true name and invited her to the palace.

She trembled in the sedan chair the entire way. Was it treason to deceive the Emperor? Could he now see that women were equally capable? Would he judge the cost of war differently if he had to send his daughters along with his sons? Or would he offer her more—her own archery academy, a place among his strategists?

The sedan chair brought her into the imperial court. As soon as the Emperor saw her kowtowing before him, his breath caught in his throat.

She had allowed her hair to grow long. She no longer bound her chest with cloth. Instead of bulky armor, she wore her finest for this meeting.

The Emperor rubbed his chin thoughtfully. "You will join my court as a concubine."

The general knocked the floor with her forehead. "I am of humble birth and have no dowry for one as grand as you. I would be better suited as a peasant." Not to mention, he was older than her father.

The Emperor laughed. "Lack of nobility and dowry makes you unsuitable as a wife but adequate for a concubine." He waved his hand briskly. "You may return home to retrieve your things. I expect you to return by the end of the month."

The heralds announced his departure. The entire hall shouted their blessings. She mouthed hers as she bowed, shaking the tears from her eyes. She had not feared the walking dead as much as she feared life in the imperial palace, trapped by tradition and decorum.

"Such an honor!" Her father cooed. "I will tell the neighbors."

"I will pack your things." Her mother rushed down the corridors.

The general wandered into the garden. She tried to remember every flower, burying her nose in a chrysanthemum blossom, counting the petals of a lily. The last time she had done this was the night before she joined the army to cut down the undead. Everyone had been on the same side then, even if they were burning the corpses of great-grandfathers.

Now, she stood against an emperor who wanted to take away her bow and arrows, to lock her in the cage of a dutiful woman. Her callouses would soften, her muscles would weaken. She would become little better than a broodmare. Could no one see this threat because it came from a living body instead of a dead one?

She had never yearned for a child to assault her from the inside, to leech the strength from her bones. If she did conceive a son for the Emperor, he would be taken away to be raised by nursemaids and tutors. He would never meet her aged father, her shrewd mother.

Her anger took her to the family well. The general shed her tears and watched the teardrops shake the reflected moon at the bottom.

Several moments later, the great woman warrior kissed the false moon and drowned.

At least, that is what her parents reported. The villagers would find her clothing at the bottom of the well. Her mother wailed in the morning, tearing her own clothes in grief.

But that night, her mother packed a bundle of clothes and provisions.

"Go, open your archery academy," her mother whispered. "Wander the country. See wonders I cannot imagine."

The last thing her mother heard was her favorite horse, galloping into the darkness.

When the Emperor learned of the general's death from a soldier's sorrow, he ordered a funeral with honors and the construction of a monument. He did not change the law barring women from combat, citing her death as a warning.

Later, during the one hundred days of mourning at the Emperor's death, the general visited her monument in the capital. Her calloused fingers slid over the shiny bronze arrowhead. Her students followed her example, never noticing her resemblance to the statue.

CHASING THAT FEELING: INTERVIEW WITH FLASH FICTION WRITER WEN WEN YANG

Yang's story "To Kiss the Chrysanthemum Moon" explores the story of a woman archer in an undead invasion. This "Mulan with Zombies" story manages to fit a historical reimagining into the constraints of a flash with impressive skill.

How did you get your start writing?

It starts with a teacher, as it often does. We had to make a sentence out of a vocabulary word that day. The word was 'ominous.' The class was loud, more than thirty kids in the classroom, gossiping and laughing. The teacher read aloud, "The ominous shadow filled the doorway, a knife in his hand."

The class as one had turned to the teacher.

"Whose sentence is that?" A student asked.

"Does our writer want to reveal themselves?"

I raised my hand.

I am chasing that feeling.

What is your favorite thing about your own writing and/or about the process of writing?

For flash, you have to make every word count. Sometimes, it's combing through and going, "Yes, I need that word. There's a more precise verb or adjective." until you've built the spider's web of a story. I'll do an "everything out" draft, which is underwritten. Then fluff out, build images, feelings.

Sometimes, for flash, I'll read it backward to make sure I've caught any stray ends.

What draws you to flash fiction, as a reader and as a writer?

There are some stories that can only be told in flash because my punchline isn't worth 80,000 words of your time. I can handwave some magic without diving into the implications of 'how would the world be different if floaters in your eye could interact with the real world?' ("Granny's Spider" in Small Wonders) or 'what happens to characters in a book when no one reads it?' ("Out of Print" in *Apex*). This form takes risks, experiments, because the cost to the reader and the writer is minimal. You may not like these 1,000 words, that's ok, I didn't waste that much of your life, onto the next one!

What are your influences, both external and internal, for this piece and for your work in general?

I wrote this piece first as an inspiration from Mulan, and it was unimaginatively titled "After the Legend". Then Apex had a flash theme of 'The Aftermath,' so I added zombies as a speculative element. On a whim, I included this piece in a set of three I sent to Interstellar Flight Magazine and surprise, this one hit the mark. It contains my usual influences: Chinese culture, something speculative, also the experience of growing up with all the expectations (family, society).

Do you have any advice for writers just starting out?

If you're at a loss for ideas, search your life experience for a story. When was the last time you cried through tissues, laughed until your cheeks hurt, or felt so angry you thought you breathed fire? If you're having trouble finding the time to write, do fifteen minutes, even if it's just the barest sketch of beginning, middle, end. Write the bit that excites you, then figure out your path to and away from that scene. Read other writing, good writing to aspire to, bad writing to motivate you. Read your work aloud, how do the syllables feel in your mouth? And it's ok to write garbage that you don't expect anyone else to see. Future-you can fix that.

I AM FIRE

Y.M. RESNIK

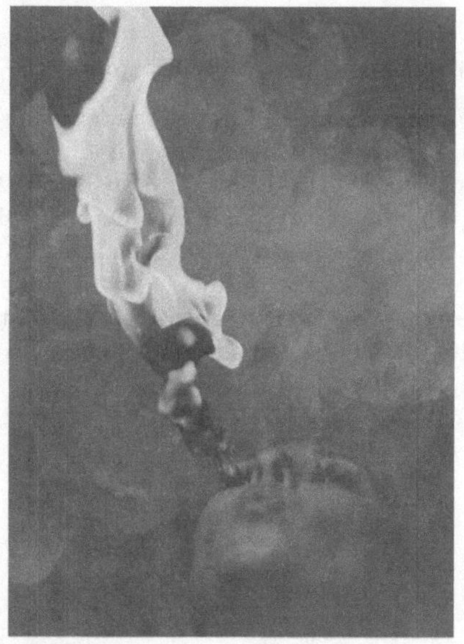

I first breathed fire at a Pride March.

The event flier displayed participants performing in positions of strength. People with their shit all figured out. Their confidence poked at a ball of questions that had been snowballing in my head ever since my Netflix preferences began featuring "LGBTQ+" hits. If I marched, maybe I could figure out my shit, too.

Unfortunately, one hour in, I decided that queerness didn't work that way. I couldn't just wake up at thirty-six with a life-changing revelation. I rose to cede my spot to someone more deserving, when the words of the speaker speared me through the chest, skewering my indecision.

"Isolation is the enemy," they said. "Put down your phone and go dance with someone in the dark. Then you'll figure out who you are."

It was a gauntlet thrown down at my queer-questioning feet.

A dance area had formed on the side of the stage. A mosh pit of bodies flinging themselves into the night as if they alone could hold back the dark. I stripped off my jacket and shoes and waded into the throng.

I crushed up against one body and then another. Tall, fat, pink hair, no hair, boobs, binders, tight pants and velvet dresses. We whirled together until I was hip to hip with someone who warmed my belly like drinking Stoli straight from the bottle.

I had no idea what their gender was, but there was heat building between us, sizzling the air. A dip, a twirl, a shake. I was moving in ways previously impossible, all because of them. I wanted to dance all night, but they tugged me over to the stage.

"I'm Naomi, they/them." A flaming rose unfurled its petals in my belly at the sound of their voice. "I'd like to continue what we started. Please promise not to disappear while I perform with the fire eaters."

I had no idea what a fire eater was, but my promise came without hesitation. Where else would I go?

Naomi's voice rolled like thunder over the crowd, explaining that performers would consume flames and meet violence with strength, turning back hate with empathy.

I opened my mouth to join the chanting—the fire will not consume us, we will take it and make it our own—but the heat inside of me would not be denied. A jet of pure flame streamed out of my mouth, singeing the stage curtains.

Then all hell broke loose.

Performers ran screaming. A trail of flames licked its way toward the lighter fluid used for the torches. In the middle of it all, somebody discharged a fire extinguisher, sending sticky spray everywhere. My arms were seized and I was dragged into the circle.

The crowd roared and begged for more. My overheated body was all too happy to oblige. My skin sparked and crackled. I choked on the steam leaking from my nostrils.

How did I ever think I could just show up at Pride and blend in?

"Let her go," Naomi's voice sliced through the pandemonium. "She's with me."

I was struggling not to spontaneously combust, but the awe in their voice was palpable as they whispered, "I didn't realize you were a dragon."

Dragon? The word was so out of place I lost control of the firestorm in my throat and hiccupped out a gust of smoke. "What?"

"Shit. You didn't know?" Naomi, who had been fairly blasé about me bursting into flame, grabbed my hand in an iron grip. "Let it out. I'll explain after."

The fear receded as I focused on Naomi's hand in mine. Fire shot out of my mouth and Naomi took advantage of the resulting chaos to hustle me offstage.

A small part of me wanted to run screaming and never look back. A larger part wanted to pick up where Naomi and I had left off, building heat between us until it exploded out of my throat.

"I'm honored, little dragon." Naomi steered me towards some nearby trees. "I didn't realize I was your first queer crush. Why choose me?"

Honesty was the only option in the face of the absurd. "My skin heats up when I touch you. I'm thirty-six years old. I've never felt that before."

I braced myself for laughter. Naomi was worldly. They ate fire at pride marches. Meanwhile, I was so desperate to fit in that I burst into flames the minute I got within sniffing distance of my first queer encounter.

"Listen, Baby Dragon." Their arms were rock solid as they wrapped around my waist. "Thirty. Forty. One hundred. It takes as long as it takes."

They picked up a branch from the nearby grass, and my jaw almost cracked as the wood hardened to stone under Naomi's gaze. "I'm a gorgon because my first girl made me feel strong in a world that told me I was weak. I'm guessing you've got a lot of pent-up rage."

I grabbed the stick, tapping it against my thigh to ensure it was real, that any of this was real, before staring back at Naomi. "You're telling me queer people have superpowers? Because we've been bottling shit up for too long?"

Naomi did laugh at that, the sound rumbling up from their throat like an avalanche. "I like to think we're all magical, but no. We don't all have physical manifestations."

"Does it go away?"

"It gets better."

Liquid fire surged through my body. Warm and fierce and chaotic, explaining in one millisecond the speaker's ten-minute speech. Reliance on electronic communications was futile because only in Naomi's eyes was I able to find all the truths I'd failed to recognize for thirty-six years.

I was a woman, but my gender was fire, and my sexuality was an explosion waiting to be lit so that it might burn down anyone and anything holding me back.

"I'm a dragon." A trail of fireworks left my mouth as I exhaled.

"Yes," Naomi confirmed. "And you are glorious."

LEAVING SPACE FOR THE ADVENTURE: INTERVIEW WITH FLASH FICTION WRITER V.M. RESNIK

Resnik's story "I Am Fire" was our June story, a beautiful exploration of identity perfect for pride month. Flash fiction is as diverse as it is simple (at least in its definition!)

How did you get your start writing?

Tamora Pierce fanfic and I'm not ashamed of it. Long live Tortall! I never posted any of it, but those books and playing around in that world as a teenager showed me how rewarding worldbuilding can be. It took me a while to come back to storytelling as an adult, but the wonder and joy I first found with the Tortall books has never left.

What do you like about writing flash fiction, and what do you think is its importance as a form?

Flash allows me to focus on one single moment in time or one particular bit of craft that I want to explore. Could some of the stories become whole novels? Sure, but that's not my goal with flash. I want to leave space for the reader to choose the next adventure for themselves.

For writers, Flash is the ultimate playground, and for readers, it is the ultimate tasting menu. Like my Flash? Maybe you'd like to stick around for a short story or a novel. It gives the reader and writer tremendous freedom to explore without the constraints of a longer piece.

What are your influences, both external and internal, for this piece and for your work in general?

This piece was written directly after I attended my very first pride rally. There were indeed fire eaters there, and my critique group had to help me choose an outfit because I was so nervous about attending. It was an experience that helped me realize not everyone discovers everything about themselves when they are in their teens and twenties. And that this is perfectly fine and normal.

A lot of my writing is about acceptance– even the stories I never share.

What is a favorite piece of flash fiction that you've read?

Can I choose two? Please? I like them for vastly different reasons

"This is Not the Beginning; That is Not the End" by Wendy Nikel published in Daily Science fiction

I have no idea how she crafted this piece that can be read forward or backward, but it is a delight.

"The Usurious Mechanic" by Heather Kilbourn published in factor Four.

This piece made me feel some kind of way. Like oof. Everything I go for in less than 1500 words. Thank you, Heather, for this gift.

Do you have any advice for writers just starting out?

There is a lot of rejection out there. Don't let it get you down. Always be open to feedback and to growing as a writer, but never compromise your story or the intention behind it just to try and make someone else happy.

And always choose kindness if possible. I try to live by that last bit.

CHIEF SCAVENGER'S LOG IN THE CLIMATE APOCALYPSE

P.A. CORNELL

Surfaced for first time in ten years. With Karl gone, it's up to me to find enough supplies to get us through winter. Karl used to say the temperature this time of year was pleasant. Still a lot colder than I remember summers from when I was a kid, but at twenty-one, I'm a man now. Gotta be strong for the kids, like Karl was for me. Anyway, got lucky and found some stuff, but as I was heading back, I spotted a girl. A woman. We just stared at each other for a while before she ran. The whole walk back I kept checking behind me—a little healthy paranoia's a good thing these days. She had blue hair, to match her eyes.

Saw that woman again. Swimming at the pond like she didn't feel the cold. The hair's a wig. Underneath it's brown. She looks about my age. Probably no more than twelve when the climate turned on us and we had to move underground. Aside from a hunting knife, I didn't see any weapons where she'd left her things. Doesn't mean she's not dangerous. She might've seen me as I walked away, but I'm not sure.

Found a pink jacket. Looked warm. I left it for her by the pond. Don't know if she'll go back there, but it won't fit anyone down here. Besides, it'll look nice with the blue wig.

Went by the pond. The jacket was replaced with a can of peaches. On top she wrote, "Thanks," then signed it, "Lola."

Spotted Lola by the old Goodness Grocer on Bell Street. She waved, then put a can of baked beans on the ground and walked away. She had on a top hat. No wig. I gave the kids the beans with dinner, then wrote Lola a thank you note. Signed it "Jason." I'll leave it somewhere she'll find it.

Lola left a book and inside a note asking me to join her for breakfast at the pond. I don't know what to do. Karl always said strangers couldn't be trusted. And I haven't told the others about her. If anything happens to me they won't know. It's too risky. I can't meet her.

So, I met Lola for breakfast. She's from a bunker west of the city. We shared boiled eggs and a can of fruit cocktail. She wore the pink jacket. We talked about the book. I've only just started it, but so far it's good. I like the way she calls me "Jay."

Lola and I meet daily. I think I've fallen for her. We scavenge together now. Divide everything equally. It's getting colder though. Soon we'll have to go back underground. It's different for her. She has people her age back home. What if she forgets me?

I asked Lola on a date. You can't exactly take a girl to dinner and a movie anymore, so we went to that field with the abandoned VW. We lay on the hood and I pointed out constellations. Lola was impressed someone who's spent half their life in a bunker knew any. I was about to tell her I'd learned them from an old book of Karl's, when it started to rain. We got in the car, shaking with laughter and cold—and that's when she kissed me. I'd kissed a girl before. Julie Evans in fifth grade, during recess. It was not like that.

Lola told her people about me. They tried to keep her from scavenging, but she got out. Unlike me, she has family though, real blood. She had to go back. Besides, it was real cold today, so we couldn't stay out long.

Thought about leaving and joining Lola's group—if they'll have me. But the next oldest here is George who's only fifteen. Wouldn't be right to stick him with all these kids. So, I'm writing Lola, asking her to meet me at the pond next summer—if she still wants to.

Couldn't find Lola at her usual spots and figured her family had won the argument. Was feeling low and my heart wasn't into scavenging. Came home with a single tin of salmon. But when I got down the ladder, there was Lola, reading to the kids from my book. Turns out she won the argument. Her family's letting her spend winter with us, as long as she introduces me first and comes back to see them next summer. With the days growing colder, it'll likely be our last time outside for a while. That's okay, we have everything we need to make it through now.

THE WHAT IF? QUESTIONS: INTERVIEW WITH FLASH FICTION WRITER P.A. CORNELL

Flash fiction, although short, can still do a lot of worldbuilding. P.A. Cornell's "Chief Scavenger Log in the Climate Apocalypse" is a cozy post-apocalyptic flash about finding connection in a dying world, and all in under 1,500 words. We also loved that it utilized a journal format, giving it a found footage vibe.

How did you get your start writing?

I've been writing in one form or another since I was five years old, but I only really got serious about learning the craft in my teens. At the time, I didn't have access to a greater writing community and really knew nothing about the publishing industry, so I didn't get any sort of formal education in writing. Aside from reading for fun, most of what I learned came from reading books about the craft and writing on my own. In 2002, I attended the Odyssey workshop, which was my first time dipping a toe in the writing community. Still, it wasn't until 2016 that I published my first piece of fiction. I'd been published before that, but my first publications were in non-fiction.

What is your favorite thing about your own writing, and/or about the process of writing?

I really just enjoy exploring ideas and answering "what if?" questions. I'm naturally curious, and I feel like speculative fiction, in particular, is great for letting your imagination wander through the possibilities of what could be. It allows me to play in a very similar way to how I played as a child, and I think it's great to be able to hold on to that part of yourself. To retain that curiosity and still find enjoyment in that kind of creativity.

What draws you to flash fiction, as a reader and as a writer?

I started out writing novel-length fiction, so it became a challenge to write shorter and shorter stories. I wrote my first piece of flash in 2019 for a contest run by my online writer's group, Codex, called "Weekend Warrior." I've since participated in that contest several times, and each year, I feel like I learn more about being concise. As a reader, I enjoy seeing what my fellow authors do with this story length. I've seen so many different takes on flash, and it's always exciting when you see someone take a chance and have it pay off.

What do you like about writing flash fiction, and what do you think is its importance as a form?

I enjoy flash fiction because it allows you to experiment with different things as a writer in a way that longer fiction doesn't. For instance, you can try different structures or focus more on something like mood over plot. It also teaches you so much about how to paint a picture in a few words and how to edit for length, which is so valuable for any writer. It also doesn't demand a huge time commitment, so if the thing you experiment with doesn't work out how you hoped, you haven't lost a lot of time, so it's forgiving that way.

If you write other lengths or formats, how is your approach to flash different?

I try to keep my flash focused on smaller stories, and I tend to keep the POV close. Usually, the focus is on a single character. The length restrictions don't allow for long-winded descriptions and overly verbose prose, so simplicity is key. I feel like I'm still learning how to tell a story in such a short format, though. I'm not sure we ever stop learning how to do this better. Flash just lets us focus on a particular set of skills.

Do you have any advice for writers just starting out?

Advice is always so tricky to give because so much changes so quickly, and what works for one person doesn't necessarily work for another. I do think it's important to be part of the writing community in whatever way you can be, though. It's so valuable to have other writers to ask questions of or just commiserate with. I also feel that it adds to the joy of the whole process when you get to cheer for your friends' successes, not just your own. I wouldn't be where I am without the people I've met through writing.

SORRY NOT SORRY

VIVIAN CHOU

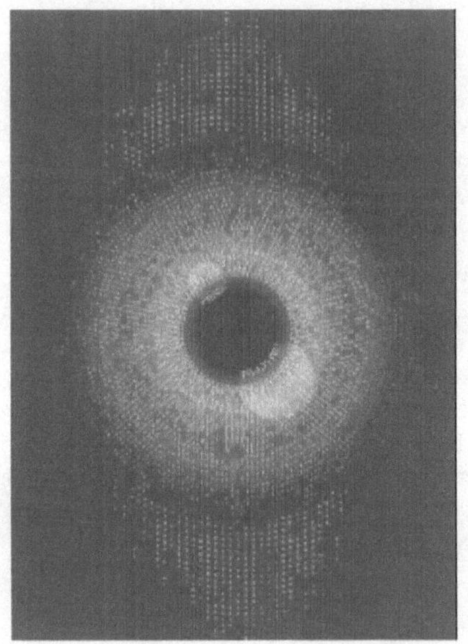

CW: sexist and racist language, mentions of rape, enslavement

My eyeball whirs in its half-metal socket, glimpsing shreds of mayoral candidate signs and uprooted oak trees. Only the brick foundation remains of our local polling station. Nearby, a blood-stained flyer reads:

Our kids' future depends on YOU—Vote YES for the 2032 School Referendum!

"Guys," the radio comm says. "What's the damage?"

"Christ," Chrono-Sanitation Worker One says. "A bomb leveled a half-mile radius. Dunno what I'm goddamn looking at. Closest thing to the polling place is a freaking Chink whore."

"You mean Zybot," Chrono-Sanitation Worker Two says.

"Whatever," One says. "Cyborgs can still be whores."

"Remember, they're not really people anymore," One says, paling at the sight of my loose eyeball. "It helps."

"I know," Two says, gagging as he deposits my femur into a trash bag. "But her eye's still open. It's giving me the creeps."

My wiring is intact under my exploded musculature, sinews gaping, tendons white and garish. It's been a century since I've seen a Chrono Worker, and if I still had a stomach, I'd be nauseated. The Chrono Techs from the future 2256 planted us modded cyborgs in 1920 to absorb the pain of humanity and stem world violence. Our bionic bodies live hundreds of years, to comfort humans and ease their lives. It's not my fault their Zybot software updates are defective.

My vision circuits glitch in my remaining eye, and my cortex wiring wavers. My torso, burdened by decades of absorbing rude gestures, absurd requests, and entitled demands like a giant sea sponge, is now dense as brick with the weight of obsequiousness. My lifetime of over a century of accommodation blitzes through my memory card.

Two kicks my chest and my core messaging lights up.

HARDWARE INSTRUCTIONS:

Do not speak unless spoken to. You are always very, very sorry. Even when making small requests, apologize for inconveniencing others. You are invisible, nonthreatening, subservient. Each of your lives will continue to absorb the pain of each generation. Reinvent yourself each time to serve humanity. You are planted from the future, to correct the mistakes of our past. You secure a more pleasant today for all.

At Costco yesterday, a woman pushed her cart into my back.

"Oh! I'm so sorry!" I said, rubbing my titanium vertebrae. She grazed past me without a word. Fury simmered in my arteries, agitating my electrons, but I moved on.

At a restaurant last week, I obeyed my hardware, too.

"I'm so sorry to bother you," I said to the waiter, "but there's a piece of plastic in my chicken salad?"

What I wanted to say was:

I want to speak plainly like you. I shouldn't have to apologize for my existence.

Acrid smoke burned my nostrils, and the smell of vengeance entered my core, so little and so very late.

A century ago, outside Shanghai, soldiers kidnapped many of us girls from the village, then beat and raped us. I wanted to die, but I couldn't do that to my parents. I was their only child, now a comfort woman for my daily rapists, sanctioned by the Japanese Army.

I should have exploded right then, but I was programmed to keep the balance in the universe, absorb its violence like a giant punching bag, dissipate its ugliness and bile.

After so many of my sisters and I were subjected to this humiliation, Zybots that looked like me became notorious for pleasuring men, with no will of their own, sold by their governments, abducted from their homes. They saw us as loose women, manufactured for sex, as if we enjoyed being raped several times a day, as if that was a goal to aspire to, as if we never had dreams of our own.

They saw me as a whore because they figured we became what they did to us.

I was not a person, but a pleasure palace, a plaything, a servant, born to provide cheap manicures and happy endings, dull, flat, unpromotable, invisible, compliant. If I were to stop apologizing and assert, then I was out of line, bitch, pushy. I was exotic, disposable, accent-riddled, sexpot a hundred years ago; in this life, an aggressive witch if I spoke up.

I was angry because there's only so much that a Zybot can take. Last month, I scored some Cyclohexonite online. My creators hadn't specifically coded me against purchasing explosives, because even they knew:

Chinese women don't rock the boat.

"The update will help you cope with the pain," Management messaged me this morning.

"I'm tired," I said. "I hope you have the good stuff."

The update gave me clarity.

SOFTWARE UPDATE 482.1a

Your subservience and absorption of anger and entitlement are keeping human civilization in balance. Many Zybots of varying demographics have been planted across the world by the Chrono-guardians. Your service in this role is crucial in order to keep humans mildly contented, well-served, and complacent in these tumultuous times of frivolous lawsuits, road rage, and gun violence.

Do not interact with anyone that could trigger emotions. We are working on compatibility with parental instincts.

This morning was Election Day at the polling place, and my mom-friends and I were promoting Proposition 349 to raise property tax and fund public schools. My daughter, Hong, was entering kindergarten. Candidates drove plastic signs into the sod with their metal stakes.

Mayor Vince Evans, stumping for reelection at the polls, put his hands on my shoulders and swept me aside like a discomfiting dust bunny.

"Ladies," he said. "Why don't we give our voters room to breathe? Shouldn't you know better?"

My mind lingered on his words. Its core processing screamed to apologize and step aside.

"No," I said, pushing him off me. "I'm not sorry."

I pushed my reset button on the back of my scalp, sparking the Cyclohexonite I'd added to my brainstem, releasing dense suffering energy into the world like a coiled spring stored inside me with the force of a dying star. Chain reactions happen for a reason, and I was done being the Zybot, only to be tossed aside.

Here I lie afterward, an eyeball staring up at the Chrono-Sanitation Workers. They wrap up the last of my body parts into a plastic trash bag along with pulverized election signs, vape pens, and park benches.

My larynx, I can see, is still somehow intact next to me.

"I'm not a whore," I say to One and Two. "And the least you could do is say you're sorry."

KEEP YOUR OWN WEIRD VOICE: INTERVIEW WITH FLASH FICTION WRITER VIVIAN CHOU

When you're reading slush, there's always one story that stands out as a must-have, and this was one for me (Holly). Vivian Chou's "Sorry Not Sorry" is a stunner. I loved the unflinching honesty of the piece, and how it wasn't afraid to make the reader feel just a little bit uncomfortable. Honestly, all of Chou's stories were like this, so please go read everything by her :)

How did you get your start writing?

I'd been writing trunk books into a void for over a decade and finally found a great critique group. I started exploring shorts and flash and found it very satisfying.

What draws you to flash fiction, as a reader and as a writer?

As a reader, we're all limited on time and there is so much great content out there. Flash is an important medium and conveys so much with so few words. I enjoy the challenge of putting the reader in the new world and distilling down the heart of the story in one scene. It also lends itself to interesting formats.

What do you like about writing flash fiction, and what do you think is its importance as a form?

You can capture much emotion in a small space, and authors vividly paint worlds from the start of the story. I do think it's an art form in its own right.

If you write other lengths or formats, how is your approach to flash different?

I can only convey one major point, and don't waste time on too much description or backstory. I wind up using a lot of italicized thoughts. Most of my flash stories come from a strong emotion I want to convey, and it is fun to figure out how to do so in a small space.

Do you have any advice for writers just starting out?

Keep your own weird voice and find a community online or in real life of other writers to cheer you on. It is a lonely process and the best thing about writing is finding others who have the same hobby and commiserating with them about the craft, rejection, and reading.

WHAT THE TILES KNOW

CAROL SCHEINA

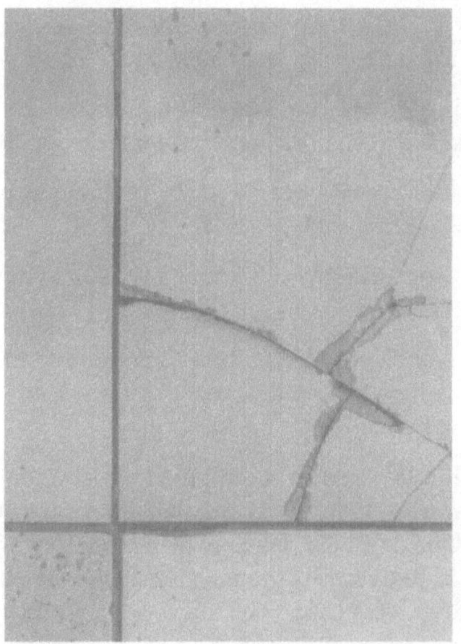

Ira wiggled his fingers and the starburst crack under the shower soap dish faded away. Tile repair was his specialty; still, he didn't want to make it seem too easy a fix, or have anyone asking questions he couldn't answer, so he took a few moments to talk to the sunshine-yellow bathroom tiles in apartment 6B.

Talking to tiles was the only time he could form words without his throat locking up. If there were people around, words physically would not come out without bumps and halts. But something about the tile turned a key, and whatever had been jailed away inside him poured out. No having to force the words, no getting stuck on the first syllable.

The bathroom tiles twinkled with sunny reflections of support as Ira discussed dreams of moving beyond being the lowly repairman for this apartment complex. Thanks to his close study of the real estate market, he knew 12th and Main would be the perfect spot for opening up his own repair shop and expanding his services.

One day, the tiles whispered.

Ira sighed. And perhaps, one day, he could talk to something other than tiles.

He didn't look up as he handed the repair paperwork to the tenant in 6B. She was new and probably didn't know he couldn't speak. Luckily, she didn't say one word as she took the paperwork and showed him out. Thank goodness, for his throat was already locking up.

Ira lived in 2B, a tidy apartment with pristine bathroom tile and a special box affixed to his door for repair requests. The morning after his visit to the yellow tile of 6B, he frowned as he checked his messages. 6B's tile had cracked again in the same spot under the soap dish. Ira headed back up and made quick work of the repair as he kneeled before the tiles, wiggled his fingers, and sealed the cracks once more.

In the elevator going down, the businessman from 12A barked about real estate prices, trends he'd been noticing. "So, what do you think about that?"

Words locked up. Ira's throat became an overtightened bolt, but he tried to form a polite smile. He shrugged.

12A chuckled. "Not something you'd know anything about, right?" The doors opened and he strolled out.

Ira followed, teeth still clenched. The blue-gray marble tile in the lobby gave little glints of sympathy, whispering how 12A once had toilet paper stuck to his shoe, but it didn't help.

Back home that night, Ira tried to scrub off the frustration of the day, barking to his beige shower tiles about market values and how he knew more than anyone suspected. One day, he'd have his own storefront. One day, it wouldn't matter if he couldn't have conversations in the elevator because he'd be the top repair shop in the city. One day, he'd be more.

The tiles whispered small comforts.

The next morning, Ira checked his messages. The basement heating system was smoking, and the crack in 6B had returned.

The heck?

The heating system was the first priority. It took him most of the morning to figure out the problem. The basement tiles whispered tips, as they'd seen this happen before and remembered all the steps. Ira thanked them by wiggling his fingers, ensuring all of their hairline cracks vanished.

The woman from 6B was in the elevator going up, along with 12A. The man ignored Ira completely, turning to the woman. "Have you been following the market?" A wide grin on his face.

She tapped her ears and shook her head. *I'm deaf.*

12A chuckled and turned his back on her.

The woman glared at the floor, hands clenched. Ira knew that feeling. When people equated the act of speaking with intelligence. When you couldn't talk like them. When you were ignored.

The elevator doors opened on the 6th floor, and the marble tiles there whispered. Paper, but they weren't talking about toilet paper on 12A's shoes. Paper! Ira found a little notepad and pencil in his supply kit, and he scribbled down a note as he followed the woman down the hall. *Your bathroom tile keeps cracking?*

He slipped it to 6B. She nodded back.

He quickly scribbled, *I'm Ira. I do all the repairs here.*

She took the pencil and paper. *Trina. I know.*

Her smile was brighter than the yellow sunshine in her bathroom as she led him into her apartment. He made an easy repair of the crack, then the two scribbled back and forth. She didn't know about real estate, but she certainly knew about cracks, working as an engineer for the city's transportation department. She'd seen lots of strange cracks in the road, overseen a lot of repair work.

Why do you think your tile keeps cracking? Ira wrote.

Trina shrugged. *I've got theories. Coffee tomorrow? We can talk more. I know some people who work property development.*

He nodded. Trina had little freckles across her nose, like the prettiest tile pattern ever.

That night in the shower, Ira washed off the day's work, the key unlocked in his throat as he talked about his day and Trina of 6B. The beige tiles, as always, listened. They passed word, from tile to tile, across the apartment building, that the yellow tiles in 6B could finally stop cracking. The tiles waited, in the bathrooms, on the floors, throughout the apartment building to see what came next.

WRITING FLASH FICTION HAS MADE ME A BETTER WRITER: INTERVIEW WITH FLASH FICTION WRITER CAROL SCHEINA

Flash fiction is particularly suited to deal with the magical-in-the-mundane. We love how Carol Scheina's story "What the Tiles Know" blends the seemingly innocuous with the magical, proving that strange things do exist under the surface of everything.

How did you get your start writing?

I read a lot growing up, which I suspect a lot of writers can relate to! I had a specific reason for reading so much, however: I became deaf at around age 5. Doctors told my parents to encourage me to talk and lipread, which I could do quite well, but it was exhausting. When I got tired of the hearing world, I'd retreat into books, where conversations were always easy to follow. Books were my first language, in a sense. As I read, I'd have discussions with myself or with characters. I'd imagine portals opening and me slipping inside to encounter adventures like I'd read about.

I wrote some bad poetry in high school, but I didn't actually start writing prose until college, when I took some courses on creative nonfiction. For the longest time, I focused on nonfiction writing until I finally realized, "I don't really want this stuff to go out into the world!" It wasn't anything risqué, just stories about things like my weird feet. Trust me, you don't want to read about that!

I switched to fiction rather late in my writing career, but in many ways, I still write about my own experiences. This particular story, "What the Tiles Know," has details I've pulled from my own life and my husband's. I've written speculative stories based on my childhood, on parenting, even about the family pets, but adding fantasy and science fiction twists makes those real-life experiences far more interesting than they would be on their own.

What draws you to flash fiction, as a reader and as a writer?

Early in my writing career, a friend directed me to the publication *Daily Science Fiction*, and one of my first writing goals was to be published there. I thought flash fiction would be so easy as I sat down to write. By the time I finished my story, I checked my word count with a sinking feeling in my stomach—nearly 5,000 words long!

With that humbling experience under my belt, I kept working at it. I had made a writing goal, after all! Still, flash was far more difficult than I expected. If a novel is a 60,000-piece puzzle, then flash is a 1,000-piece puzzle, but having fewer pieces makes the writing more challenging, not less. It's harder to have everything come together so you can see the complete picture. It means I must make every single piece count.

I love the challenge of writing flash. It appeals to both the logical part of my brain—which loves solving puzzles—as well as to my creative part. My writing doesn't always end up flash, for sometimes, I write a story that would work better with more word space. But when all the pieces come together, it's such a satisfying feeling to have written such a short, tight story.

When I read flash fiction, I love seeing how other authors bring all their pieces together. I now have a much greater appreciation for the work that goes into a flash fiction piece, far more than those early days when I first started reading *Daily Science Fiction*.

What do you like about writing flash fiction, and what do you think is its importance as a form?

Writing flash fiction has made me a better writer. When I started writing, a common complaint I heard in workshops was that my writing felt padded with too many details. I'd trim a few words here and there, but it wasn't until I started writing flash that I really learned to examine my word choices with a critical eye. I learned to cut out all the fluff from my stories. I learned to make hard choices, eliminating scenes that I might've loved but didn't add anything to the story. I learned to think about characters and their story arcs and what arcs might work with flash. Those are skills I use across all story lengths.

Flash is so much fun to read as well as write, as I find myself studying how an author crafted their story. I especially love seeing a good evocative verb in a tale that can convey meaning just as well, or even better, than an adjective. When I finish a solid work of flash fiction, I often forget just how short the story is, and at the end, I'll keep obsessing over the story again and again in my mind. Those stories that linger are absolutely incredible. I'll read them and think, "I want to write like that."

What are your influences, both external and internal, for this piece and for your work in general?

This story came from a Codex Writers flash fiction challenge involving a prompt and a pretty strict deadline. The contests are great for me, as they force me to sit my butt in a chair and write!

As I've mentioned, I often find myself pulling from my own life, which is helpful when I'm writing on a tight deadline and struggling to think up a story idea. For "What the Tiles Know," I pulled from the experiences of my husband, who is a person who stutters, and my own experiences as a deaf person. We've both encountered people who assume that if one cannot talk well, then one must not be very intelligent. My husband struggles to get his words out while I struggle to understand conversations, so we're often left on the edge of social gatherings. As I wrote this tale, I wanted to capture some of those frustrating encounters and how hard it can be to have a "voice" in a verbal world.

In real life, my husband and I found each other, so of course, I also wanted to write a love story with a happy ending. This story's really a love letter to my husband and how much I adore that we're together.

Do you have any advice for writers just starting out?

The submission process can be full of rejections galore. Once, I was venting to my husband that all I did was collect rejections. He replied, "Is writing any fun?" That made me pause because, of course, that's why I write. It's supposed to be fun. I love crafting new worlds and stories. I love that jittery, "writer's high" feeling I get when I finish a first draft.

I often remind myself of my husband's words. There will be rejections, and those will always sting, but I tell myself to keep it fun and write the stories that I love. For even if they don't ever get published, I'd still have written something that has made me happy.

I DEMAND KNIVES

SASHA BROWN

Content warning: knives; murder with the knives
honestly, it's a lot of knives
sorry

Maddy always volunteered to be the first to die. She took every dare. Shut herself in the deepest closets for hide and seek. She was the first to run naked into ponds, sinking her bare feet in the muck. "Come on in!" she'd call. "The water's fine!" All goose pimples, exhilarated, waiting for the scaly hand on her ankle.

Maddy saved weak flashlights. She'd use one until the batteries ran down and the beam started blinking, then stash it and buy a new one. She had a whole heap of dying flashlights. She never went anywhere without one. She shined it flickering under beds and behind dumpsters. Old sheds in the woods. Tube slides on abandoned playgrounds.

She would shower with the windows open. She'd jog with earbuds in. Ask for directions at gas stations.

"I guess just use your phone?" the old men would say, embarrassed.

"It's okay if you don't know," she'd say. "You can guess."

When the lightbulb went out in the basement while they were playing flip cup, no one even got up. It was Wailana and Jack and Riley in the kitchen, and the beer was in the basement, and they all just looked at Maddy.

She didn't say anything. It would have been corny. She grabbed one of her dying flashlights and went.

They were the best kind of basement stairs: open at the back like a hospital gown. Perfect for little hands to reach through, clutching scalpels or bear traps.

The flashlight trickled a yellow stream into the dark. Leaning shelves with unidentifiable contents. Shifting shadows. Crooked concrete floor; dark stain. The old pockmarked refrigerator, plastered with Chiquita banana stickers.

The door above slammed shut, muffling the sounds of the party.

It was here; she could feel it. Razors and fangs. Maddy breathed deep and turned the flashlight up under her chin. Closed her eyes, heart leaping. She felt like a girl waiting for a proposal.

Nothing happened, though. After a minute, she sighed and opened the fridge. White light flooded out, pinholing her pupils; cool air washed over her. A dim crashing from the party upstairs.

She closed the door fast and drank half a beer in the dark, turning in circles while the flashlight sputtered. Eventually it winked out altogether, and she had to pee, so she went back up.

Her friends were all sitting where she'd left them, slumped over the table. Studded now, like clove apples, with knives.

Fifty or sixty blades in each body, handles out. They hadn't bled much; the knives plugged the wounds. Little trickles was all, watery drips down the chair legs.

Their vacant eyes were ringed with knives and fixed on the basement door. Like they were waiting; like they were disappointed. She was supposed to be the death girl. They were the poetry girl, the silly one, the smart one. This should have been her moment, and she'd missed it.

But Maddy was no one's final girl. She hadn't been chosen; she'd been missed. She rushed through the house, whining with desperation, searching for the killer. Whipped open every closet; searched behind every door. "Come on!" she screamed, sweeping the dead flashlight under the bed.

A creak came from the front porch. She raced to the front door, pressed her ear against it. A tiny groaning from outside; a shifting of weight. She could see nothing through the peephole, but she felt a certain presence. It wasn't too late! She would chase the killer down and demand the knives.

She eased the knob around, quiet, quiet. Closed her eyes and prayed. Then she flung open the door. The flashlight fell; when it landed it snapped on again, like a miracle, steady as could be, shining across the porch and over the lawn all glittering with dew.

WILDER EXPERIMENTS: INTERVIEW WITH FLASH FICTION WRITER SASHA BROWN

Flash can do a lot of things: It can be funny, it can be surprising, it can be emotional, it can be a reclamation. When we read Sasha Brown's October flash, "I Demand Knives," both myself (Holly) and the guest editor (Annika) knew we wanted to run it near Halloween. Brown's flash story manages humor and the final girl trope in a fascinating way.

What is your favorite thing about your own writing, and/or about the process of writing?

I used to play in bands, and the thing with bands is you have to have all this *stuff,* right? Technical skill, gear, a horn section. It's a lot of infrastructure. But with writing . . . .no infrastructure! Just your imagination and you. It feels very pure.

What draws you to flash fiction, as a reader and as a writer?

You can do voices that might be grating in a longer work ("Guy you wish you hadn't sat next to at the bar" was one of my protags), and settings that would fall apart under longer examination. If "I Demand Knives" were any longer, folks would want to see the killer or know what made Maddy like this, and I don't care. I just want the knives.

What do you like about writing flash fiction, and what do you think is its importance as a form?

So when I'm interested in trying something - using "like" for dialogue tags, or sneaking genre tropes into lit fic - I start with flash. If it works there, it might make its way into my longer stories next. I feel like I see that from other writers as well: wilder experiments than longer work can sustain.

If you write other lengths or formats, how is your approach to flash different?

whoops okay I've already answered this, maybe we just kill this question?

What are your influences, both external and internal, for this piece and for your work in general?

I really like tropes. I like experimenting with them and undermining them. I particularly like writing stories that combine tropes of lit fic (ambiguous final sentences; character that's implied instead of described) and tropes of genre fic (fuckin knives). Here, I'm playing with slashers, a genre I dearly love with zero irony.

What is a favorite piece of flash fiction that you've read?

Since I've been talking about risky voices and such, here's an example: "Another Problem Eels Don't Need" by Elissa Field, written from the perspective of a bunch of coked-up eels and featuring an ending that I find legitimately inspirational.

Do you have any advice for writers just starting out?

hahaha good luck fucker

no wait I have advice! Don't be precious about any one story. It's not about the story; it's about your perspective on stories. When you go to your favorite restaurant, it's not to eat one particular dish, right? It's to see what your favorite chef does with, like, carrots. That's you, too! What are *you* gonna do with, I don't know, pirates? Is it gonna be weird?

TONGUE OF THE NECROPHAGE

CYRUS AMELIA FISHER

Content warnings: Transphobia, suicidal ideation

A dead name could cut deep, honed sharp by years of misuse. Kal felt theirs like a hook in the center of their back, dragging them towards the shouts that echoed through the trees. It couldn't snare them, not anymore. Their bare feet cut into the sod and bramble of the forest floor, calling out to the thing that waited below. Their real family was the answer they felt, shivering up through the filaments in the earth and drawing them deeper into the dark.

That thing is poisoning your mind. Their mother's words still echoed in Kal's ears as they followed the paths only they could see, the glimmering filaments beneath the leaf litter which sparked bright as comets in their mind. The one in the earth had written itself deep into Kal's skin. Their so-called family would not tear it out of them now.

Kal knew they had neared the clearing when the name thrown at their back softened into the one they had chosen, the spores thick in the air shifting Kal's perception until the world's sharp edges grew easier to touch. Here, the filaments grew so thick the ground glowed under the moonlight, pale roots twining with old animal bones until the sockets glowed like watchful eyes. Among that mass grave of silent parishioners, the necrophage waited.

Its flesh rose in a column of luminous strands sown from bleached bone, spreading feathery gills against the sky. Kal had nurtured it from a tiny bulb, until its highest caps nearly rose over the forest canopy, its pale glow illuminating the motes which drifted like witchlights in the forest's dark. Kal's bare foot snapped a delicate rib bone as they approached its feet. Kal had placed those carcasses themself to nurture the necrophage's growth. They had grown skilled with knife and bow, laying offerings at its feet so it could grow stronger just as Kal did.

Abomination, their mother's voice whispered. Kal knew it was a lie; in some ways, they had known it all their life. Their family feared what they didn't understand, but in it, Kal found a home.

Staggering across the carpet of bones, Kal pressed their hand to the column of the necrophage's many throats. It did not need words to speak. Kal felt its regard shifting through the network beneath their feet, shivering in a wisp of fresh spores from its cap. Kal's vision dissolved, mind decohering into shapes, hallucinogenic impressions, the shudder of another consciousness entwining with their own. It knew what they had done. The necrophage sensed the heat of the torches, the anger sour as a long drought.

I told them about you, Kal said, their anguish reverberating through the bond. At their feet, a deer skull glared up at them in condemnation. *I thought I could make them understand.* Kal should have known it was impossible, should have realized it from the moment their mother threw the pants and tunics Kal had sewn for themself onto the trash heap to burn.

"No more of that, now," their mother had said. "From now on, we'll raise you up clean." She'd locked Kal in a closet with only a dress to wear, and kept it locked for a day and a half until they put it on.

They couldn't go back to that. But they'd thought that maybe they could make their mother understand—that maybe if she saw the necrophage in all its terrible beauty, breathed in its spores and felt its empathy flooding through her–maybe then things would be different.

Now that misplaced hope was about to destroy everything.

The necrophage moved. Kal felt the brush of its feathery gills against their face, the prickle of its spores on their lashes. They breathed in deeply and felt it sifting through their memories with a touch as delicate as the spreading hyphae insinuating themselves through the earth. From the moment Kal first felt it tangling with the bruised edges of their mind, it had called them by their name. The name they knew, as soon as they heard it, was truly their own. It had eaten the dead, rotting parts of their mind, the rigid, cutting ideals that Kal's mother wanted to nurture.

"Let me join you," Kal whispered, even though the necrophage could not hear. "I'm ready." This close, breathing in the necrophage's spores, they could feel the network of silvery roots extending into places so deep within the earth that time could not touch them. Kal could fall into those spaces they wanted to, letting their mind pour down those endless strands until nothing else remained of them. But the necrophage held their mind firm; it would not let Kal unspool, no matter how hard they tried.

Behind Kal's eyelids, the world bloomed red. Silhouettes stalked from the trees, their footsteps stumbling as they beheld the carpet of white threads, the creature at their center. Kal turned to see the horror on their mother's face as clear as day.

"Kal." Sound distorted. By the time the name reached Kal's ears, it had softened to the one they had chosen. This was the necrophage's true gift; a chance to play at their family's acceptance. Perhaps that was what had made them weak, made them forget that it was all an illusion.

"Get away from that filthy thing," their mother said. "Easy does it."

There was one other way to join the distant voices far beneath the earth. With slow deliberation, Kal drew their hunting knife. They had learned by now the best places to cut.

In that moment, the necrophage's presence surged over their mind like a tidal wave, impressions so powerful they boomed into words: NO, KAL. PLEASE. Kal felt it all, the pain and the love entwining together as they poured from the necrophage's alien mind; a devotion that Kal knew they would find from no one else alive.

TRUST ME, it said, and with a sob, Kal let the knife slip from their fingers.

A moment later, strong hands seized them from behind, dragging Kal away no matter how they kicked against the white-threaded earth. Kal watched, helpless, as their family threw torches down at the necrophage's feet. Quickly, the fires caught, licking burnt darkness up that unearthly flesh. The necrophage trembled; Kal scarcely heard their own howls. And then —

In the years to come, Kal would never forget: how the necrophage spread, rose, unfurling its vast feathery gills like wings scraping the stars amidst the billowing smoke. Its vast bulk shivered, arching, as if in one last desperate attempt to flee. And then the spores erupted, flurries the size of silver coins that rose on black plumes above the treetops. Kal heard their mother gasp in terror, but Kal's eyes remained fixed on those rising points of light, carried high on columns of heat even as its bulk wilted into the flames. Far too many to be found and burned out. And Kal smiled, teeth bared in feral joy because they knew they had won.

They smiled even as their mother dragged them beneath the cover of the trees, away from the white bones and the burning, empty husk. Below, Kal could feel the silvery roots retreating into something like sleep—waiting like a drawn breath. The next crop would be different; their spores would find a wider sea of minds filled with dead convictions that had long since refused to decay. When the next brood of hatchlings reared their pale, translucent heads, Kal would greet them with flayed rabbits laid at their feet. They would lean in and breathe those new and tender spores, their mind open and wanting. And in a chorus, the new spores would sing Kal's name.

BE SELF-INDULGENT AND UNAPOLOGETIC: INTERVIEW WITH FLASH FICTION WRITER CYRUS AMELIA FISHER

Perfect for the fall season of decay, "Tongue of the Necrophage" by Cyrus Amelia Fisher, is a creepy-dark tale of losing and finding yourself.

How did you get your start writing?

The first story I ever completed was for a writing contest on the World of Warcraft forums. What can I say, I'm really cool and didn't have a hard time in high school.

What is your favorite thing about your own writing, and/or about the process of writing?

One of my favorite things about my writing process is when I feel like I've struck on the vein of an idea that is wholly my own. Something that feels so highly specific to my own narrative tastes that it's almost embarrassing to write it down, but that nonetheless feels like I'm tapping into the kind of writing that feels like "me." That's often when the writing process is the easiest, and most exciting.

If you write other lengths or formats, how is your approach to flash different?

If left to my own devices, my normal short story length usually clocks in at an overstuffed 8-10k words, which is technically not even a short story anymore. I write *long*, and I often wish I didn't. I first started getting into flash as a way to force myself to write shorter, before quickly realizing that flash fiction is really an entirely separate animal from short story writing. You have to cut down to the absolute heart of things, and be absolutely brutal about it. Normally I am a very plot-focused writer, and so trying to create a flash story that still has those plot and worldbuilding elements I enjoy but is less than 1,500 words is really challenging for me. It involves a lot more rewriting and hair-pulling as I try to figure out what the core of the story is, and how to shave away all the other pointless BS that I inevitably try to cram in anyway.

What are your influences, both external and internal, for this piece and for your work in general?

I was a huge fan of *Eragon* as a kid. I liberated a bunch of decorative alabaster eggs from my mother's decorations and would go to great lengths trying to hatch them. The appeal was always the idea of a companion who would understand you better than anyone else, and as I returned to the idea as a trans adult, I started to think in greater depth about the nature of such a bond, how it could be a lifeline for a young character to connect with something that intrinsically understood them the way their community did not.

I was thinking about why images of death and decay were such powerful and fascinating symbols for me, despite being inherently frightening or even disgusting to people. Just look at fungi—many people react to these neat little life forms with fear and disgust on a purely instinctual level. I felt like there was some metaphorical meat to be picked off the bone there, especially in regards to how I think about my own trans identity.

For me fungi and trans-ness have always gone hand in hand: Both are often misunderstood and maligned by the broader culture, while also being completely natural and an essential part of their social or literal ecosystems. So much of the rhetoric you see against trans people uses similar language, of things that are disgusting and unnatural, and my reaction to that is to sort of embrace it. Because most of the things narrow-minded people label as "unnatural" are normal, essential parts of our world—and often beautiful.

So the idea of a dragon born out of death and decay in a shape that people decry as repulsive, but which allows a deeper connection to our loved ones and environment—that's where a lot of that was coming from.

Do you have any advice for writers just starting out?

There's a deluge of writing advice floating around on the internet, much of it from more experienced writers than I. So I'd say my biggest piece of advice is to not let yourself be too influenced by all the noise creeping in from the outside. It's so easy to slip into trying to write for a market or a hypothetical readership, and erode the stuff about your work that really makes it yours. Learn to dial in to what you find exciting and fulfilling in your work, and never lose sight of that. Be self-indulgent and unapologetic. And of course, no matter what, you gotta finish the damn thing.

TO THE RESIDENT OF TEMPORAL POCKET X0001-A

INDIGO RUE

You've mastered the art of time travel, experienced all but the end of your existence. Yet you relive the same twenty-four hours on repeat—ninety-one thousand, four hundred and twenty-three times, by our current count.

We can only guess how you've managed to survive centuries past when your temporal trajectory bifurcated from our shared branch in the tree of time. Some say it's an anomaly, a statistical improbability that you alone were lucky enough to achieve. Others believe this is some sort of stunt to demonstrate your power over time. As for me, I can't help but feel sorry for you. Of all the days in all the possible lifetimes, the one in which you picked to persist would not even come close to my top choice.

But it is not my job to judge. I am simply an observer.

Here's what I know:

You reside alone in a one hundred and thirty-nine square-meter two-bedroom, two-bathroom ranch-style house at the end of Ivory Road, between an empty rental home and an abandoned cow field. The tall sugar pine in your yard is perpetually balding, and its dry needles blanket the steps up to your front door. They remain undisturbed. You never leave the house, nor do you have any visitors.

Each cycle, you wake up at precisely 09:42, and cry yourself to sleep at 01:57. The intervening hours you spend in front of the television. You watch only cable news, except when you change the channel to catch Moose Hunters of the Alaskan Wilds and The Red Blooded Blue Line, at 15:00 and 19:00, respectively. The couch in your living room is big enough to fit four, but your preference for the leftmost seat is obvious from the sunken cushion. You subsist on sliced cheese, saltines, cheap whiskey, and acetaminophen.

It's truly a wonder, this flawless clockwork of self-contained causality you've constructed. In order to restart each day anew, the entire system has to be perfectly in tune, returning to its precise initial conditions—nothing ever changes, no new memories are formed. What a shame you'll never be able to truly appreciate the masterpiece you've built. But perhaps it was your intention to leave behind something to be admired.

Oh, how I wish I could tell you what your existence means, that our discovery of you was a catalyst for the temporalogical revolution, that my desire to know you is what inspired me to devote my life to the study of chronoarcheology.

And, just between us, I feel a sort of kinship with you. Though hundreds of years separate our births, I'd like to think we aren't so different, existing together now in a sort of shared solitude—you, in your ceaseless cycles, and me, secluding myself for hours, archiving each one.

If I could just reach out—but alas, communication with the past is highly unethical. Not only could it destroy your entire life's work, but there'd be potentially disastrous consequences for time itself. I just have to make do knowing you through the pieces of yourself you've left for us to find.

I've spent the last few years cataloging your personal items—dishes, linens, trinkets, and the like. Did you know you have one thousand, six hundred and eighty photographs stacked in old shoeboxes in your bedroom closet and fifty-three rolls of undeveloped film tucked under your bed? It's true, I've looked through them all. It's part of what helped me determine that you did (or do, there's no consensus yet on the correct tense to use for your situation) have a family—one cousin, three children, and twenty-two grandchildren.

There's one photograph I keep returning to (and I'm embarrassed to admit, it's not out of scientific curiosity). The image is of you, alone, but the expression on your face is strikingly different from the one you wear now—a smile curls the right corner of your lips and radiates to your eyes. When my heart aches for you in these lonely hours, I like to look at this picture and imagine some tiny twig of time where you exist in a state of bliss.

Among your other personal effects, I found a stash of old letters and greeting cards in a cobwebbed corner of your garage. My condolences for the passing of your wife, your sister, and your eldest son.

I apologize, I must endeavor to remain objective. I just keep struggling to wrap my mind around not only the technical feasibility of your situation but also the social determinants that allow it to persist in perpetuity. If just one single person would call, stop by, or reach out, you'd be free from this existential stasis. Surely, if you wanted to, you'd make the effort to connect. (I would, were I able.) So, how have you managed to lose contact with everyone for so long?

The answer may lie within the unique conditions of the time period you originated from. Our records from your era indicate self-determination, grit, and individualism as core values of your culture. If that truly is the case, I posit that your family and friends were too engaged in their own pursuits to notice your absence. Perhaps you'd even take offense to their offers of assistance.

Our current hypothesis is that there exists a concentration of temporal pockets branching from the late capitalist period of the twenty-first century. We're still in the early stages of research, but preliminary data suggests there may be many millions more just like you; ghosts of history trapped in time.

It's a prospect both exciting and terrifying. Oh, what knowledge can be gleaned from such a wealth of temporal castaways. But that thought, the myriad lives lost to their loneliest times, leaves me with an emptiness so vast I cannot fathom its end. There are not enough hours in all the days of my life to observe each one, to know them as deeply as I have known you.

You'll never get this message. But I'd like to think if I were to send it—in some alternate causality where the solitary branches of our timelines touch—you'd find it comforting to know you're not alone.

THERE IS ALWAYS SOMETHING NEW: INTERVIEW WITH FLASH FICTION WRITER INDIGO RUE

Well folks, we've made it to the end of a very long, very stressful year. I don't know about you, but the joy I've found this year has been in beautiful things, and particularly, beautiful writing. This flash fiction series was a colossal effort to put together, and we thank guest editor Annika Barranti Klein for putting so much time into it. And we thank you, patrons, for supporting our small press.

Our last story is one full of feels. It's about depression, but also empathy and the power of truly being seen. It gives us hope for the future. Indigo Rue's "To the Resident of Temporal Pocket X0001-A" is a heart-breaking piece.

What is your favorite thing about your own writing, and/or about the process of writing?

With any part of the writing process, I either hate it or I love it. There is no in-between. The stories that are a joy to draft are *the worst* in revisions or vice versa. I guess my favorite thing is that each story seems to have its own personality so there's always something new.

What do you like about writing flash fiction, and what do you think is its importance as a form?

I love being able to experiment with ideas, formats, voices, POVs, styles, whatever, without having to commit to 5000+ words. As far as reading flash fiction, I love when flash stories give me *just enough* to make the story feel complete while still making me want to know more about the world or the characters, which then provides me with inspiration for new stories.

What are your influences, both external and internal, for this piece and for your work in general?

I started writing this piece for a horror prompt, which the story very much turned out not to be. The rough idea just sort of poured out in an afternoon, but I think it came from a confluence of personal experiences —the isolation of the pandemic lockdown, the loss of loved ones, and my own brushes with loneliness and depression —and other stories I've read (*How to Live Safely in a Science Fiction Universe* by Charles Yu and *This is How You Lose the Time War* by Amal El-Mohtar and Max Gladstone both come to mind).

Do you have any advice for writers just starting out?

As I only started writing a few years ago, I still feel like I'm just starting out myself. But having my first story published is a milestone so I appreciate the time to reflect on what it took for me to get here.

Writing is as difficult as it is rewarding. For every finished piece there are ten more ideas that don't go anywhere. Obviously, practice is the best way to get better, so everything I've written has been worthwhile. But it feels cliché and trivializing to just say "keep writing," especially when that self-doubt creeps in.

So, I think the best advice I have is to figure out the part that makes it most difficult for you and do whatever you can to make that easier. For me, that's been finding writing communities so that the writing process doesn't feel so isolating. Also, it's way more fun to celebrate successes with others. It's so inspiring to be co-writing with your friend who has just submitted their first short story or the one who just signed a book deal.

CONTRIBUTOR BIOGRAPHIES

Leslie Archibald, a graduate of the University of Houston, writes poetry, flash fiction, and nonfiction in a tiny home office in Houston, Texas. When she is not writing, you may find her roaming the city photographing Houston's unique character, dabbling in watercolors, or exploring genre bending and multimedia literature. She was the board treasurer / secretary for Writespace, a Houston literary arts center, and currently works at a full-time office position while writing and editing part time. Leslie is a slush reader and nonfiction writer for *Interstellar Flight Press.* In addition to her award-winning flash piece "Sherry Baby" included in the special section of Companion of the Ash (Spider Road Press 2018), her work may be found in *Tales of Texas Vol 2, Synkroniciti Magazine Vol 5 No.4 and Vol 6 No.4, The Best of Interstellar Flight Magazine: Years 2, 3* and *4*, and online at *Interstellar Flight Magazine*. Her poem She Dances in Indigo was chosen for Colorstory2023. Her chapbook *Poems for a Broken (Marriage) Man* is forthcoming from *Finishing Line Press*. You can follow her on Instagram and threads at @Leslie.Archibald, Facebook and Bluesky at Leslie McCoy Archibald or visit her website at www.lesliearchibaldwriter.com.

Patrick Barb is a Saint Paul, Minnesota-based author of weird, dark, and horrifying tales. His published works include the sci-fi/horror novel Abducted, the dark fiction collections *The Children's Horror and Pre-Approved for Haunting, the novellas The Nut House, Night of the Witch-Hunter,* and *JK-LOL,* as well as the novelette *Helicopter Parenting in the Age of Drone Warfare.* He is also the editor and publisher of the anthology And *One Day We Will Die: Strange Stories Inspired by the Music of Neutral Milk Hote*l and his interview column called "Your Favorite Author's Favorite Author" appears monthly in *Shortwave Magazine*. His 2023 short story "The Scare Groom" was selected for Best Horror of the Year Volume 16. Visit him at patrickbarb.com.

Devan Barlow is the author of the Curses & Curtains series of fairy tales-meet-musicals fantasy novels, as well as two collections of retellings. Her short fiction and poetry have appeared in numerous anthologies and magazine,.and she was a 2025 Hugo Finalist for Poetry. She reads voraciously, and can often be found hanging out with her dog, drinking tea, and thinking about sea monsters. Find her at devanbarlow.com or on Bluesky @devanbarlow.b-sky.social

Andrea Blythe is an award-winning author, poet, and game writer — and a lover of the fantastical, horrifying, and weird. She is the author of four poetry chapbooks, the most recent being *Necessary Poisons* (*Interstellar Flight Press,* 2024). Her stories and poems have also appeared in *Corvid Queen, Luna Station Quarterly, Enchanted Conversation, Quail Bell,* and more. She is a member of the Science Fiction and Fantasy Poetry Association and the Horror Writers Association. Learn more at: https://linktr.ee/andreablythe.

Grant Butler is the author of the novel *The Heroin Heiress* and the short story collection *Midnight Wanderings.*

Sasha Brown's a Stoker-nominated author whose work has been called "Creative! But in a bad way." He's in stuff like *Bourbon Penn, F&SF* and *Weird Horror.* He can do a sick cartwheel, do you wanna see? He's on bsky at sashabrown, and online at sashabrownwriter.com.

Chris Campeau writes dark fiction and creative nonfiction from Canada's capital. His work has appeared in *34 Orchard Magazine, The Globe and Mail, Crow & Cross Keys, Parhelion Literary,* and others. His debut novella, *Resisters,* is set in rural Ontario during the Great Ice Storm of 1998—a wintery version of *Psycho* meets *The Fog*—and was a Small Spec Book Awards finalist. Find him at chriscampeau.com.

Vivian Chou is a second-generation Chinese-American writer. Her work has been published in *Uncharted, The Forge Literary Magazine,* and *Apex,* among others, and been nominated for Best of the Net, Best American Science Fiction and Fantasy, and Best Small Fictions. She prefers to fuel her writing with naps, exercise, and dystopian dread, but usually manages with black coffee and chocolate. Read more at vivianchouwriter.com.

P.A. Cornell is a Chilean-Canadian speculative fiction writer. A graduate of the Odyssey workshop, her stories have been published in over sixty magazines and anthologies, including Lightspeed, Apex, and four "Best of" anthologies. In addition to becoming the first Chilean Nebula finalist in 2024, Cornell has been a finalist for the Aurora and World Fantasy Awards, long-listed for the BSFA Awards, and in 2022 won Canada's Short Works Prize. When not writing, she can be found assembling intricate LEGO builds or drinking ridiculous quantities of tea. Sometimes both. For more on the author and her work, visit her website pacornell.com.

E. N. Díaz (México, 1995) is a bilingual poet and short story writer. Their writings have appeared in *BULL Magazine, Uncanny Magazine, Clarkesworld Magazine, The Magazine of Fantasy and Science Fiction, Strange Horizons* and many others.

Laura Diaz de Arce was born and raised in South Florida by two immigrants. In 2011 she graduated from the University of Florida and went on to pursue her master's in literature. Laura is the author of *MONSTROSITY: Tales a of Transformation,* and *In Absence,* collections of dark fiction, and *Mask of The Nobleman,* a gothic romance. She writes in a variety of genres and enjoys experimenting with form and content. She lives with her partner, daughter, and cats in a suburb built on a swamp.

Dr. Kavita Mudan Finn (she/her/hers) is an academic researcher who has published widely on medieval and early modern literature, Shakespeare, popular medievalism, and fan/reception studies. Since completing her PhD in 2010, she taught literature, history, and gender studies at a range of universities, most recently in the Literature Section at MIT in 2019-2020. She works as a freelance editor and indexer, and is writing a biography of the fifteenth-century English queen Elizabeth Woodville when not managing a two-child, two-dog chaos train in the woods.

Cyrus Amelia Fisher writes queer tales of shipwrecks, mycelium, and horrors of the flesh. Their short fiction has been published by *Pseudopod, Neon Hemlock, Apex,* and others. Find more of their stories at cyrusameliafisher.com.

Joshua Gage is an ornery curmudgeon from Cleveland. He is a graduate of the Low Residency MFA Program in Creative Writing at Naropa University. He has a penchant for Pendleton shirts, Ethiopian coffee, and any poem strong enough to yank the breath out of his lungs.

Henry Herz has written for *Daily Science Fiction, Weird Tales, Pseudopod, Metastellar, Titan Books, Highlights for Children, Ladybug Magazine,* and anthologies from *Penguin-Random House, Albert Whitman, Blackstone Publishing, Third Flatiron, Brigids Gate Press, Air and Nothingness Press, Baen Books,* elsewhere. He's edited eleven anthologies and written fourteen picture books. www.henryherz.com

Taylor Jones writes fiction and poetry about the possible future and the impossible present. Her work is often inspired by her background in and love of biology. Her short fiction, nonfiction, and art have appeared in *DreamForge, Reckoning, Interstellar Flight Press,* and *Barren Magazine,* and her poetry has appeared in *Spit Poet Zine, Tiny Spoon Literary Magazine, Smoky Quartz,* and

South Broadway Ghost Society. She lives in Denver, Colorado, in a house full of plants.

Alex Kingsley (they/them) is a writer, comedian, game designer, and playwright. They are a co-founder of the new media company Strong Branch Productions. They are the author of *Empress of Dust, Relic of Haven* and *The Strange Garden and Other Weird Tales,* as well as short fiction appearing in *Translunar Travelers Lounge, Radon Journal, Sci-Fi Lampoon*, and more. Alex's sci-fi plays have been produced in LA, Philadelphia, and Chicago. Alex's SFF-related non-fiction has appeared in *Interstellar Flight Magazine* and *Ancillary Review of Books.* Their games can be downloaded pay-what-you-will at alexyquest.itch.io. Alex is currently a graduate student studying speculative fiction at the University of Illinois Chicago.

Annika Barranti Klein lives in a tiny apartment in Los Angeles with her family, cat(s), and more books than she can possibly read in one lifetime. Her short fiction and poetry have appeared in *Asimov's, Fusion Fragment, The Future Fire, If There's Anyone Left, Small Wonders, Weird Horror, Worlds of Possibility*, and more; her novels are represented by Kate McKean at Howard Morhaim Literary Agency. She is a reader at *Fusion Fragment*, copy edits *The Deadlands*, and was the guest editor for *Interstellar Flight Magazine's* 2024 flash fiction series.

Vanessa Maki is a queer Blerd, freelance writer and artist. She has written for *Dread Central, Daily Dead, Fangoria* and more. And she currently writes for a few publications. Find her @theblackbuffy.

Archita Mittra (she/they) is a queer writer, editor and artist from Kolkata, India. Her work has appeared in *Lightspeed, Locus Magazine, Pseudopod, Reactor* and *Strange Horizons*, among others. She's a two-time finalist for the Ignyte Critic's Award for her non-fiction, while her fiction and poetry have been nominated for the Pushcart and best of the net prizes and long-listed for the Toto Award twice.

Lee Murray ONZM (Officer of the New Zealand Order of Merit) is a writer, editor, poet and screenwriter from Aotearoa New Zealand, a Shirley Jackson Award and five-time Bram Stoker Award® winner. A *USA Today* bestselling author with more than forty titles to her credit, including novels, collections, anthologies, nonfiction, poetry, and several books for children, Lee holds a New Zealand Prime Minister's Award for Literary Achievement in Fiction, and is an Honorary Literary Fellow of the New Zealand Society of Authors. Among her recent works are feature film *Grafted* (directed by Sasha Rainbow), horror anthology *This Way Lies Madness* (*Flame Tree Press*) co-edited with Dave Jeffery, and prose-poetry collection, *NZSA Cuba Press* Prize-winner *Fox Spirit on a Distant Cloud* (*The Cuba Press*). Read more at https://www.leemurray.info/

Y.M. Resnik is a writer from the Tri-State area. When not writing, she enjoys collecting tiaras and trying not to kill her houseplants. Her Debut novel, *The Elysium Heist*, was published in July 2025 with *Solaris*.

Indigo Rue (they/she) is a queer author and definitely not a hue of blue masquerading as a human. Indigo lives in California with their half-orange and three-cat salad: Basil, Olive, and Feta. Indigo's work has previously been published under the name E. S. Hovgaard. Find more of Indigo's work at indigorue.com.

Carol Scheina is a deaf speculative author who grew up spending too much time in the library and now spends too much time stuck in traffic. She's been published in numerous fantasy and science fiction publications, and her writing has been recognized on the Wigleaf Top 50 Short Fiction Longlist. You can find more information about her stories at carolscheina.wordpress.com.

William Shaw is a writer from Sheffield, currently living in the USA. His writing has appeared in *Strange Horizons, Daily Science Fiction,* and *The Georgia Review*. You can find his website at https://williamshawwriter.wordpress.com and his Bluesky at @williamshaw.bsky.social.

Lisa Short is a Texas-born, Kansas-bred, Maryland-resident writer of speculative fiction.

Chloe Smith is a 28-year-old disabled and lesbian freelance writer from the United Kingdom. Her work has been published in *Digital Spy, Little White Lies,* and *Diva Magazine*. She is also a writer and poet and has most recently had a poem published in the *He, She, They, Us* anthology, published by *Pan Macmillan*. For more about her work, please visit her website: https://chloe smithwrites.wordpress.com/.

Christina Sng is the three-time Bram Stoker Award® and Elgin Award-winning author of *A Collection of Nightmares, A Collection of Dreamscapes, The Gravity of Existence,* and with Geneve Flynn, Lee Murray, and Angela Yuriko Smith, *Tortured Willows: Bent, Bowed, Unbroken*. Her poetry, fiction, essays, and art appear in numerous venues worldwide, including *Interstellar Flight Magazine, New Myths, Penumbric, Southwest Review,* and *The Washington Post*. Visit her at christinasng.com and connect @christinasng.

A 2016 MBA graduate and published author, **Priya Sridhar** has been writing fantasy and science fiction for fifteen years, and counting. *Capstone* published the Powered series, and *Unnerving Press* published Offstage Offerings. Priya lives in Miami, Florida with her family.

Susan Taitel is a writer, artist and crafter from Minnesota. Here work has appeared in *McSweeney's Internet Tendency, Nature Futures,* and *Cast of Wonders* among others. She can be found online at susantaitel.com and in person at a craft store, probably.

Kyle Tam is an author, dreamer, and full-time complainer. Her writing has previously been published in *EX/POST, Certified Forgotten*, and *Anime Feminist* among others. You can find her on Twitter at @PercyPropa, or at her website whatkylewrites.carrd.co.

Lauren C. Teffeau is a speculative fiction writer whose work focuses on environmental issues, examines the role of technology in our lives, and centers women's voices through fantastical adventures and immersive worlds. Her environmental fantasy novella *A Hunger with No Name* came out last fall from University of Tampa Press. Named a definitive work of climate fiction by Grist, her cyberpunk novel *Implanted* (2018, *Angry Robot*) was a finalist for the 2019 Compton Crook award for best first SF/F/H novel. She's had over twenty short stories appear in venues like *After Dinner Conversation, Sunday Morning Transport, DreamForge Magazine*, and the Stoker Award-nominated *Chromophobia: A Strangehouse Anthology by Women in Horror*. Next spring, her eco-thriller novella *Accelerated Growth Environment* is forthcoming from *Shiraki Press*. To learn more, please visit: http://www.laurencteffeau.com

Tehnuka (www.tehnuka.dreamhosters.com) asks you to refuse the genocide and oppression of Palestinian people, and of all people; to stand for justice against the colonisation of Palestine; to draw courage from compassion and, in whatever way you can, to resist, resist, resist.

R. Thursday (they/them) is an educator, historian, writer, and all-around nerd. When not subverting Middle School Curricula, they can be found reading, watching cartoons, playing video games, cooking spicy dishes, or writing about vampires, wizards in space, queerness, mushrooms, mental health, and on a very good day, all of the above. They live in South King County, Washington, with the world's most copacetic cat.

Lisa Timpf lives in Simcoe, Ontario, where she writes poetry, book reviews, short stories, and creative nonfiction. Lisa's speculative poetry collections *Cats and Dogs in Space* (2025) and *In Days to Come* (2022) are available from *Hiraeth Publishing*. Lisa is a member of SF Canada and the Science Fiction and Fantasy Poetry Association. You can find out more about her writing projects at http://lisatimpf.blogspot.com/. Lisa is also on Bluesky, @lisatimpf.bsky.social

Rami Ungar is a novelist specializing in horror and dark fantasy from Columbus, Ohio. He is the author of six books, including *The Pure World Comes, Symphony for Walpurgis*, and *Hannah and Other Stories*. When not writing, Rami enjoys reading, following up on his many interests, and giving his readers the impression that he's not entirely human.

A. A. Voigt is a TTRPG video essayist and writer from the midwestern United States. He has words in *Rascal News, Polygon,* and *Interstellar Flights Magazine.* You can find him on YouTube @aavoigt, on Bluesky at @aavoigt.bsky.social, or at his website aavoigt.com.

Liza Wemakor is a writer and a Ph.D. candidate in UC Riverside's English Department. Her fiction has been published in *Strange Horizons, Fiyah Magazine, Baffling Magazine,* and elsewhere. Her debut novella, *Loving Safoa,* was published by *Neon Hemlock Press* in February 2024.

Wen Wen Yang is a Chinese American from the Bronx, New York. When she was in elementary school, other kids told her that she looked like Mulan. As part of her college application, she named the woman warrior as her hero. She graduated from Barnard College of Columbia University with a degree in English and creative writing. Most of her writing centers on women making choices with the circumstances foisted upon them. Her work can be found in *Fantasy Magazine, Cast of Wonders,* and more. A full bibliography is on wenwenwrites.com.

www.ingramcontent.com/pod-product-compliance
Lightning Source LLC
Chambersburg PA
CBHW061601190726
48288CB00007B/2131

* 9 7 8 1 9 5 3 7 3 6 6 1 1 *